Dear Reader,

One of the questions writers often receive is "Where do you get your ideas?" In the case of *The Untamed Heiress,* the story simmered at the back of my mind for so long, I'm not sure where or when the idea originated. I just knew that someday, when the publishing world permitted, I wanted to write Helena's story.

Growing up in a cruel isolation imposed by her father, Helena Lambarth is a wild creature who comes to London with absolutely no preparation for entering the highly structured world of Regency England. Wary of society and even more wary of men, she goes her own way with fierce independence. Until Adam, Lord Darnell, her reluctant host and sponsor, begins to touch her heart by demonstrating that men of honor, courage, integrity and compassion do exist. If only he hadn't already pledged his hand to the wealthy, oh-so-conventional Priscilla Standish....

I hope you will enjoy as much as I did watching Adam melt the walls of ice Helena has erected around herself—even as her untamed spirit inspires him to find a way to meld duty with passion.

Happy reading!

Julia Justiss

JULIA JUSTISS

The Untamed Heiress

HQN™

ISBN-13: 978-0-373-77113-4
ISBN-10:   0-373-77113-4

THE UNTAMED HEIRESS

Copyright © 2006 by Janet Justiss

This edition published by arrangement with Harlequin Books S.A.

® and TM are trademarks of the publisher. Trademarks indicated with ® are registered in the United States Patent and Trademark Office, the Canadian Trade Marks Office and in other countries.

www.HQNBooks.com

Printed in U.S.A.

Also by Julia Justiss

To my editor, Margo Lipschultz, for helping to mold this story so that Helena's wild spirit shines free

The Untamed Heiress

CHAPTER ONE

THE SHRIEKING WIND whipped her tangled black hair into her eyes as the sea crashed and foamed onto the rocks behind her. Ignoring both, Helena Lambarth kept her face turned inland toward the two laborers in the field beneath the cliffs, digging steadily into the stony soil.

The grave was almost ready.

Euphoria sent her spirits swooping like gulls on an updraft. A joyous burst of laughter trilled from her throat as she finally let herself believe it.

He was truly dead. She was free.

Though she knew any sound she made should have been lost in the cacophony of surf and cawing seabirds, one of the grave diggers paused to glance up. As he raised his arm to point, the second man saw her. A look of fear passing over his face, he crossed himself and batted his companion's hand back to his shovel. An instant later the two men went back to their task with renewed vigor.

Did they think her a ghostie? Helena wondered, her lips curving in a wry smile. Or did they remember her from that grim morning nine years ago when she'd managed to escape Lambarth Castle and flee to the village, only to have a group of townsmen, deaf to her pleas for help, quickly return the "poor, mad girl" to her father.

For a moment the memory engulfed her: standing, barefoot and sobbing, within a circle of wary onlookers who murmured to each other as they took in her torn clothing, dirty face and disheveled hair.

"Such a wee lass…"

"Mind's completely gone, her papa says…"

"Her mother's fault, running off like that…"

Her lip curled as a familiar fury coursed through her. Papa's lies would keep her a prisoner no longer. Today she would leave this accursed place and search for the mother from whose side she'd been ripped just as they were about to leave her father's land. The mother who, Helena believed with all her heart, had never stopped loving her.

A movement in the distance brought her attention back to the present. The grave diggers stood, shovels in hand, as the funeral procession picked its way down the narrow track from the castle to the small graveyard. Its listing markers and barren, windswept grounds were a picture of neglect but for this new grave and one other, just inside the rusted iron gate.

A pang pierced Helena's chest as her gaze rested on that still-unsettled mound of dirt hugging the boundary wall, its occupant an interloper in death as she had been in life. If "Mad Sally," the old hermit medicine woman dead two months now, had not lived in Lambarth's woods, Helena mused, she probably would not have survived her captivity.

Would Sally have been happy for her today? Helena wondered. Though the old woman babbled nonsense most of the time, in her occasional lucid moments, she'd displayed a shrewd perception. Along with some of the villagers, who crept into the woods begging Sally's help when the local doctor's efforts failed, Helena had also prized the woman's uncanny talent as a healer.

Others believed the chanting crone possessed dark powers and avoided her—which was why her father, ever the coward, had let the woman live on his land undisturbed. Helena, though, had never known Sally to use her skills except to succor and heal.

Another pang squeezed her heart. Vacant-headed or not, Mad Sally had been her only friend, and Helena still missed her keenly.

She took a deep, steadying breath. With the demise of her father, Helena hoped that the patrol he'd set to monitor the perimeter of Lambarth land would also have departed. But whether or not she met resistance from armed guards, she vowed, only her own death would keep her another night at Lambarth Castle.

Thus sworn, she watched the funeral procession file into the graveyard. Two farm workers carried the coffin, followed by a man whose flapping black robes identified him as the vicar, and Holmes, her father's baliff.

Not expecting any other mourners, Helena was surprised to discover another person trailing the coffin. A man, Helena realized as the muffled figure drew nearer. Someone she'd never seen before.

The vicar's assistant, perhaps? Since she'd not been off Lambarth property in nine years, there were probably several newcomers to the village she hadn't met.

The man's odd demeanor, though, held her attention. Rather than focusing on the preacher, whose moving lips over the open prayer book indicated he'd begun the funeral service, the man's gaze roved up, down, around the barren graveyard, as if he were searching for something.

Or someone. A moment later his questing eyes met hers. Defiantly, Helena held his gaze. After regarding her steadily for several minutes, he nodded.

Curious now, she nodded back. The stranger gave her a brief smile, then turned back to the preacher.

While Helena watched the minister continue to read the service, her mind raced back to something Mad Sally had told her shortly before her death. Not daring to place any credence in so unlikely a possibility, Helena had dismissed as another of the old woman's crazy mutterings the claim that Helena's mother had sent someone to watch over her. Someone who'd been waiting in the village for years for her father to grow ill or incapacitated enough for it to be safe to approach her.

Could Sally's message have been true? Might this man be the one?

She mustn't let excitement carry her away, she told herself, trying to rein in her rioting imagination. However, since she intended to set off in that direction anyway, it wouldn't hurt to trail the man back toward the village—assuming her expectations were correct and no armed guards remained at their posts to prevent her leaving.

The service concluded, the minister waited only until the two mourners had each tossed a handful of stony soil over the coffin before wrapping his robes about him and hurrying out of the graveyard, shoulders hunched against the wind. Without glancing at her again, the stranger followed, leaving the two grave diggers to their work.

Watching from her rocky perch as the group dispersed, Helena hugged her thin arms around the worn bodice of her outgrown dress. Since she'd long ago grown inured to the cold of the coastal wind and mist, the shiver that passed through her frame must be hope.

"I'M SO SORRY, MY DEAR."

As if the words made no sense, Helena sat staring over the desk at the kindly visage of Mr. Pendenning, Mama's London solicitor. Except he wasn't Mama's solicitor anymore. Mama was dead.

The man at her father's funeral, Jerry Sunderland, had not known, the lawyer told her. He'd been sent to the village years earlier, after her mother's attempt to rescue her failed, with instructions to settle quietly, pursue his trade and wait until such time as he judged it safe to approach Helena with Mr. Pendenning's message.

Somehow, all through the long journey from the coast to London, she'd sensed it, though she'd forbidden her mind to even consider the possibility. Along with the lawyer's note, Jerry had given her money enough to make the trip in easy stages, but that amorphous, unnamed fear in her heart had driven her to travel night and day without rest. Oblivious to wind, rain and chill, she'd ridden much of the way on the roof of the mail coaches, unwilling to wait and reserve an inside seat on a later run. With that inner cadence pounding in her ears—hurry! hurry!—she'd done little more than numbly note the marvelous variety of terrain and the many occupations being practiced by the folk they passed on their route.

Exploring the wonders of the world now open to her was for later. Ignoring the pain in her ankles from the stiff shoes and the scratch of the rough wool cape Jerry had provided, she had clutched in her hands the slip of paper with the solicitor's address, her mind fixed on a single imperative: get to London. Find Mama.

But Mama would not be found, in London or elsewhere. For more than a year, Mr. Pendenning had just told her, Mama's brilliant smile and joyous laughter had been entombed on a small Caribbean island half a world away. The place where Gavin Seagrave, the man she'd loved and fled to, had settled after being forced to leave England.

There would be no reunion. The goal that had sustained her through beatings and isolation and deprivation, that had given her hope and steeled her to persevere, had vanished like snow in a hot noon sun.

For the first time in her life, Helena felt truly alone.

"What am I to do now?" she whispered, unaware she'd spoken the words out loud.

"Live your life, my child," Mr. Pendenning said gently. "I corresponded with your mother for years and can with confidence, I believe, offer you the advice she would have given. After her health began to fail and she accepted the painful fact that she would probably not outlive your father, it became her single goal to arrange her affairs so that once you were free, you would have the means to do whatever you wished. And though I haven't yet received the particulars from your father's attorneys, as his sole heiress as well as your mother's, you will find yourself an extremely wealthy young woman."

Helena had been listening listlessly to the lawyer's recitation, but at this, her head snapped back up. "I want nothing to do with anything that was my father's."

The lawyer ran a sympathetic glance over her thin form. "Though you did not hold him in affection, that does not alter the fact that you are still his legal heir. In addition to cash reserves, there is—"

"No!" Helena interrupted with such vehemence the lawyer fell silent. "I want nothing that belonged to him. Not one handful of earth from any property he owned. Not a penny of his wealth. I'd rather live in the streets."

The lawyer smiled. "There's no chance of your having to do that. However, you must consider that part of your father's estate consists of the land and capital that was your mother's dowry. The rest of his assets you could sell, perhaps, and invest the proceeds."

"Whatever was Mama's I will keep," Helena replied. "But nothing of my father's. Nothing. Do you understand?"

Though he gave her a dubious look, the lawyer nodded. "As you wish. But what of Lambarth Castle? It was your home and your mother's. If you do not wish to live in it, remote as the property is, I expect a buyer can be found."

"I should like the books from the library shipped to me. As for the castle itself," Helena said, turning the full force of her dark-eyed gaze on the lawyer, "I wish it to be torn down, stone by stone and beam by beam, and the rubble cast into the sea."

The lawyer's face blanched and he swallowed hard. "I…I see. And the servants?"

"By the time Papa died, only Holmes and his wife remained." Helena recalled with loathing how the two had delighted in enforcing her father's cruelty. "I suppose I cannot negate any bequests made to them in my father's will? Then they may have whatever Papa left them and not a penny more. I am a wealthy woman now, you said?"

"Extremely wealthy."

"And I may spend this wealth as I choose?"

"Your mother named me as trustee to advise you, but otherwise you may spend as you will."

"Then I should like to do one more thing at Lambarth Castle. Erect a marble monument in the burial grounds."

"To mark the grave of your father, I expect?"

Helena gave a harsh laugh. "Certainly not. The crows are welcome to him. No, the marker is for an old woman, Sally—I don't know her last name. She was a healer, and my…my friend," Helena concluded, her voice breaking.

The lawyer's face softened. "I know this must have been a terrible shock to you, leaving the only place you've ever known and traveling so far, only to find the one you were seeking forever lost to you. We've spoken of financial matters, but nothing specifically of what you will do today, tomorrow and in the coming weeks. Will you allow me to make some suggestions?"

Suddenly, Helena felt the weight of the long hours of travel with little sleep and less food. Swaying, she put a hand on the lawyer's desk to steady herself. "I…I would be grateful," she murmured.

Mr. Pendenning poured a glass of wine from a crystal decanter on his desk. "Here, sip some of this. I'll touch briefly on what I think you should do, and then you must rest."

Helena took the glass with trembling hands. "Thank you. I should be glad of some rest."

"Your mother left quite specific instructions, should all the personages she mentioned be living and amenable to her wishes. After so many years confined by your father, she wanted you to be able to travel. To study with the best tutors whatever subject you wished—music, dance, art, literature. But most especially, she wanted you to reclaim a place in Society as part of a loving family, the sort of family your mother remembered from her own childhood."

Helena's throat tightened. "While Mama was with me, we were a loving family."

The lawyer smiled. "From all that your mother wrote me and the tender regard she displayed for you all these years, I am sure you were. She would like you to have that closeness again. And so she wished for you to go live with her cousin and childhood friend, Lillian Forester."

Helena's eyes brightened. "Cousin Lillian! I remember Mama speaking of her when I was a little girl."

"She felt she could entrust her cousin—she's Lady Darnell now, by the way—to advise you on the purchase of a suitable wardrobe, to arrange whatever tutoring you might wish and, in general, to smooth your way into Society as the cultured, independent young woman she knew you would be."

To have a home…with a woman who had been dear to her mother, had known her growing up… Helena blinked back the sudden burn of tears. It would never fill the awful void left by her mother's loss, but the terrible loneliness that had devastated her when she learned of her mother's death eased a fraction.

"I think I should like that. However, what if…if Lady Darnell does not wish to take me in, or we find we do not suit?" She gave the lawyer a small smile. "I have been alone so long, I may not make a…comfortable guest. In that case, do I have funds enough to set up my own household?"

"Should it come to that, you have funds enough to set up a household in every city in England! But I don't think that shall be necessary. I took the liberty of notifying Lady Darnell that you were on your way to London. After we finish chatting, I shall send her another note letting her know you've arrived. I expect she'll immediately dispatch her stepson, Lord Darnell, to welcome you into the family."

Helena stiffened. "Lord Darnell? Why would cousin Lillian not come herself?"

The solicitor sent her a cautious look. "I expect you will not be pleased to learn this after your experiences, but in English law and custom, nearly all matters relating to wealth and family are handled for ladies by the masculine head of their household. In Lady Darnell's case, that would be Lord Darnell, the eldest son of her late husband. She resides with him."

Helena's rosy vision of a congenial family unit faded. "In that case, I should like you to advise me on setting up my own establishment. I do not wish to be part of any man's household ever again."

The lawyer nodded sympathetically. "Though I can appreciate your caution, I assure you Lord Darnell is an excellent young man—a well-respected former army officer who served during the Peninsular Wars and at Waterloo, where he performed with great gallantry. You should at least meet him before refusing out of hand the possibility of living with your cousin. It *is* what your mama wanted."

But for that fact, Helena would have rejected the suggestion without further consideration. She sat in silence for a long moment, frowning, torn between the wistful hope of recapturing something of her mother— and the hard-earned dread of being under any man's control.

"If I meet him, even agree to live under his roof, and later change my mind, I will be free to leave at any time?"

"Of course. From now forward, you are mistress of your own life."

After a moment Helena nodded reluctantly. "I suppose I can at least meet him, since that was what Mama wished."

"Excellent." Mr. Pendenning nodded his approval. "Now, I've saved the most special part for last. All the years of your separation, your mother wrote you frequently. Knowing your father would likely destroy the letters if she sent them to you, she forwarded them to me for safekeeping."

From a drawer in his desk, the lawyer removed a wooden box. "I have them all here, kept for you just as she wished. On top is her last letter, written when she knew she would never have the joy of seeing you again. In her final note to me, she asked that you read that one first."

He reached beside him to tug on the bellpull. "My assistant will show you to a room where you can be private. I'll rejoin you with Lord Darnell when he arrives. Now, can I offer you anything else?"

Numbly, Helena shook her head. "No, thank you. You've been very kind. May I have them?" She held out her hands.

Smiling, Mr. Pendenning handed her the box. "Enjoy them, my dear. Your mother loved you very much."

The precious box clasped in her hands, Helena followed the young man almost without seeing him, her heart too full of anguish, joy and confusion to speak.

Mama was lost to her forever…but her voice had not been silenced. In her hands Helena held tangible proof of the never-failing affection she'd believed in with all her heart through ten long years of separation. A priceless treasure trove of love, enclosed in a simple wooden box.

She could scarcely breathe for the emotion weighing on her chest. Tears threatened, but she held them back.

She had a story of devotion to read and she wanted to see every word clearly.

Once alone in the room to which the clerk directed her, she sat in a corner chair by the window, set the box on a table nearby and drew out the topmost letter.

My dearest Helena, I can hardly write this for the grief I feel, knowing most likely I shall never again set eyes on your precious face, clasp you in my arms or feel the beat of your heart against my breast. But I must stem my distress and persevere, for as great a burden as it is to know I will be forever parted from you, my dearest child, still more terrible would it be for you to win your freedom and have no word from me to ease your sorrow when you discover that I am gone. And so, my darling, let me tell you what I would say now, if we could be together...

By the time Helena reached the end of the letter, the words were blurring on the page and her hands shook too badly for her to refold the sheet. Somehow she managed to place the note back in the box on top of the others, stacks and stacks of letters tied in bunches with string.

Only then did she allow the anguish to wash over her in a flood of the tears she'd suppressed for so long. She wept until, limp, exhausted and desolate, she craved only rest. After tugging the curtains from their holders, she tucked her feet up under her skirts in the quiet of the now-darkened room, curled herself into a ball, buried her face under her arm and slept.

CHAPTER TWO

ADDING THE BILL TO the stack on his desk, Adam Darnell dragged his fingers through his chestnut-brown locks. He'd almost rather be back with Wellington, preparing to charge the French lines, than here in London trying to figure out how to salvage his estate from the depravations suffered during his father's long, ultimately fatal illness.

Perhaps he'd best accept the inevitable, follow his solicitor's advice and find an agreeable heiress to marry. A rapid series of knocks on the library door pulled him from contemplating that gloomy prospect.

"Adam, may I come in?" The door opened slightly and his stepmother peeked in, the ribbons on her ruffled mobcap dancing. "I hate disturbing you, but 'tis urgent!"

Wondering indulgently what new crisis had occurred to distress his flighty relative—a lost pair of eyeglasses, a dead sparrow on the garden path—Adam rose and waved her to one of the wing chairs beside the desk. "Do come in, ma'am, and save me from dealing with this pile of bills."

"Oh, those!" Lady Darnell waved an airy hand. "Burn them! 'Tis what your dear papa always did."

Which was precisely why the estate was now in such disarray, Adam thought. Biting back so unfilial a reply, he said instead, "How can you be distressed when you look so charming? Like the sun itself in that fetching gown."

Lady Darnell smiled and her china-blue eyes glowed. "Aren't you the gallant one! I must say, the moment the dressmaker showed me the yellow silk paired with this blond lace, I knew it would be perfect for me."

His widowed father's second wife, previously the relic of a baronet of very large fortune, was hopelessly extravagant, Adam thought with an inward sigh. But so tender of heart and unfailingly cheerful of spirit that it would be as churlish as it was useless to chide her for her expenditures. Nor, with him away in the army, could he ever repay the debt he owed her for abandoning all her cherished London pursuits to remain beside his ailing father during his long, slow decline into death.

Such a sunny spirit didn't need to be burdened with the details of debts and mortgages. He'd just have to make economies in other areas—and look for an heiress whose dowry could refill the family's financial well.

"The matter is urgent," his stepmother said again, recalling him to the present. "Please let me do the proper thing!"

"What is amiss?"

Lady Darnell held out a letter. "I've just received this from the solicitor who manages the property of my late cousin Diana, saying that her daughter, now orphaned, is on her way to London. He writes that it was Diana's particular wish that the child come to live with me."

Adam frowned. "Your cousin was the girl's mother? Surely it is the directions left for her care in her *father's* will that shall determine her guardianship."

"I suppose, but that is a matter for the solicitors to resolve. In the meantime, the little girl needs a home."

It sounded like a muddle that might require several weeks to work out. Still, housing a child for that short a time shouldn't put too much additional strain on his purse. "Do you wish to take her in? I don't want you to let a sense of duty force you into playing nurse-maid."

"Oh, I should love to have her! But—" Lady Darnell hesitated "—before you agree, I must inform you that Diana was involved in a rather dreadful scandal some years back. Not that anyone should hold the poor child responsible, but you know how people are. With you on the look for a wife and Charis's Season beginning, I shouldn't want some infamy committed by a connection of mine to…limit your choices."

"Then there's nothing to worry about, as I'd not consider anyone who would hold the transgressions of a mother against her child. Nor, I am sure, would Charis. So how old is the girl, and when is she arriving?"

"Soon, the lawyer said. As to her age, I cannot say. You know I am hopeless with figures! After Diana and Vincent Lambarth married, he bore her off to the family castle in the wilds somewhere, and there she remained.

Lambarth never again permitted her to come to London, not for the Season and not even to bring the child for a visit. So, although naturally one cannot condone what she did, 'tis hardly surprising, what with Lambarth keeping her a virtual prisoner in that dreary place. Right on the coast, 'twas bound to be excessively damp, do you not think?"

Adam's lips twitched, but Lady Darnell was in such grave earnest, he resisted the urge to laugh. "Just what did this dampness lead her to do?"

"Well, first you must understand that in her debut Season, Diana conceived a passion for a most ineligible young man. Though 'twas nothing ineligible about his birth—the youngest son of Viscount Seagrave—but from his earliest years, he showed himself to possess the wildest, most ungovernable character. He was expelled from Oxford the spring Diana met him, and though Lambarth had been courting her for months, once she met Gavin, she had eyes for no one else. Her family tried to dissuade her, of course. Then after being challenged by a jealous husband, Gavin killed the man in a duel and was forced to flee the country. Diana was heartbroken. But Lambarth still wanted her, so she gave in to his urging and married him."

"The union didn't prosper." And small wonder, Adam thought. What fool would torture himself by marrying a woman he knew loved another man?

"I suppose not. In any event, after more than a decade immured at Lambarth Castle, Diana...ran away. We heard she'd sailed in a fishing boat to Ireland, then taken ship to the Caribbean, where she joined

Gavin at the estate he'd settled. Lambarth refused to divorce her, though, so they were never allowed to marry under English law."

Lady Darnell paused, a pensive look on her face. "I sometimes wondered if she'd regretted leaving her husband, forced as she was afterward to live as an outcast and give up her daughter. We were close growing up, but when she married Lambarth, we lost touch."

And what of the most innocent victim of this family tragedy? Adam thought. "The poor child."

"Indeed. It must have been dreadful, losing her mama, then living so isolated before her papa died, as well."

"And you want to comfort her?" Adam asked.

Lady Darnell gave him a tremulous smile. "It's always been my greatest sorrow that I was never blessed with children. Not that you and Charis are not extremely dear to me, but by the time I married your papa, you were both nearly grown. Yes, I would very much like to care for my dear cousin Diana's poor little daughter."

This was not sounding like a "temporary" measure, Adam thought. Still, he could hardly fault his stepmother's concern, and how much could a little girl eat? By the time she needed a wardrobe full of gowns and a dowry for her come-out, she'd either have moved on to her paternal relations—or he'd have the Darnell fortunes mended.

"So when do we collect this waif?"

A dazzling smile illumined Lady Darnell's face.

"Oh, Adam, I knew your compassion could not fail! I shall reply to the solicitor immediately to fix a time."

Adam rose to escort his stepmother out. As he bent to kiss her fingertips, she pulled him close for a hug.

"Thank you, my dear," she murmured. "Your kindness will be rewarded, I'm sure. A child is always a blessing."

Recalling some of the exuberant students who had enlivened his sojourn at Eton, Adam made a noncommittal murmur. As his stepmother hurried out, he hoped the long-motherless child he was about to introduce into his well-ordered household would turn out to be a sweet, timid thing rather than an undisciplined hellion.

Only two hours after first learning of the orphan's existence, Adam found himself driving his curricle into the city to the address supplied by Lady Darnell. To their surprise, the footman returning his stepmother's note to the lawyer had brought back a second missive informing them the child had just arrived. However, as there were legal issues involved which might take some time to work out, Mr. Pendenning had suggested that rather than have Lady Darnell wait while the men untangled the niceties, the head of the household could come alone to fetch the girl.

And so, driving the open vehicle he hoped a child would prefer to the lumbering coaches she'd probably been shut up in during her journey and bearing the be-ribboned doll Lady Darnell had charged him to present as a welcoming gift, Adam prepared himself to spend the afternoon armwrestling with lawyers for the dubious privilege of adopting a child entirely unknown to him.

He certainly hoped his stepmother would be happy.

This unforeseen addition to his household underlined the imperative to get the Darnell fortunes in order, he told himself as he drove. But since he'd first considered the matter this morning, he'd had an inspiration that he hoped might spare him the humiliation of having to barter his ancient name and lineage for the hand of some newly rich cit's well-dowered daughter. As long as luck and his old childhood friend Priscilla smiled upon him, anyway.

Having been abroad for the war with France and then having leased out Claygate Manor, the Darnell country estate that bordered her father's lands, he'd not seen Miss Standish in some years. But she was still unmarried, he knew. If the plump, cheerful lass who'd loved to trail behind him on his youthful escapades, hanging adoringly on his every word, had not changed too much, he reasoned, he would have as much chance of finding marital harmony with her as with any of the other carefully coifed, capped and costumed chits about to be paraded on the Marriage Mart.

He'd have to look into calling on Miss Priscilla Standish as soon as he settled this business of the orphan.

Half an hour later he was escorted by a clerk to Mr. Pendenning's private salon, where, the young man informed him, the lawyer would join him shortly.

Knowing there would be lengthy paperwork to sort

out, Adam suppressed his irritation at the delay. The salon to which he'd been shown was dimly lit, the curtain of the single window drawn against the light. While his eyes adjusted from the bright sunlight of the brisk late-winter afternoon he'd just left, he scanned the room, his gaze settling on a newspaper left atop a side table.

He was striding to pick up the paper when a rustling noise in the corner of the room distracted him. His vision of welcoming a small, grieving moppet into the family embrace was shaken when what he'd dismissed as an assortment of black rags piled in a chair, suddenly unfolded its length and rose phoenixlike to face him.

The image of a woebegone child died altogether as the Creature approached. Sticklike legs and narrow bare feet protruded below a faded black gown more than a foot too short for her emaciated frame—which was nearly as tall as his own. Adam's shocked impression was of a walking scarecrow, until the Creature halted before him and extended one bony hand.

The girl's nose protruded beaklike from her thin face. With her sharp cheekbones, lusterless, tangled black hair and the feral dark eyes fixed intently upon him, Adam was put forcibly in mind of a bird of prey about to attack.

When the Creature's lips curved into a mocking smile, he realized he'd been simply staring at her, mouth agape, his face no doubt clearly mirroring his thoughts.

Painfully conscious of having, for the first time in his almost thirty well-bred years, failed to summon polite words of greeting, he felt hot color flush his skin. Before he could get his lips working, the Creature withdrew the hand he'd not managed to shake and made him a curtsey.

"You must be Lord Darnell," she said, her voice low-pitched and husky. "How...*charming* to meet you."

CHAPTER THREE

THOUGH THE GIRL WAS the least attractive example of femininity Adam had ever beheld, her curtsey was graceful. Moreover, the sardonic look in those snapping black eyes and the irony in her greeting told him she was shrewd enough to have guessed what he thought of her appearance.

Rather than being embarrassed, though, she seemed to derive a scornful amusement from his discomfiture as he stood, still staring, the frilly doll in one hand.

Before Adam could decide whether he was more offended or diverted by the girl's antagonism, the door opened and a short, bespectacled gentleman hurried in. Seeing the two of them facing each other, he halted abruptly.

"Oh, dear! Lord Darnell, I had hoped to discourse with you privately before…well, I see 'tis too late for that. Arthur Pendenning, sir, at your service," he said with a bow. "You've introduced yourselves, Miss Lambarth?"

"His lordship and I have indeed met," the girl replied. "As you insisted. Now, if you and I could finish our consultations, I'll be on my way."

"There's no need to hurry," Mr. Pendenning said. "Knowing that you have just finished an exhausting journey, I've ordered some refreshment. Shall we not sit together and chat while we partake of it? Please, Miss Lambarth. Lord Darnell, you will remain with us, I trust?"

Rather against his will, Adam murmured a polite acceptance. Far from appearing a grief-stricken waif in need of her relatives' support, the girl seemed almost hostile—and entirely undeferential, either to him or the lawyer. He struggled to resist the urge to let his initial shock at her appearance turn to dislike at her rudeness.

He shouldn't judge her too harshly, he reminded himself. After all, she'd had no mother to guide her for years and, Lady Darnell had warned him, by the time of his death, her late father had become practically a hermit. She probably wasn't to blame for what appeared to be a decided lack of proper maidenly deportment.

"Ah, here is the tray," Mr. Pendenning said. "Lord Darnell, Miss Lambarth, if you would both sit?"

While the servant removed the cover before bowing himself out, Adam deposited himself on the sofa and Miss Lambarth walked with obvious reluctance to perch on the edge of an adjoining wing chair.

Did she think he would bite? Adam wondered with a touch of humor, watching as she covertly watched *him* from the corner of her eye. She seemed less wary with the lawyer, who seated himself near her and began pouring tea.

Adam was about to make some light remark to try

to set her at ease when suddenly she turned toward the teapot, sniffing the air.

Mr. Pendenning extended a cup to her. Cautiously she accepted it, holding the delicate china at arm's length and inspecting the contents, then bending to sniff the liquid.

The awful suspicion that perhaps the girl was not all right in the head had begun to form in Adam's mind when, just as suddenly, she smiled. A passionate intensity lit her face, briefly imbuing her thin features with an attractiveness Adam felt almost like a shock.

Before the shaken Adam could begin to wonder at his unexpected reaction, she turned her expressive eyes on the lawyer. "Tea, is it not?" she asked Mr. Pendenning.

"Yes, my dear. Have you drunk it before?"

"Not since Mama left. But I remember it was good."

"Taste it and see what you think."

She took a sip. "Oh, yes! It *is* good!"

"Some people prefer it with a bit of cake or biscuit. Should you like some?"

She put down the cup and inspected the tray he offered her. "Cake. It is…sweeter than bread, isn't it?"

"Have you not eaten that, either, since your mama went away?" Mr. Pendenning asked.

"No. Is bread and water not the normal fare for prisoners?" she asked, a bitter note in her voice. "Augmented occasionally, when I managed to slip out and visit Mad Sally, with wild berries from the woods."

"I think you will find the cake even sweeter than berries. Do try some." Though Mr. Pendenning's tone remained light, as Miss Lambarth reached for the proffered slice, he glanced at Adam and shook his head, outrage in his eyes.

Beginning to comprehend now what the lawyer was attempting to demonstrate, Adam watched her intently, astounded by Miss Lambarth's delighted exploration of food so ordinary most Londoners of her class would scarcely have given it a second glance.

His heart contracted with pity as she tasted the cake. Once again he felt an odd sizzle of contact when another brilliant smile lit her face. "'Tis wondrous good!"

"Eat as much as you wish, my dear. You must be famished after so long a journey." Something about the lawyer's tone led Adam to think the man was referring to more than Miss Lambarth's recent trip to London.

After nibbling the cake, she tasted the biscuits. Then Mr. Pendenning uncovered another dish and gestured to it. "Have one of these, too, if you like."

Giving him a quizzical glance, she picked up one of the round objects and rolled it between her fingers. "So smooth," she said, and lifted it to her nose. "Smells sweet, like berries. Does one eat the whole?"

"No, one peels it first." Mr. Pendenning demonstrated how to section out the fruit. "It's called an orange."

Her totally unexpected, musical peal of laughter startled Adam. "Of course! Like the color. I've read about them, but the book had no illustration, so I didn't know what the fruit looked like."

"Take a bite, my dear. 'Tis somewhat sweet, like a berry, but different."

Her dark eyes alight with curiosity now, she took the piece of fruit the lawyer sectioned off for her and bit into it, laughing again as juice spurted onto her chin and she brought up her other hand to catch the drip.

The hand that, until this moment, she'd kept within the folds of her shabby skirt. As she wiped her chin, Adam stared in horrified fascination at the jagged scar that ran from the base of her thumb to her wrist.

The lawyer, Adam noted, was staring, as well. In the sudden silence Miss Lambarth darted a glance at Adam, then Pendenning. Her smile faded and her face flushed as she quickly shoved the damaged hand back into her lap.

Adam heard Pendenning's soft hiss of an explicative. "Please, do have some more, my dear," the lawyer entreated.

"Thank you, I've had enough. I'll finish the tea."

"You've had barely half a slice of cake and only a bite of the biscuit. I thought you said you hadn't eaten since arriving in London this morning," the lawyer said.

"I've had nothing since yesterday, but this was quite sufficient. I'm used to eating…lightly," she said, irony once again coloring her tone.

Lord in Heaven, Adam thought, glad that Mr. Pendenning seemed able to carry on the conversation without him, for the almost unbelievable conclusions flooding his mind rendered him speechless. Suddenly he was fiercely glad that Lady Darnell had been called upon to receive her cousin's child. After what he'd just seen and heard, even if the girl had possessed two heads and a tail, Adam would have felt compelled to take her in.

Miss Lambarth finished her tea and set down the cup. "Thank you, Mr. Pendenning. That was wonderful." She gave him a wry look. "As I'm sure was rather evident, 'twas more variety of sustenance than I've had in a decade."

"That, my dear, is something we shall shortly correct," the lawyer said, fervency in his tone. "As I hope you will agree, Lord Darnell?"

"Absolutely." Adam spoke up at last. "Although your cousin had a rather imperfect recollection of your age, Miss Lambarth," he said, indicating with a grin the doll he'd placed on the side table, "it is her most ardent wish, which my sister and I share, that you will do us the honor of agreeing to join our household."

Interest sparked in her eyes. "You have a sister?"

"Yes. Charis is eighteen—about your age?"

"I'm turned twenty," Miss Lambarth replied. "A sister…" she repeated, her gaze drifting off. "Oh, that would be wonderful," she murmured, almost to herself.

"Since Charis is as sweet as she is lovely, I believe you would find it so. Won't you make us all happy, then, and come live with us?"

Miss Lambarth looked up, staring straight into his eyes. "Are you sure you want me?" she asked bluntly. "You've seen what I look like and garnered some idea of how I've lived. I…I'm not sure I would fit into an elegant London household. As tempting as it is to contemplate living with my cousin, perhaps even having a sister, I think 'twill be better if I live on my own."

Mr. Pendenning's protest echoed Adam's. "No, my dear, that would not do at all! In our Society, unmarried young ladies do not live alone."

Miss Lambarth lifted an eyebrow and shrugged. "I am quite able to take care of myself, I assure you."

"I expect you are. That isn't the point. For a single female to live alone just isn't done."

Miss Lambarth stiffened. "You told me I could set up a household in every town in England, if I wished."

"'Twas only a figure of speech. Having the means to set up a household and doing so on your own are two very different matters."

"Mr. Pendenning, I have lived as a prisoner in another man's house for the last ten years. I intend never to be restrained by anyone again. And I care not a jot whether society approves my mode of living."

After what he'd seen and heard, Adam couldn't help but understand her reluctance. But all his protective instincts aroused, he searched his mind for some other argument to persuade Miss Lambarth to reconsider.

Before he hit upon anything, the lawyer said, "I'm sorry, I have not explained the situation very well. Naturally, one could not expect you to care about the opinion of persons you have never met. But as you are closely related to Lady Darnell, Society will expect her to offer you shelter and protection—whether or not you need them. If you do not reside with her, she will be considered shockingly remiss in her duty to you. So you see, if you choose to live alone, you will subject your cousin to severe criticism."

Although Adam didn't see why that should matter to the girl, either, her silence and the frown creasing her forehead indicated that, for whatever reason, this argument affected her. "I should not want to harm the reputation of Mama's cousin," she said after a moment.

Turning to Adam, she continued, "If I do consent to live with you, you must understand that if the…experience is not successful, I shall feel free to leave whenever I wish. Hopefully, we can rub together long enough for me to determine what I wish to do and where I want to live. I think I should like to travel, so perhaps if I leave you to set off to Europe, Cousin Lillian will be spared the censure of her peers."

"We shall just have to make sure you find residing with us more enjoyable than the prospect of taking your own house," Adam said, determined to show this waif who had been so badly treated what a blessing living with one's family could be.

She regarded him gravely. "Do you have a large library?"

Surprised once again by her abrupt change of topic, Adam said, "As it happens, my father was a bibliophile, so I believe you will find it quite extensive."

"I intend to have my books sent up from Lambarth. Will I have rooms to use at my discretion?"

"A bedchamber and private sitting room will be placed at your disposal. The library, drawing rooms and dining parlors you would share with the rest of the family."

She nodded. "If I come, you must also agree that I will pay all my own expenses. No!" she interrupted when Adam started to protest. "I absolutely insist upon that. There are certain comforts I must have and I do not intend to be beholden to you for providing them."

Thinking he'd never had so odd and blunt a conversation in his life, Adam couldn't help asking, "What sort of comforts, if I might inquire?"

"I wish to keep a fire burning in my rooms night and day. I've been cold half my life and don't intend to be so ever again."

He had a sudden vision of a small thin girl locked in a frigid room. "You may keep your fires stoked as hot as you wish," he promised, the urge to heal and protect once more tightening his chest.

A little smile played about her lips. "I want a bed with a feather mattress so soft, when I lie down I will feel like I'm floating on air. A turkey carpet on the floor so thick, my feet will sink up to the ankles, as if in a pair of fuzzy slippers. Oh, and speaking of slippers—" she turned to Mr. Pendenning "—if those instruments of torture that Jerry Sunderland provided me in the guise of footwear are representative of what I can expect in shoes, I shall remain as I am, barefoot."

The lawyer chuckled. "Not knowing your size, poor Jerry grabbed the only pair the cobbler had ready. I promise you, my dear, that the bootmakers of London can put on your feet slippers so soft and supple you would swear you *were* still barefoot."

"Very good," Miss Lambarth said. "I shall feed those shoes into the first fire I kindle in my room. And this gown, as soon as a replacement can be found."

"I've already summoned a dressmaker to wait upon

you here," Mr. Pendenning said. "She is bringing several gowns that can be quickly altered to fit. For the rest, I'm sure Lady Darnell will take you to her own mantua-maker and assist you in purchasing as many gowns as you like."

Adam had to laugh. "I can assure you she will! My stepmother positively delights in shopping. I expect my sister will also petition to join such an expedition."

"I want pretty colors," Miss Lambarth stated. "No black. And soft fabrics, like the material of this sofa."

"I'm sure Lady Darnell will be able to find you something that pleases you. So," Mr. Pendenning said, "you will go with Lord Darnell, as your mother wished?"

Miss Lambarth looked back at Adam. "A big library?"

"Quite large."

"A thick feather mattress?"

"Soft as a cloud."

"Warm rooms?"

"You can make the wallpaper curl."

At that moment a knock sounded and one of the lawyer's assistants stepped in. "Mr. Pendenning, you wished me to let you know when the seamstress arrived."

The lawyer looked over to Miss Lambarth. "Are you ready for that new gown?"

That smile transformed her face again. "Absolutely!"

"And you will accompany Lord Darnell to meet your cousin when it is done?"

After a pause she nodded. "I will go with him."

"Excellent." He beamed at the girl. "Show Miss Lambarth and the seamstress to the back office and see that they are not disturbed," he instructed his assistant.

"I'll wait here for you, Miss Lambarth," Adam told her as she walked to the door.

She paused on the threshold to look back at him. "I hope neither of us regrets this."

Something about her fierce independence sent a rush of awareness through Adam. 'Twas just compassion for her plight and anger at the unspeakable treatment she'd suffered, he told himself as he assured her, "I'm certain your stay in my home will be a pleasure for us both."

CHAPTER FOUR

AFTER THE YOUNG MAN escorted Miss Lambarth out, Pendenning turned to Adam. "Will you join me for a brandy? After the, ah, surprise of meeting Miss Lambarth, I expect you could use one. I know I could."

"I would be grateful," Adam replied.

The lawyer poured the brandy and handed Adam a glass. "I imagine you have questions for me."

"Indeed! My stepmother told me that Miss Lambarth's mother left nearly a decade ago. Am I to understand from what I've just witnessed that from that time until his recent death, her father kept her a...a *prisoner?*"

His face setting in grim lines, Pendenning nodded. "As horrifying and incredible as that may seem, 'tis true. How much of my client's story do you know?"

"Only that Lady Lambarth apparently had a...prior attachment before she married, and when after some years together, she found life with Lord Lambarth insupportable, she left him and the child and fled to her former lover."

Mr. Pendenning shook his head. "It wasn't that at all. I suppose your stepmother informed you that Gavin

Seagrave is a bit of a rogue?" When Adam nodded, he continued, "His attachment to Diana Forester was as strong as hers to him. When he learned from various sources that her marriage to Lambarth—a man he'd always disliked—was unhappy, he determined to rescue her and the child. He put men on station near Lambarth Castle, and when the opportunity presented itself one day as the two were riding, they seized them. Lady Lambarth's cries were quickly silenced once she learned who had taken them, but Lambarth chanced to be inspecting a farm nearby, heard the commotion and rode up. Her mother they carried off, but he managed to retrieve Helena."

Adam shook his head. "It sounds like a scene out of a Minerva Press novel."

"And might be equally entertaining, were the circumstances not so dire. Needless to say, my client was devastated to have her precious child trapped under the control of a man she both disliked and feared. Six months later she and Seagrave attempted another rescue."

"It was not successful, I gather."

"No. Since Helena was forbidden to venture beyond the castle gardens after her mother's flight, Lambarth discovered them before they were able to spirit her away. As he held the struggling girl, Lambarth shouted to her mother that he would see the child dead before he would let her go and that, should he ever again find strangers on his land or even in the village, he would kill her. My client believed him."

"So the child was punished for the mother's sins?"

"I'm afraid so. After that second failed attempt, Lambarth no longer allowed Helena outside the castle, even to accompany him to church. He apparently imprisoned her within the walls, meanwhile putting it about the village that, grieving for the mother who had abandoned her, the child had lost her wits—insuring that if Helena somehow did manage to escape, no one would believe her pleas for help. He also stationed guards around the perimeter of his land and had them make periodic inspections of the village and report to him if there were any newcomers."

"If she was barred from approaching her daughter, how did Helena's mother know what was happening?"

"Lady Lambarth's maid was a local girl who returned to the village after her mistress's disappearance. One of Seagrave's agents trailed the girl to London when she went to visit relations there and contacted her. They persuaded her to bring back with her a man who would pose as her cousin. Another of Seagrave's men, Jerry Sunderland. He settled in the village and practiced his trade, sending what information about Helena he was able to gather and waiting for some chance to help the girl escape. Unfortunately, Lord Lambarth insured there wasn't any."

"And so she remained a prisoner until his death."

"Yes. But though I knew she'd been close confined, even I was shocked by her appearance. I shall severely chastise my clerk for showing you in before I had a chance to warn you what to expect."

Since there was nothing Adam wished to reveal about his initial reaction to Miss Lambarth, nor could he explain the intense, fleeting response her smile had generated, he remained prudently silent.

The solicitor took a swallow of his brandy. "What she so innocently revealed during tea was even more chilling. I can only thank a merciful God that her mother never suspected the full extent of her suffering at Lambarth's hands. Truly the man's revenge was complete—to withhold from the woman who'd scorned him the child she prized almost beyond life, imprisoning the girl in such a way that her mother did not dare try to free her."

"The child he punished was his own, as well, though," Adam pointed out.

"Yes—which just illustrates the character of the man. One hesitates to speak ill of the departed, but I'm reasonably certain in the case of Lord Lambarth, it wasn't through the Pearly Gates that he entered the Hereafter. Thus, I hardly need tell you that after her treatment at her father's hands, Miss Lambarth views male authority with great suspicion. I thought at first I should not be able to convince her to try living with your family at all."

Adam stiffened. "I assure you, Mr. Pendenning, that Miss Lambarth will be treated with nothing but kindness while under my care."

"I didn't mean to suggest otherwise, my lord. And, quite frankly, before I ever suggested the arrangement to Helena, I made sure that your character was such that I need have no qualms about introducing her into your house."

"Did you!" Adam exclaimed, not sure whether to

admire the lawyer's thoroughness or resent the investigation into his background.

Obviously understanding his mixed feelings, the lawyer grinned at him. "Naturally, everyone to whom I made inquiries had only praise for your excellence. But after what Miss Lambarth has suffered, I had to be sure."

He supposed he couldn't fault Mr. Pendenning for being prudent. "I am relieved to hear it," he replied, a bit stiffly.

"Which brings us to the matter of finances. Helena is adamant that she discharge all her own expenses while she remains your guest. As I'm hoping this 'trial period' of living with you will lead to her finding a place within a warm and loving family, I do not wish to put her on the defensive by arguing that point."

"Are we to total up the cost for her soup and the washing of her linens?" Adam asked wryly.

The lawyer chuckled. "I trust she can be persuaded to let you fund the everyday necessities of life. But she will insist on paying for all her purchases outside the home. Please assure me you'll allow that."

Adam felt a guilty pang of relief. Since a young woman of Miss Lambarth's age would be much more costly to outfit than a child, he could only be grateful she was set upon bearing those expenses herself.

"If she insists. But I see a greater problem. Given Miss Lambarth's age, she should have been presented several years ago. Although, praise God, she seems quite well-spoken, despite the privations she's suffered, from what you've told me of her background, she has had absolutely no training to prepare her to enter Society."

"That is a problem indeed. For the present, she desires only to join your family. Perhaps, as she adjusts to that, your stepmother can tutor her in the behavior that would later equip her to be formally presented. As you and I both know, my lord, if she is ever to have the truly normal life her mother wished for her, she will have to be found a husband to give her status and protection."

Recalling the girl's bluntness and hostility toward men, Adam shook his head dubiously. "That's asking quite a lot—of Miss Lambarth and my stepmother."

"True," Mr. Pendennning admitted. "If she does eventually agree to a presentation, 'twill require a good deal of vigilance on your part. She's a very considerable heiress, and you would need to ensure that anyone who courted her valued Helena for herself, not just her fortune."

Given the girl's odd upbringing—and unfortunate appearance—Adam doubted even a large dowry would prompt a proposal from any suitor he would consider acceptable. But as he could hardly voice so unchivalrous a comment, he had still not replied when the lawyer waved a dismissive hand.

"But all such speculation is borrowing trouble from tomorrow, which our Lord warns us quite particularly not to do. For the present, let us get Helena adjusted to living in your household. Understanding her special background, you will take her in and treat her gently?"

"We shall do our best."

"I can ask nothing more. Thank you, my lord." The lawyer held out his hand.

Adam shook it. "Thank you for being so strong a champion for her."

While Mr. Pendenning returned the brandy decanter to the sideboard, Adam recalled the brief spark of attraction he'd felt for the girl. If anyone could work the miracle of coaxing that spark into a flame bright enough to make Miss Lambarth capable of catching a husband, it would be his stepmother. But a miracle it would be. He was by no means sure he wished to commit his stepmother to attempting it.

But, as the lawyer said, such concerns were far in the future. He had no doubt that regardless of the girl's deficiencies, for the love Lady Darnell still bore Helena's mother, his stepmother would receive her gladly and lavish her with affection.

At that moment a knock sounded at the door and Miss Lambarth walked back in. Though the modest blue round gown hung loosely on her bony frame and thin arms, her legs were decently covered and the color made her face look less sallow. A plain straw bonnet capped her tangled black hair, which still appeared in dire need of a comb's ministrations. Apparently the dressmaker had not thought to bring shoes or gloves, for the girl had on what could only be the crude farmer's boots she'd complained about and had tucked her damaged hand within the folds of the gown.

She curtseyed to them. As he bowed in return, Adam noted again the grace of that motion. Apparently her late mother had had time to teach the girl at least something of proper behavior. Perhaps the task of making her presentable might not be as impossible as he feared.

"I expect I'm ready—if you still wish to take me home with you," she added, looking to him.

Did he detect a hint of anxiety in her tone? Adam gazed steadily into Helena's dark, black-lashed eyes—undoubtedly the girl's best feature—and smiled. "Of course I do. I expect by now Lady Darnell will have worn a hole pacing the carpet, so anxious is she to welcome you."

Helena lifted an eyebrow dubiously before turning to Mr. Pendenning. "How can I thank you, sir, for all you have done for Mama and me?"

"It was a privilege to serve so loving and devoted a lady," Mr. Pendenning replied. "Having now met the courageous lass who inspired that devotion, I don't wonder at it. If I can do anything more for you, Helena, call on me at any time."

The girl nodded, her concealed hand fidgeting with a pleat of her gown. "Do…do you suppose I might come see you from time to time?"

"I shall be very offended if you do not visit me often!" He walked over to her and took the unblemished hand she offered. "It will be all right, you will see," he said softly. "Your mother was a very wise lady. She would not entrust your future to someone unworthy of the task."

Swallowing hard, the girl nodded. "I'm not so sure *I* am worthy of it."

Before Adam could add his reassurance that all would be well, she turned to him, her diffidence vanishing beneath the cool demeanor she'd exhibited at their first encounter. With a trace of the same irony in her tone, she said, "Shall we go then, Lord Darnell? I shouldn't wish to keep my *impatient* cousin waiting any longer."

HELENA TRIED NOT TO let her spirits sink as she followed the tall, broad-shouldered Lord Darnell from the room—leaving the sanctuary of the man who'd known and served her mother for a doubtful reception by a dimly remembered relative who lived in a wholly unfamiliar world.

Head high, Helena Lambarth, she told herself. Lord Darnell might have the muscular frame of the soldier he was reputed to be, but she could defend herself if necessary. She'd faced down worse bullies. And unlike her father and his baliff, he had no idea what she was capable of if cornered.

He certainly *appeared* attractive enough, with his handsome face, wavy hair the color of ripe chestnuts and clear green eyes. She'd even felt some…sensation pass between them, something that sent a shiver to her stomach, though it didn't seem menacing.

Still, her father had been handsome, too, in his way. She better than anyone should know how little appearances meant. Except that Lord Darnell's face also looked kind—not something she ever could have said about her father.

Besides, she was free now—*free.* Though custom might say Lord Darnell could dictate her actions, he had no legal authority to compel her to do anything. It would take her some time to learn the passages of the house to which he was conveying her, but she was sure she could figure a way out of its confines if she had to, just as she had ferreted routes out of the stone tomb of Lambarth Castle. Unlike her miserable years at Lambarth, however, if she should need to escape, she had no doubt that Mr. Pendenning would stand her advocate.

Besides, as the lawyer had reminded her, Mama had chosen these people to care for her. Her trust in Mama's love and wisdom had sustained her for years. She didn't intend to start doubting it now.

So she had no reason to be apprehensive as she set boldly out on this new adventure—or so she tried to convince the small child inside who, though she refused to acknowledge it, hungered desperately for acceptance.

To distract herself from her nervousness, once Lord Darnell's curricle set off, she bent her intellect to carefully observing every detail of the London scene. After she returned monosyllabic answers to his first few comments, Lord Darnell transferred his attention back to his restive horses and let silence reign between them.

The horses were magnificent, she noted with approval. Having learned to ride from practically the time she could walk, Helena had sometimes wandered down to the castle stables during the nights when she escaped her barred room. Mad Sally had taught her that animals could communicate with humans, if one had an eye to see and an ear to listen. Helena's visits with these fellow wild creatures, penned up as she was and forced to do a master's bidding, had always brought her solace.

She would be able to buy her own horses now, she realized, the thought cheering her.

If it became necessary for her to find her way out of London, however, escape would be more difficult. From the moment she'd caught her first glimpse of the city from atop the mail coach as it rounded the heights, she'd marveled at the sheer size and complexity of it. As Lord Darnell drove, she noted again what a twisted tangle of streets, carriages, laden wagons and scurrying pedestrians it was.

The library at Lambarth Castle had contained atlases of the globe. Surely there were maps of this city, as well. She made a mental note to obtain one on her next excursion.

For the trip to the Darnell town house, she'd put back on the stiff leather shoes she'd worn from Lambarth—which she intended to remove at the first opportunity and feed to the fire. And though the blue dress she now wore was softer and warmer than the rag she'd arrived in, she anticipated with great eagerness being able to enter an elegant shop like the ones they were now passing and order a whole wardrobe of shoes and gowns made to fit her alone.

The humiliation she had forbidden herself to feel when Lord Darnell first saw her, revulsion writ clear on his face, heated her now. She'd not see him again, she vowed, until she looked presentable. Or at least as presentable as someone of her thin, bony frame and plain face could.

Although the first purchase she made would be a comb and brush, she decided, fingering the twisted mat of hair beneath the straw bonnet. After deciding to declare his daughter "mad," to further bolster that claim, her father had thrown her mother's silver set off the cliffs.

With a bittersweet smile, she remembered her disappointment the first time she'd managed to escape the castle and make her way to Mad Sally's hovel. She'd hoped to tidy herself, but found the old woman was as much a stranger to grooming as Helena had been forced to become.

Small wonder the villagers had stared when she stumbled into their midst a short time later.

Undoubtedly her aunt also possessed a tub in which she could bathe, as had Mama. Oh, to feel truly clean again! Whatever the cost of having servants bring up the necessary containers of heated water, she would pay gladly.

She was still imagining the delights of hot water and scented soap when Lord Darnell's voice interrupted her.

"We're arriving now in St. James Square," he said as he signaled his horses to a walk. "Darnell House is third from the left on the northwest side."

Despite her brave resolutions, Helena's stomach dipped as she studied the brick building with its elegant inset pilasters. A moment later Lord Darnell pulled up the horses, a livried servant coming to their heads.

After a footman helped her to alight, Helena took the arm Lord Darnell offered her and ascended the steps to the front door—which was opened before they touched the handle by yet another servant attired in formal black dress.

"This is Harrison," Lord Darnell said as the man bowed them in. "Without his supervision, our household would cease to function."

"Thank you, my lord, and welcome, Miss Lambarth. The ladies are expecting you in the south parlor."

While Helena marveled at the quantity of servants employed in the Darnell household, an older lady bearing a vague resemblance to Mama rushed into the hall. "Oh, Adam, I just couldn't wait—"

Catching sight of her, the woman stopped in midphrase. As her gaze traveled down Helena from the cheap straw bonnet to the stiff leather shoes, her smile faded, her cheeks paled and her eyes widened.

"Lord in Heaven!" she exclaimed. Then she swayed, her eyes fluttering shut, and crumpled to the floor.

It was a scene out of Helena's worst fears: Lord Darnell leaping to catch his stepmother before she hit the marble paving, Harrison calling out for assistance, an elegant young lady who must be Lord Darnell's sister rushing into the hallway to stop short in dismay.

Perhaps the sister will swoon, too, Helena thought, trying to ignore the pain that lanced through her as her vague hopes of a warm reception dissolved like Lady Darnell's welcoming smile.

Crossing her arms over her bosom, Helena looked at Adam, staggering under the burden of his semiconscious stepmother, and raised her eyebrows. "Are you still sure you wish to offer me a home, Lord Darnell?"

CHAPTER FIVE

THE YOUNG LADY, WHO HAD pale blond curls and her brother's warm green eyes, turned to her. "Of course he does! I'm Charis, Lord Darnell's sister. Let me escort you out of this confusion while Adam attends to Bellemere."

There was no mistaking the sincerity of the girl's tone. Prepared to offer a waspish reply, Helena was left with nothing to say. A gratitude she didn't want to feel warmed her chest and angrily she blinked back tears.

Promising herself she would exit this dwelling as soon as possible and make her way back to Mr. Pendenning's office, Helena let the girl escort her into the parlor.

"Please, will you not sit? Though I shouldn't wonder at your wishing to bolt for the door, thinking you'd arrived at a house out of bedlam!"

There seeming nothing else to do; Helena took a chair.

"Let me apologize for so appalling a welcome," Miss Darnell continued as she seated herself. "Lady Darnell has the sweetest of temperaments, but a very nervous disposition that sometimes overwhelms her—

and she has been beside herself all afternoon with impatience for your arrival. Pray, do pardon her! When she recovers, she will be mortified at having made such a scene."

Not sure what she should answer, Helena simply nodded.

"Should you like some tea? We didn't know whether you would be hungry when you arrived."

"Mr. Pendenning gave me refreshments at his office."

"Are you tired, then? Adam said you had a very long journey—from Cornwall, was it? Oh, but here I am, chattering on when you must be wishing only to rest until dinner. Shall we go upstairs, then?"

Not sure she could bear an interview with the "recovered" Lady Darnell, Helena knew she should take her leave immediately. But the short nap at Mr. Pendenning's office had refreshed her very little. The idea of having a place to temporarily lay her head held such appeal she was not able to refuse it.

"I should like to rest," she admitted.

"Let me take you up straightaway, then. Adam is the most delightful of brothers," Miss Darnell continued as they left the room and began mounting the stairs, "but he is a *man*." Miss Darnell glanced back at Helena with a mischievous look. "I've often longed for a sister. Oh, I do hope we shall become great friends!"

Though Helena returned her gaze searchingly, once again she could read nothing but sincerity in the girl's open manner and friendly smile. Too weary to worry over the matter any further, she entered the bedchamber to which Miss Darnell conducted her, conscious only of the clarion call of sleep.

"Ring the bell when you're ready and a maid will escort you back downstairs," Miss Darnell said as she pulled the curtains closed. "Now, rest well, for I warn you, when you join us again, I shall be full of questions!"

To which, Helena thought as she sank gratefully down on a bed as soft as Lord Darnell had promised, she was not sure she had any answers acceptable for the ears of a sheltered young maiden.

THOUGH HELENA HAD INTENDED only to close her eyes for a few moments, when she reached consciousness again, she was dismayed to find the room in almost total darkness. She sprang up, a little fear darting through her. If what happened in the next few minutes solidified her determination to leave, would she be able to find her way back through the tangle of streets to Mr. Pendenning's office? Would anyone even be there at such an hour?

Before she could decide whether or not to tug the bellpull, her chamber door opened and a maid peeped in.

Spotting Helena standing by the bed, the girl bobbed a curtsey. "Begging your pardon, miss, but mistress wished me to see if you was awake yet. The ladies be waiting for you downstairs. If ye be ready, I'll show you the way."

"Mistress" presumably being Lady Darnell, Helena hesitated. She might as well get the meeting over with.

If 'twas unpleasant…well, she'd already determined to leave. But she would do so properly, after expressing her gratitude to Mama's cousin for her courtesy—not sneaking out like a prisoner breaking parole.

Mentally armoring herself for the confrontation, Helena followed, then paused on the threshold while the girl announced her. Taking a deep breath, she walked in.

She found Charis Darnell sitting on the sofa beside her mother's cousin. Before Helena could utter a word, Lady Darnell jumped up and hurried to her.

"My dear Helena, please forgive me! My wretched nerves. I had worked myself into such a state waiting for Adam to return with you that when I perceived you at last, such a look of poor Diana about you, I was quite overcome!" Lady Darnell held out her hands. "Please tell me you'll pardon an old woman's foolishness and let us start over."

Hesitantly, Helena offered her hands. To her surprise, the woman seized them and pulled her into a hug.

The soft brush of blond curls against her cheek…a scent of roses…the warmth of a rounded female form holding her close… All these touched something deep within her, flooding her with memories of a loving embrace.

After a moment of shocked surprise, Helena returned the pressure of the older woman's arms. She clung fiercely to Lady Darnell, the contact fulfilling a craving for closeness she was only just realizing she possessed.

After several moments Lady Darnell loosened her grip and moved Helena to arm's length, gazing with loving intensity at her face. "You do have the look of Diana about you," she said softly.

"Do I? I always thought I looked nothing like her. I am so dark and she was fair, like you."

"'Tis not so much coloring as in the way you carry yourself, your profile, the tilt of your chin."

Still not quite sure she dared believe it, Helena said, "You do want me to live with you, Lady Darnell?"

"More than anything! But 'Lady Darnell' makes me sound like some sort of forbiddingly strict chaperone, which I assure you I do not intend to be. Adam and Charis call me Bellemere, after…something French, I believe."

"'Belle-mère'—stepmother," Helena supplied. "Or 'beautiful mother,' which is even more appropriate."

Lady Darnell dimpled with pleasure. "How sweet of you, child! I'm glad to see Diana taught you something of languages before she…" Coloring a little, Lady Darnell rushed on. "Well, I do not doubt it, for she was very clever! When we were girls, I always looked on your mama like a sister. I would be very pleased if you would call me 'Aunt Lillian.'"

"You must call me Charis and I hope you will let me call you Helena," Lord Darnell's sister said as she came to join them. "We are so thrilled to have you here."

Amazingly, it seemed they really did want her—despite her ungainly form and unattractive face, her mangled hand and tangled hair.

Mama had been right after all.

Swallowing the lump that clogged her throat, Helena at last managed to reply, "I should be honored to call you Aunt Lillian and Charis."

"Good, that's settled!" Charis said. "My brother shall be Adam, but I don't expect we'll see much of him. Once Bellemere announced her intention to summon an army of linen drapers, bonnet makers, cobblers, dressmakers, hairdressers, glove makers and such, he told us he expected to be frightfully busy for at least a month!" She grinned at Helena. "Sit down and let us start planning."

"Yes, please do," Aunt Lillian said as she led Helena to the sofa and took the seat beside her. "I had Cook hold dinner, not knowing when you would wake. While it is prepared, you must tell us what *you* wish to do."

It had been so long since anyone had asked Helena what she wanted that for a moment she was too surprised to reply. A rush of gratitude filling her, she said, "Since I know virtually nothing of how to conduct myself in Society, I shall need you to teach me. I should like tutors, too, for the pianoforte and history and literature and all those subjects I have not been able to study since Mama left. Of course, I wish to have gowns and shoes and all such necessities made up as soon as possible.

"But first, I waited so very long to be reunited with my mother, only to discover I will never see her again. Please, Aunt Lillian, would you tell me about Mama? Everything you remember, from the very beginning!"

Lady Darnell gave her a tremulous smile. "Of course, my dear. We first met when Diana just five years old…"

AFTER HIS STEPMOTHER'S disastrous reaction to Helena Lambarth, Adam had borne the afflicted woman to her bedchamber. Leaving her maid to minister to her, he'd hurried back downstairs to be told by the butler that both Charis and Miss Lambarth had retired to rest until dinner. Realizing there was nothing further he could do for the moment, Adam headed for the library.

Although Helena appeared to better account in the blue gown than she had in the rag she had been wearing when he'd first cast eyes on her, the impression she made was still startling. Lady Darnell's fainting fit was his own damn fault, he acknowledged with a gusty sigh as he sat behind his desk. He should have anticipated such a strong reaction from his sensitive relation and, while waiting at the lawyer's office for Helena to have her dress fitted, sent his stepmother a warning.

Too late for that now. Still, he knew Lady Darnell's desire to take in the girl was heartfelt and genuine. Hopefully once over the cataclysmic shock of meeting Helena, she would deal better with her.

He certainly hoped so, for otherwise he had no idea what he would do with her. Though he'd promised her a warm welcome, he could hardly insist that his stepmother care for someone she held in abhorrence. Nor could he, in good conscience, send the girl away to live alone in London.

Pushing that worry aside, he opened his account books to tackle the more immediate problem of finding somewhere the money to make the repairs his agent had written were essential for the tenants at Claygate Manor.

His humor soured further as he played that financial shell game. Several hours later, after resolving the matter as best he could for the moment—and promising himself he would look into the courting of Miss Standish with all speed—he closed the ledgers and headed to the parlor to see if his stepmother had recovered enough to present herself for dinner.

Pausing on the threshold, he spied the three ladies on the sofa, Miss Lambarth and Charis sitting to either side of his stepmother and leaning toward her as she spoke.

"Lord Lambarth pursued your mama from the moment she appeared at her first ball," Lady Darnell was saying. "Diana liked him well enough…until Gavin Seagrave arrived halfway through the Season. Oh, the look on her face when she saw him—and he her! I was standing right beside her, and knew with dismaying certainty that very instant that theirs would be a Fatal Passion!"

"Why dismayed?" his sister asked. "The Seagraves are connected to an earldom, are they not?"

Adam shifted his gaze to Helena. Her lips parted in a half smile, her eyes glowing, her whole face and body radiated the dynamic intensity that had struck him when she smiled at him in the lawyer's office. A vibrancy so luminous one actually did not notice the thinness of her face and frame.

But more than that, she looked *happy*. A deep sense of satisfaction settled in his gut and he offered a swift prayer of thanks that despite their inauspicious beginning, the ladies were obviously now on cordial terms.

Quietly he retraced his steps. Since he was promised

to dine at his club anyway, he'd leave Helena to bask in Lady Darnell's memories of her mother and consult his stepmother about her future later.

HALF AN HOUR LATER, Adam entered White's. His return from the army was still recent enough that several gentlemen, former Oxford mates or London acquaintances whom he'd not yet seen, came up to greet him, slowing his progress to the dining room where his best friend Bennett Dixon awaited him.

Dix rose and tossed down his newspaper as Adam approached. "At last! I'd about given you up!"

After shaking his friend's hand, Adam threw himself into the chair opposite. "Sorry. I was skirmishing with the account books and lost track of time."

Beckoning to a waiter, Dix nodded. "Devil of a job, bookkeeping. Hope you won the battle."

"Barely. Johnson wrote informing me that the roof of the dining parlor at Claygate leaks. Not wishing to scare off the new tenants who will soon arrive, 'tis imperative to repair it. I can't afford to lose the rent." Sighing, he shook his head. "And to think, I used to believe all I need do was get my carcass back to England before some Frog dragoon skewered it, and all would be well."

After ordering dinner, Dix looked back at Adam, sympathy in his gaze. "A bloody shame, your father wasting away as he did. Stands to reason everything went awry, with no hand on the helm for so many years."

"Enough bleating about finances. Let me tell you

the most exceptional news." After pausing to sip his wine, Adam recounted the circumstances behind the arrival of Helena Lambarth. "So," he concluded, "after collecting her from the lawyer a few hours ago, I conveyed her home."

"How old did you say she is?"

Adam swallowed another sip. "Twenty."

"Twenty! And unmarried?" Dix's eyes immediately brightened. "Is she attractive?"

Adam recalled the response she'd briefly sparked in him. Still, he could hardly describe her as a Beauty. "I doubt she'll ever be accounted a Diamond, though I'm confident her appearance can be improved. You see—" he glanced around to confirm that no one was near enough to overhear "—the poor girl has been ill-nourished and badly treated. Indeed, my stepmother about had palpitations when she first saw her. However, learning that she must assist the chit in acquiring a complete new wardrobe soon rallied Bellemere's spirits. We don't yet know whether the girl will wish or be able to go about in Society, so don't mention her existence to anyone just yet."

Dix nodded. "You can rely on my discretion." After suspending the conversation while their waiter served dinner, he continued, "No wonder you're in a pucker, having this additional charge placed on your income."

Adam chuckled. "Not a bit! Apparently the chit has been left quite a lot of money, which she insists upon using to purchase her own kit. Rather an…independent sort," he said, having difficulty finding words to adequately convey Helena's unusual essence.

"An heiress, eh? Maybe I need to take a look! Unless you have an interest there yourself."

Dismissing the brief flare of warmth that question generated, Adam laughed outright. "Heavens, no! Even if I did, 'twould hardly be fitting, with her practically my ward. Nor would I encourage you to dangle after her. Helena's father treated her with such severity that, at the moment, she's very wary of men. No, the solution to my financial woes will have to come from some other quarter. In fact, I have someone in mind and wish your opinion."

Dix nodded. "Hate to see anyone forced into leg shackles, but one can't allow the family holdings to be sold off. So, who is the heiress you're considering?"

"Miss Priscilla Standish."

Din gave a low whistle. "Setting your sights rather high! Rumor says Miss Standish has refused a number of eligible offers these last few Seasons. Don't know the chit myself—I don't run in the elevated circles her family frequents! Her parents are said to be regular Tartars, especially the mother, but since the girl's fortune exceeds that of any other maiden in the Marriage Mart, I suppose they can be particular. What makes you think you've a chance to win this female Golden Ball?"

Adam shrugged. "We were neighbors growing up. She always had a fondness for me."

"A childhood attachment—that's an advantage no other contender can boast," Dix approved. "That might do it, for even the officious Mrs. Standish can't fault your breeding. And the chit's fortune is certainly large enough to offset your lack of one. Am I to wish you happy, then?"

Adam laughed. "That would be a bit premature! I've not even called on her yet, and I haven't seen her in years. She, or Mrs. Standish, may show me the door—for being the fortune hunter I am." Adam feared his light tone wouldn't entirely mask his bitterness at being forced into that role.

"It isn't 'fortune hunting' when the suitor is well-born, handsome and of superior character!" his friend returned loyally.

"Thank you," Adam replied, the sting slightly eased. "But 'tis what I am for all that. Still, if I can steel myself to perform my duty with dispatch, I may be able to provide enough of a dowry that Charis, at least, will not have to concern herself with finances when 'tis her turn to choose a mate. And it will be satisfying to see Darnell land restored to what it was in my grandfather's day."

Dixon nodded again. "Might as well look to the positive. So, when do you begin the siege?"

"Tomorrow. In the meantime, though, I must postpone the trip to the card room I promised you earlier and return to consult Lady Darnell about our new houseguest."

Their meal finished, the two friends stood and shook hands. "Let me know if there is anything I can do to help," Dix offered. "And promise me I'll be the first to meet your mysterious guest, once you judge it possible!"

"You'll be bid to her very first dinner." Running through his mind one more time a vision of Helena as she appeared at the lawyer's office, he added, "But don't expect the invitation anytime soon!"

AFTER RETURNING FROM WHITE'S, Adam went in search of his stepmother. After discovering she was in her sitting room, he proceeded to the door and begged leave to enter.

Lady Darnell greeted him from the secretary, where she'd been writing notes. To his relief, her eyes were bright, her cheeks their normal pink hue, and her smile welcoming. Apparently she had recovered from the distress occasioned by her first glimpse of Miss Lambarth.

He walked over to kiss her hand. "You are looking much better than when I left you, dear ma'am. I'm so sorry to have foisted Miss Lambarth on you unprepared."

"And I must apologize for acting such a looby! I didn't mean to be so hen-hearted. 'Tis only that I was horrified to see how badly she had been neglected." As she said the words, tears welled up again in her eyes.

Adam patted the hand he still held, his concern for her returning. "Are you sure you wish to undertake her care? You are in no way bound to do so, you know. 'Tis not a frightened child we are talking about, who could be cosseted and tucked away in the schoolroom, but a young woman who, by right of birth, ought to be out in Society. Given her total lack of preparation for such a thing, it seems impossible that she could be schooled in the proper behavior by the start of this Season. You spent years at Papa's bedside. I would not have you exile yourself from Society again. We can hire tutors for Miss Lambarth."

Dashing her tears away with one hand, Lady Darnell shook her head. "Turn the poor child over to strangers, when she's just found her family? Certainly not! If I could bear standing by, watching your dear papa dwindle into a shriveled husk of the man he'd once been, I can tolerate Helena's appearance now. Despite all that she went through, she is a bright, clever girl. She will learn how to get on quickly enough, and with proper nourishment, her looks should improve. Her mama was quite the beauty."

"If anyone can make her appear to best advantage, 'tis you!" Adam said, encouraged by Lady Darnell's assessment. "Still, as you know far better than I, the rules of the ton can be a trap for the unwary. I shouldn't wish you to suffer for the social lapses that she will inevitably make, inexperienced as she is."

Lady Darnell waved a hand. "One of the benefits of age, my dear, is the freedom to ignore the opinions of Society. My friends, who will all know her circumstances, will understand, and I care nothing for the rest. That is, as long as you and Charis aren't embarrassed by it."

"Since I have no doubt that Charis will capture some discerning gentleman's affections long before Helena is ready to make her appearance, and I may be on my way to being settled myself, you needn't worry on our account. I only wish to make sure you are assuming this burden not out of a sense of duty, but because you truly wish to."

It was a testament to his stepmother's absorption with Helena Lambarth that she didn't immediately task him for details of how he meant to get "settled." Oblivious to all else, she continued, "'Twill be a challenge to my skills—and a delight. While you were working, I sought her out to apologize for my rude reception. We had a very pleasant chat. Oh, how I do see Diana in her! Teaching her proper deportment may be easier than you imagine, for she has already begged me to instruct her."

Lady Darnell patted her eyes one last time. "When I think of what Lambarth made Helena suffer, Diana's kin all unknowing! No wonder the child wants nothing to do with any of her father's family."

"It shall be as you wish, then. Mind, she and her lawyer insisted that all expenses for her upkeep should be paid from the proceeds of her mama's estate, so you needn't be outfitting her from your pin money."

Lady Darnell's enthusiasm faltered. "Oh, dear. Must I follow a strict budget?"

Adam chuckled. "Quite the contrary. From the figures I was shown, the girl might just be the wealthiest young woman in England. Buy whatever you think needful."

Lady Darnell clapped her hands and gave Adam one of her most brilliant smiles. "Excellent! Mark my words, Adam, when I am done with Helena, you shall not even recognize her!"

CHAPTER SIX

EARLY THE NEXT MORNING Helena left her chamber to share breakfast with the two ladies who had been so welcoming. After experiencing the confusing array of tastes and scents at dinner the previous night, she was happy to discover that the first meal of the day consisted of toast and tea served informally in the breakfast room.

More than her cordial reception, Lady Darnell's stories about Helena's mother had established between them the intangible link of kinship. Feeling more loved and accepted than she had since the loss of her mother, Helena vowed to do her utmost to fit into Aunt Lillian's world.

Eager to begin that process, as they sat sipping tea, Helena asked, "Shall we go to the dressmaker today?"

As she spoke, both women's gazes went to the damaged hand she had unconsciously brought up to support her cup.

Deciding the first step in her resolve would be to set their minds at rest about her hand, Helena tucked it back in her skirt and said, "As I expect you've noticed, I also have an immediate need for gloves."

After a glance at Aunt Lillian, Charis said tentatively, "Does…does the thumb still pain you?"

"No. The accident happened long ago. But it left the hand rather unattractive. I should like to conceal it as soon as possible."

"And so you shall," Aunt Lillian said sympathetically. "Rather than go to the shops in person, however, Charis and I agreed it would be better to have the merchants call upon you here. You can then make your first public appearance after you've had your hair styled and your new wardrobe completed, and have had some schooling in the behavior that will be expected of you as a young lady in London. I'm afraid you will find the rules a bit more restrictive than those you have been used to in the country."

She would have to be exiled to the polar reaches of the planet to move in an environment more restrictive than that from which she'd escaped, Helena thought sardonically. But her kindhearted aunt didn't need to learn that. "Please, do instruct me," she replied. "I don't wish to make errors and embarrass the family."

Though the teeming city just outside beckoned beguilingly, Helena told herself she could tolerate being confined for a few more weeks. Should her resolution falter before Aunt Lillian pronounced her ready to greet the ton, she need only recall the shocked revulsion that had wiped the polite greeting off the face of Adam Darnell.

She intended to carefully avoid that particular gentleman until she could be sure that the response she evoked in him at their *next* meeting was more positive.

"We shall be happy to tutor you!" Lady Darnell said, pulling Helena from the humiliating memory. "I have already dispatched a note requesting my favorite mantua-maker to wait upon us this afternoon. Before she arrives, Charis and I will go to the shops and bring back a selection of shawls, gloves, shoes and undergarments from which you may choose. And I shall tell Harrison to contact his usual employment agency to find you a lady's maid."

The last item in this list drove the smile from Helena's lips. "I've always waited upon myself, Aunt Lillian. I don't wish to have a stranger." And she had a compelling reason not to bare herself before one, as well.

"Helena, a maid is a necessity!" Charis said. "The simple round gown you are wearing now is…adequate, but your new clothing will require someone to adjust and pin it properly, to lace you in and out of your gowns and stays."

Inspecting the morning gowns worn by her two companions, Helena realized Charis was correct. The bodice of the gowns closed in the back with tightly drawn laces extending from the high waist to the neckline. It would be impossible for her to manage lacing them alone.

"You mustn't worry," Aunt Lillian said. "Any candidate the agency sends will have excellent references."

Any candidate with excellent references would likely be contemptuous of an employer who knew as little as Helena did about gowns and fashion. To say nothing of the other…

"I would rather employ someone just starting out, as I am. Could not one of the maids already here serve?"

Aunt Lillian frowned. "I suppose if you would feel more comfortable being assisted by someone within the household, Harrison might assign one of the house-maids until you feel ready for a proper lady's maid."

Perhaps she might request to have the maid who had summoned her for breakfast, Helena thought, bright-ening. The girl appeared young enough, perhaps, to not immediately recognize the deficiencies in Helena's up-bringing, and her merry smile suggested a sunny dis-position. But she, too, would probably be shocked when she saw Helena unclothed.

That sobering thought extinguished the delight Helena had been feeling at the prospect of a new wardrobe. "Must I disrobe to be measured for gowns? I have not undressed before anyone since my mother left."

Both women looked at her in surprise. "Surely you had some female to assist you," Aunt Lillian said.

Helena shook her head. "My father did not risk exposing me to anyone with feminine sensibilities," she said dryly. "The sole servant I saw after Mama left was the baliff who…helped enforce my father's dictates." The less said the better on just what those dictates had been.

"You've existed since your mother's departure with no female company at all?" Charis asked, clearly taken aback.

"None at all." A more pleasant memory intruded and

Helena smiled. "Except for the old medicine woman who lived in our woods—a hermit who'd been there as long as anyone could remember. However, as she dressed all by guess, she was of no assistance in matters of fashion."

"You poor child," Aunt Lillian said, her voice shaking a bit. "But you mustn't worry. In this house, you need do nothing that makes you uncomfortable. The seamstress can measure you in your shift and your maid need only assist you into your gowns. You can manage a night rail alone."

Relieved, Helena nodded. "Thank you for understanding, Aunt Lillian. But my shift is so old and worn I should be embarrassed to meet the dressmaker in it. Might it be possible for you to purchase something for me before she arrives this afternoon?"

"Of course. Right after breakfast, Charis and I shall proceed to the corsetiere and order a selection of garments to be brought here for you to inspect, while we continue on to the glove and shoemakers. Before Madame Sofie arrives, you shall feel presentable in shift, gloves and slippers."

Helena rose to hug her aunt. "How can I thank you?"

Lady Darnell kissed her forehead. "By enjoying yourself. We want you to be happy with us, child."

Emotion rose to choke her throat and for a moment Helena could not speak. For nearly as long as she could remember, the intent of those closest to her had been to make her as *unhappy* as possible. She almost needed to pinch herself to believe she was awake and this was real, not the dream she'd dreamed every night of the life that would be hers when at last she was with her mother again.

That would never be possible now, but Mama, dearest Mama, had arranged something almost as wonderful. Grief and gratitude swelled in her chest.

"I shall do my best to be happy," she said at last, "but you must do your parts. Mr. Pendenning assures me that Mama has left me the vastest of fortunes. It would delight us both for you two to choose new garments, too."

Charis gave a peal of laughter. "Since Bellemere loves nothing better than new fashions, I expect we shall all be blissfully happy."

Lady Darnell rose. "Come, Charis. If Helena is to be ready to meet Madame Sophie this afternoon, you and I must get to work." She turned to Helena. "Should you like to rest in your chamber until we return, my dear?"

"Might I go to the library, ma'am?"

"'Tis Adam's domain, but since he is to be out most of the day, you may certainly inspect it if you wish."

"Are you a great reader?" Charis asked.

Helena paused, trying to frame the most innocuous reply. "I spent my happiest hours after Mama left in the library," she said. Which was true enough.

"I do love the works of Mrs. Burney," Charis said, and sighed. "The events were exaggerated, of course, but oh, how brave were the heroes and how fiendish the villains!"

Once again, Helena hesitated before answering. Heroes truly were the stuff of fiction and as for villainy... The images flashed into mind before she could stop them: the restraints, the whip, the airless, lightless priest's hole where she had nearly lost her wits.

Shaking off the memories, she replied, "Isolated as we were, Mama taught me to love reading, but she preferred Scott, Shakespeare and the poets. Also the French philosophers—Pascal, Montaigne, Voltaire. Though truly, I read almost everything—travel journals, philosophy, mathematics. I would love to explore foreign lands."

"You sound like quite the bluestocking!" Charis said. When Helena looked at her, uncomprehending, she explained, "A lady of vast education is known by that term—not a very complimentary one. I'm afraid it isn't considered admirable for a lady to be too learned."

Helena widened her eyes. "Society values ignorance?"

"Not precisely. I'm making a muddle of this." Charis looked to Lady Darnell. "Could you explain, ma'am?"

"Of course a young lady can't be ignorant," the other lady replied. "She must be able to manage a household, stitch and embroider competently, and deal with servants and tradesmen. 'Tis desirable that she sing and perform pleasingly on the pianoforte or the harp and play well at cards. Some competence in reading French or Italian is also permissible, but a lady shouldn't fatigue her mind with too much book-learning."

Helena laughed ruefully. "Then I've acquired almost

no useful knowledge at all. I haven't set a stitch in years and have no idea how to get on in Society or manage a household. But if learning is so despised, why does anyone keep a library?"

"Oh, 'tis quite acceptable for *gentlemen* to be educated. But the gentler sex isn't equipped to comprehend foreign tongues or study ancient literature—gods and goddesses cavorting about in the most unseemly fashion! And gentlemen don't admire a lady who seems too…knowing."

That she could believe, Helena thought acidly.

"You are far braver than I," Lady Darnell continued. "I do not stir from London without two grooms to ride post and John Coachman on the box with his blunderbuss! To think of you traveling all alone on the mail coach is enough to give me palpitations, to say nothing of envisioning you in heathenish foreign lands!"

She shivered. "Pray, do not speak of it again. Having just found you, it is our earnest hope that we can make you so comfortable that you shall never wish to leave us. But enough," she concluded as Helena sat mute, overwhelmed for the second time by Lady Darnell's generous affection. "We must be going, Charis, if we are to complete our commissions and return betimes."

After the ladies left, Harrison led her to the library. For the next hour, Helena explored with delight the treasures of this well-stocked room.

What a marvelous retreat this would make! she thought, selecting several volumes from the shelves. However, if this were Lord Darnell's domain, she would not have unlimited use of it. She would have to ask Harrison every morning about his master's schedule for the day.

Her inventory of the library's holdings complete, she gazed around the room, taking in the sofa and two wing chairs before the hearth and the massive desk in the corner. Adam Darnell's desk, of course.

Though her first impression told her this man would not be her enemy, best to learn as much as possible about the master of the household in which she now resided. Curiously she walked over to inspect his desk.

A stack of ledgers occupied one corner; an inkstand, quills and nibs were set at the center above several sheets of blank paper. To the other side was an assortment of books—Plato, Cicero and Voltaire, along with *The Compleat Farmer* and *An Account of Operations at Holkham Estate*.

If the desk were an indication of the character of the man who used it, Adam Darnell was neat and organized, a careful landlord and something of a scholar. He was certainly handsome, she recalled, some unnameable something stirring within her at the memory, and he seemed kind.

Still, it might be wise to explore the remainder of the house before the ladies returned. One never knew when a speedy exit might become imperative, and in such an event, one could not count on using the front entry.

However, with a dressmaker coming this afternoon, Helena's most pressing need was to determine if the friendly parlor maid would be suitable to serve her. Even if the maid never saw her without her shift, at some point in the apparently laborious dressing process, that garment might slip—and the maid who viewed her back would need to be prepared and staunchly loyal to her service.

Leaving her chosen volumes for later, Helena exited the library and followed the hallway to a door that led to a flight of service stairs. As she expected, these ended on the ground floor next to the kitchen.

Within that ample room, a mob-capped woman tended a pot over a large iron cookstove while two other women chopped vegetables at a center table. At a smaller table to one side, Harrison sat across from an older lady in a dark dress with a set of keys pinned to her apron.

Conversation ceased and every occupant of the room turned to stare as she walked in. She sensed immediately that she had trespassed outside her proper domain.

Harrison jumped to his feet. "Excuse me, Miss Lambarth, I didn't hear you ring. What do you require?"

"Excuse *me,* all of you, for coming here uninvited, but I have a bit of a dilemma that I hope you can help me solve." Helena addressed herself to the dark-robed woman. "You are the housekeeper, Mrs. Baxtor?"

"Yes, miss," the woman replied, curtseying.

"As I did not bring one with me, I need a lady's maid. I should prefer not to hire some unknown person out of an agency and wondered if I might instead speak with the girl who waited on me this morning—Molly, I believe?"

The butler and the housekeeper exchanged glances. "Harrison takes care of hiring help, miss," the housekeeper replied. "Molly is just a lower housemaid and hasn't been trained for such work. If you step up to the parlor, I'm sure Harrison can discuss your requirements."

Harrison bowed. "If you will follow me, miss?"

Nodding to acknowledge the curtseys of the staff, Helena dutifully left the room. So much for her distant memories of going with her mama to the kitchen to sample Cook's fruit tarts, she thought ruefully. Not only had she obviously stepped out of place, she had stumbled into a hierarchy that did not readily admit change. Housemaids, apparently, did not turn overnight into ladies' maids.

She would find no allies among that lot, Helena concluded, recalling the startled and mildly disapproving faces. But then, the household would go as the master dictated, as she ought to know well enough by now.

She must try a different tack, she decided as she trailed Harrison into the parlor. It would probably be better anyway to hire an outsider beholden to Helena alone for her position. But not, she was adamant, an experienced woman who would know instantly how out of place Helena was.

As Helena seated herself, Harrison said, "You would like me to inquire about a lady's maid, miss?"

"Mr. Harrison, let us be blunt. My error in invading the kitchen must have confirmed what a man of your stature probably saw at first glance—that I wasn't trained as befits one of my station. Lady Darnell will be helping me address those deficiencies, but while she does so, I do not wish to engage a dresser who would immediately note my inexperience. I should like to talk with Molly and see if she has a relation I might hire. I hope I could then rely on your guidance in instructing a new girl in her duties."

Harrison nodded. "Better to bring in a newcomer than raise a maid here above her station. Naturally, I shall assist anyone you hire. I'm sure Mrs. Baxtor will, too."

"You will have Molly sent to me, then?"

"Yes, miss. I expect Mrs. Baxtor can spare her from her work for a few moments."

After pronouncing the last without a quiver of irony, Harrison withdrew. But as Helena waited for the maid to appear, memories of a conversation overheard on the way to London suddenly sparked another, better idea.

In addition to allowing her to personally select her employee, this alternative would insure that the person she chose would owe her position to Helena alone—and probably be grateful enough for the opportunity that she would work hard and ask no questions.

Best yet, Helena would be able to see at least a little of the city immediately. Indeed, by slipping out to hunt for a maid now, she could enjoy a freedom of movement that, based on what Aunt Lillian had just told her, she would probably have to forfeit once she'd been transformed into a young lady of fashion. A thrill of delicious anticipation energized her.

At that moment Molly entered and curtseyed. "Baxtor says you was wanting me, miss?"

"Yes, Molly. I have an errand to do and require a companion familiar with the city. Do you know how to get to St. Marylebone?"

"St. Marylebone?" the girl echoed. "'Tis rather far north of here, not near the shops or nothing. Are you sure that's where you was wishful of going?"

"There's a…business there I need to visit. You can show me the way?"

"I can, but you'd best be ordering out the carriage. 'Tis rather long a walk for a young lady."

"I shall not be going as a fine young lady—at least outwardly. Lady Darnell does not want me to go about until my wardrobe is complete, but this matter cannot wait. If you can procure me a plain cloak with a hood, I can go there and back without attracting any notice. I will compensate you well."

As the implications of Helena's traveling incognito registered in the girl's mind, her friendly smile faded. "I don't think Lady Darnell or Mrs. Baxtor would look kindly on me, iff'n they knowed I helped you sneak out."

"If anyone should discover us—which they will not—you need only tell Mrs. Baxtor that I ordered you to take me. She already knows I am a bit…odd."

Molly giggled. "My, what a to-do it was, you coming down to the kitchen without a by-your-leave! John the footman told me ol' Baxtor's eyes was as big as dinner plates!" As if suddenly recalling to whom she was speaking, she blushed. "Meaning no disrespect, miss!"

Waving off the girl's apology, Helena said, "Just before dark, while Lady Darnell is resting and the staff prepares dinner, we will slip away. Can you go today?"

Molly shook her head. "Oh, no, miss. Not today."

A sympathetic anger uncurled inside Helena. "Does the master keep you confined here? Is he harsh?"

Molly looked at her uncomprehending. "You mean—Lord Darnell? Oh, no, miss! He's been ever so kind every time I've seen him, even when he come up behind me one morning as I was bringing Eckles—that's his valet—his shaving water and I dropped the pitcher and it shattered all over. But he was sweet as honey on a biscuit about it, and wouldn't even let Eckles scold me, saying it was his own fault for startling me so." The girl sighed. "He's terrible handsome, too."

So he was, Helena thought, remembering the odd little quiver he'd evoked in her. Relieved to have her innate distrust put to rest and her favorable first impression of Lord Darnell confirmed, she said, "Can you take me tomorrow?"

"I couldn't get away until my half-day on Thursday."

"Shall we say Thursday, then? If you come to my room before dinner tonight, I will give you money to make the preparations and reimburse you for working on your half-day. We shall have an adventure!"

Molly looked as if she did not find the idea of an adventure especially appealing. "I reckon I can do it, miss, but you...you're sure we won't get in no trouble?"

"None at all, I promise," Helena said, giving the girl her most persuasive smile. She considered adding that the homemade knife she always kept strapped to her thigh—and her ability to use it—would guarantee a trouble-free trip. Judging by what she'd seen of London so far, however, such expertise was probably unusual among young ladies. No sense having Molly find her odder than she'd already shown herself.

After setting a time to meet the girl later, Helena dismissed the maid and went to fetch her book from the library. How much she'd accomplished in a single morning! The process of acquiring a wardrobe had begun, she'd discovered the room she would make her personal retreat and soon she would find a personal servant to be her ally in the household. Best of all, in a very few days she would embark on her first excursion.

Suddenly life seemed more exciting and full of opportunity than she'd ever imagined possible back at Lambarth or in the dark hours after learning of her mother's death. A pang of sadness muted her enthusiasm as she remembered the lady whose wisdom had led her to this household—and to a family that actually seemed concerned about her happiness. To this household whose master, she thought, recalling Darnell's handsome face and kind eyes, might just prove that honorable men existed after all.

CHAPTER SEVEN

WHILE HELENA ACQUAINTED herself with his home and staff, Adam made a number of business calls, ending with a visit to the Standish mansion on Grosvenor Square. Though the ornate drawing room was full of guests, Miss Standish looked up and smiled when she heard him announced.

The heiress would never be described as a Beauty, but Adam was pleasantly surprised to discover that the plump little girl who'd followed him about like an eager puppy had grown into an attractive young woman, her smile engaging, her pale blue eyes intelligent, her blond hair charmingly arranged. Her wealth was revealed by the excellence of her gown's cut and fabric rather than by a showy effusion of trimming or a superfluity of jewels.

His first impression favorable, after paying his respects to her mother, Adam walked toward the sofa where she sat surrounded by guests. To his gratification, upon seeing him approach, she waved him to a chair.

If, while she made polite chat with her other guests, the young lady occasionally slid him a glance under her lashes, Adam was also covertly inspecting her. Some of the anxiety that had tensed his shoulders and settled in an ache at his temples eased, for not only was her appearance pleasing, her behavior was exemplary.

He observed none of the capricious airs or haughtiness of manner often exhibited by a young woman who knew herself to be a sought-after matrimonial prize. On the contrary, she gave equal attention to both the young men paying her court and two prosing dowagers. While deftly parrying the fulsome compliments of several highborn peers, she also offered a few kind words to a stammering young man from a minor family whom she might have snubbed with impunity.

Adam's impression of Priscilla's mother, stridently directing the conversation around her, was less positive. But Mrs. Standish had already been a stiff, overbearing woman in Priscilla's childhood—which was why her daughter had escaped Standish Hall to follow Adam whenever possible.

If he discovered that he and Priscilla still suited, they'd not be living under her mother's thumb anyway, Adam reminded himself. Waiting for an opportunity to move closer, when the dowager at Miss Standish's elbow said goodbye, Adam swiftly commandeered the vacant seat.

Turning back from bidding another guest farewell, Miss Standish saw him and smiled again. The odd impression struck him that, though pleasant enough, even up close her smile lacked the magnetism of Miss Lambarth's. He shook off the thought as Miss Standish addressed him.

"Captain Darnell—or I suppose I should say 'my lord'? I understand you've left the army. So sorry about your poor papa, by the way. He was a fine gentleman and you must feel his loss keenly."

"Thank you, Miss Standish, I do. But now that Bonaparte is corralled at last, 'tis good to be home."

"And your friends must delight to have you here unharmed. Though I applauded the bravery that had you mentioned in the dispatches, I did fear for your safety."

So she'd kept track of him. Despite himself, Adam was touched. "That was kind of you—given that more often than not, when you were scolded for some mischief when we were children, 'twas I who'd led you into it."

"Ah, but the adventure was always worth the scold," she replied, her smile deepening and a glow in her eyes.

Adam had been the recipient of feminine admiration often enough to recognize it in Miss Standish. Heartened by that excellent sign and seeing no reason to proceed by half measures, although she had just refused several other supplicants this favor, he continued, "If you dare risk your mama's censure again by driving out with a gentleman whose only claim upon your kindness is an attachment from youth, let me escort you to the park this afternoon. I regret that the war and the…exigencies of my family led to our losing touch, and should like to reestablish our bond."

There could be no mistaking his intent. For a moment, the little group around her fell silent—

doubtless marveling at his temerity. Her smile fading, Miss Standish simply stared at him, and Adam feared he might have been too bold.

But his circumstances were urgent, he told himself as he awaited her answer. If she felt herself above renewing their relationship, better to find out right now.

Despite that brave conclusion, he was relieved when Miss Standish finally replied, amused reproof in her tone, "I see that time has taught you neither patience nor prudence, Lord Darnell."

"No, ma'am. War rather teaches a soldier to value audacity and surprise."

She laughed outright. "Two qualities I would have thought you amply supplied with from the beginning! Very well, Lord Darnell. I will drive with you."

Ignoring the mutters of disapproval from his vanquished rivals, Adam fixed a time. Hardly daring to believe he had progressed so far in a single morning call, he bid Miss Standish and her mother goodbye and departed.

Given the partiality the heiress had just shown him, if in the relative privacy of his curricle they were able to reestablish the easy camaraderie of their childhood friendship, he thought exultantly, he might wrap up this courtship business and have Claygate on the road to recovery sooner than expected.

LATER THAT MORNING, Helena put aside her book to receive the corsetiere's assistant. Marveling at the fineness of the garments, she fingered each one with delight as the girl lifted them from the boxes: feather-

light linen shifts, petticoats and stays embroidered with
tiny bows and blossoms, night rails of silk whose
lushness whispered against her skin. Rejecting only the
flannel items, she told the shopgirl she would take all the
rest.

After nuncheon, Lady Darnell and Charis returned
with new treasures: gloves of kid, chamois and net in
every shade of the rainbow; slippers and half boots of
French kid; twilled silk and Norwich wool shawls;
fans of wood, bone and ivory with intricate painted
panels. The ladies also brought a few hats that could
be trimmed to match her gowns and would do until she
could visit the shops herself.

Soon after, the mantua maker arrived with her
samples. Determined after years of rough homespun to
drape herself in the softest and most delicate of weaves,
Helena was persuaded only after much argument to
accept some sturdier cotton cloth for day wear.

Helena then further distressed her aunt by rejecting
all the material in the white and pale shades they
informed her were the colors considered most suitable
for young ladies. She instead selected cloth in gold,
scarlet, deep blue and coral hues. Worse yet, in her
aunt's opinion, after reviewing fashion plates, Helena
refused to consider any style cut low over the back or
bosom.

In vain did Lady Darnell argue that though the
designs might seem a bit immodest to a girl who was
country-raised, in London such gowns were worn by
ladies of every age. As ashamed of her scarred back as
she was of her mangled thumb, Helena could not bring

herself to tell the kindhearted Lady Darnell the real reason she refused to consider more revealing styles. Saying that such shoulder-baring gowns would make her cold, the only plausible excuse she could think of to try to placate her aunt, Helena then traced over the styles she liked best, proposing alterations.

After considering Helena's suggested changes, Madame Sofie became her unexpected ally, holding up a hand to silence Lady Darnell's renewed protest. "No, your ladyship, the young miss speaks truth. The neckline just so, in this gold silk, will be different from what others wear, but will much become mademoiselle, with her elegant *taille*. She will not follow fashion, she will lead it."

Fortunately—since Lady Darnell still looked skeptical—Charis agreed with Madame Sofie. "'Tis brilliant, Bellemere! Helena's gowns shall be *of* the prevailing style, not *in* it, and completely unique. Beside her, all the ton Beauties will look insipid!"

Helena cared nothing about setting fashion. She only hoped that when she met Lord Darnell again, wearing one of her lovely new gowns, she would see approval, rather than disgust, in his eyes.

Despite Charis's agreement and the dressmaker's firm support, Lady Darnell continued to wring her hands at the thought of dear Helena throwing away the chance to display her youth and beauty to best advantage. Only by insisting they had spent time enough on Helena's needs and must now discuss new garments for Charis and Lady Darnell were they able to turn her thoughts in a more cheerful direction. The rest of the

afternoon passed agreeably in that endeavor, with
Madame agreeing to have several designs completed
for Helena within the week.

After the dressmaker's departure, Harrison brought in
the tea tray, bending low to murmur to Lady Darnell
before bowing himself out. Frowning, her aunt turned to
Helena.

"My dear, Harrison just told me you paid a visit to
the kitchens today in search of a temporary maid."

She was about to be chastised for her sins, Helena
thought, armoring herself against the coming scold ·
and resentful of Harrison for immediately reporting her
breach of decorum. But then, what had she expected?

A frisson of dismay dissipated her annoyance.
Having once again demonstrated just how untutored
she was, would Aunt Lillian's warm affection for her
cool?

Ready to suffer any punishment to retain her aunt's
good will, she replied in her most penitent tone, "Yes,
ma'am, I did, and I do apologize. From the staff's
reaction, I saw immediately that I had made an error."

"You should have let Harrison handle it."

"So Mrs. Baxtor informed me. I tried to leave as
quickly as I could once I realized my error, but I'm
afraid the housekeeper must think me rather odd. I am
sorry, Aunt Lillian. I didn't mean to upset the household."

To Helena's immense relief, Lady Darnell patted her
hand. "Don't refine too much upon it, my dear! I suppose
it must have seemed quite logical for you to inquire
about it yourself. But such things are not done directly."

"So the housekeeper also informed me," Helena said.

Lady Darnell chuckled. "Mrs. Baxtor is a bit tart-tongued, but vastly efficient! You must treat servants fairly and with respect, but at a distance. Although it might seem otherwise, if you are too familiar, they will think you do not know your place and disdain you for it."

Helena smiled wryly. "They are right. I do not."

"But you soon will! Harrison said you made quite a good recovery. You mustn't fault him for reporting the matter to me, for if you had not already won his respect, he would not have done so! He told me that with a bit of guidance, he expects you will make an excellent mistress. Which is quite a tribute, my dear, considering you have been with us barely a day."

"I hope I will ever follow your guidance."

"I am sure you will," Lady Darnell replied, squeezing Helena's hand. "Now, shall we have our tea?"

Having armed herself to suffer serious chastisement, it took Helena a moment to realize that Lady Darnell considered the matter settled. Still rattled by the encounter, Helena sipped her tea silently, unable to remember when she'd last made any error for which she'd not been severely punished. A bit more of the hard shell in which she'd had to encase her emotions softened as a wave of gratitude flooded her.

While she pondered the marvel of her aunt's forbearance, Charis and Lady Darnell discussed the various entertainments offered by the Season and how much Helena would enjoy them when, several weeks hence, she was gowned, coifed and confident enough about her mastery of ton etiquette to attend. A riot of contending emotions roiled in her chest as she listened—awe at the easy dismissal of her error, surprise at Harrison's unexpected championship, relief that she had not altered Lady Darnell's affection.

Just then Charis mentioned a dinner the two ladies were to attend that coming Thursday. Recalling what she had planned for that day, Helena felt a pang of guilt.

A moment's reflection, though, convinced her that it was essential she follow through with her engagement. 'Twas fortunate, then, she reflected as she sipped the rest of her tea, that she'd had years to perfect her skill at evasion, for if Lady Darnell were to discover the nature of this coming excursion, her sympathetic aunt would doubtless be much less understanding.

WHILE THE LADIES WERE TAKING tea, Adam was calling in Grosvenor Square to take Miss Standish to the park.

The lady first impressed him by keeping him waiting only a few minutes. Then, garbed in an unadorned carriage dress of medium blue that intensified the hue of her eyes, blond curls peeping out from under a fetching bonnet that framed her oval face, her understated elegance and modest demeanor again elicited both his admiration and approval.

After he'd handed her up and remounted himself, he signaled the horses to start and turned to her. "I must thank you for overlooking the impetuosity of my request and agreeing to drive out with me anyway. You would have been quite justified in putting this upstart in his place by refusing, if only to gratify your other suitors."

She gave him a rueful half smile. "Perhaps 'twas as much to put *them* in their places that I did accept."

Adam returned the smile. "I'm also well aware that it was quite a mark of favor to have your mother receive me—particularly given my family's current situation."

"Which is precisely why I wished to drive with you. Rather than spend several morning calls trying to beguile me with empty flattery, you come right to the point. I had hoped time had not robbed you of the direct manner I remember so fondly. I am glad to find it has not."

"If you wish plain speaking, then I must say I am delighted to discover that a young lady as sought after as you are still retains the unaffected manners and common sense *I* remember with such fondness. Along, I expect, with a mischievous desire to sometimes do the unexpected."

"Alas, I can seldom allow myself that indulgence! Now that we are so much in Society, I owe Mama and Papa good behavior. But though I shall never be a Beauty, neither am I a fool. I tire of having to smile and demur at the compliments of highborn suitors whom I know, did I not possess a fortune, would never give me a second glance."

"The more fools they," Adam retorted.

Miss Standish's eyes glittered with a sheen of tears. "Thank you," she said quietly. "That is the other reason I agreed to drive out with you. Once you knew and liked me for myself. Oh, I know if I did not possess a fortune, you probably would not have sought to rekindle our old friendship, but I also believe—and I cannot say this of any other man of my acquaintance—that my being an heiress would never be your most important motive for doing so."

Taken aback and a bit humbled by her bluntness, Adam replied, "Thank you for your confidence in my character. Let me reaffirm that regardless of my family's needs, I would never seek to win the favor of a lady I did not also admire and respect."

"Now that we've settled that," she said, brushing at the corners of her eyes, "we can both be comfortable. Let me tell you again how happy we are that you are finally back in England. Your father was a good neighbor to us and we grieved at his suffering. How hard it must have been for you, compelled by your duty to remain so far away!"

Adam nodded, heartened to discover how well she understood his dilemma. "With Bonaparte's generals still wreaking havoc in Spain and Portugal, I couldn't simply desert my post. Despite his infirmity, Papa commanded me to remain with Wellington where I might do some good, as he said there was nothing anyone but God could do for him. Still, it was…difficult."

"Difficult, too, to return to find your estate in disorder." When he looked over, startled, she pointed out, "We said there would be only plain speaking between us."

Not so sure he liked blunt honesty after all, Adam said wryly, "I hope that not the whole of Society is privy to the true state of our fortunes."

"I'm sure it is not!" she reassured him. "But remember, we are neighbors. With Claygate Manor so close, Papa couldn't help but notice the property deteriorate over the years. Then when we heard it was to be let out… Not that you should blame poor Lady Darnell, who I expect did the best she could, but being by nature rather frivolous and lacking the firm hand on her household Mama has taught me to exercise, the decline was perhaps unavoidable."

Before Adam could begin to take up cudgels in his stepmother's defense, she added, "But one cannot expect a lady to master estate matters. Besides, under the most distressing circumstances, she remained a helpmate to your father through the whole of his long illness. Mama often pointed to her as an excellent example of wifely devotion. I only hope I may serve my own husband as well someday."

Lips twitching, Adam was about to retort that he didn't much relish the idea of languishing for years on a sickbed while his wife lovingly tended him. But Priscilla's expression was so serious that, not wishing to offend her, he refrained from voicing that observation. "You will be just as excellent a wife to the gentleman fortunate enough to secure your hand," he said instead.

Miss Standish gazed at him with a warmth that surprised him, even as it gratified his masculine sensibilities. "Then I must wait for the right gentleman to solicit it."

At that moment he drove onto the carriageway at Hyde Park, where the throng of vehicles and strolling pedestrians required him to refocus his attention on his horses. As they made their slow progress about the park, however, it soon became clear just how marked a favor Miss Standish had bestowed on him.

All down Rotten Row, the ladies or gentlemen whom they stopped to greet smiled at Miss Standish— and gave Adam frankly speculative looks. Although their conversation on the drive home was general rather than personal, Miss Standish describing for him the many activities he and the Darnell ladies could expect to enjoy during the Season, Adam began to wonder if taking Miss Standish driving had been such a wise idea after all.

He had the uncomfortable feeling that somehow in the space of a single afternoon he had catapulted from renewing an acquaintance to raising expectations among Society—and perhaps in the young lady—that an offer from him was imminent. And while he was certainly looking at her as a possible wife, he didn't wish to have his hand forced.

Given that vague discomfort, when the young lady thanked him for the drive and then invited him to dine with her family three nights hence, Adam almost refused.

However, if he truly wished to get to know her well enough to decide whether or not to make that offer, it only made sense to accept. Having done so and given her his compliments, Adam drove off.

He was still examining his mixed feelings about courting Priscilla when he arrived at his club to meet Bennett Dixon for dinner. Before he'd even taken his seat, his old friend came over to pound him on the back.

"You were always one to rush your fences," Dix said, grinning. "So when am I to wish you happy?"

Trying to ignore the highly interested stares of a number of other club members, Adam said, "You are referring to my driving Miss Standish in the park—an event which was, apparently, witnessed by all the world and his brother?"

"Dash it, man, you can't drive at the Promenade hour and *not* be seen by everyone," Dix replied.

"Perhaps, but I must have missed something during my sojourn in foreign lands. Since when did a drive in the park become tantamount to a proposal of marriage?"

"When the lady accepting that solo invitation is Priscilla Standish," Dix replied. "Given the vastness of her fortune, the chit can look as high as she likes for a husband. Not wishing to discourage any of the desirable contenders still manning the lists—and to keep the current suitors dangling—her parents have never before let the girl drive out with just one gentleman. Miss Standish must have raised quite a fuss to persuade them to allow it. You might as well have had heralds riding before you, announcing the banns."

At that moment two dandies crossed the room, holding out what Adam recognized, with a sinking feeling, as the club's betting book. "Care to enter a wager, Dix?" one of them asked, winking at Adam. "Odds are better than even that our hero here will be engaged by month's end."

Dix turned to grin at Adam. "See? Even I didn't believe you could rout the competition so quickly."

Adam took a swallow from the glass of wine Dix offered him. This was what he'd wanted—wasn't it? He should be pleased at how quickly matters seemed to be progressing.

He needed a well-born, attractive lady he respected and admired who could manage his household and give him an heir. Miss Standish was all that, as well as a friend from childhood. And she was rich. What more could he ask?

It wasn't as if he were waiting to fall in love. He'd experienced that heady infatuation once or twice in his salad days. The inevitable wrenching disappointment had taught him 'twas an indulgence best avoided by mature gentleman with familial obligations.

Still, a fiancée would doubtless expect him to dance attendance on her, limiting the time he would be able to spend with his family. Also limiting his ability to provide Charis, his stepmother—and their houseguest, once Bellemere deemed her presentable—with an escort.

The image of Miss Lambarth's dark eyes and captivating smile flickered in his mind. He'd not seen her since he brought her home from the lawyer's office. For a brief moment, he wondered how she was progressing.

Dismissing that concern, he assured himself he'd not been too precipitous, jumping with both boots into the business of courting Priscilla. But as he parried the gibes of his friends, he couldn't quite stifle the little voice at the back of his head warning him that the impetuosity that had had saved his skin on several occasions as a soldier might not have served the civilian quite so well.

CHAPTER EIGHT

THE FOLLOWING THURSDAY afternoon, Helena stood by a normally unused garden gate, the plain dark cloak Molly had smuggled to her masking her unmistakably genteel gown. A joyous excitement coursing through her, she congratulated herself on the preliminary work she'd done the previous two nights, rising after the other occupants of the house were abed to silently explore the town house from attic to cellars. She now knew the location of every exit, every window overlooking a tree branch, every sheltered corner within the garden where a person could secret herself.

Confident that she and the maid could slip away and back without anyone observing them, she'd spent the morning studying the London map an obliging footman had obtained for her. Even should Molly, who was still less than enthusiastic about the proposed expedition, fail to appear, Helena would be able to navigate her way to St. Marylebone.

Best of all, Lady Darnell had announced at nuncheon that she and Charis would spend the afternoon making calls. Certain now that her absence would not be noted, Helena had returned to her chamber and rung for Molly to inform her they could leave as soon as the maid finished her chores.

The soft pad of approaching footsteps told Helena that the maid had decided to accompany her, despite her reservations. Reveling in the prospect of an afternoon free to achieve her most pressing purpose, she put a finger over her lips to caution Molly to silence, then placed a sovereign in her hand and led her through the gate.

They scurried down the mews without incident and made it to the hackney stand, where Helena engaged a carriage. For the length of the short drive to St. Marylebone, Helena kept her face pressed to the window, noting the street names and observing every detail.

Throngs of vehicles crowded the roads, carriages and wagons and street vendors with carts calling out their wares. Equally diverse were the people, from housemaids shaking out feather dusters to dustmen hauling refuse to richly dressed ladies and gentlemen descending the steps toward glossy carriages with crests painted on the panels....

When the jarvey announced they had reached their destination, Helena promised herself that someday soon, she would slip out on her own and explore the teeming diversity that was London. But now, to find a maid.

After paying the jarvey to wait for them, she set off, Molly at her heels. But the girl stopped short as she looked up at the large building fronting Paddington Street. "Miss, you sure the address is right? This be the St. Marylebone workhouse."

"Then my directions were correct," Helena replied, pleased at her navigation skills.

The maid planted her feet, her eyes widening. "You mean to…go in? Whatever for, miss? 'Tis naught but a bunch of paupers and thieves, half of 'em stricken with awful diseases! If you wish to contribute to the poor relief, better you do it at St. George's vestry."

"I mean to contribute—by offering employment," Helena replied. "I need a maid. Since the inmates of this place are looking for work, I imagine I can find one."

"Oh, you're bamming me!" Molly said, relief in her voice. "Baxtor said you was wanting a maid. Harrison will find you one from Mr. McClaren's agency…."

As Helena shook her head gently, Molly's words trailed off. "Oh, miss, you cannot be thinking to hire someone outta there! We could all be murdered in our beds!"

"Molly, the workhouse isn't a prison for cutthroats, nor what I believe you call a 'flash house,' where young criminals gather. I had it from the lips of a clergyman serving on the Board of Directors of the Poor for St. Marylebone that in their workhouse the unfortunates of the parish are trained for useful employment. Father Roberts said St. Marylebone is a model institution."

Helena omitted mentioning that she'd overheard this information in a conversation on the mail coach between the reverend and a passenger with views similar to Molly's. "Is not offering one such deserving girl a chance to better herself more desirable than putting coins in the poor box?"

"No disrespect to Father Roberts, but the poor box be a heap safer," Molly muttered.

"I shall be very careful," Helena promised. "If no one seems suitable, I can send Harrison to the agency. But now that we are here, I will take a look." And unless the reverend had perjured himself irredeemably, she would hire someone. Perhaps a girl as eager to escape her prison of poverty as Helena had been to leave Lambarth Castle.

"Had I known you was coming here, I'd not have agreed to bring you," Molly retorted, reluctantly trudging after Helena. "Iff'n the master finds out I led you to such a place, he'll turn me off for sure."

Would Lord Darnell be concerned if he thought she'd been placed in danger? Helena wondered, distracted by recalling the intent gaze he'd fixed upon her in the lawyer's office.

Then the stooped old man at the door asked them their business, took their cloaks and led them to the director's office. That official questioned Helena closely about her purpose and background before summoning a child to guide them to Mrs. Smith, the inmate who supervised the instruction of the older girls.

After passing through a large room filled with emaciated, bedridden adults their young escort cheerfully informed them were "the bad sick who'll likely die," they entered the girls' ward. Here, the floor was newly swept, the rows of beds neatly made and thankfully empty.

The child led them onto the porch. A thin woman of indeterminate age, a clean but ragged shawl wrapped about her, stood supervising the work of a number of girls bent over washtubs or hanging linen on drying racks.

Mrs. Smith looked up. "Ladies, may I help you? 'Tis laundry day, as you see. The girls earn a few pence while learning to wash and iron. Are you from the parish?"

"No, ma'am," Helena replied. "I am Helena Lambarth and this is Molly. We reside with my aunt, Lady Darnell, in St. James Square. I'm newly arrived in London and wish to hire one of your girls as my personal maid."

The thin woman's smile brightened. "I imagine any one of them would jump at the chance of such employment."

"I should like to watch them for a while, if I may."

"Stroll with me. The girls will continue working, assuming as I did that you're from the parish committee."

While Molly waited on the porch, Helena walked around the courtyard with Mrs. Smith, observing how some of the girls lounged about, not returning to their tasks until Mrs. Smith drew near. Her attention was drawn to a tall girl who ignored the visitors and continued her scrubbing, a boy beside her handing her linens and soap as needed.

"Who is that girl?" she asked Mrs. Smith.

"Nell Hastings, with her brother Dickon," the woman replied. "Her father, a soldier, died at Waterloo. Her mother took in laundry, but worn down by grief and overwork, she, too, died last winter. Nell's a fine girl, but she won't do for you. She's determined to keep what's left of her family together. I doubt she would consider employment that would take her away and leave Dickon here."

"Let me speak with her anyway," Helena said, already beginning to wonder how she might hire the brother, as well.

Mrs. Smith called the girl over. Helena watched approvingly as Nell walked to them, her manner neither hurried nor ingratiating. "How can I help you, ma'am?"

"The lady wants to talk to you," Mrs. Smith told her. "Excuse me, miss, while I see to the other girls."

"You want to hire out washing, miss?" Nell asked as Helena walked her back to her washtub. "We launder and mend fine garments. Our rate is quite reasonable."

"Can you embroider and alter gowns, as well?"

"Yes, ma'am. Madame Beaumont's dress shop in Mayfair sends me work when they have too many orders to finish."

"Your father was a soldier?"

A shadow of sadness passed over the girl's face. "Yes, ma'am. Papa was a sergeant in the Ninety-fifth Rifles. He died last summer, and Mama after him."

"Why did you not seek shelter with other family?"

"Mama and Papa's kin live up north—I don't know where. It seemed best to stay in London and hope for work here."

Her decision all but made, Helena nodded. "Thank you, Nell. I must discuss the matter with Mrs. Smith."

"Yes, ma'am." Nell curtseyed and went back to her scrubbing.

When she began questioning Nell, Helena had set the coin purse from her reticule on the bench beside the girl's washtub. Leaving the purse, she sought out Mrs. Smith.

"I wish all the girls were as diligent as Nell," the matron said. "Some, I'm afraid, want only to sneak off to the main building where the boys stay. Then there's Jane." She indicated a thin girl with a vacant expression. "A sweet child, but not…all there."

While Mrs. Smith spoke, Helena covertly watched Nell. A moment later, as the girl wiped her hands, her brother gathered up Helena's purse and the two walked toward her.

"Miss, you left this. Dickon, return it to her, please."

With evident reluctance, the brother handed it over. "You kin count it iff'n you like, but 'tis all there."

"Thank you," Helena said. "I'm sure it's all there."

"Told ya we couldda kept a coin," the boy muttered.

"No, Dickon. 'Twould not be honest. You know that."

Though the dress the seamstress had brought Helena at the lawyer's office was unadorned, the material and workmanship proclaimed its quality. After looking Helena up and down, the boy said, "She's rich enough not to miss a copper. I couldda bought us apples on the street."

"Where you should not go anyway!" Her face coloring, Nell explained, "Dickon chafes at my keeping him here with the girls—but I'm afraid of what he learns from the boys."

"Whereas you possess the finest of scruples," Helena said, pleased the girl had passed her little test. "Nell, I need a lady's maid. Would you like the position?"

The girl's eyes widened. "You mean, work for you,

miss? Oh, yes! But…would I have to live at your house?"

A moment's reflection told Helena she could not keep the girl's origins secret if Nell traveled back and forth from the workhouse. "Yes, that would be necessary."

"Take it, Nell," the boy urged. "I kin take care of m'self."

Clearly distressed, Nell looked from Helena to her brother. "I should love the job but…but I promised Mama we would stay together. I can't leave Dickon here alone."

Interrupting the boy's protest that he was old enough to fend for himself, Helena said, "If I promise to find a place for him, too, would you accept the job?"

Nell's face cleared. "We would both live at your house? Oh, that would be wonderful!"

"Excellent. You shall start tomorrow. Report to the kitchen and ask for Molly." Helena pointed to the maid waiting on the porch, who offered Nell a halfhearted wave. "I will find a place for Dickon within the week."

"Thank you, miss!" Nell cried. "We'll work hard and not disappoint you, won't we, Dickon?"

From the boy's mutinous face Helena gathered he would prefer to remain at the workhouse, where he might run with his fellows without his sister's close supervision. "Master Dickon, what sort of work would you like?"

"I dunno, miss. I've only ever helped with washing."

"Yes, but that's women's work, isn't it? We shall have to find you something more fit for a man."

The boy drew himself up straighter. "Though some think I'm still a child—" he threw a resentful look at his sister "—I'm big enough to do man's work."

"Being a soldier's son, I'm sure you are. 'Tis settled, then. Nell, I'll see you tomorrow."

"Thank you again, ma'am. I know what an opportunity you're giving us. You'll not regret it, I promise!"

"Bless you, Miss Lambarth!" Mrs. Smith said softly as Nell, a beaming smile on her face, hurried her brother back to the washtub. "I know you'll be happy with her work."

"You will watch out for Dickon until I send for him?"

Mrs. Smith sighed. "I shall do my best. He is a handful, that one. But I believe I can keep him out of mischief for a week. God bless you, miss, for helping these poor forgotten babes!"

"Thank you, Mrs. Smith, for caring so much about them." Touched by the woman's probably thankless efforts on her indigent charges' behalf, Helena impetuously handed the woman the rest of the coins in her purse. "Spend some of this on yourself, now, not just on your children!"

Mrs. Smith's thanks following them, Helena collected Molly and returned to the waiting hackney. Once they were seated within, Molly burst out, "Miss, whatever am I to tell the household when that girl shows up tomorrow?"

"You needn't volunteer where she came from. Just tell them she is someone you know."

Molly gasped. "I couldn't lie to Harrison!"

"It's not a lie. You met her today."

Molly shook her head, her face still distressed. "Someone's bound to find out. I'll be sacked for sure!"

"No one shall find out," Helena said bracingly. "Nell will work hard and earn everyone's respect. After a few weeks no one will care where she came from."

"If she or that ne'er-do-well of a brother don't rob us blind first."

"If your suspicions prove correct, I will turn them over to the magistrate without a qualm. If anything untoward does happen, I shall accept full responsibility."

Molly shook her head. "Harrison will still sack me."

Helena grinned at her. "If your worst fears are realized, I shall hire you back myself. Now, here is another guinea to soothe your worry with ices at Gunter's."

After a moment's hesitation, Molly took the coin. "Iff'n I do get sacked, Ma would say I'd be better off going to the workhouse myself than taking that job. You be the most unusual lady I've ever met, and that's the truth."

If you only knew, Helena thought ruefully, watching the Marylebone workhouse fade from view as the carriage headed back toward Mayfair.

CHAPTER NINE

THREE WEEKS LATER, in great good humor, Adam ran up the front steps of the Darnell town house and swept inside, tossing his coat, hat and cane to the butler.

"Are the ladies at home?" he asked Harrison.

"They just returned from their afternoon calls."

"Would you have them join me in the Green Salon? At once, please."

Harrison didn't flicker an eye at the unusual summons. "Yes, my lord. Should I send refreshment?"

"Have James bring up a bottle of Papa's best claret. And Harrison," Adam continued, grinning as he placed a gold coin in the butler's hand, "you may wish me happy."

Harrison permitted himself a small smile. "Excellent, my lord. Allow me to convey my own and the staff's best wishes to you and Miss Standish."

Adam trotted up the stairs to the parlor chuckling at Harrison's congratulations. Trust one's servants to know everything that was going on without one's having to utter a word, though given the time he'd spent calling on Miss Standish, Harrison's surmise was hardly a wild guess. However, his steward's additional

demands for funds to cover the repairs at Claygate
having spurred Adam to suppress his initial misgivings
and conclude his courtship with unusual speed, he
expected his news would elicit a bit more surprise from
the ladies.

As he went from the landing into the hallway, he
caught a glimpse of a tall, dark-haired figure disappearing around the corner. Probably his stepmother's ward,
he thought, though the girl vanished before he got a
good enough look to be sure. Come to think of it, he'd
still not seen Miss Lambarth since the night he'd
brought her home. He felt an illogical sense of disappointment at having missed her once again.

He'd seen evidence of her presence, though, in the
library, where Harrison told him she spent a great deal
of time. She'd added a thick Aubusson rug in front of
the sofa by the fire. He grinned as he remembered their
conversation in the lawyer's office, wondering if she
kept the fire in her chamber hot enough to curl the wallpaper.

True to Lady Darnell's word, his stepmother had
handled every detail of Miss Lambarth's care, sparing
him having to make any decisions about her and
keeping the herds of tradesmen his valet complained
about from inconveniencing him, for which he was
most grateful. Not that he'd spent much time at home
to be inconvenienced.

He entered the parlor, poured himself a celebratory
brandy and downed a bracing sip. He trusted Lady
Darnell had made her cousin's child feel welcome—
and hoped she'd made progress in schooling the girl on

how to behave in Society. Since Priscilla was to become his wife, Adam should introduce Miss Lambarth to his fiancée. Indeed, the girl ought to be present when Lady Darnell invited the Standish family to dine, as she was certain to do once she'd heard his announcement.

A moment later Charis hurried in, Lady Darnell on her heels. "What is it, Adam?" his stepmother cried, an anxious expression on her face. "Is something amiss?"

"On the contrary, everything is excellent! Please sit, ladies. I know you will be relieved to learn that the…troubling times we've suffered since Papa's death are at an end. An hour ago I proposed to Priscilla Standish and was accepted. I hope you will wish us both happy."

Lady Darnell's frown dissolved into a smile. "Adam, you sly dog!" she exclaimed, coming over to give him a hug. "I'd heard from my friends that you had an interest there, but being so preoccupied with Helena and with the Season just begun, I had no idea you meant to move so quickly!"

"Why impose some artificial delay? Priscilla assured me she has had her fill of being courted as one of society's leading Belles and is as eager as I to formalize our engagement. And though I'm sure there are any number of excellent young ladies making their bows this year, I've no interest in a chit straight out of the schoolroom."

The footman's arrival with the wine halted conversation while the bottle was opened and poured. Holding up his glass, Adam said, "To Priscilla

Standish! A lovely, accomplished young lady whom I hold in the highest regard and affection. May she make me as excellent a wife as I shall earnestly endeavor to make her a husband."

After his sister and stepmother had answered his toast, Adam continued, "I hope you will both welcome Priscilla to the family with as much warmth as I trust she will soon extend to you."

Nothing that though his stepmother was beaming at him, Charis looked pensive, Adam extended an arm. "I'd have a hug from you, too, sister!"

She smiled then and came over to embrace him. "Miss Standish is very rich, isn't she, Adam?"

He kissed the hand he still held. "Yes, sweeting, although I hope you don't think so poorly of me as to hint that I proposed to her only for that reason."

"Of course not. I know you were friends when I was still in the nursery," she said.

"Yes, and a merrier-spirited little girl you could scarcely imagine. The scrapes I led her into! You were too small to remember them, I suppose."

"I didn't meet her until the beginning of this Season. She…she doesn't seem very lively now," Charis observed.

"Naturally she is upon her best behavior when she goes about in Society—as I expect you to be!" he said, a niggle of unease troubling him at his sister's lack of enthusiasm.

Lady Darnell intervened with the observation that she must give a dinner so that the families might become better acquainted before the ball Miss

Standish's parents would doubtless host in honor of their engagement. After a discussion of possible dates, Lady Darnell excused herself, leaving the siblings alone.

Wishing to dispel his lingering uneasiness, Adam said, "I'm a bit disappointed that you aren't more enthusiastic about my news. You mustn't worry that my taking a wife will distance you from my affections! Your welfare will ever be one of my primary concerns. Indeed, my settling my future so early in the Season frees you to enjoy your own. Though your dowry still won't be what I would wish it, you may concern yourself solely with judging a suitor's character, without concern for the size of his purse."

"As you could not?" Charis asked bluntly.

"You mustn't think that!" Adam returned. "True, 'tis important to the restoration of Claygate that my bride be wealthy, but truly Priscilla is the choice of my heart."

"Is she? How can you be sure, with the Season scarcely begun and you having played no part in Society since you joined Wellington years ago? There might be…other ladies in London who are rich, accomplished and attractive. Some fascinating lady who would completely enthrall you. For excuse me, dearest brother, but when you speak of 'regard' and 'affection' I cannot believe your heart is truly engaged."

Squelching the smidgeon of doubt her words evoked, Adam gave her an indulgent smile. "I may not have described what I feel for Priscilla in terms as rapturous as those contained within the pages of one of your Minerva Press novels, but my affection for her is real. And more substantial a base for a lasting marriage, I believe, than more poetically intense emotions."

"'Twas not in the pages of a novel that I learned of devotion, but by watching Bellemere and Papa," Charis countered. "She loves London, yet during Papa's life she was completely content to remain at Claygate. On the very few occasions when she went to town, he fretted the whole time she was away. And though some may think her frivolous and empty-headed, when he fell ill, she nursed him with untiring devotion, refusing to turn over his care even to his valet, and sank into a melancholy for months after his death. Indeed, 'twas not until Helena arrived to occupy her that she has seemed more like her old self. Can you avow such intensity of emotion for Miss Standish?"

"Sounds rather uncomfortable," Adam replied, wishing he'd never broached the subject. "Perhaps in my salad days I fancied myself violently in love with some dashing creature or other, but it always ended in disillusionment. I suppose ladies possess more sensibility, but gentlemen don't experience such excess of feeling—at least not one of my mature years with an estate to set to rights."

"So you say," Charis replied, looking unconvinced.

Anxious now to end the exchange, Adam kissed her cheek. "With my future settled, we should discuss which of the young men you've met thus far you admire most."

Though the lift of her eyebrows told him Charis recognized quite well that he was trying to turn the subject, she said, "I do thank you for sparing me having to marry wealth. I only wish you did not have to do so! But since you ask it, I will try to be happy for you and welcome Miss Standish with sisterly affection."

"I know you will." Having had no luck with his first diversionary tactic, Adam tried another. "You mentioned Miss Lambarth a bit ago. How is she doing? Will she be ready to appear at Bellemere's dinner for Priscilla?"

At once Charis smiled. "She is doing wonderfully! I think when you next meet her, you'll be delighted with the changes Bellemere has wrought."

"Our stepmother has ever been a wizard at equipping a lady to look her best—as the recent additions to your wardrobe attest! If we don't have a crowd of young bucks worshipping at your feet within a week of your formal presentation, the young men of London must be blind."

"Worshipping at my feet as you assure me a mature gentleman would not? Then I must hope for young suitors!" Charis replied with a giggle.

"I'm relieved to hear of Miss Lambarth's progress. I was hoping I wouldn't have to present to Priscilla a girl whose odd behavior made her appear attics-to-let."

To his surprise, Charis's smile faded. "Helena is nothing of the sort!" she retorted hotly. "Indeed, I believe her mind to be brilliant! All her tutors have expressed their astonishment at the breadth of her knowledge of literature, philosophy and mathematics. She performs splendidly upon the pianoforte, which is amazing since she confided that she had not played at all since her mother left! She's even proficient at fencing—"

"Fencing?" Adam interrupted, eyebrows raised.

Charis colored. "She has a dancing master, too, and is becoming just as proficient at that. She's a most unusual girl, who interests herself in almost everything."

Adam had a swift, disturbing vision of a thin waif trying to defend herself at sword point. Shaking it off, he said, "So I observed when we first met. But if we can sit through the length of a dinner without her embarrassing us in front of Priscilla, I will be content."

Charis stiffened further. "If she should do something…not quite right, it would only be because Bellemere has not thought to instruct her about it or our way of doing it does not seem logical. Her mind is very precise. And she learns with amazing speed—Bellemere never has to correct her for the same mistake twice." Charis smiled. "'Tis most entertaining to see our everyday habits and behavior through her eyes!"

"You are quite her champion," Adam observed wryly. "I had hoped she could be like a sister to you. If you have become fond of her, I am glad of it."

"I love her! She has a dry wit and is wonderfully kind, though I know I'm not nearly as clever as she is. I'm never bored in her company. She has such a novel perspective—one never knows what she will say or do next."

Given how exacting Priscilla's mother was, this last confidence was not precisely reassuring. Adam said a quick prayer that the upcoming dinner—meant to show his prospective in-laws that his breeding, if not his finances, was fully worthy of their daughter—did not turn into a disaster, courtesy of his stepmother's unpredictable ward. "Well, I hope she'll not be too entertaining in front of Mrs. Standish. She's…rather conventional."

Charis made a face. "Overbearing and opinionated, I would describe her—but as she is to be your mama-in-law, I shall say no more."

"If you are indulgent of Miss Lambarth's lapses, I expect I shall be, as well. But I must be off. I'm to dine at Grosvenor Square, then meet Dix at White's, where I expect to toast my engagement handsomely."

Charis wrinkled her nose. "Which means you will drink to excess and return home too foxed to stand."

Adam laughed as he gave her a hand up from the sofa. "And what would you know of that, minx? I shall certainly celebrate this early and providential solution to our difficulties, and be happier still that you may enjoy your Season without my having to worry about expenses."

Arm in arm, the two siblings strolled into the hall. After rising on tiptoe to kiss Adam's cheek, Charis said, "I shall be happy, too—if it all works out somehow." And with that cryptic remark, she walked away, leaving him staring thoughtfully after her, a tiny bit of unease still lodged in his chest.

LATE THAT EVENING, garbed in one of her new silk night rails under a dressing gown of fur-lined emerald satin,

Helena descended to the library after chatting with the ladies upon their return from the musicale they'd attended.

'Twas nearly the last event they would go to without her, Aunt Lillian had told her this afternoon. Now that Helena's wardrobe was complete and since she had so quickly assimilated the essential rules of social behavior, her aunt wanted Helena to start accompanying them on morning calls to Lady Darnell's friends, two of whom, Lady Jersey and Mrs. Drummond Burrell, might be counted upon to send vouchers for the all-important assemblies at Almack's. Once Helena appeared there, she could expect a flood of invitations to routs, musicales, dances, balls, masquerades and alfresco breakfasts.

Though Helena was more interested in attending the meetings of the Mathematical Society, the concerts of the Philharmonic Society and the art exhibition of the Royal Academy, she had dutifully expressed her anticipation of these delights. If it gave Aunt Lillian pleasure to escort Helena to her favorite entertainments, Helena would do her best to appear agreeably entertained.

Her first evening engagement, her aunt had also told her today, would be here at Darnell House at the dinner Aunt Lillian was giving in honor of Lord Darnell's engagement to Miss Priscilla Standish.

Though there was no reason she should be, Helena had been surprised—and inexplicably disappointed— upon hearing of Darnell's engagement. She had to admit he intrigued her, probably because he seemed so different from the few men she'd known growing up. She'd hoped to get to know him better once Aunt Lillian pronounced her ready to appear in public—since, remembering all too vividly his reaction upon first meeting her, she'd been careful to avoid him during the month she'd spent under his roof.

But the family shouldn't expect to see much of the newly affianced gentleman, Charis—who hadn't seemed very enthusiastic about the engagement, either—had told her this afternoon. At least, Helena thought with a sigh, when she did meet Darnell again, he should be pleased by the improvement in her appearance.

Reaching the library, she entered and crossed to the sofa. Harrison having confirmed that Darnell would be out late celebrating, she'd asked the staff to build up the fire and bring in the extra candelabra she used when she stayed up late reading. Noting as she lit the candles that the blaze of heat from the hearth made the fur-lined robe she'd worn to ward off the chill in the rest of the house unnecessary, she slipped off the garment before turning to inspect herself in the mirror beside the fireplace.

She *was* much improved, Helena decided as she studied her reflection. Nearly a month of Cook's wholesome fare had filled out the hollows under her cheekbones and added an attractive rounding to the shoulders and bosom outlined by the clinging silk of the full-sleeved, high-necked night rail. Her hair was still too unruly, her body too tall and her eyes too large and prominent for beauty, but she would do, she decided.

Her wardrobe would certainly be exemplary. Though some might disapprove of the colors, not the most exacting could fault the gowns' meticulous construction or the splendor of the materials. For subtle improvements in the design, her new maid could share much of the credit.

Nell had more than justified Helena's risky choice of a workhouse employee. Not only was the girl as wonderfully clever a seamstress as she'd claimed, she possessed an innate sense of style that marched with Helena's own tastes, allowing her to suggest adding touches that enhanced the simple beauty of the gowns. Willing to work at whatever Helena set her, modest, quiet and unassuming, she had settled into the Darnell household without stirring a ripple of dissent. Even Aunt Lillian had pronounced herself impressed by Nell's competence.

With her careful ear and observant eye, Nell also reported to Helena the news about town and within the servants' quarters, giving Helena a welcome source of information about the outside world since, not wishing to chance being discovered, Helena had not again ventured out.

Though, she concluded as she poured herself a glass of wine, after three weeks of enforced inactivity, she would almost be willing to join the Christians in the ring at the Roman circus just to escape the house.

Her new employee's most valuable attribute, though, was her willingness to answer any questions that occurred to Helena's active mind without becoming distressed, embarrassed or offended.

Of necessity, Helena had been obligated to reveal to Nell something of her past. In turn, Nell told Helena about a soldier's vagabond life and the deep affection that bound his family together, even when separated by distance and time. The two had formed a bond much stronger than that normally found between a lady of the ton and her maid.

Glancing at the splendidly polished copper fender by the hearth before her, Helena had to sigh. Sergeant Hastings' son Dickon had not found his place within the Darnell household with nearly the ease of his sister. Indeed, it seemed for a while that Molly's dark predictions about Nell's brother were going to come true.

Initially thinking to use the boy as a tiger when she drove out, Helena had sent him to the head groom. But since she'd not as yet been able to acquire her horses or carriage, the boy had little to occupy him. He'd quickly succeeded in committing a variety of transgressions, from converting a purloined leather saddle girth into a slingshot to pepper the laundry maids with pebbles to attempting to teach the pot boy to gamble using buttons he'd stolen from the wash. The harried grooms soon washed their hands of him, prompting Harrison to quietly advise Helena that something else must be found to occupy the boy or he would have to be sent away.

Summoning the lad after his latest transgression— and doubtless after he'd received a blistering scold from his sister—she'd taken advantage of his penitent state to exact Dickon's promise to behave himself and work diligently if she found him some other suitable task.

Helena had then used every ploy she could devise to persuade Harrison to take the boy on as a sort of apprentice footman. Only her assurance that she would not contest the child's banishment if he abused his position—and her avowal that Dickon was awed by the prospect of being tutored by so eminent a personage as Harrison himself—finally induced him to agree.

In the two weeks since, the boy had certainly lived up to his promise. The brass on every door handle and knocker was as shiny as mirrors, while the iron grates and hearth utensils gleamed with a fresh coating of oil. Harrison was so impressed with Dickon's efforts that he'd allowed the boy, under his supervision, to begin polishing the silver.

Of course, Helena thought with a smile, the fact that Dickon followed Harrison about, hanging on his every word and, despite Harrison's outward protest but obvious gratification, saluting him every time the butler gave him an order, hadn't hurt his cause. When Lord Darnell entertained the family of his new fiancée— who, Nell had confided, were said to be very high in the instep—his home would shine from entry hall to attics.

The dinner at which, to reflect credit on the two ladies she had come to love so dearly, Helena was determined to be on her most careful behavior.

The blaze of candles adding to the fire's warmth, Helena set down her wine with a contented sigh and snuggled back against the silk pillows with which she'd strewn the couch. Enjoying the sensual glide of the fur-lined satin over her silk gown, she settled the robe over her lap and opened her book.

Several hours later the muffled thump of the front door closing echoed through the silent house, pulling her from her reading. It was followed by the sound of bootsteps ascending the stairs in an unsteady rhythm.

Probably Lord Darnell, she thought. From the sound of his uneven footsteps, he must have left his revels well in his cups.

Which the staff had predicted, Nell had told her tonight when she brought Helena's night rail. Agog with chatter about the rich lordling's daughter their master was to wed, all had agreed that the master would celebrate heartily as, Harrison had observed, was only fitting for a gentleman who had Done his Duty to his Name to Marry Well and Save his Estate. Since apparently, Nell further confided, the Darnell family had been nearly under the hatches.

Surmising that meant the Darnell finances were at a low ebb, a fact of which she'd previously been unaware, Helena understood a little better why Lord Darnell had suddenly decided on matrimony. It also made Helena very glad she was paying her own expenses and had insisted on sharing the dressmaker's bounty with Charis and Aunt Lillian.

Expecting Lord Darnell to continue his unsteady progress up to his chamber, Helena went back to her book. Not until the candles on the table beside her flickered in the sudden breeze from the open door did she realize that the footsteps had continued, not up the stairs, but to the library—where Lord Darnell now stood on the threshold, staring at her.

CHAPTER TEN

SOME FIVE MINUTES EARLIER Bennett Dixon had pushed an unsteady Adam Darnell out of a hackney. "Splendid party," Adam said as Dix half-guided, half-hauled him up the town house entry stairs. "Immensely gratified, old friend."

Dix chuckled as he braced Adam against the front door. "I doubt you'll thank me come morning. I expect you'll have the devil of a headache—a fit beginning to your new life under the cat's paw."

Adam shrugged. "You're just jealous of my charm. 'Tis good to know one has successfully concluded so important an endeavor."

"Growing up with parents who could scarce stand to be in the same room, I may have a jaundiced view of the married state," Dix admitted. "And, Lord bless you, you did make short work of fulfilling your duty. Would that Heaven might provide you some suitable reward! However, I shall be even prouder if I manage to get you to your chamber without us both falling down the stairs."

"No need, Dix," Adam replied, waving off his friend. "I can proceed from here. If you'd tasted some of the brew we drank in Portugal, you'd not worry over me after a few bottles of excellent port. I bid you good night—or morning," he concluded, offering Dix a salute that was only slightly off the mark.

"As you wish," Dix said. "Just be careful not to let that new ball and chain trip you on your way upstairs!"

Weaving a little, Adam made it through the front door, shucking his greatcoat as he walked, then up the first flight, banging his shins into the balustrade only once. Congratulating himself on that feat, he was about to tackle the second flight when a glowing half moon of light emanating from under the library door caught his attention.

Had someone left candles burning? The realization that such negligence might lead to the catastrophe of a fire cleared some of the alcohol fumes from his brain. Removing his foot from the first step, Adam turned and headed down the hall to open the library door.

The rush of heat that greeted him made his pulse leap in panic until his eyes registered that, though the fire roared lustily, it was fully contained in the hearth.

His heartbeat had just started to slow when he saw the girl reclining on the sofa. Her hair, a shining fall of blue-black alive with dancing copper highlights, framed her face and cascaded over her shoulders where she lay propped upon a profusion of pillows. A white silk night rail outlined her form from the collar high on the graceful curve of her neck down over the round of her shoulders and even fuller swell of her breasts before disappearing beneath the robe of emerald satin spread over her lap.

After a moment spent staring at the rise and fall of those perfect breasts, his stupefied gaze rose again to the oval of her face, the skin almost as pale as the silk of her gown. The vaguest hint of recognition formed in his brain as he completed his inspection of the high cheekbones tinged with a hint of a blush, the narrow nose, the pert mouth whose full lower lip begged to be nibbled. Had he seen her gracing someone's opera box?

Her large, black-fringed dark eyes regarding him in return, the Vision smiled. "Welcome home, Lord Darnell," she said, the low-pitched, throaty murmur of her voice as arousing as the rest of her.

For a moment, disoriented, he cast a startled look about. But, yes, that was his desk in the corner, Papa's portrait as a young man hanging above the hearth, his sofa before the fire upon which the young woman reclined. However she happened to get here, this exotic beauty was definitely addressing him in his own library.

And had said library not already been as warm as a summer noon in Portugal, he would still have felt the heat now popping out in beads of sweat at his forehead, rushing through his body, pooling low and turgid in his loins. Struggling to prompt his dazzled brain to function, he wondered how this rare beauty had ended up in his library.

A reward from Heaven? Dix's comment suddenly recurred to him. But why would his whimsical friend send such a creature to his home?

Pushing aside that interesting but, at the moment,

superfluous question, Adam approached the sofa. Could he get the lady up to his chamber without waking anyone, or would it be better to simply bolt the library door before partaking of the enjoyment that lush body promised?

Given the need for stealth, the warmth already blanketing the room and the throbbing intensity of his erection, here and now seemed the most sensible choice.

"Have you been sent to help me celebrate?" he asked, finding his voice at last. "I see you have wine already."

"I wasn't precisely 'sent,' but I should be happy to drink a toast," she responded in that velvet voice.

"I've had wine enough and more, but I suppose we could start with that," he returned, heading toward the sideboard to pour himself a glass. "Though I am more interested in exploring your…other skills."

"Other skills?" she asked, tilting her head coyly to study him. "And…what might those be?"

Ah, so she was clever as well as stunning. Too bad he'd imbibed too much to match her wit. "I was hoping you would…demonstrate them. But first—" he approached the sofa and set his full glass down on a side table "—why not help me get more comfortable?" Having undone his coat buttons as he'd ascended the stairs, he now pointed to the buttons at his waistcoat.

Her eyes followed his gesture and the pale cheeks pinked further. Her show of innocence and her throaty chuckle sent another bolt of lust through him.

"It appears you are already…comfortable enough, my lord. Perhaps I'd best bid you good night."

This was progress! Adam thought, grinning. "An excellent idea!" But as he stepped forward, intending to pull her into an embrace, the girl lifted one slim hand and, rather than reaching for him, tucked a lock of ebony hair behind her ear.

Her fingers rested against her head, her thumb extended. A thumb that bore a long jagged scar running from her palm to beneath the wrist of her night rail.

Adam halted as he tried to force a brain numbed by alcohol and lust to search out the meaning of that damaged thumb. Then, like a blow to the solar plexis, recognition hammered into him.

This girl was not an exotic ladybird hired out of one of London's most exclusive brothels by a naughty Dix to celebrate the end of his bachelorhood. Unless he'd gone totally out of his senses—and he felt that he was just now and unfortunately far too late returning to them—this was his stepmother's virginal relative, the "child" he'd invited into his home practically as his ward.

Miss Helena Lambarth.

The enormity of the mistake he'd almost made left him speechless. But she was not, and the certainty that he'd mistaken her calling grew stronger with every word as she thanked him for the use of his library, apologized for the excessive heat within it and assured him that she herself had provided the funds for the extra candles and coal expended. Her final salute, with the last sip of the wine in her glass, to him and his fiancée sealed the matter.

He was still staring, openmouthed in dismay and

regret, when with one last remonstrance that he not forget to extinguish the candles before leaving the room, she stood, slipped the satin robe back over her shoulders, curtseyed and walked out.

For a moment after she exited, he still did not fully believe that the tall scarecrow he'd brought home from Mr. Pendenning's office and this exquisite, sensual creature could be the same woman. His gradually sobering brain worked at summoning up the likenesses: slender figure, dark hair and eyes, high cheek-bones...the damaged thumb. That last detail sealed the identification, for he could not image two women possessing that same unique pattern of scarring.

The implications of his conclusion were so dire that rage erupted, coursing through his still-aroused body. Bellemere had certainly outdone herself, he reflected bitterly. Somehow she'd coaxed the spark of attraction that had singed him in the lawyer's office, not to a flame, but into a full-blown conflagration that had nearly cindered reason and sanity right here in his library. 'Twas just what he needed as a newly engaged man—a breathtaking siren living under his roof.

Angry at himself for the idiocy he'd almost committed and at the capriciousness of fate, he snatched up Miss Lambarth's empty glass and hurled it into the fire.

ADAM ROSE LATER THAT MORNING, his head as painful as Dix had predicted. But his physical discomfort was minor compared to the dismay engendered by recalling the encounter in his library with Miss Helena Lambarth.

By now, his rage at fate had cooled while his fury and chagrin at having made a bloody fool of himself had intensified. He was exceedingly lucky that Miss Lambarth, confronted by a foxed lecher she barely knew, had not run from the room screaming to lift the rafters, awakening his aunt and requiring him to provide some extremely embarrassing explanations.

The only sop to his self-esteem in that disaster of an encounter was that she had not. But that didn't mean his next meeting with the girl would be much more comfortable. Somehow he was going to have to come up with an innocuous but convincing explanation for his odd behavior.

No such explanation had yet occurred. In the interim, recalling how he'd ambled toward her, soliciting her help in disrobing, made him cringe.

And he'd thought her show of innocence a sham to further inflame him. Beseeching a merciful God for deliverance, he could only hope she was indeed too innocent to fully understand what he'd been about.

By the time his valet had, in merciful silence, shaved him and provided a mug of his infallible morning-after remedy, Adam had decided the adage that the more disagreeable the task, the better to complete it swiftly applied in full force here. Since he knew from the servants' chat that Miss Lambarth normally rose early and took breakfast in the small back parlor, he decided he would go immediately, hoping to catch her alone and make his apologies before the rest of the family arrived.

Served him right for being so proud of leaving the

management of Miss Lambarth to his stepmother. If he'd expressed the least interest in her progress, instead of being so focused on his own affairs that he'd merely been grateful to escape any responsibility for overseeing hers, he would have met her a dozen times the last few weeks, instead of being blindsided in his own library by her miraculous transformation.

After dressing with meticulous care for the role of avuncular elder brother, Adam descended the stairs, setting off a clanging in his head which present circumstances rendered even more unpleasant than Dix had predicted.

As he walked to the breakfast room in his still-reduced mental state, he entertained the craven hope that Miss Lambarth might have decided to take a tray in her room. But alas, as he entered the breakfast parlor, he spied her at the sideboard.

Instead of a silk night rail and a satin robe, the girl was outfitted in a shimmering turquoise material that might have done justice to a ball gown, except that once again the garment covered her from her toes to the tip of her chin. Having apparently heard him enter, she half turned, fixing those large, thick-lashed eyes on him, her body outlined in profile against the dark sideboard behind her, which emphasized the slenderness of her figure and the fullness of her breasts.

Heat flushed his skin and he felt an immediate stirring in his loins. Destroyed in that single glance was his fond hope that his inebriated brain had overreacted to last night's display of satin and silk.

In the tepid sunlight of a gray London morning, Miss

Lambarth exuded just as much sensual allure as she had by firelight. Desire, no less potent for being entirely unwanted, coursed through Adam as he watched her, that lush lower lip, the exotic gleam of those dark eyes, that demure gown buttoned up over a swell of bosom. Into his head flashed the memory of those breasts cloaked in a thin veil of silk, a hint of the nipples outlined.

Sweat popped out on his forehead and his neck cloth seemed suddenly too tight.

He would just have to put those images out of mind, he told himself, sternly commanding his body to desist. Not only were they unseemly, given that Miss Lambarth was practically his stepmother's ward, but he was now engaged to another woman.

Cursing under his breath, he summoned a smile. His life, he realized grimly as he advanced into the room, had just become a great deal more complicated.

CHAPTER ELEVEN

HELENA FELT HER SMILE falter as Lord Darnell stared at her, his expression growing ever grimmer. And yet, though his countenance remained forbidding, the flash of intensity she saw in his face before his eyes became hooded reminded her of his appearance last night in the library.

She'd been startled when the door opened, but relaxed immediately once she recognized the intruder. After living in Lord Darnell's house for nearly a month, hearing naught but tributes to the excellence of his character from his stepmother down to the kitchen maid, she'd not been alarmed at encountering him alone, even in his inebriated condition. Indeed, she found the obvious signs of his impairment diverting, an amusement that deepened as it became apparent he had no idea who she was.

She'd even felt a sweet, novel sense of feminine satisfaction that her appearance was so changed he'd not recognized her. Until something about the intentness of his scrutiny had brought her up short, made her breath catch. His gaze resting on her bosom had driven color into her cheeks and made her nipples tingle.

Though she'd already been warmed by the fire, a wave of heat that seemed to emanate from deep within had washed through her.

She'd found him unexpectedly appealing when they first met at the lawyer's office, but the odd sense of connection she'd felt then was a mere nothing compared to the cataclysmic reaction he'd evoked last night. His gaze this morning had roused those sensations once again.

Though unprecedented, the feelings seemed to produce more a sense of…excitement than alarm. She must ask Lady Darnell later what they signified, Helena decided as she gathered up her plate.

At the scrape of the china against the marble-topped sideboard, Lord Darnell winced. Remembering the vivid description Dickon had given her of the condition suffered the next morning by gentlemen who celebrated too freely, she suppressed a smile and proceeded to the table.

"Good morning, my lord," she said, keeping her voice low. He gave her a short bow, wincing again as he straightened, and she was hard put not to giggle.

"Miss Lambarth, let me apologize for my…intrusion last night. I hope you will forgive my…forwardness."

"Since 'twas I who trespassed in your library, there's nothing to forgive. And I take it as a testimony to Lady Darnell's efforts to improve my appearance that you did not immediately recognize me."

Her amusement deepened when he colored, obviously still embarrassed by his mistake. "'Tis true that you look nothing like the woebegone orphan I escorted here a month ago. A most…charming transformation! Still, I should—"

Before he could continue—or she could question him about the strange energy that had connected them last night and again just now—the door opened to admit Lady Darnell, who stopped short as she saw them together.

"Adam, what are you doing here so early? You've spoiled my surprise, you wretch! I had planned to present the 'new' Helena to you today before Miss Standish and her family arrived for dinner. She is transformed, is she not?" Lady Darnell demanded, coming over to give Helena a hug.

"She is indeed," Lord Darnell said, his voice tight.

Lady Darnell's cat-in-the-cream-pot smugness dissipated a bit at the coolness of his tone. "But utterly charming, do you not think?" she pressed.

"'Tis a triumph, Bellemere. She is exquisite."

With a trill of satisfied laughter, Lady Darnell went over to embrace her stepson. Though she seemed pleased by his response, Helena noted again how grudging was the tone in which the compliment had been delivered.

As she stared at him over the head of Lady Darnell, whom he held still encircled in his arms, his eyes darkened and some wordless current passed between them.

She felt it vibrate into the core of her being and was nearly certain he felt it, too. She knew just as instinctively as he stood watching her, the smile he'd put on for his stepmother vanished from his lips, that he was not happy about it.

Which meant he probably wouldn't be willing to discuss whatever it was, certainly not in front of Lady Darnell. Putting away that interesting observation to reflect upon later, Helena said, "You are both too kind! I shall always be a tall Meg with too long a face, but Aunt Lillian and the dressmaker have managed so cleverly, I am at least presentable. But now, Aunt Lillian, you must tell us about dinner tonight and what we can do to help."

Something like relief flashed through Lord Darnell's eyes and the taut set of his shoulders relaxed a fraction. "Yes, Bellemere, please do! Although I expect the most helpful thing I can do is stay out of the way. The groom is always *de trop* when ladies plan such things, is he not?"

Lady Darnell laughed. "He need only remember the hour at which his fiancée wishes him to present himself."

While Lady Darnell bantered with her stepson, Helena watched Adam Darnell with a curious eye. Had he feared she would reveal last night's intoxicated behavior to his aunt? Had that behavior—and the looks that passed between them—been somehow inappropriate?

More questions to ponder, Helena concluded. But though Lord Darnell had become marginally more at ease as the conversation moved past their meeting, confirming her impression that he did not want Lady Darnell to know of the incident in the library, he still appeared anxious to quit her presence. He was now explaining to her aunt how various commitments required him to leave immediately after breakfast and would keep him away until practically the time his fiancée and her family were to arrive.

"Of course you are busy," Helena intervened. "Charis and I can help Aunt Lillian with whatever must be done."

"Thank you, child, but you have lessons this morning and afternoon, do you not? I don't wish you to miss them."

"Greek and dancing, which I can postpone until later. Lord Darnell's engagement dinner is more important."

"'Lord Darnell' sounds so formal!" Lady Darnell interjected, turning to her stepson. "Do you not think that, within the confines of the house, it would be more comfortable for Helena to call you Adam?"

The glance he sent Helena told her he wouldn't find such intimacy comfortable at all. Wishing to save him having to invent some excuse, Helena said, "We know each other so little, Aunt Lillian. Can I not call him Darnell? If I'm accustomed to addressing him so, I would not risk slipping into unseemly familiarity when we are in company. If that is agreeable to you, my lord?"

"Whatever makes you feel most at ease, Miss Lambarth."

Helena suppressed a chuckle, since it was *his* comfort rather than *hers* in question. It appeared he recognized that fact, was even grateful for her assistance, for he gave her a tiny nod and smiled.

Unlike his previous polite expressions, the genuine warmth of it lit up his face and magnified several-fold the enticement of his already handsome countenance. As she had last night, Helena caught her breath as his potent appeal settled over her, evoking once again those odd feelings in her body—and a potentially more dangerous desire to move nearer to him.

So this is what attraction feels like, she thought. But though all she'd seen and heard in the last month told her Lord Darnell was every bit as kind, generous and caring as he appeared, her innate protective instincts warned that it wouldn't do to let down her guard.

After all, her mama, a very intelligent lady, had failed to realize the menace posed by Vincent Lambarth until it was too late for them both. Or perhaps, having lost the man she'd truly loved, her mama's instincts had been dulled by grief?

But she needn't make too much of her reaction to Darnell, Helena reminded herself. With him engaged, 'twas unlikely she would see him often and even more unlikely that they would be alone when they did meet. Dismissing a pang of regret over losing before it began the chance to build any closer relationship between them, Helena turned her attention back to her aunt.

Clearly disappointed at not having coaxed them to greater intimacy, Lady Darnell continued, "It shall be as you prefer, of course. But this dinner is also your first appearance in Society and I wish you to have time to prepare. Indeed, I believe Adam has invited someone special to meet you. Bennett will attend, won't he, Adam?"

Lord Darnell looked startled, as if he'd forgotten that fact. "Yes, Dix will be present."

"Bennett Dixon," Aunt Lillian explained, "Adam's best friend since childhood. They were at Eton and Oxford together, then joined the same Hussar unit. We credit dear Bennett with helping Adam come through that dreadful war unscathed. He's almost as much a son to me as Adam."

"Dix and I have always looked out for one another," Lord Darnell affirmed with a smile.

"With Adam's future settled, we must turn our attention to Charis's presentation—and yours, dear Helena. Adam, you must prevail upon Bennett to dance with the girls when they are presented at Almack's— and you must, too, if Miss Standish permits. We can make Helena's formal introduction at the ball we've been planning for Charis. Oh, we shall all be so merry!"

Helena regarded her aunt fondly. Charis had confided to her how much Lady Darnell had enjoyed being one of Society's foremost hostesses before her husband's long illness forced them to withdraw to the country. Helena was as glad as Charis that the rounds of shopping and social calls, which Helena privately thought must be rather boring, had pulled her aunt from her grief.

"Of course, I shall be happy to participate in any way you wish, dear aunt. But please, let the presentation ball be for Charis alone. 'Tis an event she has surely been anticipating for years. I don't wish to reduce by even a fraction the attention that should be hers alone."

"Kind sentiments!" Charis said, entering the breakfast room at that moment. "But quite impossible, my dear! Once society has glimpsed what a lovely, unusual lady you are, we should be trampled by gentlemen demanding your presence should we be foolish enough to try to keep you hidden. More important," she added, giving Helena a hug, "I shall enjoy the ball much more with you there to share in it."

Touched, Helena hugged Charis back. "As you wish."

"You girls will be a sensation!" Lady Darnell predicted, beaming. "The gentlemen of the ton will stumble over each other to come courting. Perhaps we shall have *three* weddings to celebrate this year!"

That comment abruptly cut short Helena's enjoyment of her aunt's enthusiasm. If Aunt Lillian were planning her presentation as a prelude to a bridal, Helena had better put a period to that notion immediately.

"I shall delight in wishing both Darnell and Charis happy. But, Aunt Lillian, I have no intention of marrying. Not this Season. Not ever."

In the silence after her pronouncement, all three Darnells turned to stare at her.

"Did Darnell not tell you?" Helena demanded. "I informed him at our very first meeting that I intended eventually to set up my own household. Dear as you all have become to me, that intention is unchanged."

Recovering from her chagrin, Lady Darnell said, "I— I suppose I can understand that your…unfortunate upbringing may have given you a wariness about gentlemen, but when the right one appears, you will change—"

"It did and I won't," Helena interrupted, determined to exterminate any hope her aunt might try to salvage on the matter of matrimony. "I'm sorry, Aunt Lillian, but I am absolutely adamant."

Suddenly realizing that her implacable opposition to wedlock might make her appear even odder than her not-of-the-prevailing-fashion gowns, she reluctantly added, "If my desire to remain unmarried will embarrass you or the family, perhaps I should begin looking for another residence at once."

To her relief, both Lady Darnell and Charis immediately protested. After promising they would respect her wishes but still earnestly desired her to remain with them and participate in Charis's Season, she acquiesced and the discussion turned back to the dinner this evening.

Lord Darnell, however, Helena noted, said nothing.

After avoiding looking again in her direction, he finished his coffee, bowed to the ladies and quit the room.

Something of the morning's brightness left with him.

Still, with him gone, before the ladies parted for their morning activities she could question them about those odd feelings Lord Darnell generated in her.

"Aunt Lillian, what does it signify when a man gazes at a lady intently?"

Lady Darnell set down her teacup and chuckled. "You must have been reading Charis's novels! In your case, I expect it would mean the gentleman was admiring your fine eyes—and lovely they are!"

"What if he were staring at my…person," she elaborated, substituting at the last moment that more innocuous term for breasts.

Lady Darnell's pleased look faded. Her brow furrowed, she exchanged a glance with Charis and then replied, "Your…person? Do you mean some man has been…ogling you?"

Before Helena could answer, her aunt's eyes widened and she wailed, "That trip from Cornwall all alone! Oh, I feared you might have suffered indignities, traveling so far without even a maid to lend you consequence! Did some man make offensive overtures? And that short gown! The sight of your bare ankles must have inflamed him!"

"My bare ankles might…inflame someone?" Indeed, her own odd feelings in Darnell's presence had been accompanied by a profound sense of warmth. "With what kind of heat?"

Looking even more distressed, Lady Darnell said, "It could mean the man has a desire to…to touch you, a dangerous offense which one must be ever vigilant to prevent, which is why unmarried young ladies do not venture anywhere without at least a maid to protect their virtue."

Another thought occurred and Helena frowned, unable to reconcile her aunt's differing advice. "You say that the sight of my naked ankles might engender dangerous heat in a man. But did you not urge me to order gowns that would reveal my chest and shoulders?

Would not baring those more intimate parts elicit even more undesirable heat?"

"Well, I suppose," her aunt allowed, "but 'tis not undesirable to incite warmth in a *proper* gentleman."

"A ton gentlemen, you mean? It is permissible for that sort of man to give me heated glances?" Helena asked, trying to discern exactly what was considered proper.

"Yes. No! That is, it is quite acceptable to display, only before true gentleman who are well-bred enough not to attempt to take liberties, a…a physical loveliness that excites the sort of admiration that would encourage that gentleman to court you for his wife."

Finally Helena made the connection. "Ah, so a gentleman who stares in that way desires me for breeding."

"Helena!" Lady Darnell cried, fanning herself. "You must never say such a thing! Oh, Charis, where are my smelling salts?"

While Helena stood, dismayed at the havoc her simple question had created, Charis found the vineagrette and waved it under Lady Darnell's nose. "Calm yourself, dear ma'am! Let me assist you to your room."

"Aunt Lillian, I am so sorry!" Helena cried.

Moaning, fingers to her temples, Lady Darnell did not reply. Over her stepmother's shoulder as she led her away, Charis said softly, "She will be fine after she's rested. I'll come back in a trice and try to explain."

As there seemed nothing else to do, Helena waited for Charis to return, feeling both guilty and exasperated. No wonder Lord Darnell had not wanted to discuss this before his stepmother. It seemed Society had complicated rules to govern what nature handled much more directly.

A few minutes later Charis appeared. Waving aside Helena's apology, she said, "Bellemere's nerves are easily overset—only recall the afternoon of your arrival! I expect that answering your question must seem to you quite straightforward, but as I suppose you've surmised, 'tis a matter of great delicacy generally not mentioned in Society. Usually a girl's mama tells her how to properly elicit and respond to a gentleman's…interest, but I expect you never received such instruction."

"Will it distress you to explain?"

Charis smiled ruefully. "I can share the little I know, but girls aren't told a great deal. I learned more watching the horses at Claygate Manor than my mother ever divulged! Gentlemen, of course, know more, but—"

"One cannot ask them," Helena finished.

Charis laughed. "Exactly! They seem to…desire women, an impulse, from what I've gathered, akin to what stallions feel for mares. 'Tis apparently a very strong impulse, for girls are warned never to be caught alone with an unrelated man unless they are betrothed. If some man has directed lustful glances at you, tell Adam. Now that you are living with us, 'tis his responsibility to protect you."

It hardly seemed politic to reveal that 'twas Lord Darnell with whom she had exchanged the lustful glances. "Am I in danger from such a man?"

"This part is more complicated," Charis admitted.

"'Tis acceptable to excite a gentleman's desire, for he knows he may not act upon his impulses unless he pledges to wed the lady who arouses them. It would be dangerous to elicit desire in a man not of your class, for whatever his intentions, you could not marry him. Fathers or brothers guard their female relations from men such as that."

"Then men must suffer these feelings of desire until they marry? It sounds most…uncomfortable."

"Well, there is a class of women who…who earn their living by satisfying men's desires." Charis's cheeks, already pink, reddened further.

Fascinated, Helena said, "Do you know such women?"

"Heavens, no!" Charis replied with a giggle. "'Twould be most improper! A gently bred lady is not supposed to know such creatures exist. If you should notice one riding in the park or at the opera, you must pretend you haven't seen her, even if she is quite obvious."

Shaking her head at such willful ignorance, Helena said, "So it is permissible for a gentleman to gaze at you with desire—or for you to desire him, if you are to marry?"

Putting a hand to her hot cheeks, Charis gamely replied, "Yes, though 'tis quite brazen to admit it! An engaged couple is permitted to kiss and embrace, which sounds quite delightful. Brazen or not, I want the man I marry to desire *me,* not some grasping hussy in an opera box. But of course, a young lady must never—"

"Speak of it," Helena finished wryly. "No wonder poor Aunt Lillian was so distressed! Thank you, Charis, for daring to enlighten me. Now, do you suppose Aunt Lillian is calm enough that I may go beg her pardon?"

"Yes, let us go up," Charis agreed, looking relieved to be done discussing so obviously embarrassing a subject.

How was a woman to know how to respond to desire, Helena wondered as they climbed the stairs, if she was never to speak of it—not even to the man who desired her, or whom she in turn desired? It seemed a stupid sort of reticence that must surely lead to misunderstanding.

And how did a man mate with a woman? With the wild intensity of a stallion with a mare? Just thinking of Adam Darnell mounting her, his hands on her breasts, his teeth at her neck, set her blood coursing and sent a tingling warmth to her breasts, between her legs. She could well believe, as Charis had timidly confirmed, that a woman wanted a man to desire her.

Must a lady be wed to slake her desires? Obviously it was not required for men to be, since women existed to serve that sole purpose. Was desire elicited only by one particular person? A stallion, she knew, would mate with any willing mare. Were men and woman like horses in this?

It seemed her original question only led to more. Which, she now knew, she could not ask of Lady Darnell or even Charis, who had already told her all she knew.

How unfortunate she could not query Lord Darnell. The possibility that he found her desirable both excited and disturbed her. Was she so unconventional that to Darnell she seemed like one of those women meant to slake a man's lust? Yet Charis also said that since Helena was now a part of his family, Darnell would feel obligated to protect her from the desires of ineligible men.

Even from his own?

For being promised to another, he could not wed her—even if she wished to wed, which she did not. Though, she thought a bit wistfully, the idea of marrying a man who both desired her and was as honorable and compassionate as Adam Darnell appeared to be almost tempted her to reconsider her stance. But, no, marriage was out of the question for a number of excellent reasons.

What a muddle! she concluded as she knocked on her aunt's door. No wonder the attraction between them made Darnell so uneasy.

CHAPTER TWELVE

AT THE DINNER THAT EVENING which was to mark his triumph, Adam Darnell sat tense and disgruntled, trying to keep his attention from being drawn from his fiancée and her mother beside him to Miss Lambarth, placed near his stepmother and Mr. Standish at the other end of the table.

He could try to tell himself he was only concerned that she might embarrass Priscilla by using the wrong fork or spilling her wine. But that was a lie and he knew it.

He simply couldn't rid himself of a sense of her presence. An unwanted, intangible awareness of her annoyed him constantly, like the mosquitoes that on many a Peninsular night had whined about his head, unable to be ignored or successfully swatted.

Nothing in her behavior should have drawn his eye, for she used all her utensils correctly and properly performed every ritual of courtesy. Her conversation was perfectly conventional as she prompted Mr. Standish to discuss the land management techniques he employed on his estates. But though her unadorned gown of violet silk covered her up to her chin, she said nothing outlandish and committed not the smallest breach of etiquette, no amount of proper behavior could mask the passionate intensity she radiated to every man in the room.

The slightly protruding eyes of Priscilla's first cousin and her father's heir, Francis Standish, never left Miss Lambarth's face…though fortunately did not drop to her bosom, which would have required Adam to plant him a facer. Nor could Priscilla's father, prosing on about tares and staves, tear his gaze from her as she smiled and nodded.

Even Dix, between making conversation with his dinner partners, took every opportunity to turn and watch her…like a hound eyeing a beefsteak he'd like to devour, Adam thought sourly.

How could he not? Without making any overt attempt to do so, still the girl exuded sensuality.

Given what he knew of her father's treatment of her, Adam supposed he could understand her initial refusal to consider marriage. But marrying her off would be the best, most socially acceptable way to dispose of her and the damnable temptation she posed—and the sooner, the better.

Despite her determination not to marry, Adam knew there were any number of ton gentleman of excellent character. Surely one of them, when she got to know him better, could lure her into matrimony.

And into his bed—the lucky dog, he thought with a sharp, unwanted stab of jealousy.

Until then, however, Adam could figure no way out of his obligation to let her remain in his house. After

casting a clandestine glance down the table and receiving in just that quick look a sense of connection as
sharp as a shock, he felt he would almost rather be back
in Belgium, riding all day through the mud while
dodging a hail of shot and canister, than here in
London, having to rub shoulders with Helena
Lambarth in the close proximity of his house.

As the dinner progressed, he discovered that his
problem was more than mere lust. He noted how Miss
Lambarth deferred to Mr. Standish and, though the
man was a dead bore, prompted him with questions and
appeared completely absorbed in his answers. Nor
could he help but notice that she'd made pains to
include Priscilla's shy cousin Emily in the conversation, rather than taking advantage of the curiosity even
the female members of Priscilla's family felt about her
to make herself the center of attention.

That was kindness and modesty indeed, which he
had to admit justified Charis's high praise for the
girl. Even now, his sister and stepmother sat smiling
their approval at her exemplary behavior. The fact
that Miss Lambarth had been so completely
embraced by those ladies ought to relieve him, since
it meant he'd not be consulted save on the most important decisions concerning the girl. Yet the obvious
affection in which those ladies held her only demonstrated how sterling a character she must
possess—something he'd rather not have to acknowledge.

Adam suppressed a curse. He didn't *want* to like or
admire Miss Lambarth. 'Twas bad enough that he was

forced to continue offering her the hospitality of his home, where she could so effectively cut up his peace.

To make matters worse, it had quickly become apparent that Priscilla had taken an immediate dislike to her. The moment his fiancée had set eyes on Miss Lambarth in the parlor before dinner, she had stiffened. Which, he supposed, was mostly his fault. Priscilla had been led to expect the girl would be an ill-behaved, scrawny orphan.

In the short time between his discovery of Helena's transformation and the party tonight, Adam had tried to think of a way to warn his fiancée that Miss Lambarth was now radically different from the half-starved waif who had elicited his compassion in the lawyer's office. However, caught in the throes of trying to control his strong physical response to the girl, he'd been afraid if he attempted a description, he would end up uttering something either too brief or too detailed.

Wanting at all costs to avoid the horror of having Priscilla, who was no fool, sense how intensely the girl affected him, as they sat together this afternoon in a sheltered alcove in the Standish garden, he'd limited himself to just the innocuous observation that his stepmother and Charis had managed to effect a marked improvement in the girl, which he hoped his fiancée would appreciate. Of course, they could not expect in just a few weeks to truly bring her up to snuff, so he trusted Priscilla would be kind enough to overlook any lapses.

Squeezing his hand, she had replied that she hoped

she would always treat every member of his family with the graciousness he expected of his wife—and lifted her face toward his.

He'd given her the kiss she obviously expected. And tried to ignore the fact that this brief salute upon her lips had not stirred his blood to anything like the pulse-pounding, heat-inducing furor Miss Lambarth had provoked tonight merely by walking into the room.

Which meant he must continue to avoid, to the extent possible, being in the same one with her. What bitter irony, he thought glumly, that the home for which he'd longed all through the hell of Waterloo and the long months of duty in Paris was no longer the haven he'd dreamed of, but a trap that might tempt him to the worst of follies—at least until he could fight his mind free of the spell cast by Helena Lambarth.

His nerves on the raw, Adam sighed with relief as Lady Darnell rose and signaled the ladies to withdraw. At last he could relax over a badly needed glass of port.

He had scarcely filled his glass when Dix strolled over, delivered a sharp punch to his side and introduced the very topic he wished to avoid. "Wretch!" his friend exclaimed. "Lady Darnell's ward is exquisite! The only reason I shall not immediately challenge you to fisticuffs is that you allowed me to meet her first."

That intent, heated glow in his friend's eyes had not been provoked by Miss Lambarth's conversation. Slim as the possibility was that Adam might have been mistaken about her effect on other men, he didn't relish having his assumptions confirmed. "Need I remind you that she is a lady and under my care?" he asked stiffly. "I expect you to treat her as such."

"Of course!" Dix replied, sounding a bit affronted. "I'm a gentleman, after all. 'Tis well that you are already vigilant about men who aren't, however. I shall be happy to help you protect her—and you needn't worry that I'll drool all over her, as I feared young Standish was about to during dinner."

Anxious to end a conversation that only deepened his annoyance, Adam said sharply, "Perhaps you should remember the destination to which admiring a young lady might lead."

Dixon merely chuckled. "I admit, I've hitherto scoffed at marriage, but since you've hurtled the breech, perhaps it's not quite the disaster I've always envisioned it. And with a prize that alluring…"

Allure, Adam thought acidly. If one could bottle the essence that surrounded the girl, women would storm the shops to purchase it.

Adam's future father-in-law walked up. "I say, Darnell, 'tis quite an interesting chit your stepmama's taken up. I'd heard she was odd and ill-dressed, but I found her nothing of the sort! Asked quite knowledgeable questions about my estate. Ah, ah, taking little puss."

Standish's eyes held the same gleam as Dix's, Adam noted with disgust.

"Rumor at the clubs says she's quite an heiress! I suppose I should be glad my gel brought you up to scratch before she arrived." Standish cleared his throat. "I trust, despite her presence, you'll remember what's due my Priscilla."

Though he might be inwardly struggling with his attraction to the girl, not even from his future father-in-law would Adam tolerate such a questioning of his honor. Fixing Mr. Standish with the cold stare that had, in his army days, reduced many a subordinate to stammering incoherency, Adam said softly, "What do you mean to infer?"

Flushing, Mr. Standish took a step back from the menace in Adam's eyes. "Nothing at all! Just…making conversation. So, what is the chit worth, anyway?"

Still bristling, Adam replied, "I am not her guardian. Her assets were placed in trust with her mother's lawyer, who led me to believe she was well provided for."

Standish gestured toward his heir. "The way Francis stared at her all through dinner, I'm sure there's an interest there, eh, my boy? Should she come into wealth, 'twould be a good match, don't you think?"

Francis glanced toward the door through which the ladies had exited, a salacious look on his face. "I just might be persuaded to fix my interest there."

The thought of the oily Francis getting his hands on Helena was so nauseating, Adam was once again tempted to plant the man a facer.

"Not a responsibility I'd want, watching over a girl with her looks," Mr. Standish continued, giving Adam a collegial slap on the back. "I expect you'll be beating off the gentlemen. You'd be wise to get her wed before some rake tries to, ah, sample her charms."

Telling himself that Standish meant well, Adam reined in his temper. "I'll be sure to give your advice the weight it merits," he said, striding to the sideboard before irritation tempted him to say something unwise. Meeting him there, a sympathetic Dix rolled his eyes as he refreshed Adam's glass.

"Have no fear," his friend murmured. "I'll carry her off myself before I'd let fish-faced Francis have her."

He ought to be glad of Dix's assistance. But instead of relief, the knowledge that while he must avoid her, his friend might freely solicit Miss Lambarth's company angered Adam so much he had to bite back a sharp reply.

Suddenly rejoining the ladies and bringing this evening to an end seemed like a good idea after all.

IN THE PARLOR, HELPING Aunt Lillian prepare to serve tea, Helena waited for the party to be over. As she'd feared, once the novelty of eating dinner in company faded, the meal had become rather tedious.

After introductions and some stilted chat in the parlor, they'd proceeded to the dining room, where Mrs. Standish had stridently directed the conversation at her end of the table and Mr. Standish monopolized the talk at his. Interested in estate management, Helena had remained mostly silent as the man prosed on while she nodded and smiled until her cheeks ached. Still, she thought it rather poor behavior on the part of this supposedly elevated member of the ton that he'd hardly let Lady Darnell utter two sentences all evening.

On her other side sat Miss Standish's cousin Emily, a meek slip of a girl clearly intimidated by the relations with whom she resided. Feeling sorry for the girl, in the few moments her own attention was not demanded by Mr. Standish, Helena had attempted to get her to talk.

The only person of interest besides her aunt and Charis was Darnell's friend Mr. Dixon. Though he sat too far away for her to engage him in conversation and properly devoted his attention to his dinner partners, occasionally she'd caught him gazing at her. Each time he gave her a wink, as if he were amused by a joke he wished her to share. Perhaps when the gentlemen returned she might have a chance to speak with him.

Darnell himself had ignored her. Though he played the gracious host, responding to all the sallies directed at him by Mrs. Standish and his fiancée, his strained expression seemed to indicate he was not enjoying himself. As for Miss Standish, even the most sanguine observer could not have interpreted the occasional look she directed at Helena to be either approving or congenial. Besides which, in Helena's opinion, Darnell's fiancée seemed far too ready to second every strident opinion her mother uttered.

If that behavior gave any evidence of the way in which her character was evolving, Helena felt sorry for Darnell.

The parlor door opened and the gentlemen filed in, followed by the butler with the tea tray. As the men gathered at the table awaiting their cups, Helena bent her attention to performing her task, not wishing to embarrass her aunt by spilling anything or mixing up the orders.

A shadow fell over her fingers. She looked up to

find an unsmiling Miss Standish before her. "What a lovely gown, Miss Lambarth, and of such unusual styling! I recall my governess used to prefer gowns cut high upon the throat like that. As it is not quite what is currently in fashion, I expect dear Lady Darnell must have a great fondness for you, to indulge your whims in such a matter."

Looking over from the cup she was filling to smile at her aunt, Helena replied, "I could not wish for someone more loving or considerate."

"Sometimes we are too indulgent of those whom we fancy. Mama has always warned me to guard against it, especially with children. You've been out in Society too little yet to know, Miss Lambarth, but what appears to be a harmless indulgence within one's family can be interpreted by larger Society as encouraging the inappropriate."

Helena's smile faded. Although she'd tried to overlook the subtle criticism of Miss Standish's first remarks, she could not ignore this further gibe, not only concerning her taste, but Aunt Lillian's judgment, as well.

"And 'tis such an unusual color!" Miss Standish continued. "I suppose it becomes you better than the white or pale shades normally thought suitable for a young lady embarking upon her first Season."

Helena gazed at Miss Standish, her eyes narrowing. Darnell was in the corner conversing with Mr. Dixon, but all the other guests were lingering by the tea table, listening to their exchange. Though Helena cared not at all what Society thought of her, she was incensed by the indirect criticism of the aunt who'd lovingly accepted an ill-bred orphan into her home and heart.

Knowing that returning the first sharp reply that sprang to her lips would probably increase the breathless interest with which their audience was following the conversation, she bit back her observation that 'twas fortunate that Miss Standish was beyond her first few Seasons, since pales would not become her, either. "I do prefer colors," she said instead.

"At least you are out of black, which is such a difficult color to wear. It has been a year since your father's death, I assume?"

At the mention of her father, the last shreds of Helena's good will evaporated. "Miss Standish, I chose this color and material because the weave of the silk pleased me. And though it has not been a year since my father's death, I would never be so hypocritical as to wear mourning for him."

"Oh!" Miss Standish exclaimed, appearing to be taken aback. "How very…outspoken you are, Miss Lambarth! I suppose, having lived all your life in the country, you are not yet familiar with London customs. I beg you will not repeat that remark in any less intimate a family group than this, for such blatant lack of respect for your late parent would be considered most improper."

"Miss Standish, do take your tea," Aunt Lillian said nervously, holding out a cup. "I fear it is growing cold."

With a satisfied smile, Adam's fiancée accepted the tea and moved away. Still seething, Helena resumed serving the rest of the company.

Perhaps she'd better begin looking for new lodgings immediately, since she most certainly wished to be established elsewhere before Adam Darnell brought home *this* bride. If the new Lady Darnell were going to be as unpleasant to Aunt Lillian and Charis as she'd just been to Helena, she would urge both ladies to depart with her.

When she looked up again a moment later, Bennett Dixon was watching her. "'Tis a task that requires a good deal of concentration, isn't it?"

"Certainly for one with as little practice as I," she flashed back.

He grinned at her, as if he were amused by her sharpness. "I don't know how you ladies manage it. When I serve punch at Christmas, I spill it all over the cup. Lady Darnell, would you be so kind as to release your charming assistant? I've been wanting all through dinner to converse with her."

Lady Darnell, who'd been looking distressed since the interchange with Miss Standish, brightened. "Of course. Helena, did I not tell you Bennett was eager to meet you?"

Just then Francis Standish walked up and Helena suppressed a moue of distaste. Bennett Dixon's easy, casual elegance appealed to her far more than Standish's overly fussy appearance and pompous air of self-importance.

"Ho, Dix, 'tis not fair to steal away the debutante of the evening, whom I, too, long to engage in some small chat."

Before Helena could point out that Charis was the

debutante and his cousin the dinner's honoree, Mr. Dixon replied, "You'll soon be part of the family, Standish, able to run tame in the house whenever you wish. We not so lucky fellows must seize such opportunities we can. Miss Lambarth?" Grasping her elbow, he pulled her away.

As soon as they were out of earshot, Helena murmured, "Though I thank you for the rescue, 'twas rather managing."

"Excuse me if I've offended you!" He grinned again and sighed lustily. "But I fear you are correct. I expect it stems from too many years in the army."

"You served with Darnell, Aunt Lillian told me. Where were you posted?"

"We saw action through most of the Peninsular war, then at Waterloo." He paused, a shadow passing over his face. "'Twas often a bloody business, which I'm sure Miss Standish would pronounce not a proper topic for a lady's drawing room. But at times I still miss the camaraderie of the unit and the sense that one was engaged in a business more important than oneself. And the uniform, of course, which the ladies found very dashing."

She laughed, as she was sure he meant her to. "You were in the hussars, were you not? You must know horses, then. Now that my aunt will be permitting me to go about, I wish to purchase horses and perhaps a carriage."

"Do you drive?"

"Nothing but a pony trap, and not for many years. I may have to learn all over again. But I can begin riding again as soon as I can obtain a suitable mount."

"Tattersalls would be the best place here in the city to look for one. Should you like me to make inquiries?"

"I should be much obliged! Or…is that something I shouldn't ask you to do, even though you are a very old friend of the family?" She smiled ruefully. "I expect Darnell has warned you I grew up with little supervision. Lady Darnell has been doing her best to rectify my faults, but there are so many rules! I could ask Darnell to assist me, but I imagine he shall be fully occupied dancing attendance on his fiancée and her family."

"Poor Adam," Mr. Dixon murmured.

Helena was surprised into a chuckle. "How very unchivalrous, Mr. Dixon!"

Coloring a bit, he returned, "You must allow her mama to be a bit…overwhelming. I much prefer present company."

"You are quite the gallant, sir! But—would it be acceptable for you to look into acquiring horses for me?"

"Quite acceptable," he confirmed.

"And you would not consider it an imposition? Please do tell me if it is, for I've procured an excellent map of London and am sure I could find the place myself."

"No imposition at all. I go to most of the auctions anyway, which, I'm afraid, are not attended by ladies."

"Then however is one to—" Stopping herself before she voiced her opinion of the idiocy of that stricture, Helena continued, "Thank you for the warning. I shall need all I can get, if I am to avoid falling into behavior that might reflect badly upon poor Aunt Lillian." She cast a bitter glance across the room at Miss Standish.

Following the direction of her look, Mr. Dixon squeezed the hand that rested on his arm. "I hope to become *your* good friend, as I am Adam's."

"I should like that," Helena replied, smiling. Mr. Dixon was a man, of course, and therefore suspect, but it appeared he might make an amusing companion. His engaging manners and easy friendliness were particularly appealing after Miss Standish's enmity.

"With Darnell occupied elsewhere, it would be most helpful to have a trusted gentleman's advice on matters of propriety and fashion." Since it would be better not to approach Darnell himself, she thought, recalling the peculiar sensations they seemed to evoke in each other.

Mr. Dixon bowed. "I would be delighted to offer you a masculine perspective on whatever matter you wish to discuss. Shall we begin immediately? Drive with me in the park tomorrow and I can show you the types of vehicles available while you point out the horses you prefer."

"If Aunt Lillian agrees, I would be delighted."

At that moment, smiling in approbation, Aunt Lillian called to them. "Helena, dear, Miss Standish and her family are departing. Come help me bid them goodbye."

As a member of the family. Helena understood at once the significance of the gesture and a pang of bittersweet affection pierced her chest. Aunt Lillian might not have the biting wit to engage Miss Standish in verbal combat, but she intended by her actions to show Adam's betrothed that she fully embraced her unorthodox niece.

"Shall we set a time for the drive?" Mr. Dixon asked, interrupting her reflections. After settling the matter, he bowed. "'Twas my very great pleasure to make your acquaintance, Miss Lambarth. Until tomorrow."

He bent over her hand. Beyond his lowered head Helena saw Darnell, fiancée on his arm, staring as Mr. Dixon saluted her fingers. A disapproving frown creased his brow.

A look sizzled between them. Turning away, Helena shrugged off the sensation. Darnell could hardly object to the attentions paid her by his good friend. And despite the intensity of their reaction to each other, his breeding impulses must now be focused on Miss Standish.

Somehow Helena could not help feeling that would be a very great waste.

CHAPTER THIRTEEN

THE FOLLOWING DAY at nuncheon Aunt Lillian announced they would begin the round of social calls necessary for Helena's introduction to Society. First on the list was Aunt Lillian's old friend and Society leader, Lady Jersey.

While Lady Darnell retired to ready herself for the excursion, Charis asked Helena to stay with her for a few minutes in her sitting room.

"We've not had a chance to chat since dinner last night. What did you think of Miss Standish?" Charis asked after they'd seated themselves before the hearth.

Not knowing how Charis felt about her brother's fiancée, Helena answered carefully, "I found her attractive and very...self-assured."

Charis sniffed. "Indeed! Adam said Miss Standish used to be a lively child. If she was, I can't help thinking she has grown rather stodgy. And she seems always so...measuring, as if she is constantly assessing my actions and finding them wanting. And I thought it most unkind of her to call attention to the fact that you do not wear mourning, which anyone who knows what transpired with your father would perfectly understand, but which might well be thought improper by those who do not."

Helena smiled wryly. "I don't think Miss Standish likes me very much."

Charis tossed her head. "I expect not. You are just as rich as she is, and much more beautiful."

"Me?" Helena shook her head dismissively. "With her blond hair and light eyes, I thought Miss Standish very lovely. And dear as you are to claim so, no *disinterested* observer would ever call me beautiful."

"Perhaps not in the conventional sense," Charis admitted. "You possess something more—a sort of intensity that makes you seem so…alive, it is almost as if you are in motion even when you are sitting still."

Helena laughed out loud. "What a fanciful notion!"

Charis chuckled. "Fanciful perhaps, but 'tis true. Gentlemen certainly notice it! Last night they could scarcely take their eyes from you." She paused, gazing into the fire for a moment. "No wonder that man on the mail coach stared at you. He must have sensed that…passion in you, even before you looked as lovely as you do now."

"And you are a great goose!" Helena said roundly. "If the gentlemen stared last night, I expect, as Miss Standish was at pains to point out, 'twas because of my oddly styled gown of inappropriate color. And if the company had not already been well acquainted, *you* would have been the center of attention, for you were by far the prettiest lady present. I believe Aunt Lillian was correct in predicting your Season shall be a huge success!"

"Though I fear I cannot like Miss Standish very much, I expect I should be grateful that Adam fixed his interest with her, for with the promise of her wealth to help restore Claygate, he will now be able to provide me a dowry. Not enough to make me acceptable to the highest sticklers, but I don't seek a grand match. I would rather wed the choice of my heart, or not marry at all."

"If no man claims your heart, you must come live with me after Darnell installs Miss Standish here. But I suspect such a dreary single fate will not be yours."

"Oh, I am certain *your* life shall always be exciting, whether or not you marry! But I'm not so brave. I should prefer marriage to remaining unwed, if I can find a kind, sensible man who cares for me and wishes to retire to a pleasant country estate like Claygate—where we shall raise a bevy of children to idolize their daring Aunt Helena."

Warmed once again by Charis's affection, Helena replied, "Then let's hope daring Aunt Helena doesn't spoil their future mother's chances of wedding the man she chooses by creating some awful scandal! Now, we must go change our gowns if we are to be ready to leave." With a hug, Helena left Charis and proceeded to her chamber.

An hour later they entered Lady Jersey's crowded drawing room. While they waited to speak with their hostess, Helena noticed their small party was drawing the attention of a number of the guests, who, while trying not to appear to be doing so, were definitely scrutinizing her.

Recalling Miss Standish's hostility last night, Helena wondered if Darnell's fiancée had begun circulating stories about his odd houseguest. Before she could decide how she should deal with that possibility, her aunt secured their hostess's attention.

After introductions and an exchange of greetings, Lady Jersey frankly inspected Helena's gown. "Unusual, Miss Lambarth, but quite becoming."

"Then it does suit me," Helena replied, amused by the relative hush as the guests nearest them strained to overhear the conversation, "for I fear I, too, shall prove to be rather unusual. I hope, having long stood her friend, you will not hold my social lapses against Lady Darnell, who is taking great pains to try to civilize me."

Lady Jersey chuckled. "Your concern for your aunt speaks well of her efforts, Miss Lambarth. Being such a contrast to the norm of milk-and-water misses, I expect you shall cause a stir." A little smile played about her lips. "I shall greatly look forward to witnessing it."

After leaving their hostess, Lady Darnell led them toward a fashionably dressed matron holding court in the opposite corner of the room, murmuring that she was delighted she would be able to present Helena to another of the Almack patronesses, Princess Esterhazy.

As they walked, Helena noted a finely dressed older watching her. Since they'd entered Lady Jersey's parlor, each time Helena looked around during a pause in the conversation, she'd caught the woman staring at her.

"Aunt Lillian, who is the lady in the green dress?" she asked, pointing her chin in the woman's direction.

Turning where Helena indicated, Lady Darnell gasped. "Oh, my! 'Tis…'tis Lady Seagrave, my dear. The mother of the gentleman whom…"

"My mother loved," Helena finished, now inspecting the woman as avidly as that lady had regarded her. "Should I approach her?"

"I can introduce you if you like, but it wouldn't be wise to encourage the connection. Though 'tis many years since the…unfortunate events transpired, if you associate with Lady Seagrave, some may remember what circumstances forced your poor mama to do, and think badly of her."

A decade of anger sizzled in Helena. "'Tis my father Society should think badly of!"

"Indeed, my dear, but when a marriage doesn't prosper, 'tis always the woman who is blamed. Then, too, Lady Seagrave might resent you. If your mama had not taken refuge with her son, perhaps he might have been able to return to England. 'Tis best not to stir up old troubles."

Her aunt was probably correct, Helena thought, unable to read what emotion lay behind Lady Seagrave's enigmatic expression. In any event, since Lady Darnell was clearly uncomfortable about introducing them, Helena would not trouble her by insisting on it.

But she couldn't make herself turn away without acknowledging the challenge of Lady Seagrave's steady regard. Drawing herself up to her full height, she gave the woman a gracious nod. With the faintest of smiles, Lady Seagrave returned it, leaving Helena still uncertain of the woman's opinion of her.

Then, swallowed up in the crowd of gentlemen around the princess, Helena lost sight of the woman. Lady Darnell explained as they drew closer that, like the princess's husband, many of the men here were diplomats, the Englishmen having returned to London to consult with the government.

When they were halfway through the group, a tall, blond gentleman chanced to look their way. His dark eyes lighting, he eased his way toward them.

"How are you, ma'am?" he asked, bowing over Lady Darnell's hand. "You may not remember me, for you retired to Claygate soon after Adam and I became friends, but he and I were at Oxford together. Nathan Blanchard."

"Of course I remember you, Lord Blanchard!" Aunt Lillian responded with a smile. "Allow me to present you to Adam's sister and my niece, Miss Lambarth."

"Miss Lambarth, a pleasure. But surely this blond angel cannot be Adam's little sister! I seem to recall at our last meeting a child with long pigtails, some sort of furry creature in arms and a quantity of mud."

Charis blushed. "Lord Blanchard, children grow up."

"But few grow so enchanting! Lady Darnell, you must permit me to call while I'm in London."

"You will be welcome at any time," that lady replied, looking pleased by Blanchard's reaction to her charges.

"Will I find Adam at home, or is he still with the army in Paris?"

"No, he returned about a month ago. He will be delighted to see you—in such time as he can spare from his betrothed. He has just become engaged to Miss Standish."

Lord Blanchard raised his eyebrows. "Adam captured the hand of the elusive Priscilla Standish? He's been quite busy! Tell him I shall seek him out to present my congratulations. And I hope to see you ladies again soon."

After exchanging a few words with the princess, who gave Helena a gracious smile, Lady Darnell shepherded the girls to the door. Pronouncing herself highly satisfied with the call, Lady Darnell decided to treat the party to ices and return home. She expected Miss Standish and her mother to call to thank her for the dinner party, she told them, and wished to rest before they arrived.

Understanding her aunt's need for repose before having to receive Adam's fiancée and her tiresome mother, Helena was doubly glad she would be driving out with Mr. Dixon—and thus had an excuse to avoid being present during the Standish ladies' visit.

Helena's escort arrived promptly at the arranged time. Determined to escape before Darnell's fiancée arrived, Helena descended minutes after Harrison sent up his card.

"Miss Lambarth, you astound me!" Dixon exclaimed as she entered the parlor already garbed for the drive. "I've scarcely had time to warm my hands at the fire."

"Perhaps you should invest in warmer gloves, sir," she responded with a chuckle as he shepherded her to his phaeton. "Before you commend my punctuality, however, I must confess it is due more to the desire to avoid…certain callers than to an unusually high degree of promptness."

It took him only an instant to puzzle out her meaning. "In that case," he replied with a grin, "I'm surprised you were not waiting in the foyer!"

The open vehicle into which he assisted her had a narrow bench seat suspended high over very large wheels. She admired the view offered by its superior elevation while Mr. Dixon scrambled up to take the reins.

"I hope the height of the phaeton doesn't alarm you," he said as he set his team in motion. "Though it may appear the seat is suspended a dangerous distance from the ground, 'tis quite safe—with a competent driver at the ribbons. You needn't worry I shall overset you."

"I doubt you could have gone through a war intact if you were that ham-fisted. I love the carriage! I shall obtain one myself as soon as I learn to drive it."

A bit of coolness in his tone, he replied, "I beg your pardon, but even at the risk of incurring your displeasure, I couldn't allow a *female* to drive my rig."

She looked at him in surprise. "Are females not permitted? How tiresome! Then I shall hire a carriage and pay John Coachman to teach me. I have vast experience driving a pony cart and expect the same principles apply."

Looking at first a bit taken aback at her blithe disregard of convention, he recovered to produce a smile. "If you are that determined, let me offer to tutor you. A high-perch phaeton is a gentleman's vehicle and, without wishing to appear a braggart, I expect I have more experience at handling one than a coachman. My vehicle is better maintained, my horses of higher quality, than any you might hire."

Helena slid him a laughing glance. "But, Mr. Dixon, you just said you could not allow a female at the ribbons."

"A female in general, no, but a serious student would be an entirely different matter," he replied promptly.

"Ah, but I would not wish to risk your superior horses or vehicle at the hands of a clumsy, inexperienced driver."

"With my guidance, your handling would not be clumsy."

The debate continued until they reached Hyde Park, Helena maintaining she could not impose upon his time and would feel more comfortable learning in a hired vehicle, Mr. Dixon insisting she would learn better and more quickly with him as her instructor.

As they entered the park, Helena exclaimed at the beauty of the large open expanse with its tended carriageways and verdant greenery. Taking his place in the long line of vehicles, between greeting acquaintances, Mr. Dixon pointed out various styles of carriages.

After a half hour of slow progress, Helena's initial enthusiasm began to dissipate. "'Tis very well to look at thoroughbreds, Mr. Dixon, but if this is the only place in London one can ride, I shall need nothing more spirited than a plodding old pony."

He smiled at the exasperation in her tone. "One doesn't come to the park during the promenade hour to ride, but to see and be seen."

"There is better riding to be had at other times?" Helena inquired hopefully. "'Tis truly a waste of fine carriage trail to dawdle about in this fashion."

"You prefer galloping *ventre à terre,* I suppose?"

"Is there any other way?" she returned with a grin.

Mr. Dixon laughed. "I suppose not. Early morning is best, I understand, if you wish the park to yourself."

"So I shall come only then. Do you prefer your phaeton to riding—or are you not an early riser?"

He turned to gaze into her eyes, his own darkening with something of the look Darnell's had possessed as he'd stared at her in his library. "I could be...if the spectacle were sufficiently arousing. Do you keep country hours?"

Feeling more uneasy under Dixon's intense scrutiny than she had at Adam's, Helena's cheeks heated. She was almost certain her escort was referring to more than a morning ride. Perhaps Charis had been right when she'd said Helena elicited a passionate response from gentlemen.

Not sure what she ought to do about it, Helena kept her response strictly mundane. "'Tis not fashionable, Aunt Lillian told me, but I fear I do rise very early. I'm a rather restless soul, as I suppose you've noticed. Despite the slow pace of the drive, 'tis wonderful to be outside again after being tethered to the house for weeks."

"You spent much of your youth out of doors?"

Into her head flashed the image of the barred room, the airless, lightless priest's hole. "Not enough. I was often...constrained to be indoors and vowed that someday I would spend as much time driving and riding as possible."

"Adam tells me your home is on the coast? I expect the weather often forced the ladies indoors. Were you condemned to take your exercise strolling the Great Hall under the disapproving eyes of your ancestors?"

Since there was little she could or wished to say about her home and upbringing, she replied instead, "My mother's passion was raising thoroughbreds. As she was the foremost horsewoman in three counties, I sat a pony before I could walk and practically grew up in the stables. I can't wait to begin riding again."

If he noted her evasion, he did not comment on it. "Then as we progress at our shamefully slow pace, you must point out the horses that interest you."

For the next half hour they exchanged observations on the points of the various bays, bloods and grays under saddle of the passing riders. They had nearly finished their first circuit of the park when a congestion of horsemen and vehicles gathered about one carriage brought their already slow progress to a complete halt.

Seated in the central carriage was a woman with white-blond hair wearing a scarlet gown and pelisse with the lowest décolletage Helena had ever seen. At this distance she could not ascertain the color of the woman's eyes, but her lips and cheeks were so arresting a rose, Helena knew she had to have resorted to a rouge pot.

"Who is that lady?" she asked her companion— whose enthralled gaze, she noted, was fixed on that very subject.

As if startled, Mr. Dixon turned quickly back to her, his fair skin flushing. A guilty look in his fine blue eyes, he cleared his throat as if uncertain what to say.

"Is she one of the pleasure women?" Helena asked. As Mr. Dixon's face flushed even redder, she waved off his garbled response. "I suppose she must be. My apologies! Charis did warn me I should not mention such women."

While her escort remained speechless, Helena shook her head and sighed. "I must say, it seems there are a great number of interesting topics one is 'not supposed' to discuss. But I have embarrassed you, so I promise to at least pretend to avert my eyes and return the conversation to more proper channels."

Though, Helena thought as she made a show of primly directing her eyes straight ahead, she might have to figure out a way to meet the woman. Ladies of that class were probably the only members of her sex with either the willingness or the experience to discuss the fascinating topic of men, women and desire.

The knot of carriages moved apart and they were able to ease past the vehicle. She turned to find Mr. Dixon's frankly assessing gaze on her. When she lifted an eyebrow inquiringly, he chuckled and shook his head. "You are a remarkable lady, Miss Lambarth," he said, the color in his cheeks beginning to recede. "Gentlemen do not discuss certain…topics with ladies to spare their more delicate sensibilities. However, since you appear more curious than embarrassed, I hope that, despite my reaction a moment ago, you will feel free to ask me any question you wish."

"Even on 'forbidden' topics?"

Though his cheeks colored again, he replied firmly, "Especially on forbidden topics. I greatly admire individuals who think freely, not meekly accepting rules simply because Society dictates them. Ask me anything."

Studying him and deciding his offer was genuine, Helena nodded. "I shall do so, then. Is that not the entrance we came in? I expect we can return now."

"So soon?" He looked startled. "Have I been that poor an escort?"

"You have been charming," Helena assured him. "'Tis just that, due to that restless nature I described, if I'm forced to endure this maddeningly slow pace much longer, I fear I may leap from the carriage and run screaming out of the park—a scene that would have to embarrass you as much as it would distress Aunt Lillian. To avoid so dreadful a prospect, would you take me home? I shall not return to the park unless it is deserted enough for me to ride as fast as I wish."

"I hope you'll allow me to accompany you."

"But you said you prefer not to rise early."

"I said I'd come out early for the right reason."

She grinned. "You believe you can keep up—once I'm mounted on the excellent horse you shall find for me?"

He returned another of those heated, hungry looks. "I believe I am up to the challenge."

"*Ventre à terre,* the complete circuit?"

Mr. Dixon put his gloved hand over hers and turned to look into her eyes, his own smoldering with intensity. "I shall look forward to it with utmost anticipation."

She was struck again by how much the heat of his gaze resembled the look in Adam Darnell's eyes that night in the library. But instead of being mesmerized, Helena had to resist the urge to move away. Gently removing her hand from his, she replied, "Very well. So, what is your opinion of the dissolution of the Italian states?"

Tacitly accepting her retreat, during the drive back to St. James Mr. Dixon talked with her about the recent initiatives put forth in the international discussions. By the time they reached the Darnell town house, as impressed by Mr. Dixon's knowledge as she'd initially been by his charm, Helena hoped he would indeed turn out to be the friend he showed promise of becoming. He left Helena with a pledge to inspect the current offerings at Tattersalls for her.

She had just arrived in her chamber, where Nell waited to take her pelisse and bonnet, when after a short knock, Dickon rushed into the room and skidded to a halt.

"Miss, I be so terrible sorry!" he cried, wringing his hands. "I never meant to mull things up so." Turning to his sister, he added, "I'm sorry for you, too, Nell!" With that, he buried his face in his hands and sobbed.

Exclaiming with alarm, Nell gathered the weeping lad into her arms. Before she could extract any information from him, there was another knock and Charis entered.

Her face distressed, she came over to Helena. "Is it true, what Harrison told Bellemere? It upset her so, she suffered another of her spasms."

Casting a glance at Helena's two servants huddled together in the corner, she lowered her voice to a whisper. "Did you really hire Nell and Dickon out of a workhouse?"

CHAPTER FOURTEEN

AFTER HER CALL ON his stepmother, Adam had driven his fiancée to the park—where he had the dubious pleasure of seeing, at a distance, his best friend so absorbed in chatting with Miss Lambarth that he failed to notice Adam.

The other gentlemen riding or strolling about had certainly noticed Miss Lambarth, her pale oval face luminescent as a pearl above the emerald satin of her gown, displayed as upon a stage in that ridiculously high excuse for a carriage. The progress of Dix's phaeton seemed to Adam to have created nearly as great a stir as that of the Divine Alice, a Fashionable Impure whose great beauty was exceeded only by the high cost of her upkeep.

His disgruntlement was not eased when Priscilla patted his hand and said she thought it very bad of Mr. Dixon to show off Miss Lambarth almost like a man would flaunt…another sort of creature. Perhaps Adam ought to put a word in the ear of Lady Darnell or his friend, since the poor untutored girl obviously didn't realize that riding about in such a vehicle, with only the gentleman's groom as a chaperone, might make her appear quite "fast."

That probably wasn't reason enough for him to feel so tempted to knock Dix's teeth down his throat, but Adam was too irritated to want to examine the impulse any further. Impatient to go home and make sure Dix had taken her straight back to St. James Square, he had to force himself to calm down and accept Priscilla's offer of refreshment.

He had just taken a seat beside his fiancée in the Standish parlor when a footman entered, bearing a note from his stepmother. From what little he could decipher of the wildly crossed lines, Lady Darnell implored him to Return Immediately to Deal With a Matter of Grave Import.

"I'm sorry, Priscilla, but I shall have to beg off. Something has arisen that requires my immediate attention."

"That phaeton! I hope there hasn't been an accident."

Alarm flashed through Adam before he recalled that, unstable as the phaeton might be, with Dix at the reins an accident was most unlikely. "I trust not, but Bellemere implores my assistance, so go I must."

"Of course you must! You will report back later and set my mind at rest? Dear Lady Darnell will be my mama-in-law soon, and I am most concerned for her welfare."

Although Adam balked at the idea of "reporting" to anyone, he could hardly fault his fiancée's concern. Curbing his irritation at the wording of her request, he agreed to return when the problem was resolved.

Wondering what could have set off his volatile stepmother this time—and despite his instinctive resentment of Priscilla's assessment, grimly certain that it must have something to do with Helena Lambarth—Adam collected his curricle and drove home with all speed.

His stepmother, when he begged admittance to her chamber, practically fell into his arms. "Oh, Adam," she cried, leaving off weeping into her handkerchief as she ushered him to a seat, "I can scarcely breathe, I am so upset! You must talk with Harrison and discover the Truth."

"The truth of what, ma'am?" he asked, but his stepmother did no more than open her lips before another sob shook her. "I cannot speak of it! Talk with Harrison, I beg you."

Had that rascal Dickon done something truly awful this time? Adam asked himself as he left his stepmother's chamber. He'd dismissed the lad's previous escapades as the follies of a boy with too much imagination and too little employment, but if the child were causing more commotion, he would have to go. Returning to his library, he summoned the butler, who managed in a few terse sentences to convey the essentials of the dilemma.

Small wonder the staff was in an uproar, Adam thought, astounded by the news. He stood speechless while Harrison continued, "When the lad mentioned by chance that he'd lived in the workhouse, I immediately tasked him about it, then confirmed the truth of what he'd divulged with his sister and Molly. I have failed you, my lord, by not inquiring more particularly into the references of employees brought into this house. If you feel you must dismiss me along with them, I shall understand."

"I'll have no talk yet of dismissal," Adam replied, trying to reason his way out of the coil. "Have the pair given poor service? Done shoddy work? Thieved?"

Harrison shook his head. "On the contrary, my lord, their work has been exemplary. If they both had not affirmed the truth of it, I never would have believed they came from such a place."

"So they did not deny or dissemble when you taxed them about this? Their honesty speaks in their favor. What would you recommend about their continued employment?"

Distress was clearly written upon Harrison's normally impassive countenance. "I've grown fond of the lad, I admit. But the staff is most upset, and I cannot have the household disturbed. The two entered under false pretenses and I suppose they must go."

"Would there be a disturbance if they stayed?"

"I—I cannot say. I suppose it would be better if they left. I'll see to the lad's references myself."

"You would give the boy references, yet you want him dismissed?"

Harrison waved his hands helplessly. "I shall do as you direct, my lord."

Could no one make a decision? Adam wondered with exasperation. But since his stepmother was incapable of confrontation and the butler clearly wished to avoid it, as head of the household he would have to settle this business himself. So, much as he would prefer to avoid Helena, before he did anything, he ought to discuss the matter with the person who had introduced this problem into his house.

"Will you send Miss Lambarth to me, please?"

"At once, my lord," Harrison said, obviously eager to leave the solving of this imbroglio in his hands.

'Twas bad enough that his stepmother's ward had cut up his peace. Now she had disturbed the tranquility of his household. What rubbed most, he thought sardonically as he waited for Miss Lambarth to appear, was that he might be forced to admit to Priscilla that she had been correct in the concern she'd voiced the first night she met Helena—that the girl's lack of breeding could cause difficulties for his family. An opinion that at the time, reading into it a criticism of his stepmother, he had fiercely resented.

He wasn't sure what he'd expected to see in Miss Lambarth's face when she answered his summons— Embarrassment? Shame? Penitence? He was definitely not prepared for the rigidly upright figure who stormed through the door, her whole being radiating angry defiance.

Instead of the siren who'd enticed him, she now appeared a Valkyrie ready to do battle. He wasn't sure which guise was more arresting.

Given the girl's agitation, Adam decided it might be best to avoid a direct confrontation. Trying instead for a wry, half-humorous tone, he said, "Well, the cat is among the pigeons now. I suppose the news is true?"

Apparently she'd been expecting hostility in return,

for the mildness of his remark seemed to surprise her. Her wariness dissipating a trifle, she said, "Yes, it's true."

"How did you come to hire employees in a workhouse?"

"I told everyone from the start that I didn't want a proper dresser who would look down on me. From remarks made by a clergyman traveling on the mail coach, I guessed that a girl from the workhouse, if she were honest and willing, would be grateful for employment and work more diligently than someone Harrison deemed 'suitable.' And so she has! Have you heard a word of complaint about Nell or Dickon since they came here?"

Adam thought of the grooms' protests about the mischievous boy. "Not really, but—"

"Doesn't Dickon practically worship Harrison and do whatever he bids the instant he commands it, always trying to do more to win his favor? At this moment, the child is hidden in my wardrobe, weeping his heart out knowing that the man for whom he has been toiling has rejected him. Knowing his disclosure means he and his sister will be forced to leave the place he has just now begun to think of as home. And why? Because he was idle or encroaching or dishonest? No—for the sin of having been orphaned."

"That makes you angry," Adam said, impressed by the fierceness of her loyalty to and concern for the boy.

"It makes me furious! But I expect that's merely my 'unconventional' background, which instilled in me more respect for what a person does than for his position in the world. I *am* sorry for upsetting Aunt Lillian and disrupting your house. But I am not in the least sorry for hiring Nell and Dickon, nor do I have any intention of letting them go. Since that apparently will cause problems here, I will have them go elsewhere until I can obtain other lodging for us, a search I shall begin immediately."

It was a golden opportunity to send the girl packing and put an end to his struggle to resist her—but he couldn't make himself seize it. "You would abandon Bellemere, after all the care she has given you?" he asked, pulling out that argument to mask his own reluctance to see her go. "It would break her heart!"

For the first time her defiant expression softened. "I don't mean to be ungrateful and I…I should miss her, too. But what else can be done?"

Relieved, he gave her a wry grin. "I expect she intended me to convince you to let Nell and Dickon go. Ah, Miss Lambarth, it truly would have been easier on everyone if you'd just let Harrison handle the hiring of your maid."

In an instant she changed from angry to imploring. Stepping forward to seize his hand, she cried, "My lord, if only you had been there! Seen how diligently they labored in the workhouse laundry! Their father died for England, their mother from overwork trying to provide for them. Stranded and alone with no family to take them in, they had no choice but the workhouse, though it meant giving up what little hope they had of finding employment elsewhere."

Her gaze dropped and her voice faded almost to a

whisper. "I know what it is to be shut away, shunned by good Society, with no hope of assistance."

She stared into the far distance, seeing memories he could only guess at, while the hand she seemed to have forgotten seared his palm and sent heat through every nerve. But before he could think what to say—could bring himself to detach those slender fingers—she looked back up and, to his relief and regret, pulled her hand away.

"Once I saw Nell and Dickon and learned the facts of their situation, how could I *not* help them?"

He had come prepared to echo Harrison's advice and, at the least, finagle her consent to the firing of her unsuitable employees. But a wave of compassion for Nell, the boy—and for her—overcame him. How many years had Helena existed, shut away after her mother's flight? Feeling, with good reason, abandoned by the world and betrayed by those who should have cared for her.

It hadn't been right—not for her. Not for the two unfortunates she'd chosen to rescue. Perhaps his years in the army, where he learned to judge men not by birth but by actions, had instilled in him, too, a share of her "unconventional" opinion, but he had seen vagrants who enlisted for a shilling become outstanding soldiers, and pampered sons of the nobility bolt at the first sound of the guns. It wasn't fair to dismiss Nell and Dickon, whose service in his household had been exemplary, for the misfortune of becoming orphaned.

And so he found himself telling her what, ten minutes earlier, he never would have imagined saying.

"Don't leave, Miss Lambarth. Bellemere and Charis would be much more distressed by your going away than they could ever be by knowing that your maid came from the workhouse."

She stared at him as if she couldn't believe what she'd just heard. "But…but what of Harrison? Cook and the housekeeper? I won't keep Nell and Dickon here because *I* wish to stay, only to have them shunned by the staff."

"I shall inform Harrison that, having judged both of them valuable employees despite their origins, I want them retained. As we both know, he has a fondness for Dickon and, I suspect, will secretly rejoice not to have to discharge him. As for the rest, I expect my staff to treat each other with respect and will tolerate nothing less."

"You would do that? Why?"

He gave her a smile and shrugged. "Because you have convinced me 'tis right."

She stared at him a long moment, as if not sure whether to believe him. Then, when he was on the point of telling her she could leave, a brilliant smile lit her face, transforming her already arresting features into a beauty that stole his breath.

"Thank you, my lord. I promise you will never regret showing mercy." Her smile turning roguish, she added, "And I will earnestly try to cause no more havoc in your house! Now, I will go prostrate myself before Aunt Lillian and beg her pardon, too." After a deep, straight-backed curtsey that would have done honor to the queen's drawing room, she rose and swept out the door.

As if she'd cast a spell over him, Adam stood immobile for several moments after her departure. In the lawyer's office he'd pitied her. In his library that night he'd desired her. Now in these last few minutes she had reached him on yet another level. Bypassing his irritation over the problem of his lust and dispelling his resistance to thinking well of her, she'd brought him to a profound admiration and respect for the girl who'd fought isolation and captivity to find freedom. The girl who, even at the cost of giving up her home with the aunt who loved her, was ready to fight just as fiercely for the unfortunates in her care.

He'd never met anyone remotely like her. He was beginning to fear he would never judge any woman her equal.

He shook his head as if to clear it of her sorcery. He must talk with Harrison, though he suspected convincing the butler would not be overly difficult. That done, he could trust the head of his staff to ensure Nell and Dickon were properly treated by the rest of the household.

Then, he thought with a grin, he would go see whether Miss Lambarth had managed to cajole Lady Darnell with the same passionate thoroughness she'd used to win him over.

His smile faded when he remembered he'd committed himself to returning to see Priscilla. Putting off that visit would worry her and sending a note, which he was highly tempted to do instead, might be interpreted as slighting her concern. With a sigh, he concluded he would have to wait until later to see what miracles Miss Lambarth had worked on his stepmother.

An hour later, Harrison fully on board and the household quieted, Adam returned to the Standish town house. He was shown immediately to the parlor, where Priscilla had apparently been awaiting him.

"Ah, you are here at last! I've been so worried! Do tell me all is well."

He kissed the hand she offered and followed her to a seat on the sofa. "Yes, 'twas nearer a trifle than a serious problem. As you may know, Lady Darnell has a…nervous disposition and sometimes becomes agitated by things, which, when one examines them in more detail, are not truly alarming."

"I am glad to hear it! What was the problem, if I might inquire? Living together as we shall soon be, I should like to make sure I do not do something similar and upset your dear stepmother."

Adam chuckled. "I am certain you would never do anything like it."

"Like…what?" Priscilla persisted.

He had not intended to mention specifics, but in view of Priscilla's concern and laudable desire to accommodate herself to his household, perhaps he should inform her. Briefly he summarized the cause of the commotion.

Appearing much shocked, Priscilla exclaimed, "You wrong your stepmother, Adam, in calling that a 'trifle!' I'm surprised even a girl with as little training as Miss Lambarth would have—but I shall try to give her the benefit of the doubt, which I admit is somewhat harder to do after learning how greatly she distressed Lady Darnell. In any event, I trust you speedily dismissed the miscreants."

Miss Lambarth might have little training in the niceties of ton behavior, but she'd swiftly seen to the right of a much more important matter—and defended it eloquently. Shocked at his fiancée's lack of compassion, Adam's newfound admiration for Helena made it difficult for him to refrain from committing what he instinctively knew would be the mistake of defending her. Instead he said stiffly, "Both employees have given stellar service. Why would I dismiss them?"

Priscilla's eyes widened. "You didn't dismiss them? Creatures out of a workhouse? Adam, you can't be serious! How could Lady Darnell or Charis feel safe, knowing such persons were creeping about?"

"My dear," he said in some exasperation, "we're speaking of a serving maid and a ten-year-old boy— hardly villains to inspire fear."

His fiancée would not be mollified. "Vice knows no age limits, Adam. I've heard such institutions are breeding grounds for all manner of debauchery."

Adam tried to hold on to his patience. "These two have been under close scrutiny in my service for more than a month without exhibiting the slightest tendency to vice."

Priscilla sniffed. "Doubtless they are clever enough to wait until the household is lulled into complacency before showing their true colors. Adam, I implore you to get rid of these…vermin immediately!"

"As you do not know the particulars, I will take your advice as well-intentioned," Adam said tightly.

"But I am master in my house and will do as I feel proper."

"Indeed!" Priscilla retorted, obviously not happy to have her recommendation dismissed. "I trust, at least, that before I enter that house as your bride, Miss Lambarth and her…exceptional employees will have moved elsewhere."

"Of that, you can be certain," Adam confirmed grimly.

More unsettled than he should have been over the squabble, Adam stayed for only a few more minutes before excusing himself with the need to complete some estate business. He rode back to St. James Square in a pensive mood. Though just a day ago he had longed for Miss Lambarth's departure, now the thought of her leaving caused a hollow feeling in his chest. Such a remarkable girl…and they would not have the chance to become friends.

But the necessity of her leaving was more than just the simple fact that, should Miss Lambarth not end up marrying before his own nuptials, she and Priscilla could never live in the same house. Under the unusual circumstances that had prompted their meeting today, he'd managed to be in the same room with her without the attraction that always simmered just beneath the surface erupting to complicate matters. But he shouldn't fool himself into believing that the respect engendered by his recent glimpse into her character would make submerging his desire easier in future.

Prudence dictated that while she remained in his house, he must continue to maintain his distance and treat her in the offhand, elder-brother manner one would expect him to display toward his stepmother's niece.

No matter how tempted he was to get to know this intriguing girl better. A temptation only a tad less dangerous than the desire she evoked in him.

CHAPTER FIFTEEN

SEVERAL MORNINGS LATER, Adam rose early. Rather than take coffee in his room, as had been his habit since the arrival of his houseguest, he prepared to descend to the breakfast parlor. Tonight Miss Lambarth would make her first appearance with the Darnell ladies at a ball given by another of Lady Darnell's Society friends. Though his stepmother had told him not to worry about escorting them to the event, he'd decided to honor his sister's debut and his stepmother's reentrance into Society by returning after dinner with his fiancée to take them to the ball.

Though she knew Miss Lambarth would be a part of the group, Priscilla had been entirely supportive, a gracious gesture which had done much to smooth over the tension that had lingered between them since their disagreement over his handling of his domestic debacle. More cheerful than he'd felt for some time, Adam planned to surprise his stepmother with the news over breakfast—and incidentally, take the opportunity to chat with Miss Lambarth, whom he'd not seen since their interview several days previous.

Conscious of his resolve to deal carefully with that

lady, he resisted the impulse to enter and perhaps find her alone. Not until he heard his sister's voice along with her husky tones did he proceed into the room.

"Adam, what a surprise!" Charis cried, coming over to hug him. "To what do we owe this pleasure?"

Nodding to acknowledge Miss Lambarth's curtsey—though it hadn't required that gesture for him to notice her, for he'd felt her presence the instant he walked in—he returned the hug. "Must I have some hidden purpose to take breakfast with my favorite sister?"

"I should hope not, though despite the fact that the house has been free of merchants for over a fortnight, we've seen very little of you. The obligations of an affianced gentleman, I expect!"

He allowed his gaze to return to Miss Lambarth, garbed this morning in a plain, high-necked gown of deep rose-apricot—its hue like that of the banked coals glowing on the hearth. And like them, she radiated a warmth and energy that urged one to draw nearer. Dismissing the whimsical analogy, he said, "Miss Lambarth, I see you've reconciled with the ladies?"

She smiled slightly, a hint of the expression that had captivated him at their previous meeting. "Aunt Lillian is still not entirely happy, but I've been most penitent. Have I not, Charis?"

"If you're referring to Nell and Dickon, Adam, after Helena explained to me how they were circumstanced, I understood perfectly why she felt it essential to hire them. A brave decision on her part, do you not think?"

While Helena shook her head in demurral, Adam replied, "Risky, certainly."

"I shall endeavor to do nothing else to distress Aunt Lillian," Helena asserted. "I am even being careful in my conversation when we go out, that I not embarrass her."

"I don't think you need to worry about that," Charis said. "Since her drive with Mr. Dixon a few days ago, Helena has been surrounded by admirers at every call we've made. I think she shall be the hit of the Season!"

Adam found the notion curiously distasteful. But if she was to marry, which was the best solution for them both, he would have to cease resenting her admirers.

"I'm merely the latest curiosity," Helena countered, "soon to be forgotten when the next oddity appears." She chuckled. "Or when the arbiters of Society find someone else to correct. 'Scarlet is not a color to be worn by a damsel in her first Season,'" she intoned.

As Charis burst into giggles, Adam was taken aback, for she had mimed perfectly the intonation and pitch of Mrs. Drummand Burrell, a redoubtable Society patroness.

When he turned to his sister, eyebrows raised, Charis said, "She captures Princess Esterhazy and Lady Jersey just as well, Adam. Tell him what 'Silence' replied when you were told that, Helena."

Her eyes alight with mischief, Miss Lambarth switched to Lady Jersey's softer tones. "'Not by ordinary damsels, Charlotte, but Miss Lambarth is quite exceptional.'"

"You've a definite talent for mimicry, Miss Lambarth," Adam said with admiration.

The light in her eyes faded and her voice went dry. "In my youth, I sometimes found the skill quite useful."

He could only imagine to what end she'd employed that gift—to evade her father, perhaps? He wished he could ask—but revealing details of what she'd endured would upset his sister and, if that grim line about her mouth were any indication, wasn't something she would relish retelling.

Before he could speak, her smile returned. "Although it is the dress, rather than the voices, of Society's notables I find fascinating. Mr. Byng, in his pastels accompanied by his poodles. Lady Wimbleton, whose bonnets remind me of those illustrated in a book in your library about the court of Marie Antionette."

"Surely not that exaggerated," Adam protested.

"But they are!" Charis confirmed, giggling again. "Birds, fruit, feathers, plumes all together atop a huge construction of straw and net."

"Incredible," Adam said with a shudder.

"All too real," Helena affirmed. "Only look!" Putting down her cup, she snatched up a leaf of the previous day's newspaper, then strode over to pluck a bit of charcoal from the hearth. With the charred piece she quickly sketched the profile of a woman with a long nose, protruding lips and fantastic headdress displaying all the previous items plus a quantity of lace and bows.

"Why, 'tis her very image!" Charis gasped. "Helena, you are so clever!"

As Adam wondered to what use that talent had been put during her grim youth, Miss Lambarth shook her head. "Not at all. Sketching helped pass the time when I was…forced to be idle."

"When have you ever been idle?" Lady Darnell's voice came from the doorway. "Adam! How delightful to see you!"

After kissing his stepmother's hand, he protested, "You both speak as if I've become a stranger to my dearest kin. I see I shall have to breakfast with you more often."

"That would be lovely," Lady Darnell said.

"If Miss Standish can spare you," Charis added, an edge to her voice.

Did his sister feel abandoned? Adam wondered with a pang of guilt. He *had* been avoiding the house—for reasons he could hardly confess to Charis. But though his nerves continued to hum with the awareness of Miss Lambarth's nearness, this visit had otherwise gone well. Perhaps as he got to know her better and the searing impression of the courtesan in his library was overlaid by images of her as a lady of quality, his baser reaction to her would dissipate. So he could chance spending more time with the ladies.

"Actually, 'twas upon that topic I wished to speak. Priscilla and I both agreed that the great occasion of you ladies attending your first ball demanded an escort. So after dining with her tonight I would like to return here, if you will grant me the privilege of escorting the loveliest ladies in London to Mrs. Cowper's ball."

He felt amply rewarded when Charis's face lit. "Oh, Adam, that would be wonderful! I've been so nervous, but I shall feel much more confident with you at my side."

The little sister he ought to protect had been apprehensive, and he too absorbed in his own problems to notice, he thought with a surge of guilt and regret. "I wouldn't wish to be anywhere else. I know I've…neglected you of late. Please forgive me, Charis."

"'Tis very kind of you and Miss Standish," Lady Darnell said. "But after the gentleman of the ton see my girls at their first ball, I doubt that they will lack for escorts. You need not fear we shall trade upon your fiancée's generosity too often."

Though he ought to be pleased at the picture of other men standing in for him, freeing him to escort his betrothed, for some reason he was not. Dismissing that illogical reaction, Adam turned the conversation to fixing the time for their departure and took his leave.

His baby sister had grown up, he thought as he walked out, feeling suddenly older and a bit wistful. Though he'd wrestled with details of finances and dowries, not until this moment had it truly struck him that soon, some man would claim Charis as his wife and remove her from Adam's house and care forever.

The bittersweet thought of losing her made him appreciate more keenly what she must have been feeling since his engagement. He vowed to savor the time they had left before each took lifelong vows pledging their primary allegiance to another.

He would be proud to stand beside her as she made her debut. And with a curiosity still tinged by jealousy, he admitted he was intensely interested in observing Miss Lambarth's launch, as well.

WITH A SENSE OF ANTICIPATION, Adam returned to Darnell House that evening to collect the ladies. Bennett Dixon had promised to join their party. He'd also had a note from his friend Nathan Blanchard, newly returned to town and whom he'd not yet encountered, saying he would look forward to seeing Adam at the ball and standing up with each of Darnell's ladies.

Obviously watching for him, Lady Darnell hurried down to greet him the moment he crossed the threshold. Her eyes bright with happiness and excitement, she blushed as he complimented her great good looks and stylish toilette of deep green satin, admonishing him to save his pretty words for the young ladies.

Taking his arm, she turned him to watch as Charis slowly descended the stairs, twirling for his inspection as she reached them. "So, how do I look, big brother?"

"Like a fairy princess!" As truly she did, from her blond curls done up with pearls and gold ribbon to her gown of white silk trimmed with tiny clusters of pearls to the golden slippers on her dainty feet. With the respectable dowry he could now provide, Adam thought fondly, Charis should have no lack of suitors.

After giving his sister's hand a kiss, Adam turned his gaze back to the landing, wondering in what guise the unpredictable Miss Lambarth would appear. He started when he heard her voice coming out of the shadows to his left.

She emerged from the darkness of the hallway and he literally caught his breath. In defiance of tradition concerning the proper dress for young maidens, she was garbed from toe to chin in shimmering gold cloth. As she glided toward them with the proud carriage of an empress, her dark eyes and ebony hair gleaming above the flash of fabric, his dazzled brain conjured up the image of a pagan queen, a gilded Cleopatra.

She halted beside him, near enough that every nerve tingled. It took him several minutes to get his galloping pulse and shaky breathing under control.

So much for becoming used to her attractiveness, he thought wryly. Given its effect on him—he who had been primed to expect the unexpected—he could only wonder at the reaction her appearance would provoke at the ball.

Still, as he angled his head to give her a covert inspection, he had to confess one small disappointment. Bad as it was of him, he'd hoped for a glimpse of the shoulders and bosom normally exposed by a ball gown. But though its color might shock, like her other gowns, this one covered her to the tips of her ears. However, he couldn't help notice how the golden halo of fabric outlined every curve against the darkened hallway.

He didn't realize he'd stood silent for some minutes until Charis said, a bit impatiently, "Don't you see, Adam? Helena and I are complements!"

Pulling himself from his absorption with Miss Lambarth's figure, he noted the pearls and white ribbon twined in her dark hair, the clusters of ribbon-trimmed pearls adorning her otherwise plain gown.

"Innocence and… Eccentricity," Miss Lambarth said, her husky voice warm with humor. "I believe steel is the preferred metal for armor, but I shall make do with gold."

Did she fear her unconventional attire might incite Society's wrath? Adam wondered. "'Tis your admirers who will need to armor themselves against your brilliance," he countered. "You ladies are magnificent— all of you."

"Lady Jersey herself predicted Helena would be a sensation!" Charis said.

Helena grinned. "I believe she said I should cause a 'stir,' which is not quite the same. But—" she gestured to her gown "—at least Society shall see at a glance that I do not intend to launch myself into the Marriage Mart. If I achieve that, dressed as I please, without alienating Aunt Lillian's friends or Charis's suitors, I shall be content. If not—" she turned to address Lady Darnell "—I shall withdraw from Society before I cause you further damage."

"Nonsense," Lady Darnell replied. "You shall consider only how much you will enjoy the ball. Now let us be off!"

Watching the reflection of Miss Lambarth's gilded collar in the carriage lamp as the coach carried them to the ball, Adam found that, like Lady Jersey, he was curious to see the "stir" Miss Lambarth would provoke. If she did encounter the disapproval she seemed to expect, he would intervene. No less than Charis was she under his care.

Such a plucky lass, fighting for her charges one moment, facing down Society in her gold dress the next! A fierce protectiveness welled up in him. As much as he could, he would try to insure her first ball was a success.

Though his nerves still danced at her nearness, the awareness had settled to a barely perceptible hum. Now that he'd moved beyond being blindsided by her allure, perhaps if he concentrated on extending to her the same support and protection he owed his sister, they might get on comfortably.

Despite her provocative choice of dress, he didn't think she'd need that protection tonight. She was well-born, possessed of an unusual and arresting beauty—and reputedly very rich. Save for a few of the highest sticklers, he expected Society would warmly embrace her.

He'd rather not speculate on Priscilla's reaction.

The scrutiny began as soon as they entered the ballroom, conversation near them ceasing as they walked by, all eyes turning to inspect them as they passed.

And then the gentlemen began to approach. Adam barely had time to claim his betrothed before a group formed about the ladies, all earnestly desiring introductions.

He'd about reached the limit of his patience in presenting the never-ending gaggle of admirers when his old friend Nathan Blanchard appeared. Using, Adam noted with a smile, his diplomat's skills, he threaded his way through the crowd and insinuated himself at the head of the line.

"Nathan, how good to see you again!"

"Wonderful to see you intact, as well, especially after the carnage of Waterloo," Blanchard replied.

"You'll remember my stepmother, Lady Darnell?"

"I had the pleasure of meeting her again a few days ago. How charming you look, ma'am. I'd been waiting for the crowd to dissipate—to no avail! Never before have I been so happy to exert the claim of prior friendship. Miss Darnell, Miss Lambarth, you are both ravishing. Although, Adam," Blanchard said, turning back to him, "your sister is far too beautiful to have so inelegant a brother. And much too poised to have just emerged from the schoolroom."

"Lord Blanchard, I see you have studied the art of diplomacy all too diligently," Charis replied, a blush tinting her cheeks as she curtseyed to his friend.

"'Tis nothing but the truth," Blanchard countered. "Miss Lambarth, I hope we shall have a chance to chat. I've heard so much about you."

"I hope you dismissed much of it," she replied. "Probably not one in three of Society's on-dits are true."

Blanchard laughed. "You're both of independent mind and perceptive. You will favor me with a dance later?"

Adam noted that Priscilla, standing at his side, was tapping her toe with impatience. Having been much courted for several years, she was not accustomed to being overlooked by a fine young gentleman. To Adam's relief, she brightened when Nathan, with a finesse that augured well for his career in the diplomatic corps, bowed over her hand, saying he'd saved the most important lady for last, as she was the special girl who was to make his good friend the happiest man in England.

Next, Bennett Dixon appeared out of the crowd. After shouldering a string of disgruntled gentlemen out of the way, he joined their group, then volunteered to entertain the ladies while Adam and Blanchard procured refreshments.

"Sorry I wasn't able to catch you earlier," Nathan said as they walked off together. "I did want a word with you—and I suppose this will be our best opportunity tonight. First, congratulations on securing the hand of Miss Standish! A lovely, accomplished girl who should make a fine mistress for your house. 'Tis also a match which should go a long way to curing your financial ills."

"You know of them, too?" Adam said with a sigh.

Blanchard shrugged. "It's my business to know what's going on, at home and abroad. But now that you're settled so brilliantly, might you do as much for me?"

"You are looking to marry?" Adam asked, surprised.

"If one hopes to rise in the diplomatic corps, one must entertain, and to do so properly, one needs a hostess as poised as your Miss Standish—and a wife as rich." His gaze drifted back to the ladies they had just left. "Your sister would be a lovely ornament to an embassy party."

Adam understood fishing when he heard it. "She would ornament any gathering," he replied with a fond pride. "Regretfully, though her character is deserving of the highest accolades, I doubt her dowry would be sufficient for your needs. My 'brilliant' match will allow me to rearrange estate funds to provide her a portion, but I couldn't describe it as more than 'modest.'"

"No rich relations to settle money on her?"

"Alas, no."

"You're quite sure?" When Adam nodded, Blanchard said, "What a pity. She is the most entrancing girl I've met in years." After another lingering glance in Charis's direction, he heaved a sigh and shrugged. "No sense torturing oneself dreaming of the impossible, I suppose. Thank you for your honesty. Have you other suggestions?"

Though there was one quite obvious possibility, Adam found himself loathe to suggest it. But then, he thought, brightening, Miss Lambarth hardly possessed the background and social experience essential for an ambassador's wife. "My stepmother's ward is reputed to have the wealth you seek, but though she displays a keen wit, I'm afraid her rather…odd upbringing would not make her the best choice for a diplomat's hostess."

Blanchard laughed. "That outrageous gold dress! Throwing it into the face of society's beldames, isn't she? She's strikingly attractive, and if intelligent, I expect could be taught the necessary social skills. Though Dix seemed ready to mill me down if I didn't cede my place beside her."

"I suspect he finds her novelty attractive. In any event, he's pledged to help me watch out for her so that her inexperience with Society customs doesn't lead some reprobate into trying to take advantage of her."

Blanchard nodded. "A wise precaution. Given how alluring she is, someone less than a gentleman, or a gentleman too much in his cups to know better, might mistake her behavior as an encouragement to take liberties he'd dare not attempt with a more conventional girl."

"Indeed," Adam replied with a shudder, Blanchard's comment echoing his greatest fear as her defacto guardian.

"Perhaps I should get to know her better."

He felt a curious reluctance to encourage his friend, but that was silly. Miss Lambarth must marry someone, and were she to wed Blanchard, she would be well settled—and frequently abroad, out of temptation's reach. "Do that."

They had collected their cups and were walking back to rejoin the ladies when, from the entrance to the ballroom ahead of them, a girl in a golden dress dashed out. After a wild-eyed glance to either side, she turned and fled down the hallway away from them.

"What the deuce?" Blanchard exclaimed.

"'Tis Miss Lambarth!" Adam cried. Had some man pressed her too closely while he was chatting idly with Nathan? Had Dix? Concern and fury erupted in his breast.

"Tell the ladies I shall return shortly. I must go after her." Depositing his collection of cups onto a hall table, Adam sprinted off in pursuit.

CHAPTER SIXTEEN

SKIDDING INTO THE HALLWAY, Helena took a great gulp of the cooler air. After a quick glance down both sides of the hallway revealed a cluster of guests approaching from the left, she turned and ran in the opposite direction.

She simply couldn't tolerate that overcrowded room a second longer. Her throat dry and her head aching as she'd waited for Darnell and his friend to return with the wine, it had seemed that with every moment the noise grew more deafening, the air more stifling.

Finally, as Mr. Dixon was introducing someone to Charis, his words lost in the babble of sound, the sea of faces had started to swirl about her, making her dizzy. The gasp of air she took didn't seem to reach her lungs, sending an icy tingle of panic skittering through her.

When the dizziness intensified and little spots began to dance before her eyes, she'd been seized by an irrational, irresistible need to escape. Brushing past Mr. Dixon, she'd fought her way through the milling crowd and darted for the door.

At the end of the hallway now, she halted, gasping.

If this house were similar to Darnell's, the doorway nearest her should open into a salon or library. Hoping to find it empty, she eased the door ajar.

Thankfully, the darkened room appeared deserted. A faint glow emanated from the window, which must overlook the street. She stumbled across the room, yanked back the curtains, then unlatched and pushed open the casement.

Cold air carrying the faint scent of wood smoke and horse streamed over her. From the street below came the murmur of voices and low laughter. Livried servants manned their posts beside the torch-lit entrance while on the roadside beyond, men in greatcoats huddled around a fire.

How she wished she might be out there, free to slip away under the camouflage of darkness!

For several moments she simply stood, letting the chill and quiet slow her pulse and soothe her nerves. Not since the day the villagers had forced her back to Lambarth Castle and her enraged father had shut her inside the priest's hole had she felt such blind panic.

That day she'd screamed until she lost her voice, pounded on the oak panel until her fists were raw, then slid down onto the cold stone floor sobbing until, exhausted by fear and grief, at length she'd slept. She'd awakened with a fury-fueled determination to brave the blackness and find the way out. Which, the next time her father imprisoned her there, she had.

Despite his intent, the incarceration had not broken her spirit. In fact, being shut up in the priest's hole had forced her to conquer her fear of the dark and sharpened her sight so she could now find her way about in all but the most lightless places.

She leaned on the window ledge, her face lifted into the onrushing air. Escape today had been much simpler. She'd just begun analyzing what about the ball had so frightened her when a hand seized her shoulder.

With a cry, she swiveled to face her attacker, bringing her free hand up to scratch at his face.

"Miss Lambarth!" the man cried as he blocked her blow. "It's me—Darnell!"

His voice registered even as she swung. Thankful his swift countermove prevented her from mauling his face, she pulled her arm free. "Darnell! You...you startled me."

"Are you all right?" he demanded. "I saw you run from the ballroom. Did someone hurt you? Tell me!"

She shook her head. "No. It's just it was so...close. All those people, crowding around me. The noise, pounding in my ears. I—I couldn't breathe. I had to get away."

"No one...assaulted you?"

"No. There were just...too many people. Did you bring the wine?"

He peered at her for a moment, as if trying to determine if she were truly all right. Then he threw back his head and laughed. "No, I dumped the glasses on a table when I saw you run off. You gave me such a fright! Have you recovered? Do you think you can walk?"

Diverted by the rare sound of his laughter, she couldn't help smiling, too. "I feel much better."

"I had Blanchard tell Bellemere I would fetch you.

Did you explain to her why you had to leave so suddenly?"

"No." Feeling like a small child caught in some mischief, Helena said, "I—I couldn't think. I just ran."

"Let me escort you to the refreshment room for that wine punch and then return you to the ballroom. Belle-mere will be worried."

Helena wasn't sure why the ballroom had affected her so profoundly, but she did know she wanted no more of it. "I don't want to go back. If you summon me a hackney, I shall go home. I find that balls are not to my liking."

"I can't send you off in a hired carriage at night alone! If you will not return to the ballroom, wait here. I'll find Lady Darnell and—"

"Please don't! She will try to persuade me to stay— or feel duty-bound to accompany me. And if she goes, Charis might feel she had to leave, too. They were both so looking forward to this ball, I don't wish to spoil it for them. I shall be perfectly fine returning home on my own. Tell her…tell her I had the headache. I do, a little."

Darnell sighed and shook his head. "London streets at night are not safe, even in a hackney. If you must go, I shall have to escort you. Let me fetch your cloak and send a footman to tell Lady Darnell what is transpiring so she doesn't worry."

"You needn't accompany me! What would Miss Standish think, were you to abandon her at the very first ball since your engagement! She would never forgive me."

"Not forgive my taking care of a lady in my charge? I should rather think she would insist that I escort you."

Was Miss Standish's sense of duty that strong? Helena wondered. Or did Darnell simply not know how much his fiancée disliked her? Though the girl was certainly not the partner Helena would have chosen for Darnell, neither did she wish to create trouble between them.

"I don't want to argue," she said after a moment. "Please, I should feel much easier returning alone than knowing I have dragged you away and ruined your evening."

"We are at an impasse then, for I cannot enjoy my evening knowing you are traveling alone through London."

Before she could think of some other argument to persuade him, he laughed again. "Come now, Miss Lambarth, let's cry pax! In the time we've spent brangling I could have already had the carriage waiting. I can escort you home and be back so quickly I shall hardly be missed."

It appeared he was truly adamant about seeing her safely home. Though Helena still considered his escort unnecessary, she could not help being touched. When had a man other than the lawyer ever concerned himself with her safety? And, as Darnell said, they wasted time arguing.

"Very well, then," she said, turning to close and latch the window. "Let us go."

He gave her his very attractive smile. "Excellent. Thank you for being so reasonable."

"And doing what you wish?" she asked wryly.

Grinning, he offered her his arm. "Precisely. Your hand, please, Miss Lambarth?"

Cautiously she placed it on his, tensing as a little tingle traveled all the way up her arm. Distracted by her reaction, she barely noticed how within a few moments, he had a message sent to Lady Darnell, secured their wraps and escorted her to the Darnell carriage.

For a time after the vehicle set off they were both silent. At last, feeling ever more badly about forcing him away from the ball, she said, "I'm sorry to have been such a bother. I'm not usually such a coward."

In the flickering light from the carriage lamp, he found her hand and patted it. "I'm sure you are not," he assured her. "But this ball would be described as a 'sad crush'—and you are unused to crowds."

She wrapped her fingers around his, luxuriating in the contact. "I can't remember ever being in a room with more than a dozen people. 'Twas the reason I rode on the coach roof to London—I couldn't tolerate being confined inside."

"You rode outside all the way to London? No wonder you still looked half frozen when I met you!"

"I'd been half frozen for ten years—in every way," she replied, realizing the truth of it as she spoke. "Until you invited me into your home. Thank you, Darnell."

His eyes scanning her face, he said softly, "I'm so glad I…we…have been able to provide the warmth you need."

So captured was she by the intensity of his gaze, it

took her a moment to realize the carriage had stopped. How had they traversed the distance to Darnell House so quickly? she wondered. Though she knew he must return to the ball, she found herself reluctant to say good-night. Perhaps he was as bewitched as she, for when she rose to alight, he looked startled.

"You will note we encountered neither footpads nor highwaymen," she said over her shoulder as she stepped through the door a footman held open. When Darnell rose to follow her, she made herself say, "You needn't see me in. I doubt I shall be attacked before I reach the door."

Despite her words, he exited after her. "I am not in the habit of dropping ladies off on the street. John, walk the horses, please," he instructed the coachman. "I shall return directly."

Pleased despite herself to still have his escort, her senses heightened by his closeness, Helena was handing over her cloak to a footman when Harrison appeared. "Miss Lambarth, is something amiss?"

"Nothing serious," Darnell replied. "Miss Lambarth had the headache and wished to return home early."

"Shall I summon Nell to attend you, miss?"

"No, I'm not ready to retire. I should like to read in the library—if you do not object?" she asked Darnell.

"Not in the least. I'll walk you up."

In a silence overlaid with the intensity of the connection between them, she slowly climbed the stairs, once again reluctant to reach her destination and have to send him on his way. Finally, as he opened the door for her, she could delay his departure no longer.

"Thank you for your consideration in handling Aunt Lillian and taking me home," she said quietly. "I suppose I must now insist that you return to the ball."

He sighed. "I suppose you must. But I shall go at ease, knowing you are safely deposited in my library."

Helena thought of the night she'd first encountered him here—and wondered if he were remembering it, too. Perhaps so, for as he motioned her inside and walked her to the hearth, she felt the strength of the current already flowing between them intensify.

They reached the sofa by the fire, but instead of bowing and leaving, as he should, he lingered, gazing at her. Watching how the glow of the fire played over her face, her lips, as she was watching it illumine his?

To try to diffuse the tension building between them, she said a little nervously, "Might I beg one last favor? In future, could you screen my invitations and recommend only those entertainments which will be less crowded?"

"I'd be happy to—though that will limit your outings, since many of the ton events are quite large."

"I've no need to attend a party every night. And will you help me convince Aunt Lillian and Charis to go out and allow me to stay at home with my books?"

"If you are sure that is what you want."

What she wanted… Knowing she dared not stare at his lips and say what she wanted, she looked into the fire. "You…must go now. Pray convey my apologies to Aunt Lillian and particularly to Miss Standish for having taken you away from her. And…thank you." She couldn't keep herself from looking up one more time into his face—

that handsome face with its straight nose, determined chin and gray-green eyes that was fast becoming far too dear to her. "I think you are the kindest gentleman I've ever known."

For a moment he did not reply. His hazel eyes seemed to glow with the fire's heat as he bent toward her. "I wish I could be more than 'kind.'"

Something sweet and heavy pooled in her chest, made her limbs feel hot and liquid. Her eyes on his, without conscious volition, she rose on tiptoe and lifted her face as his lips descended.

She felt the warmth of his breath against her mouth and closed her eyes. And then, suddenly, cool air washed where his breath had heated and her eyes snapped open.

"You are right. I must go," he said, his voice sounding strained. "I bid you good night, Miss Lambarth."

"And I you, Darnell." But she whispered those words to his back, for he had already paced to the door, where he exited without a backward glance.

Heart pounding, feeling somehow…bereft, Helena sank down on the sofa. She sat motionless, staring into the fire, her thoughts, like the flames on the hearth, flitting in all directions while her pulse calmed and the sensations coursing through her body slowed and ceased.

The book Helena had been reading lay on the side table, but at the moment, it didn't tempt her. Pensively she rose and went to pour herself some wine, trying to order her thoughts.

She supposed Darnell must be correct about her reaction to overcrowded rooms. In future she would restrict her social engagements to musicales, dinners, routs or card parties involving no more guests than could be accommodated in a dining room or large salon.

Once again he'd surprised and touched her, as he had over the matter of Nell and Dickon. In high dudgeon when he'd summoned her, she'd gone to confront him certain he would rebuke her and order their dismissal. Instead he'd listened to her—and changed his mind, not seeming to think it a weakness to alter his opinion based on the arguments of a mere girl. She had been surprised—and grateful.

Nor had he chided her tonight for her overreaction, argued with her to return to the ball or mocked her cowardice. Instead, despite the disturbance he had to know it would cause with Miss Standish, he had insisted on seeing her safely home.

He truly was the nicest man she'd ever met—including Mr. Pendenning. But the kindly lawyer did not inspire in her the sort of feelings Adam Darnell had incited tonight.

As for the culmination of their interlude in the library tonight, Helena wasn't sure what to think. Darnell had been about to kiss her, she was certain. And she had certainly *wanted* him to kiss her.

Just remembering the enchantment of his nearness, the warmth of his breath on her lips, revived those powerful sensations and sent them once again spiraling through her body. She shifted restlessly, the silk of her gown sliding over her skin and making it tingle.

How would it feel were Darnell's fingers, rather than the silk, skimming over her body?

Her breathing shuddered and her nipples tightened, while warmth pooled between her thighs. So this must be desire, she thought. She wanted more, to experience rather than imagine his closeness.

But that couldn't be—for either of them. He was pledged to Miss Standish and so would not allow himself the pleasure of kissing her—as wonderful as she suspected it would be. So strong was her response to him, she knew it was wiser that she not kiss him, either.

She'd observed enough of her mother's horse-breeding operations to guess where desire between a man and a woman would lead. Though she'd vowed not to marry so she might never again be legally bound to another man's rule, she'd forsworn wedlock at least as much from the conviction that she must never take a husband to her bed and bear a child.

A child who carried the tainted blood of a man who had abused and imprisoned his own daughter.

Still, she thought, the sweet sensations continuing to hum through her, she would like to *taste* desire, if only for a kiss. Did this odd, compelling excitement exist only between her and Darnell?

The fact that Darnell was about to wed and bed another lady argued that the feeling was not exclusive between one particular man and woman. Though she'd not felt as strong a pull to anyone else, perhaps she might feel attraction to another man. Perhaps she should invite a kiss that would give her a sample of passion.

Perhaps with Mr. Dixon? He was appealingly handsome, an interesting companion—and had pledged to satisfy her curiosity even on "forbidden" matters.

Helena had a strong suspicion the business of kissing fell into that category.

She would definitely pursue this with Mr. Dixon. Even though, she thought with a sigh as she picked up her book, she would much rather kiss Adam Darnell.

CHAPTER SEVENTEEN

NOT WISHING TO HAVE to explain herself that evening, Helena retired to her chamber before the Darnell party returned. But knowing her aunt would be concerned—and having had sufficient time to work out her explanation—she was ready when, just before noon the next day, Lady Darnell sent Nell to ask that she join her in the back parlor for nuncheon.

To Helena's surprise, she discovered as she walked in that Adam Darnell was present, as well. Though he gave her only a polite nod, the glance that passed between them was nearly as potent as a touch.

Assuring them she was feeling quite recovered, Helena explained her abrupt departure from the ball, after which Lady Darnell asserted she was glad Adam had found Helena before she managed to go off alone in a hackney.

"And I can only hope Miss Standish accepted my apology for dragging him off so precipitously," Helena replied.

A small frown briefly creased Darnell's forehead before he said, "She understood your position perfectly and will, I know, rejoice to know you are feeling well again."

So she might not distract Darnell's attention, Helena concluded. 'Twas well that lady had not witnessed what had nearly happened between them in the library. Helena felt her cheeks flush, remembering, and from the sudden spark in Darnell's eyes before he turned away to busy himself with his coffee cup, she suspected he was recalling it, too.

"I'm so disappointed you felt compelled to leave the ball," Lady Darnell said, pulling Helena's attention back to the present. "Such a crowd of gentlemen! I lost count of how many begged for introductions and were quite dismayed that you left before they could secure one."

Darnell frowned. "I expect 'twas exactly that crowd who brought on Miss Lambarth's headache, Bellemere."

"So you told me last night," Lady Darnell said, looking back to Helena. "Though perhaps 'twas just the heat. The room was so stuffy, I felt a bit faint myself."

"I've thought about it carefully and have concluded, as Darnell posited, that 'twas indeed the crush of people that disturbed me. I grew up in such…isolation, I suppose I cannot be easy with so large a group about."

"But as you grow more used to Society, perhaps—"

"No, Aunt Lillian," Helena interrupted. "I am sorry to disappoint you, but I disliked the experience intensely and do not wish to repeat it. But you mustn't feel you or Charis need avoid balls on my account. As I told Darnell, I shall be perfectly fine at home with my books."

"But, my dear, how shall your suitors get to know

you—and you them, if you spend your evenings hidden away?"

Helena gave her a level glance. "Aunt Lillian, as I have already assured you, I have no desire to marry. 'Twould be both dishonest and unkind to any purported suitors for me to appear at functions which might lend credence to the notion that, despite my declaration to the contrary, secretly I wish to wed."

"But, my dear!" Lady Darnell began, only to be silenced by a stern glance from Darnell. "Well, I do not mean to tease you about it. We just want you to be happy."

"Bellemere agrees with me that you should attend solely those entertainments you find appealing," Darnell interposed. "Is that not so, ma'am?"

"Yes, Adam," she replied, not appearing too happy with the approval he'd obviously coerced. "But," she said, brightening, "the Season is just begun. No doubt you shall find many other functions more to your taste."

"I'm sure she shall," Darnell said. "You enjoy music, do you not? Bellemere has invitations to several musicales, which are generally held in a drawing room and attended by no more than several dozen guests."

"That sounds delightful," Helena said, relieved to see her aunt's face brighten. Grateful to Darnell for lending her the assistance he'd promised, she turned and mouthed a silent thank-you.

He smiled at her, which warmed his green eyes and set the hint of a dimple playing in his cheeks. Checking a strong desire to touch it, she tucked her hand in her gown.

Her aunt was extolling the talent of London's singers when Harrison entered, announcing Mr. Dixon was below. Darnell excused himself, but Aunt Lillian pronounced herself ready to accompany Helena to the parlor.

Their guest bowed as they entered. After an exchange of greetings, Mr. Dixon said, "I am delighted to see you have recovered, Miss Lambarth! The ball was a tedious affair after you left."

While Aunt Lillian smiled her approval of his fulsome compliment, Helena had to chuckle. "Now you are being ridiculous, Mr. Dixon. The rooms were packed to the chandeliers with guests, half of them quite lovely ladies."

"But none with conversation—or questions—as interesting as yours," he replied. "Should you like to look at some horses? The stock for Tattersall's next auction is in the stables. We could inspect them today."

"If Aunt Lillian permits, I should be delighted!"

"Of course, my dear," Aunt Lillian replied.

After fixing a time to return for her, Mr. Dixon took his leave.

Excited at the thought of finally being able to drive and ride again, she changed her gown and was waiting impatiently when her escort returned. Within a few moments he'd helped her into his phaeton and they were off.

"You are fortunate to be seeking horses at this moment," Mr. Dixon told her as he guided the carriage down the crowded street. "Several gentlemen whose enthusiasm for gaming outreaches their skill have recently suffered reverses that require them to part with their cattle. Randall's selling off some fine riding hacks, and Bridgeman has a beautiful pair of carriage grays."

"I can view all the horses now?"

"Yes. Let me know the ones you prefer and I will bid for you since, as I believe I mentioned, ladies do not attend the auctions." He looked over with a smile. "Ladies generally do not visit the stables, either. I was rather surprised Lady Darnell agreed to let you do it."

"She knows how keenly I desire to purchase horses—and probably realizes that I would insist on choosing them myself. Thank you for braving censure by escorting me."

"'Tis my pleasure. I admire your independence, and certainly wouldn't wish someone else to choose *my* horses."

In perfect charity with one another, they reached the auction company's stables. Nostalgia mingled with the ache of grief to temper Helena's enthusiasm as she walked with Mr. Dixon and Masters, Tattersall's head groom, through the stable block. How many times as a child had she accompanied her mother as she instructed the stable boys or showed off her yearlings to prospective buyers?

Mulling over the relative merits of the saddle horses she'd seen, Helena had lagged behind the men when a tall black gelding in the next box stall caught her eye.

A broad chest, straight legs and well-muscled haunches suggested the strength and stamina she desired in a mount. Beyond that, however, something about his stance and wary, almost feral eyes attracted her. As if reciprocating her interest, the horse paced the stall, then turned back to her and tossed his head.

Going to the stall door, she put out a hand, encouraging him to draw closer. Slowly the horse approached, nostrils extended as he scented the air. Murmuring to him, Helena remained perfectly still, letting the horse accept her presence. Finally he allowed her to stroke his velvet neck.

So absorbed was she in getting acquainted that when Dixon's voice sounded from right behind her, she jumped, prompting her equine friend to jerk away, snorting.

"Come along, Miss Lambarth. Masters wishes to show us that pair of grays I mentioned for your carriage."

"What is this horse's name, Masters?" she asked.

"Pegasus, but it outta be Devil! He's not a fit mount for a lady, miss."

"Why not? Is he ill-tempered? Ill-paced?"

"His paces be smooth enough and he's not mean-spirited, exactly. He's just powerful strong with a mind of his own. The stable boys say he'd as soon run 'em into the side of the stall as walk through the door."

Helena chuckled. "He won't tolerate being ignored or underestimated. Spirit and stamina are essential in a mount—else, why ride? Mr. Dixon, I want this horse."

The two men exchanged uneasy glances. "Miss Lambarth, he is splendid," Mr. Dixon acknowledged, "but if Masters says the horse is…difficult, please respect his opinion."

"Indeed, I do! But neither of you have seen me ride. Masters—" she turned to the groom "—as I've already told Mr. Dixon, my mother bred horses. I've been in the saddle since before I could walk, riding everything from a pony to a green horse under saddle for the first time. I beg that you will both respect my knowledge of what I can handle."

"If you say, miss," the groom replied. "I'll just go on ahead and let you discuss it with the gentleman."

"Coward," Dixon muttered, watching the groom retreat. "Now, Miss Lambarth, pray be reasonable!" he said, turning back to Helena. "You've admitted you haven't ridden in years. Wouldn't it be wise to choose a more docile mount?"

"Undoubtedly," Helena agreed. "But I want this one. In dealing with horses—and men—I trust my instincts, which have never yet failed me. Pegasus and I shall suit perfectly—and gallop like the wind, shall we not, my beauty?" she crooned to the horse.

After a sigh, Dixon shook his head. "I'm sorry to be disobliging, but I cannot in good conscience try to obtain this horse for you. Now, the bay mare or the gray—"

"Please, Mr. Dixon, you needn't apologize! I shall simply bargain for him myself."

Dixon's momentary look of relief was succeeded by one of consternation. "But you cannot, Miss Lambarth! Have I not already explained—"

"You have, quite clearly," Helena interrupted. "But based on my assessment of the horses available, I have chosen the one I believe will suit me best. Was it not to ascertain that very thing that you brought me here?"

"Yes, but—"

"Then you can hardly expect me to settle for another horse, simply because others like it better. That would be neither logical nor intelligent."

"But…but Miss Lambarth," Dixon continued, looking rather desperate. "Adam would have my head if I purchase so highly unsuitable a lady's mount for you!"

"Since you have already said you have no intention of doing so, you may be easy," Helena replied. "I shall purchase the horse myself, saving you Darnell's wrath."

"He'd likely demand pistols at dawn were I to allow you to risk soiling your reputation by taking part in the auction," Dixon retorted.

"Then I fear I *have* imposed upon you most shamefully, for one way or another, I intend to have this horse. Perhaps you could tell Darnell I was so ungovernable you washed your hands of me? In any event, I must catch up with Masters and inquire how to go about bidding. If it is impossible for a female to enter the auction room, I must hire him to bargain for me."

She turned to walk away. With a growl, Dixon caught her shoulder. "This is blackmail, Miss Lambarth!"

"Indeed, I do not mean it so," she countered, suppressing a chuckle. He had done her a great favor and she ought not to be amused by his dilemma. "I'm sure Masters can find a hackney for me, if you wish to follow my advice and disavow all responsibility for the proceedings."

"As if that would matter a farthing to Adam, after I

brought you here. He'd be more likely to shoot me where I stood for abandoning you." Looking both aggrieved and chagrined, he swept his hand across his perspiring brow. "Very well, Miss Lambarth, if you must have this horse, I suppose I must buy him. But only if you promise you will not ride him without myself and your groom present."

Helena decided to allow him that one concession. "If you feel it necessary, Mr. Dixon. But I do assure you, I can handle the horse." She lost the battle to restrain her mirth and a chuckle emerged. "I expect you no longer admire this 'free-thinking individual' quite so much."

He gave her a half-resentful, half-amused glance. "Since you have so neatly hoist me with my own petard, I can't in fairness begrudge you the victory. In future, though, I will be on my guard!"

"I should like to continue our friendship, but I am what I am, so 'tis best that you are forewarned," she replied. "But come, let us discuss something we can agree upon. If the grays are as admirable as you say, I shall bow to your advice and purchase them."

Though Mr. Dixon was still somewhat disgruntled, it appeared he was too fair-minded to hold a grudge, for by the time she approved the grays, they stopped for ices at Gunters and arrived back at St. James Square, he had recovered his good humor.

"Behold me whole perhaps for the last time, Miss Lambarth," he said as he escorted her up the steps. "I return to Tattersalls to complete your commission, and when Adam sees the riding hack I've purchased for you, it shall likely be grass for breakfast between us."

"If he quarrels with anyone, it should be with me,"
Helena replied, giving him her hand to kiss. "By now
he should know I form my own decisions, even in the
face of well-intentioned advice to the contrary."

"Perhaps. But I intend to insure my will is in order,
just in case!" With a bow, he left her at the door.

BEING ENGAGED WITH HIS MAN of business the afternoon
of Helena's excursion to Tattersalls and spending that
evening escorting his fiancée to a ball, Adam didn't
learn of Helena's purchases until he arrived at his stables
the following morning. As he brought Adam's horse, the
head groom asked whether the master meant to join
Miss Lambarth and Mr. Dixon in the park, where they
were putting Miss Lambarth's new mount through his
paces.

"Ah, so she purchased a horse, then?"

"Aye, sir. The auction folks brung him by late yesterday. Rather a handful fer a lady, I'd a'said, iff'n
anyone was to 'av asked me."

Though Adam had intended to return to the solicitor's office, the groom's remarks made him uneasy.
Lady Darnell had told him Dix had offered to help
Helena find a mount. Adam had been happy she would
have Dix's expert opinion—even though he could not
rid himself of the tiny nugget of resentment that Dix
could escort Helena as often as he wished, actively
pursuing his acquaintance with this intriguing lady,
while Adam had to keep his distance.

Though he'd certainly failed to do so during that
episode in the library. He'd thought he'd succeeded in

armoring himself against the attraction that always sparked between them. He'd resisted her looking like a goddess in her gold dress, had even steeled himself to suggest her to Nathan as a possible match. So how had she broken through his defenses?

Perhaps it had been the scare her flight from the ballroom had given him. Or the aftermath of the almost uncontrollable rage that had burned in him at the possibility that some man had frightened or imposed upon her. Or perhaps the compassion he'd felt at seeing her in distress, or the satisfaction he'd experienced at being her rescuer, had lured him into letting down his guard.

Whatever breached his hold over it, when they reached the library, elder-brother concern had been swamped by desire, his mind overcome by memories of her garbed in white silk, lounging on his sofa, her sensuality calling to him like a siren's. Nay, 'twas worse this time, for while that first night she had been surprised and hesitant, this time she had seemed to respond to the heat in him, leaning up for the kiss he'd almost been mesmerized enough to offer.

Ah, yes, she'd appeared eager to explore the desire she incited. But it was not for him to initiate her into passion's embrace. He shook his head and shuddered at how close he'd come to dragging an innocent into scandal—his guest, a girl he was supposed to be protecting! Far better that Dix choose her horses, Nathan escort her to parties, Charis and his stepmother keep her company. Lest honor prove too fragile a curb on an attraction that had just shown him how unexpectedly it could flame out of control.

Still, she was in his care. If his groom, whose knowledge of horses he trusted, disapproved of the one she'd bought, he ought to check on her. Surely, he thought with a touch of disgust, in broad daylight in the park he'd manage to keep his appetites under control.

Leaping into the saddle, Adam set off for the park.

It was early enough that Hyde Park was virtually deserted when he guided his horse through the gates. After scanning the carriageway and seeing no one, he set off down Rotten Row. At the crest of the first hill, he spied a rider in the distance. A rider in a scarlet habit poised sidesaddle on a huge black horse, a description that proclaimed her identity even before he saw Dix's chestnut gelding trotting beside her.

Anxiety mounting, Adam kicked his horse to a canter and went in pursuit. Just as he reached them, the skittish black, apparently spooked at hearing a horse approaching from behind him, veered sideways off the path and reared up, trying to unseat his rider.

Fear chilled his blood and a cry of warning caught in his throat. He watched in horror as Miss Lambarth fell backward, expecting at any moment to see her tumble beneath the dancing hoofs of her mount. But in the next instant he realized that, rather than being tossed to the ground or grabbing in panic at reins and saddle, Miss Lambarth had purposely thrown her head back—laughing.

"Excellent, my beauty," she cried, and then must have commanded the horse to repeat the trick, for in the next moment he rose up again, forelegs pawing the air.

Adam realized that, far from being carried off, Miss Lambarth was in complete control of her mount. And what a spectacle they presented! The rearing black horse, the scarlet-clad woman riding him so easily the two seemed almost to merge into one, like an ancient pagan deity. The feral excitement of the two half-wild beings crackled in the air.

The elemental attraction Helena exuded washed over Adam in a powerful wave that stood every hair on end, dried the breath in his throat and engulfed him in an irresistible urge to tame and possess.

"Magnificent, isn't he?" Miss Lambarth exclaimed, her eyes bright and her smile brilliant as she settled the horse back on four hoofs. "I just had to see if he would rear on command. Now for a gallop!" At the tap of her whip and the urging of her heels, the horse wheeled and exploded into a run.

When Adam managed to tear his gaze away from the racing horse and scarlet-clad rider to look over at Dix, his friend was still staring fixedly at Miss Lambarth, apparently oblivious to Adam's arrival. Mirrored on Dix's face Adam saw the same awe and lust still churning in his own breast.

A primal, instinctive jealousy fired him to rage. "Hell and the devil, Dix, have you lost your wits? Whatever possessed you to allow Miss Lambarth to buy such a horse? I thought she was about to be trampled!"

Startled, his best friend whipped his attention over to Adam. Strong emotion must still be roiling in him, as well, for his normally easygoing face turned hostile.

"But, you notice, she was *not* trampled," he responded. "In fact she handled the horse as well as you or I would have, and better than any woman I know. Despite that, I did everything in my power to prevent her buying Pegasus."

"Pegasus? The beast should be named Charon, since he looks apt to ferry her straight to Hades! And I note how successfully you dissuaded her. Heavens, man, her dress makes her singular enough. Do you not realize that making a spectacle of herself on that beast, as intriguing as you may find it, could tarnish her reputation? If you have so little regard for protecting her good name, I shall have to forbid your escorting her!"

"She would command attention regardless of her mount. Galloping a flashy beast in the park will not harm her reputation as much as bidding for the horse at Tattersalls, which, I assure you, she threatened to do if I refused to bargain for her. Besides—" Dix eyed him narrowly "—I suspect you enjoyed that 'spectacle' quite as much as I. There's something about her that wraps a fist about a man's throat so he can scarcely breathe." Dix shook his head. "I may have to marry her before she drives me crazy."

"Maybe you need to stay away from her," Adam retorted.

"Maybe you need to take your own advice," Dix flashed back. "I've seen how you look at her. At least I'm free to act. May I remind you that you're engaged? I suggest that you hie yourself back to your fiancée and stop trying to put blocks in the path of those who value Miss Lambarth as much for her spirit as for her...passionate beauty."

At that moment Helena came galloping back and pulled up the black beside them. Cheeks flushed from the wind, eyes alight, she once again exuded a sensual allure that tightened Adam's chest and sped his pulse.

"What cowards they are, Pegasus," she said, patting the horse's lathered neck. "They didn't even try to catch us. But you see," she continued, looking over to the men, "he will be quite docile now. He needs to run, not be shut up in a box stall for days on end."

Still glowing, she turned to Dix. "I can't thank you enough for obtaining him, Mr. Dixon. Darnell, I hope you've not been taking Mr. Dixon to task for purchasing me such a spirited mount. As you have seen, I have no trouble managing him. Indeed, we understand each other perfectly."

Before Adam could reply, after a pointed look at him, Dix said, "No, we've just been agreeing that the two of you create…an arresting picture. But so appealing, I hope you will allow me to ride with you every time you go out, to keep the importunate from bothering you."

She laughed. "Stuff! No one could catch us anyway! Though, if you choose to ride early enough, Mr. Dixon, I shall be pleased to have your escort. Now, let's have an easy canter to cool Pegasus down before any more riders arrive in the park. You will accompany us, Darnell?"

"No, Miss Lambarth. I was on my way to my solicitor's and just happened by. I shall leave you in Mr. Dixon's—" he gritted his teeth over the word "—capable care."

After exchanging a curt nod with his friend, Adam wheeled his mount and headed out of the park. Dix's sharp words stung, all the more so because they were true. Adam *did* desire her. In fact, so jealous and furious had lust rendered him, it had taken all his control and breeding to cede her escort to Dix and ride out of the park.

Hie himself back to his fiancée, indeed! Thank heavens Miss Standish did not rouse him to such uncomfortable excesses of emotion. Riding a firestorm from anger to lust to jealousy and back would not be a comfortable way to live. Much better to have a wife whom one respected and admired, who inspired one with more temperate emotions.

Or was the fact that Miss Lambarth could spark in him feelings—both lust and respect—so much more intense than those roused by his fiancée a warning that he might have been too precipitous in his choice?

Had his engagement to Priscilla been a mistake?

Shocked and dismayed by the thought, Adam's mind fled from that conclusion. Since his engagement was a fait accompli and could not be broken, there was no point pursuing such reflections, he told himself firmly. He would leave Miss Lambarth to Dix and fix his thoughts on the business that took him to his solicitors.

Forcing himself to begin mentally reviewing reports on acreage and yields, he absently directed his horse toward the City. But that awful snippet of doubt, like a burr on a saddle blanket, stuck at the back of his mind and refused to be dislodged.

CHAPTER EIGHTEEN

IN THE LATE EVENING ten days later, Helena sat on the sofa before the library fire, reading—or rather, attempting to read. An edgy restlessness had made it nearly impossible for her to keep her mind on the story. After realizing she'd just looked over the same Greek phrase a fifth time, she gave up and put aside the book.

She poured herself a glass of wine, but the warming liquid worked no better than the book in quelling the sensation that made her feel like a caged beast.

So anxious was she for fresh air and activity, she'd almost agreed to accompany Charis and Aunt Lillian to the ball tonight. But stifling in noisy, overcrowded rooms would not banish the agitation that drove her to spring up and pace the library.

Even at the musicales she was ringed about by too many people. The desire for freedom and solitude had become an almost physical ache. How she yearned to go out all alone, as she had roamed through the night forests of Lambarth!

Small chance of that. It seemed that a gently bred girl could not step out her front door unaccompanied.

Her aunt insisted that if she wished to go anywhere, she take the carriage along with Nell and a footman.

She had hoped riding Pegasus would quell the sense of being trapped that had grown more acute with every day she spent in London. But though she had a wonderful mount to gallop, she'd found that even when leaving at dawn, she was required to bring along a groom, whose presence precluded going off afterward to explore the city. And once it become known that she went early to the park, she began encountering not just Mr. Dixon, but a crowd of other men.

Some were bold enough to call at the house, though her blatant indifference discouraged all but the most persistent—notably Dixon and Lord Blanchard. Both stopped by almost daily, but having quickly noted how often the diplomat's glance strayed from her to rest on Charis, Helena was quite sure Blanchard didn't come to see *her.*

When she'd teased Charis about their caller, her friend had replied with a sigh that Helena must be mistaken. Blanchard's duty required him to wed a woman of wealth, and he was too noble and courteous to raise hopes he would be unable to fulfill. Charis had then quickly turned the subject, leaving Helena unable to determine the exact depth of her friend's feeling for the handsome diplomat.

Though she might not be certain of Charis's thoughts on matrimony, she was still certain of her own. But despite her boycott of balls and refusal to attend Almack's, it seemed the ton had not been persuaded that she had no intention of bestowing her hand—and the fortune she reportedly possessed—on some persistent suitor. At the few Society functions she did attend, she found herself thronged by single gentlemen, from callow lads just out of Oxford whose downy chins had scarce seen a razor to bewhiskered widowers on the catch for a rich new wife.

She could only imagine it was the challenge of a woman who dressed to please herself and turned up her nose at matrimony that continued to capture their attention.

Or perhaps, she mused, whatever it was about her that brought the lustful looks to their faces—and Darnell's.

She paused by the hearth, its heat recalling the maelstrom of sensations Adam inspired in her. A memory that did nothing to soothe her agitation.

Oh, to have been born a man, who might go anywhere at any time of day or night! From exclusive clubs to gaming hells and brothels, all of London was accessible to them. Whereas a lady couldn't even inquire about, much less explore, such places.

Places a girl might learn the secrets of desire.

Her pacing having produced no results, Helena decided to slip down to the kitchen. Perhaps a bit of Cook's good ham would calm her enough that she could sleep.

She moved silently down the service stairs into the kitchen, where the banked fire and a lantern turned low beside a dozing footman provided a fitful illumination. She was about to enter the larder when a stealthy scratching sound at the door made her freeze.

Slowly she backed to the wall, reaching as she retreated for the homemade dagger she kept tied to her leg. She had the knife drawn and ready to strike when the kitchen door opened and a small figure crept in.

Dickon! Relief and amusement filled her. Nell or Harrison would likely provide the boy a close acquaintance with a leather belt, were they to discover him sneaking back in the middle of the night. What had he been up to?

Helena waited until the boy, his eyes on the sleeping footman, was abreast of her. Then she sprang out, pinching his nose closed with one hand and applying pressure with the thumb of her other hand to the vulnerable spot beneath his windpipe, as Mad Sally had taught her. With him incapacitated, she whispered in his ear, "Hush! It's Miss Helena. Come with me to my chamber."

She held the boy until she was sure he understood her command before releasing him. Hand to his throat, he silently followed Helena up to her room.

Safely within, she turned to face Dickon. "What were you thinking, creeping about like that? If Charles had awakened, Harrison and Nell both would have your hide!"

"Charles don't never rouse. When he's on duty, I can always get out and back with no one the wiser."

"So you've done this before?"

Realizing his mistake, Dickon tried at first to deny it, but at length admitted that, in the past few weeks, he'd slipped out frequently.

"And what do you do out there?"

"Meet up with me workhouse mates and go for a

taste of blue ruin and some cards. Maybe earn a copper standing outside where toffs are having their to-dos, holding their horses." He shuffled nervously. "You ain't going to turn me in to Nell or Mr. Harrison, are you?"

Helena's reflection that Nell had been wise to try to remove Dickon from the influence of St. Marylebone was swiftly succeeded by a more exciting idea.

"I really should tell Nell. But perhaps I shall keep your secret…if you agree to help me."

"Anything, miss!" Dickon said eagerly.

"First you must obtain me some boy's clothing. Then I want you to take me to some of the places you go."

Dickon stared at her. "In the middle of the night, with you dressed as a lad? You're mad, Miss! I couldn't never do such a thing!"

"You needn't bring me to play cards or drink with your mates, where my chances of being found out are greater. I just want to be able to walk alone, without a maid and footmen on my heels. Watch where gentlemen go, observe what they do. What safer way than to dress as a lad—who goes everywhere and attracts the attention of no one?"

"But them streets ain't safe by half, even for such as me," he objected. "There be some very bad men about!"

"We shall avoid the most dangerous areas. I can't imagine the cutpurses working the crowds by the theaters would bother us. If the worst occurs, I have my knife and can use it. I did well enough tonight, didn't I?"

"Maybe," Dickon said, rubbing his throat where her thumb had pressed. "But I still can't help you. Nell and Mr. Harrison would have my head iff'n they found out."

"They'd be scarcely more happy if I tell them you've been sneaking out. At the least, Nell would insist you promise not to do so again. Whereas, if you agree to take me, you may keep on with your excursions. I shall expire if I cannot escape the house and explore without the baggage of petticoats, maids and footmen! Didn't I stand up for you and Nell with Lord Darnell?"

"Aye, you did, and right grateful I am." Continuing to rub his throat, Dickon studied her, as if trying to judge how desperate she was—and therefore how likely to tell on him if he refused her request.

"What's to stop you from ratting later, once you've had your fill of exploring?"

"Ah, but I couldn't, for if I revealed your wanderings, you could reveal mine. I wouldn't wish to distress Lady Darnell by having her learn of them any more than you want Nell to know of yours. So your secret would be safe, safer than it is now," she pressed. "Even if I agreed now not to tell Nell, with nothing at stake for me, I might inadvertently let something slip later."

"I expect Lord Darnell would pack you off to a nunnery if he was to learn you'd done something so outlandish."

"Exactly. So, Dickon, what shall it be? More adventures? Or a word in Nell's ear and restriction to the house forever?"

Dickon eyed her resentfully. "You don't give me much choice, do you, miss?"

"Excellent!" Helena cried. "Can you have the clothes by tomorrow night? Miss Charis and Lady Darnell are to attend another ball, and Darnell of course is escorting his fiancée, so they will all be out until very late."

Though Dickon agreed to her plan with far less enthusiasm than she felt, before she dismissed him he agreed to smuggle the clothing to her, then meet her at midnight inside the chamber overlooking the garden.

From where, Helena thought exultantly, they could easily descend, by way of the sturdy tree branch she'd already discovered, into the garden and out the side gate she'd used for her excursion with Molly. Their chances of discovery under cover of night were slim.

Though there had been wolves and the occasional poacher, Lambarth's woods at night had held few perils. London was much more dangerous, but as she'd assured Dickon, she intended to be very cautious. But to compensate for the risk, she would have the joy of being truly free, almost on her own, and able to explore the vast city beyond the drawing rooms of Mayfair.

Helena had not felt such excitement since, full of anticipation, she had boarded the mail coach for London.

THE FOLLOWING DAY, after spending the evening pacing the library until it was late enough for Nell and the other servants to be abed, Helena returned to her room to don the boy's clothes Dickon had smuggled to her.

So anxious had she been to set out on her adventure, she'd had great difficulty masking her enthusiasm—or her impatience for the ladies to leave. After both Charis and Aunt Lillian remarked at dinner how agitated she seemed, Helena was forced to voice a fervent desire to return to the Greek work she was currently translating that rather exceeded her actual appreciation for the text.

She dressed herself quickly and slipped down the hallway into the guest chamber overlooking the garden. Moments later a soft knock heralded Dickon's arrival. After rebutting with as much patience as she could muster his last attempts to dissuade her from the excursion, she opened the chamber window, clambered onto the nearby branch and bid him follow.

"Cor!" Dickon whispered after they had made it safely to the ground and through the hidden side gate. "You be right good at tree climbing!"

"I never imagined how much easier it would be, unhampered by petticoats." Helena chuckled. "If ladies ever discovered how much more serviceable breeches are, they would never again wear skirts! Now, I should first like to visit a tavern, the sort where common folk go."

"Whyever for, miss? It ain't like you was wanting to drink blue ruin and play cards."

"But I do wish to taste it. Although I expect it would be best for me not to linger long enough for a game of cards. Where do you usually go?"

Dickon sighed. "There's a place not far—Fancy Jim's. 'Tis a hell where some of the gents go to play and drink deep. I expect you'll be safe enough if you stay out in the stable yard with my mates."

"Excellent! Let us go at once."

With the clip-clop of passing horses and vehicles, the occasional illumination from streetlamps and carriage lamps, Helena found London at night to be neither as quiet nor as dark as Lambarth's woods. Proceeding on foot allowed her to pause and inspect the house and shopfronts that interested her while Dickon looked on patiently and attempted to answer her avid inquiries.

Enjoying herself immensely, Helena was happy to remain in the stable yard of Fancy Jim's, where Dickon introduced her as the "new boy" at his master's house. Listening silently to the lads' banter, some of it delivered in a cant she could barely comprehend, she waited while Dickon went inside to procure them some drink.

She quickly found blue ruin not at all to her taste. Much to Dickon's consternation—and the amusement of his friends—she spat out the mouthful she'd taken, pronouncing it "nasty stuff," and dumped the rest onto the cobblestones before Dickon could stop her.

Once her guide finished quaffing his own mug, they set off again, Helena proposing they continue to St. James Street. As it was the site of several famous gentlemen's clubs, she explained, Aunt Lillian told her ladies were not permitted to stroll there. "I should like to observe the clubs from the outside, perhaps discover what about them engenders in gentlemen such a fascination and loyalty."

"No secret to it," Dickon replied. "They got good victuals, high-stakes cards, fine port—and no females to make a fuss about 'em. Now, miss, it ain't a good idea to go there. Seein' as how some of the toffs 've seen me at the house, I might be recognized."

"We won't stay long and you can stand in the shadows," Helena countered, already setting out in that direction.

Running after her, Dickon muttered a curse on all women and their unreasonable ways.

Surprised to find how close together the two most famous establishments were located, Helena lingered first outside Brook's, where the chat among the arriving and departing gentleman seemed to concern mostly corn bills, enclosures and the excesses of the Prince Regent. She then crossed the street and sauntered toward White's. From the bits she overhead here, it appeared this clientele concerned itself more with gaming and gossip.

She was about to slip away when two men rode up and she heard Lord Blanchard's voice, followed by his companion's reply extolling the loveliness of Miss Darnell.

Despite Dickon's frantic hand gestures signaling her to retreat, Helena couldn't keep herself from approaching. When Blanchard's friend swung down from the stirrups while Blanchard remained mounted, Helena scurried over. Pitching her voice to mimic the tones of a street urchin, she called, "'Old yer 'orse fer a penny, gov'ner!"

Scarcely gazing at her, the man tossed her a coin, handed her the reins and turned back to Lord Blanchard, who never even glanced in her direction.

"Don't look daggers at me, Nathan," the gentleman said. "If you've no real interest there, you can hardly object if other respectable gentlemen pursue her."

Blanchard sighed. "I know. I only wish I *could* pursue my interest, but you know how I am situated. My family, my career, all require me to marry a woman of wealth. Even though I would rather wed an angel."

The other gentleman laughed. "She is one, isn't she? Since someone else must win her, it might as well be a fine fellow like me! Come join me and drink to my efforts."

Blanchard smiled grimly. "Thank you, but no. I may wish you well, but I'm not saint enough to drink to the prospect of her wedding another."

"You could drink to the prospect of finding your heiress. Perhaps Miss Darnell's friend, Miss Lambarth?"

"Ah, Miss Lambarth." Blanchard laughed. "The beautiful and unique! I give thanks for her daily, since her presence at Darnell House allows me to call there as often as I wish."

The other gentleman shook his head. "She's more than I'd want to handle, lovely and rich though she be. No, give me a sweet, quiet, biddable wife."

"I pray you may find one—as long as she's not Miss Darnell." Tipping his hat to his friend, Blanchard wheeled his horse and trotted off.

Handing Blanchard's friend back his reins—and accepting another coin—Helena paced slowly toward where Dickon waited, her mind churning. So Lord Blanchard *was* in love with Charis! Could her friend secretly love Blanchard, as well—but knowing his circumstances, have despaired of his making her an offer?

If so, Helena thought, excitement putting a skip in her step, she might just have a solution.

CHAPTER NINETEEN

NOT WISHING TO PROLONG the rather strained evening he'd spent with his fiancée, Adam declined Priscilla's invitation to come in and left her at her door. Deciding that a long walk in the cold air might help clear his mind, he sent his carriage home and set out for White's.

All night he'd been plagued by recurring memories of his last encounter with Miss Lambarth in the library. He had seen little of her since that meeting, and always in company. Still, to his annoyance, several times at the ball tonight his pulse had raced when he glimpsed some dark-haired lady or heard a husky female voice. Which was ridiculous, since after Miss Lambarth's panic at her first ball, he knew she would never attend another.

Much to his stepmother's distress, Miss Lambarth had also continued to refuse to go to Almack's or to any large gathering. Although Priscilla had privately warned him that Miss Lambarth's spurning of the many invitations she received would lead to her being ostracized, quite the reverse was occurring. The novelty of a lady who refused the most exclusive of invitations had every hostess vying to devise parties that might lure the heiress to attend.

Certainly she had no lack of escort when she did go out. Dix, with whom Adam's relations had remained cool since their exchange at the park, was quick to offer his arm and often Nathan joined the party. Indeed, every time Adam went to his club, gentlemen waylaid him, pleading to be presented to Miss Lambarth. Several presumptuous cawkers had even asked his permission to propose to her.

He'd dutifully presented the former and sent the latter packing, informing them that for now Miss Lambarth refused to entertain any offers. That fact was a source of both anxiety and a secret, guilty pleasure.

Though now that he'd shown himself again how quickly his supposed self-control around her could disintegrate, it would be far better if Miss Lambarth married and removed herself from Adam's life. Of late, he was tense and edgy around Priscilla, viewing her actions with a critical eye.

Was it because of the doubts he couldn't quite shake that his fiancée seemed different to him, or had she truly changed since she'd accepted his suit? Was it only because he'd now observed Helena's unique response to his world that Priscilla seemed almost stultifyingly conventional?

Before they'd left the Standish mansion last night, Priscilla had accepted her cloak from one footman, her fur muff from another, without seeming to see those servants at all. Her only thanks had been directed to the butler.

Thinking back, he could not remember her speaking to any of the Standish minions save her maid, the butler and the housekeeper. He couldn't imagine her descending to the kitchen or personally interviewing a servant.

Her behavior when they were alone together also troubled him. Where at first Priscilla had seemed as eager as he to slip off into the garden, he didn't think it was just his imagination that she now seemed to avoid such opportunities. Just yesterday, perhaps to prove to himself that he found his fiancée as appealing as…another lady, he'd tried to entice Priscilla into some passionate kisses. Chastising him for disarranging her gown, she'd pushed him away, telling him her mother had recommended they limit themselves to chaste kisses until *after* the wedding.

Were Miss Lambarth in his arms, he didn't think she would have dipped her head to take his lips on her forehead instead of her mouth.

Now that he thought about it, he'd seen little evidence since their engagement of the adventuresome little girl he remembered so fondly. The child who'd once delighted in escaping her mama's supervision now seemed all too often to preface or end her speeches with "Mama said…"

When he'd half humorously taxed Priscilla about it after that rebuff in the garden, she'd quickly become defensive. "Mama reminded me that I am soon to be a married lady and must comport myself with more dignity. If I seem to quote her overmuch, 'tis just that I wish to be as excellent a manager of your household as she is of ours and seek to learn all I can from her."

"Is there to be no spontaneity, then? No—" he kissed her fingertips "—disappearing into dark alcoves together?"

"Spontaneity, Mama says," she replied, removing her fingers from his, "is usually ill-bred behavior someone is trying to pass off as innocence. I hope I am beyond that."

There being nothing to object to in her observations, Adam was silent. Yet his feeling of disquiet remained.

Trying to rid himself of it, he'd sought out his fiancée for a third waltz tonight, only to have her send him on to her school friend, Lady Cordelia. Mama, she said, believed 'twas not seemly for them to dance together overmuch, as they would soon be married and ton couples did not spend every moment in each other's pockets.

Would two people attached to each other, on fire for each other, not burn to claim one another as often as possible, particularly for the dance that was as close to intimacy as one might come in a ballroom?

Were Miss Lambarth his to claim, Adam didn't think he would allow her to waltz with any man but him.

Suddenly the disinterested affection he'd previously thought most likely to promote lifelong marital happiness no longer seemed so appealing. What would life be without the boiling rush of desire, without irresistible passion, with…polite kisses on the forehead?

Lud! he thought, stomping his foot in disgust. He sounded like Charis reading one of her Minerva Press novels. He'd made his choice and could not now, in honor, go back on it—nor could he subject Priscilla to the ridicule of being jilted. So that was the end of it.

He was approaching White's when he spied Nathan Blanchard on horseback, talking with another gentleman. Not in the mood for chat, Adam halted, waiting for the two men to finish their conversation.

As he stood there, his gaze idly scanning the street, something about the lad holding Blanchard's companion's horse caught his eye. He leaned forward, a shock rippling through him, then cursed under his breath.

He really was in need of strong brandy if he was now seeing Miss Lambarth even in the figure of a street urchin.

Nathan rode off, the other man reclaimed his horse, and the boy ambled back across the lane. Once again, in defiance of all logic, something about the strolling figure set all his senses stirring. He must be a candidate for Bedlam, because as vociferously as he argued with himself that such a thing was impossible, he found himself irresistibly compelled to cautiously approach the boy.

He'd almost convinced himself that even the intrepid Miss Lambarth would never have either the audacity to attempt, nor the ability to carry through, such a disguise when another boy emerged from the shadows. With the full glare of a streetlamp upon him, Adam had no trouble recognizing the lad—the ever-resourceful Dickon, Harrison's pet and bane of the head groom's existence.

So the boy was sneaking out to meet his mates—no great harm in that. Adam had just decided to dismiss his ridiculous suspicions and head back toward his club when Dickon's whisper carried to him on the still night air.

"'Cor, you about seized up m'lungs, going right up to the toffs like that! What if one of 'em had recognized you?"

"But they didn't," came a low-pitched reply that froze Adam in midstride and made his heart stop. "In any event, I'm ready to depart. Let's go to Covent Garden. I should like to find a lady I once saw in the park—the Divine Alice, I think they called her."

While his heart stuttered and began beating again, he heard Dickon reply that they'd seen enough for one night and there weren't no way they was going to visit a fancy woman. The two had proceeded down the street before Adam's brain resumed working and feeling returned to his limbs.

Despite the logic that dictated Miss Lambarth couldn't possibly be gadding around London dressed like a boy, he knew with absolute certainty that she was.

But what should he do about it?

Dismissing his first reaction, which was to run after them, seize her in his arms and haul her off, probably protesting, to a hackney, he scoured his mind for a more prudent response. On no account did he want to do anything that would draw the attention of the patrons at White's to himself and the "lad" walking with Dickon.

Blessing his experience as a dispatch carrier for Wellington on the Peninsula, when on several occasions he'd had to practice stealth to avoid alerting French pickets, Adam surreptitiously began following them.

Fortunately, Miss Lambarth and her escort made no

attempt at concealment. Keeping in the shadows, Adam was able to trail them at a distance. They headed toward Picadilly, by their gestures still arguing, Miss Lambarth apparently reluctant to end the evening and Dickon anxious to return to St. James Square, in which direction he continued to point.

Adam let them round the next corner ahead of him, debating whether he should hang back to see if Dickon won the argument or catch up to them and, as quietly as possible, convey Miss Lambarth home.

His heart skipped a beat again when he reached the corner and did not see them, then kicked back into rhythm when he spied them walking down a side alley—thankfully in the direction of home. But before he could rejoice that Dickon had convinced her to return, from the back of a tavern, a large man stumbled out into the alley.

Fear speeding his steps, Adam closed the distance separating them. He was still fifty paces away when the man approaching Miss Lambarth from behind caught her arm.

"Hey, there, m'fine young gent," he said, looking her up and down. "Ain't you the pretty one? I likes pretty boys, better 'n most anything. Fer a copper, I'll show ya just how much."

A murderous rage filled Adam, the likes of which he'd not felt since Waterloo, when a French dragoon had slashed the squadron mate beside him out of his saddle. Teeth gritted, a growl in his throat, he fisted his hands to attack.

But before he could take a step, in the flickering

light from the torches beside the stable entrance, Adam saw a flash of silver. In the next instant, Miss Lambarth had a slim, curve-bladed knife pressed against the throat of the beefy man who'd accosted her.

"You'd best leave 'pretty boys' alone, sirrah...lest I render you incapable of offering your services to boys or girls," she said in a low, menacing voice.

Eyes bugging out as he stared down at the knife, the man let go her arm. "No need to stick me, now! Didn't mean ye no harm!"

When Miss Lambarth lifted the blade away, the man scrambled backward. Eyes still on her and Dickon, who paced after the fellow, a large rock in his hands, the man stumbled over the cobblestones, then turned and scuttled back into the tavern's stable yard.

For a few moments afterward, Adam heard only the sound of his own gusty breathing. Then Dickon's voice broke the silence. "R-reckon it's time to go home," he said shakily.

His heart still hammering against his ribs, Adam sprang back and flattened himself against the building behind him. Light-headed now that the fury had left him, he watched them continue down the lane.

After they had drawn far enough ahead, he resumed following at a discreet distance, letting out a sigh of relief when at last they reached Darnell House and slipped into the garden by a side gate he had forgotten existed.

He stared at the closed gate, bracing his suddenly shaking hands against the garden wall. That momentary weakness was quickly succeeded by another wave of fury—directed this time at Miss Lambarth. How could she be so reckless, so heedless, so blithely unconcerned about the hideous scandal that would result had someone discovered her—or the terrible danger she'd courted, skulking about London at night with only an idiot boy for protection?

At the same time, he had to acknowledge the ingenuity she'd displayed in contriving so unique a means of escaping the restrictions Society placed upon young maidens—and her cool, quick-witted courage when confronted by a potential attacker. He couldn't imagine any other woman possessing either her daring or her resourcefulness.

Now that she was safe, he hoped that grudging admiration would help him get through the lecture he intended to deliver without strangling her.

Or—her wildness and his fear for her unleashing a need he was finding difficult to control—without hauling her into his arms and kissing her as senseless as he'd felt upon recognizing her outside White's.

Trying to crush that primitive impulse, as he had before numerous battles, Adam stood motionless for several minutes, focusing only on drawing in and exhaling slow, deep breaths.

By the time he had his emotions back under control, he figured Miss Lambarth should have been in the house long enough to have changed out of her disguise and returned to her usual late-night reading in the library.

Adam set off around the corner. Their imminent confrontation was a battle he must win. Trotting up the

front steps of Darnell House, he scarcely acknowledged the greetings of the sleepy footman who opened
the door, his concentration already focused on the maddening, exhilarating woman who awaited him in the
library.

But when, after a brief knock, Adam paced into that
room, he found it deserted. Apparently after reaching
the safety of her chamber, with a sudden return of
prudence, Miss Lambarth had remained there.

For a moment Adam stood irresolute before the cold
hearth. Much as he longed to charge up the stairs and
pursue her, even at this late hour he could hardly do so
without some servant remarking upon it, nor for the
same reason could he ask one to summon her. He no
more wanted to raise a ruckus here that would require
explanation to Lady Darnell than he'd wanted to draw
attention to the diabolical girl by accosting her in front
of White's.

With a growl, Adam paced to the sideboard, poured
himself a generous glass of port and downed the whole.

Though he sincerely hoped her altercation tonight
had terrified Miss Lambarth as much as it had him, he
couldn't count on it. It was imperative that he make
sure she understood the excellent reasons that required
she not indulge in any further such nighttime excursions. But with her already abed, he could think of no
way to make that happen. Not tonight.

Groaning, he dropped into the chair behind his desk
and put his head in his hands. Somehow he was going
to have to devise a way to speak privately with her
tomorrow. Though seeing her alone in daylight was not

much safer than accosting her here, in the room where she'd first inspired him with this life-complicating passion, it was unthinkable that he include anyone else in the meeting.

Even as he regretted that fact, a heated, guilty awareness pulsed in his veins at knowing that for a time tomorrow, he would have her all to himself again.

AFTER SLEEPING BUT LITTLE, and badly, Adam returned to his library early the next morning. The imperative to talk privately with Miss Lambarth weighed on him—but he'd still not figured out how to bring that about without involving or alarming Charis or Bellemere. He supposed he could wait until this evening after the ladies went out to try to catch Miss Lambarth reading in the library…unless she slipped out first for another tour about London. No, he didn't wish to chance that.

Before he could decide how best to proceed, a knock sounded at the door. Anticipation flashed through him—but Miss Lambarth was most unlikely to seek him out. Shaking off the thought, he bid the supplicant enter.

To his surprise, Dickon entered the library and begged for a few minutes to discuss a matter of utmost urgency.

Adam suspected he knew quite well what urgent matter Dickon felt compelled to discuss. "What is amiss, Dickon?"

After studying Adam's stern face for a moment, the boy said, "Miss Helena, she can get a body to do things he don't really want to do, you know?"

Did he ever! "Continue."

"She caught me sneaking in after midnight one night. Well, the short of it is, she told me she'd been feeling stifled, getting to go nowheres but to them lady meetings, always with other folks, never out on her own. She threatened to tell Nell on me unless...unless I promised to take her exploring with me. So last night I—I did."

Releasing some of his pent-up frustration, Adam barked, "Are you out of your mind, boy?"

"I never wanted to! And she didn't go togged out like a female neither, but in boy's clothes. Can make her voice sound just like one of my mates, she can." Dickon chuckled. "Even Lord Blanchard didn't recognize her."

"Thanks be to God! I ought to have you transported."

"I didn't let her talk me into taking her to a brothel, much as she wheedled me! And I did come tell you, when sure enough nobody would have found out otherwise." He looked up at Adam, his eyes appealing. "Miss Helena wouldn't listen to me if I begged her to stop, but you could order her to stay home, couldn't you?"

Dropping his gaze, he added with a sigh, "I expect you'll want to turn me off, and I can't hardly blame you. But I figured you had to know."

Adam waited, but Dickon said no more. He had to admire the boy's loyalty in protecting his mistress by revealing only the bare fact of her transgression and omitting the more damning—and dangerous—matter of the man who'd accosted her.

A shudder passed through Adam at the memory. Decided it was better not to let Dickon know he'd seen them by questioning him about the incident, he tipped the boy's chin up. "Master Dickon, a lad who knows the difference between what is important and what is not is a valuable employee I should not wish to lose. I will keep your secret—but I suggest in future you confine your wanderings to more suitable hours. You may go."

"Aye, sir!" Dickon bowed, looking much relieved. "You'll talk to Miss Helena?"

"If you please, ask her to join me immediately."

Dickon sighed again. "When she learns I've scarpered on her, she's like to can me herself. But I'll fetch her right quick." With another bow, he left.

Adam let out a long breath. Bless Dickon, both for his honesty and for providing Adam with the perfect means to summon Helena discreetly. Though when he did confront the wretched girl, she would probably reply that no one had specifically instructed her that she was not to wander about the city after midnight in boy's clothing.

Lady Darnell would have palpitations.

He hoped he would be convincing enough to persuade her never to do so again. Though he wasn't about to confess so to Dickon, he was certain that attempting to *order* her to refrain would be a waste of breath.

A few moments later another knock sounded. He closed his eyes, letting the surge of heightened sensation that telegraphed her presence roll over him as she entered.

She made him a deep curtsey. "What have I done now, that you must needs summon me?"

Garbed in a gown of teal-green, every dark curl in place, she looked lovely enough to steal his breath, the very picture of a young lady of quality. It seemed impossible that a few hours ago she had wrestled with a miscreant in a dark London alley.

Shaking his head, he said, "What do you think?"

She put a finger to her cheek and appeared to consider the question. "Was it that I told Lady Jersey yesterday, after she'd commented on my having so many admirers despite my distaste for marriage, that Society is like a great cat? Speak sweetly and try to lure him to you and he disdains to approach, but ignore him and he jumps into your lap."

Despite the urgency of what he needed to discuss with her, Adam laughed. "Anything else on your conscience?"

"Is it because I gave Viscount Framingham's wandering hands a smack at the musicale two nights ago?"

"He did what?" Adam straightened, instantly incensed. "I shall have to break every one of his fingers."

"You may spare Freddie's fingers," Helena replied with a chuckle. "I scratched him so hard he bled on his blue satin breeches. I doubt he'll trouble me again."

"I'm relieved to hear it." Tamping down his anger over Framingham's lecherous advances, Adam made himself focus on the more serious matter at hand. "The event that concerns me occurred…rather late last evening."

He wasn't sure how she would respond to his probing. To his relief—since he didn't want to put her immediately on the defensive by announcing he'd seen her—she gave him a sheepish glance. "I suppose Dickon talked to you? I thought he was wearing a guilty look this morning. He told me over and over last night what a fright I'd given him."

"He wasn't the only one! I saw you, too."

Her chin jerked up and her eyes widened. "*You* saw me? Where?"

"Outside White's…holding a horse for a gentleman who was talking with Lord Blanchard."

To his gratification, a flush stained her cheeks. "Oh, my. Well, I suppose I can only be glad you did not drag me off by my heels on the spot."

"Believe me, I was sorely tempted to do just that! But I didn't dare risk creating a disturbance that would have drawn attention to you."

"I suppose I must thank you for your restraint. Shall I now wait quietly while you berate me?"

"If I thought railing at you would be effective, I'd give you the jobation of the century! Especially after having followed you home."

But though her cheeks flamed redder, she merely said, "I should congratulate you on your skill. You are obviously better at stealth than I."

Incensed that she still would not acknowledge the seriousness or folly of her escapade, Adam jumped up from his chair and exploded. "If you weren't terrified out of ten year's growth when that ruffian accosted you, you should have been! I assure you I was!"

Too agitated to sit back down, he started to pace the room, looking back at her as he spoke. "Hel—Miss

Lambarth, surely you must realize what you did was incredibly dangerous! What if that man had been joined by others? What if he—or someone else—had discovered you were a female, out in the dead of night with only a small boy to defend you?" His words pouring out in a furious rush that gave her no time to reply, he continued, "Even setting aside the peril of it, how do you think Bellemere would feel if someone whispered to her that they'd seen you roaming the London streets in boy's dress?" Shuddering at the hysterical scene that would inevitably result from such a disclosure, he demanded, "How *could* you do such a thing?"

In a silence broken only by the ticking of the mantel clock, they stared at each other. "I'm certainly glad you don't intend to lecture me," Miss Lambarth said at last.

But before he could erupt again, she waved him to silence. "It wasn't wise—I see that now," she admitted.

"Why run such a risk? Dickon mumbled something about you feeling 'stifled,' but you must know you are free to go out whenever you wish, with a proper escort. Whatever possessed you to creep about in the dead of night?"

She knotted her hands and gazed down at them. "You know that my father kept me…close confined. You probably don't know that I eventually found a way to escape every prison he devised. I taught myself to pick locks and discovered every exit through Lambarth's walls. After I'd been locked in for the night, I would leave the castle and walk about the grounds. Or visit Mad Sally, an old medicine woman who lived in the woods and was my only friend after Mama left. I should have gone as mad as she was reputed to be if I hadn't had her to talk with. So you see, wandering about at night is quite natural for me."

Adam had to admire her indomitable spirit even as he deplored the circumstances that had compelled her to escape her own home. "But you have many friends here."

"Acquaintances merely, most of them more interested in my fortune than my character. Besides, I've spent so much of my life alone that to be always among a crowd of people makes me feel—closed in. Here, I may ride or visit only with an entourage. Sometimes I…I simply must be outdoors, alone and free to move about on my own."

"Surely you see how perilous it is to do so here."

She nodded. "I didn't realize just how perilous until last night. I now acknowledge there are good reasons for the rules that prevent girls from going out unaccompanied. Which I imagine you will now forbid me to do."

"I haven't that right. But I will most earnestly implore you not to do so, for your own safety and the peace of mind of all who care about you."

"That is a pledge easily given! I promise I will not do so again. Though," she added with a sigh, "I'm not sure what I shall do now when I feel hemmed in."

Her agreement was a huge burden lifted. Uttering a swift prayer of thanks that she had proven so reasonable, he finally felt calm enough to cease his pacing. Waving her to a seat beside him on the sofa, he said,

"Perhaps it is partly London itself that makes you feel caged in—the tall buildings that cut off the horizon, the throngs of people wherever you go. An excursion into the countryside might refresh you—to Hampton Court, perhaps. One can go by boat down the Thames. The gardens will be almost deserted this time of year. And it has a maze. Find the center and you may rest there, breathing in the scent of fresh air and evergreens and feeling you are the only person on earth."

To his satisfaction, her face lit. "I shall ask Aunt Lillian if we may go."

"Let me know if she does not care to take you. I…" No, much as he would enjoy escorting her, he must not offer—even if his fiancée could be persuaded to make a party of it, which, Priscilla not being fond of the country, he doubted. "I can arrange an escort. Mr. Dixon or Lord Blanchard would be happy to squire you and Charis."

Head tilted, she studied him as he spoke. Suddenly self-conscious, he went silent.

To his surprise, Adam found himself feeling, not an intensification of desire, though the nearness of her still hummed in his veins, but an odd…wistfulness. How he would love to row with her down the river, watch her eyes light with pleasure at the extensive gardens, tease her through the maze. Sit with her at the center, content to watch her happiness. Happy to be with her.

Slamming his mind shut to the ramifications of that strange feeling, Adam was fumbling for something else to say when Miss Lambarth smiled—not the breath-stopping siren's smile, but a tender curve of the lips that squeezed his chest and made him want to cradle her in his arms.

"You are very kind," she said. "You will not say anything to Aunt Lillian about my—?"

"Heavens, no! That shall remain our secret."

"Thank you." Her serious mood passing, she chuckled. "I promise to try hard not to disturb your peace again."

He laughed with her, humor hardly easing the ache in his chest. "I believe I've heard that pledge before."

"Never fear! Soon enough, I shall leave for good and disturb you no longer. My lord," she said, and curtseyed.

After she exited, Adam ran a trembling hand through his dark hair. In Lambarth or in London, the thought of her in peril horrified him. Yet though he deplored her rashness, he could not help but admire her fearlessness. A girl who carried a knife and could use it! Lady Darnell would indeed have palpitations.

Nor could he resist reaching out to help when she confessed her need for solace.

It was good that she must leave soon. For, Lord save him, as he had the night she fled the ball and despite his fine words about sending her off with Dix or Nathan, *he* wanted to be the one to console and protect her.

Staring into the flickering flames on the hearth, Adam observed bleakly that reining in his lust was hard enough. Must he grapple also with a growing sense that she was a unique soul he hated to lose?

CHAPTER TWENTY

HELENA LEFT HER MEETING with Adam Darnell pensive and unsettled. The idea of leaving the city had been instantly appealing. Though she would prefer to go with Darnell, he'd quickly caught himself before making that offer, which was just as well. Miss Standish would doubtless put a damper on such an expedition, if she agreed to go at all.

Besides, Helena only wanted Adam's company if she might have him to herself, able to take his arm and stroll the pathways until they reached the center of the maze. Where, hidden away, she might draw close—and kiss him.

A flush of heat rose in her. No, she had better not claim his escort to Hampton Court. But though attraction had sizzled between them as fiercely as ever this afternoon, she'd also felt linked on a different, deeper level. The temptation to a touching of flesh was both intensified and enriched by a touching of minds.

She'd been amazed that Darnell seemed to comprehend her poorly articulated feelings of restlessness. Having discovered her secret excursion, once again he'd tried neither to bully nor intimidate, but to understand—with an empathy she had not experienced since her mother's flight.

Adam Darnell was almost bringing her to believe that men existed who could be not just desired, but admired and trusted. Admired, trusted—and loved, as she had loved her mother and now loved Aunt Lillian and Charis? If that were true…what would that mean to her plans for the future?

A swell of longing intensified the now familiar desire still spiraling in her belly.

But the only such man she'd met was Darnell, and he was spoken for. Having already several times examined the implications of that fact, she locked her roiling emotions away and forced her mind to focus on the most intriguing information she'd overheard outside White's.

Deciding to search out the truth of it, she went to Charis's chamber, where she found her friend still at her dressing table, absently combing her hair.

"What a slug-a-bed you've become!" Helena exclaimed with a smile, gesturing to the mantel clock.

"I haven't your energy, Helena! Though I noticed you weren't up to greet us when we returned last night."

Helena squelched a guilty pang at the reason for that omission. "Hurry, now! Your beaux will be calling soon."

Charis shrugged. "Charlbury and Lord Newsome will stop by, probably. Mr. Dixon, of course, but he comes to see you."

"And Lord Blanchard, I expect," Helena said, noting

how Charis looked quickly away, her fair skin coloring. So her friend was definitely not indifferent to Blanchard.

"Lord Blanchard comes to see you, too," Charis said.

"I hear he's hanging out for a wife. What do you think of him?" Helena asked.

Charis glanced up quickly, looking surprised and more than a little dismayed. "Would you consider his suit?"

"It isn't me that his eyes rest on when he sits in our parlor...but a lovely blond lady," Helena pointed out.

Charis dropped her eyes. "I admit I like him far better than any other young man I've met. But it doesn't matter. He *is* looking for a wife, and Adam has already warned me he must wed a rich one. I shall have but a thousand pounds. A man with Lord Blanchard's position and connections can do much better than that."

"He is in the diplomatic service and liable to spend much of his time abroad. Didn't you tell me you'd prefer to marry and settle at a snug country estate?"

"I do prefer Claygate to London. But...how exciting to travel in foreign lands! Such a vast responsibility to represent the interests of one's country abroad."

"Would *you* accept an offer from Lord Blanchard?"

"'Twould be like a dream come true," Charis admitted. "But 'tis impossible. Adam told me so weeks ago, when I first hinted I would like him to call. Why do you ask?"

Helena grinned. "No reason—except that I wish to

keep abreast of what will make my almost-sister happiest." Giving Charis a hug, she rose and headed for the door.

"I'm sure he would be willing to offer for *you,* if you gave him the least encouragement," Charis said with a cheerfulness that sounded forced.

Helena laughed. "Heavens, no! I'm merely the excuse that allows him to call so often. I expect if he thought for a moment I actually believed he was courting *me,* he would hire the next available transport and flee back to Vienna!"

While Charis disputed that assessment, Helena blew her friend a kiss and walked out. A rising excitement distracting her from her own unsettled emotions, she skipped to her room and penned a note, then summoned Dickon to deliver it and wait for an answer.

Her note found its recipient and generated an immediate reply. An hour after her talk with Charis, Helena sat at a table at Gunter's, Nell discreetly behind her. Moments later, Lord Blanchard rushed in.

Scarcely waiting to complete the usual greetings, he blurted, "Excuse me for being abrupt, but you said the matter was grave and involved Miss Darnell. Is she well?"

"I didn't mean to worry you," Helena replied, not at all sorry to have provoked that telling demonstration of concern. "Yes, she is quite well."

Blanchard exhaled a gusty sigh. "Thank the Lord. Then with what might I assist you in her regard?"

"Lord Blanchard, I fear I am also about to be rather abrupt. But I need to know if the…story I've heard of your deep regard for Miss Darnell has any truth."

For a moment Blanchard looked away. "I hope," he said at last, "I have not raised expectations that, sadly, circumstances do not permit me to satisfy. Though I have tried to maintain a proper distance, she…she is so enchanting, it is very difficult to pretend myself indifferent." He looked up suddenly, his eyes widening. "Pray, assure me I have not caused her any distress!"

Ignoring the question, Helena said, "Am I to understand, then, if a, um, distant relation were to settle a rather large sum upon Miss Darnell, you would like to know?"

He frowned. "But Adam assured me she would have no dowry but such funds as he could wrest from the estate."

"Yes, but what if it *happened* that Miss Darnell were to become the recipient of, say, fifteen thousand pounds?"

After staring at her, perplexed, a slow smile formed on his lips. "If she were dowered with a penny over ten thousand pounds, I should be the happiest man in England."

Helena smiled back. "I recommend you call on her tomorrow. I believe she may have interesting news." She rose and extended her hand. "Thank you for meeting me on such short notice, Lord Blanchard."

Blanchard seized her hand and kissed it fervently. "If you mean what I think you mean, Miss Lambarth, you are an angel and I will thank you to my dying breath."

Helena retrieved her hand. "You may thank me,

Lord Blanchard, by remembering, once you *possess* an angel, to treat her accordingly."

"I will worship her all my life!" he vowed as Helena curtseyed to his bow and bid him goodbye.

Highly satisfied with that interview, Helena proceeded to Mr. Pendenning's office. After a short wait, his clerk ushered her in.

"Miss Lambarth!" He took her hands and looked her up and down, smiling broadly. "How wonderful you look! I knew living with Lady Darnell would be good for you."

"You were right. She and Charis have become as dear to me as my mother." Better to say nothing of Lady Darnell's intriguing stepson, Helena thought, suppressing a sigh. "Speaking of Charis, I have finally decided what I wish to do with that unwanted inheritance from my father."

SHORTLY AFTER NOON the next day, Adam Darnell stared at the lawyer's note in his hand, too shocked to speak.

"It's true, then, isn't it?" Charis asked, her face radiant with excitement. "Adam, you will allow me to accept it, will you not? Lord Blanchard has just arrived, asking to speak with you. Helena told me he would call. Oh, please say it's true and you will give us your blessing!"

Numbly, Adam looked up. Of course he could not deny his sister's happiness—or his friend Blanchard's, for that matter. Not for so small a thing as his pride.

"Send Nathan in," he said.

Charis sprang up and seized him in a hug so tight

his neckcloth almost choked him. "Oh, best, most wonderful, most excellent of brothers!"

The smile on Nathan's face as he came in was almost as brilliant as the one worn by Adam's sister. "I expect you know why I've come."

"I knew you admired Charis, but I admit, I never expected a declaration."

"That was before a certain relative intervened. Cousin Cornwallis, I believe her name is? Or so Miss Lambarth just informed me."

"Cornwallis," indeed, Adam thought, recalling the location of Lambarth Castle. "What if there is no endowment?" he asked, trying to check his irrational anger.

Nathan's grin faded. After regarding Adam for a thoughtful moment, he shrugged. "So be it, then. I've come to realize a lifetime of happiness with someone you adore is worth far more than advancement in your career. Adam, have I your permission to ask Charis for her hand?"

Feeling a bit ashamed, he replied, "Of course, Nathan. I shall be proud to call you 'brother.' And by the way—the endowment, in the amount of fifteen thousand pounds, has already been deposited to my bank. Call upon me later and we shall set the lawyers to drawing up the settlements."

Blanchard's smile returned. "Charis *and* the dowry? 'Tis almost too wonderful to comprehend! Though I can understand your…disgruntlement, a little. A man has his pride. Suffice it to say, I shall always be very grateful to the eccentric nature of your distant connection, Miss Cornwallis, for choosing to bestow so generous a gift on her only living unmarried female relation."

"So those were…ah, yes, the rather unusual terms," Adam replied. "I appreciate your discretion. And I wish you both very happy."

Blanchard whacked him on the back. "We'll name the first boy after you, I promise!" he said, and hurried out.

Adam sat down and stared into the fire. A low-burning, proper fire now, not the obscene blaze of heat a certain young lady preferred. A young lady whose generosity he had to grudgingly admire, much as that largesse now chafed and embarrassed him.

At least it appeared the story of the fictitious Cousin Cornwallis would spare him having the whole world know that a slip of a girl had bestowed on the sister he was supposed to provide for the funds—and joy—he could not.

Just then the door was pushed ajar and that same dark-eyed lady beamed at him. "As if you hadn't already guessed, Charis and Lord Blanchard are now engaged. She sent me to ask you to join them in the parlor."

"Should I not first go down on my knees and humbly offer my thanks to 'Cousin Cornwallis'?" he asked, unable to keep the bitterness out of his voice.

Her smile dimmed. "Perhaps, but since from what I understand, that lady lives somewhere near the Irish Sea, 'twould rather delay your arrival in the parlor. I doubt that Charis wants to wait that long to share her joy. Besides, I believe Charis's joy is all the thanks Miss Cornwallis would require."

At least she didn't intend to rub his nose in her benevolence, which was some relief. Still stung, though, he replied, "I rather wish Cousin Cornwallis had mentioned something to me before dispensing her money so liberally, but tell Charis I shall be down directly."

Miss Lambarth stilled, her eyes scanning his face. "Why would you wish that?"

"Because as head of this family, 'tis *my* responsibility to protect my sister and assure her future!" he retorted savagely, furious that she did not understand what any girl with the least degree of breeding would have known. Of course, it would never have crossed the mind of a gently bred girl to intervene without consulting him in the first place—nor would such a girl possess resources in her own name she could draw upon. "You can't expect me to be truly grateful to be shown how poor a job I was doing."

"I didn't mean to embarrass you or flout your authority. Isn't it enough that Charis shall be able to marry where her heart is, without thought of fortune?"

"Of course I am gratified that she will be happy. If you will excuse me, ma'am, I will go tell her so." He rose from his chair, his illogical fury, resentment and chagrin untouched by her explanation.

"I am sorry you are angry. But I am not sorry about Charis's gift." As she stood aside to let him pass, she added fiercely, "If I were meek and conventional and biddable, I'd be dead."

Even this reference to the indignities she'd suffered

caused him to hesitate but momentarily. For once, fury burned hotter than attraction. Brushing past without any desire to touch her—unless it be to wring her neck—Adam stormed down to the parlor.

The raptures of his sister and her new fiancé, so occupied in gazing and smiling at each other it soured his stomach, led Adam to take his leave as soon as possible.

At first he thought to go to his club. But realizing that the glad tidings would soon be out and not in a humor to deal with speculation over his sister's great good fortune, Adam decided instead to visit Miss Standish.

She would appreciate hearing about the betrothal before some gossip mentioned it—and would never suspect the true origin of his sister's bequest, assuming as she would that Adam had charge of any matter concerning his family.

To his smarting pride, that conventional turn of mind suddenly seemed very appealing.

ADAM GREETED PRISCILLA in her parlor with more enthusiasm than he had for some time. He was also gratified when she herself suggested a stroll in the garden, where she allowed him several thorough kisses.

"So, we are to have some spontaneity after all?" he teased, tracing a finger on her reddened lips.

"Perhaps," she replied. "My friend Lady Cordelia says that sometimes a lady must relax her own standards when 'tis necessary to…to fight fire with fire."

Adam didn't wish to ask to what she might be referring. "You can incite quite a blaze all by yourself," he responded, dropping another kiss on her forehead.

"You seemed rather disturbed when you arrived, despite the wonderful news about Miss Darnell," Priscilla said, taking his arm as they strolled down the garden path. "Is something distressing you, Adam? Can I help?"

How nice to have a lady inquire what *he* wanted, instead of taking matters into her own hands, Adam thought, still disgruntled. However, his fiancée did not like Miss Lambarth, and though at the moment he was irritated with her, he didn't think it wise to admit that to Priscilla.

"A small matter," he said. As if fifteen thousand pounds were small! "If I seemed…distracted, I apologize."

"You never need do that! I am concerned by anything that concerns you. 'Tis my role now to ease your burdens—as much as a mere female can, of course."

He could not help but appreciate that selfless avowal. "I hope you shall let me carry your burdens, too."

"I shall endeavor not to add to yours! I imagine overseeing Miss Lambarth is trying enough. Such a…a headstrong girl. Excuse me, but I must feel that to be dangerous trait, given her sad lack of proper upbringing."

If she only knew. "It can be vexing," he admitted. "I'm only a man, hardly an expert on managing females, yet with Lady Darnell's nerves so delicate, I hesitate to consult her even when I sometimes feel at a loss."

It was a great relief, he found, to express some of his frustration. Which he'd been unable to voice to his stepmother without spilling details that would only upset her, nor to Charis, who was far too much Miss Lambarth's champion ever to admit any fault in her.

"As if you did not have enough responsibilities without having to supervise so unruly a girl! Francis tells me she recently bought a most unsuitable riding hack—a horse Randall sold as being completely unreliable."

"Yes, she managed to coax Bennett Dixon, whose judgment I would have thought more sound, into bidding on the horse for her. Not learning of the deal until it was already complete, and as I must admit she *is* a good enough rider to control the beast, I did not countermand it."

"She should have consulted you, not Mr. Dixon!"

That glowing affirmation was balm to his injured sensibilities. At least his fiancée respected his position as head of the family and trusted his ability to manage its affairs. "'Tis done now, so I will say no more."

"I hope that is the last of her wild starts!"

For a moment he saw Helena again in his mind's eye, galloping away on the fractious black. Shaking his head, he sighed. "Even that horse wasn't as bad as—"

Catching himself with a start, he closed his lips. As satisfying as it had been to air his displeasure, this story would be better kept to himself.

"There was worse?"

"Nothing, really. I should not have mentioned it."

She patted his arm. "Dear Adam! I know you don't wish to distress Lady Darnell with your worries, but I am made of much sterner stuff. I would be honored to receive your confidences and provide you with what I flatter myself to be a sensible female's perspective."

Now he really was in the basket. Searching rather desperately for an excuse Priscilla might accept, he said, "'Tis a matter of great delicacy I'd rather not mention."

His luck was out. Looking wounded, Priscilla removed her hand from his. "I see. I had thought that as I am soon to be your wife, you would feel you could trust me, but I see I was mistaken. Excuse me for my effrontery."

"It's not that I don't—" he began.

"Please, Adam, you needn't explain. If you do not wish to consult me, that is your choice entirely." She turned away from him, the picture of injured dignity.

Grinding his teeth at his stupidity in stumbling into this dilemma, Adam pondered what to do next. After Priscilla's tender declaration of concern, he was loath to hurt her feelings, as he obviously had just now. She *was* to be his wife, after all. And with her punctilious standards of behavior, surely she wouldn't wish any word of Miss Lambarth's shocking adventure to escape, tarring as it must the family of which Priscilla would soon be a part.

Perhaps he could get by relating just a bit of the story. "If you are sure you don't mind my imposing. I know I can count on your discretion in not repeating a syllable, even to your mother."

Looking mollified, Miss Standish glanced back at him. "Nothing I can do for you would ever be an imposition."

He took a deep breath. "'Tis just that I discovered Miss Lambarth has…slipped out at night to explore the city."

Priscilla gasped and her eyes widened. "Slipped out? Without a proper chaperone, you mean? But how…how hoydenish to go about with—what, only a footman? What if someone had recognized her—or the Darnell livery?"

"She didn't take a livried servant. And I don't think she'd be recognized."

"As distinctively as she dresses, and her so tall? I would not be so confident. Oh, how awful! No wonder you were so upset. Only think of poor Lady Darnell's distress if someone saw the girl and reported back to her!"

"I'm certain there's little likelihood of that."

"How can you be certain? Did she have the foresight to go out cloaked and masked?"

"Ah, no. But she was…disguised."

Miss Standish stared at him. "Disguised? As…as a servant? Oh, Adam, that's even worse!"

"No, no, she was disguised as a lad. I'd be amazed if anyone managed to recognize her."

Priscilla's eyes widened ever more. "She went out into the city…dressed in *breeches?*"

Wishing now he had followed his first instinct and gone to his club, Adam nodded. "You understand why I should not wish a word of this breathed to anyone."

"Of course not! 'Tis atrocious behavior, even for one as unprinci—unschooled as Miss Lambarth. My papa would lock me in my room on bread and water for such a stunt!"

Adam recalled Helena's description of being forced into the blackness of the priest hole. "I rather think being restrained for too much of her life is what led her to do this in the first place," he replied grimly.

"But you can't mean to let her go unpunished after such a flagrant breach of decorum."

"I can hardly punish her severely without telling Lady Darnell the reason. Something, I'm sure you'll agree, I wish to avoid."

"Poor lady! She'd have an attack of the vapors at least! But you must do something to show the girl that such behavior cannot be tolerated, or sooner or later, she will drag the family into a scandal that cannot be hidden."

"Now, Priscilla, I've given her enough of a scold that I think she is suitably chastened."

"And I think you are much too indulgent with her, Adam. You must not let her take advantage of your kindness and good nature—as she did the night of Mrs. Cowper's ball, dragging you away on some ridiculous pretext."

"'Twas no pretext. We already discussed this, my dear. I thought you understood."

"I understood how humiliating it was to be left without an escort for half the evening while my fiancé went off with another woman—and her dressed like…like some foreign hussy!" Priscilla cried.

Though he'd never flinched on the battlefield, Adam now felt the strongest desire to cut and run. How had the discussion gotten so out of hand?

Wanting urgently to end it, he said, "Priscilla, calm yourself. Such…vehemence isn't like you."

Miss Standish exhaled a shuddering breath. After a moment of uneasy silence, she said, "Pray excuse me for allowing my…my feelings to run away with me. Shall we go in now? Mama will be wondering what has become of us."

"By all means, my dear," Adam said, wondering the same thing himself.

And he had thought the artillery barrage at Waterloo daunting. Silently wishing a pox on all women—and men foolhardy enough to confide in them—Adam led his fiancée out of the garden.

THE FOLLOWING MORNING, after checking his cravat one more time, Adam descended to the breakfast parlor with a small package in his hands. After extracting himself from the inquisition Miss Standish's mother had given him about his sister's unexpected bequest, the less probing questions and more sincere congratulations offered him when he'd finally reached his club had helped soothe his disgruntlement over Miss Lambarth's conduct. The masculine camaraderie and several good bottles of claret, however, had not settled his unease over discovering that Priscilla held Miss Lambarth in much greater aversion than he'd thought.

Their nasty quarrel had also shocked him into realizing that, while claiming to bow to his authority, Priscilla was probably trying to manipulate him by her rationed kisses, her pouts—and her anger when he did not accept her advice. There was something to be said for Miss Lambarth's directness and lack of feminine wiles.

He'd also had time to ponder why he'd been so unreasonably incensed by Helena's gift. Her usurping of his authority and then acting without consulting him would have irritated under any circumstances, but should not have wounded him as they had.

Part of his anger, he'd decided, had been the chagrin of discovering that an outsider had realized before he did that Charis's happiness depended on wedding Blanchard. He should have been the one to make that union happen.

More muddled were his wildly mixed feelings about having hurtled into the breach to offer for Priscilla. He'd needed to repair the family fortunes, of course, but in large part his haste had been motivated by the desire to stabilize their finances and to provide a dowry for Charis. So that she would not have to consider wealth when choosing her life's partner.

Miss Lambarth's bequest had rendered that sacrifice unnecessary. Would he have taken a different a path, had *he* been free to choose? For though it shamed him to admit it, another part of his anger had been a keen envy of the joy so evident on the faces of Blanchard and his sister—a joy he'd not felt at any time during his own engagement.

Finally, he'd allowed injured pride and the vanity fanned by Priscilla's soothing words to lead him into betraying Miss Lambarth's trust. For that indiscretion, he was even more ashamed. And though the small gift he'd found for her was hardly recompense for so grievous an error, it helped to assuage his guilty conscience a little.

The excited chatter emanating from the breakfast parlor indicated that his sister and stepmother must be discussing wedding plans. Not hearing Miss Lambarth's huskier tones and anxious to get the apology over with, he was relieved as he entered to spy her by the sideboard.

Elegant this time in a riding habit of sapphire velvet, she was sipping coffee and smiling at the ladies. After greeting everyone, he quickly approached her.

She started to move away as he walked up. He stayed her with a touch to her elbow—a touch that seared as if his fingertips had skimmed bare flesh instead of cloth.

Trying not to let that contact distract him, he said in a low voice, "Pray let me apologize for my hasty words yesterday! 'Twas stupid pride on my part. Your gift was discreetly done and has guaranteed the happiness of my beloved sister. Thank you again."

To his surprise, she squeezed the hand that had touched her elbow, sending another shimmer of sensation through him. "Let me apologize in return. Though it seems obvious now, it never occurred to me to consult you." She smiled slightly. "My previous experience has not led me to confer with anyone before taking action…nor instilled in me the belief that the head of the household's first thought is the happiness of those in his charge. I'm sorry if I embarrassed you."

His heart lightening, he was about to recommend they put the matter behind them when Lady Darnell looked over. "Adam, what have you in your hand? An engagement gift?"

"No, 'tis a trifle for Miss Lambarth. After one of our previous discussions, I thought she might enjoy it."

Lady Darnell clapped her hands. "Oh, famous! Open it at once, Helena!"

Adam stood watching as, after a surprised glance at him, she removed the tissue and stared down at items.

"'Tis a set of drawing chalks," he explained.

"Conte and charcoal. How perfect!" Charis exclaimed. "Now she shall truly be able to display her talent."

Wonder in her eyes, Helena looked up at Adam. "I hardly know what to say."

"'Thank you' should suffice," Charis said with a giggle. "Have you never had a present before?"

Miss Lambarth's gaze wandered to the window and, to Adam's dismay, tears shimmered in her dark lashes. "Just before she…left, Mama gave me a brightly colored parrot. Father turned it loose in the garden. A hawk got it."

While Charis and Lady Darnell gasped, she turned to offer Adam the smile that transformed her face from arresting to breathtaking. "'Thank you' is paltry, but it shall have to do until I can think of something better."

"Your enjoyment—and the enjoyment your sketches will give us all—is thanks enough," Adam replied, the glow of her gratitude warming him right to his toes.

Recovering her composure, his sister said, "Helena, will you accompany Bellemere and me to shop for fabric this morning? If my wedding clothes are to be ready before Nathan must return to Vienna, we have to begin at once!"

"Give me a few moments to change into something more suitable." Wrapping the chalks back in their paper, she raised shining eyes to Adam. "Thank you again, Darnell."

Absurdly pleased to have made her happy, he bowed as she walked out. "Your servant, Miss Lambarth."

After the other ladies left, Adam proceeded to the library. Settling behind the desk, he smiled at the sight of Miss Lambarth's book by the sofa. How glad he was to have made peace between them.

He supposed he should call on Priscilla to try to smooth over *their* disagreement. But, deciding to put off what would probably be an uncomfortable meeting, he pulled out his account ledgers. He was reading through a report from his steward when a feminine scream split the air.

Charis's scream.

Dropping the paper and knocking his chair out of the way, he bolted up the stairs.

CHAPTER TWENTY-ONE

SHOCKED BY CHARIS'S scream into dropping the stick of charcoal with which she'd been experimenting, Helena looked back to see the girl standing on the threshold of her chamber.

"Oh, Helena!" Charis whispered. "Your back!"

Helena jerked her half-buttoned dressing gown up over her shoulders. "I'm sorry! I was about to change, but—"

At that moment Lord Darnell charged through the open door. "Charis, what is wrong?"

She turned to her brother and burst into tears.

Cursing silently as Darnell pulled his sister into his arms, Helena felt the accusing look he threw her over the girl's shoulder almost like a blow. "Nell, help Lord Darnell carry Miss Charis to her chamber," she ordered curtly. Sick at heart, she picked the broken charcoal off the floor and sat back down.

A few moments later the knock she'd been expecting sounded at her door and she bid Darnell enter.

"What the devil was that about?" he demanded. "I could get nothing sensible out of Charis."

Slowly, Helena rose from her chair. Unbuttoning the

top fastenings of the dressing gown and lowering it to expose her shoulders, she turned and let him see the scars.

Swiveling to face him again, she recoiled at the shock and revulsion on his face. "I expect you understand better now why I insisted on hiring a maid out of a workhouse. And on wearing fashions that cover me to the chin."

When still he said nothing, she added harshly, "Is it not standard practice among the best families for erring daughters to be horsewhipped?"

"It is...unspeakable," he said, horror in his voice.

Her defiant facade beginning to crack under his scrutiny, she fought back tears and whispered, "Then let us speak no more of it." Fingers trembling now, she turned away and buttoned the dressing gown up to her chin. When she looked back again, Darnell was gone.

AGHAST AT HAVING DISTRESSED CHARIS and unable to deal with explaining the incident to Aunt Lillian, as soon as Nell returned, Helena bade the girl assist her into a promenade gown and sent the maid to summon a hackney. She would go to Hatchards, stroll in the park while it was still unoccupied, mayhap visit the British Museum.

Lord Blanchard was to fetch Charis and Aunt Lillian to dine with his family this evening, an event Helena felt would guarantee Charis recovered from her shock. Needing time to think what she should do next before encountering any of the family again, Helena did not plan to return to St. James Square until they had all left for the evening.

But when, hours later, she wearily climbed the stairs to the library, she found Adam Darnell sitting within.

Stopping short, she said, "Darnell! I was certain you would have already gone out. Excuse me for intruding."

Seeing again in memory his expression of distaste and horror, she wanted only to remove herself from his presence. But as she curtseyed and backed away, he rose.

"Please, Miss Lambarth, don't go! I promised Charis I would not leave until I had spoken to you."

Probably to demand she quit the house before the ladies returned, Helena thought. At least, ever honorable, he had the courtesy to deliver that order to her face.

Thinking to spare him what must be an unpleasant duty, she said quickly, "You needn't say anything! I feel terrible about the…incident this morning. Please believe I never wished to distress any of you."

Waving him to silence when he opened his lips to reply, she continued, "Having heard that avowal several times already, I hardly expect you to believe it. Suffice it to say, I've caused enough commotion in your household. I've initiated plans to move elsewhere as soon as Mr. Pendenning can obtain a suitable house. If…if you prefer that I leave immediately, I shall find a hotel—"

"Miss Lambarth!" Darnell exclaimed, finally cutting her off. Through the mist of moisture suddenly clouding her eyes, it appeared he gestured toward the sofa.

"Come warm yourself by the fire. You really must cease this business of threatening to leave us."

While he stood watching, Helena numbly took a seat.

"First, let me offer you an apology from Charis and myself. Our reactions cannot help but have wounded you—and you obviously have been wounded enough."

The smile she tried to give him wobbled badly. "Ah, but I was a very disobedient child."

"Were you the devil's spawn himself, it would not excuse such treatment!" he spat out.

"What did you tell Aunt Lillian?"

"You needn't worry you've upset her. Charis, clever girl, told her she'd been pierced in a, ah, sensitive place by a pin from her gown. By the way, as soon as she recovered, she rushed back to your room, only to find you already departed. She charged me to beg you to remain with us so we might ensure no one ever harms you again."

That expression of concern when she'd been expecting repudiation weakened Helena's tenuous control over her emotions. "You—you are all…so kind," she murmured, her throat aching with unshed tears.

Shaking his head, Darnell paced to the hearth before looking back at her. "I knew that day at the lawyer's office that you had suffered. But I never imagined… No wonder your mother ran away! My God, how did you survive?"

"The beatings didn't start until after she left—when Father discovered I'd escaped after he'd locked me in. I expect he wanted to frighten me into never trying again, though he knew 'twas unnecessary. The townspeople, believing me mad, had already returned me to him the one time I made it into the village."

"He did stop, though. Those scars…were not recent."

Helena smiled grimly. "I think he drove me mad in truth, a little. The last time he beat me, I grabbed the whip, determined to bear no more. Though it nearly took my thumb off, I held on, then jerked it free with my good hand. I warned him if he ever came at me again, I would use it to fight back." She looked down at her damaged hand. "It healed badly, as you can see. If it hadn't been for Mad Sally and her potions, I expect I would have died."

Wonderment filled his eyes as he shook his head. "You amazing girl! Did no one suspect? No visiting relations?"

"No relations ever visited. Perhaps you understand why, when you first met me, I had little use for family."

"I hope you know now you have one that loves you."

Helena swallowed hard. "Thank you." Save upon hearing of her mother's death, she could not recall when she'd last wept. But despite her stern command to desist, one of the drops brimming at the corners of her eyes insisted on welling up and sliding down her cheek.

Though she turned her face away, Darnell came over to sit beside her. "Ah, Helena, don't cry," he said softly.

All her life she'd met punishment and anger with defiance. But hearing her name on Darnell's lips for the first time, so tender it sounded like a caress, tore at the defenses she'd erected to survive loneliness and abuse. To her dismay, that first tear was joined by another and another.

And then, without her knowing quite how it happened, she was in his arms, cradled gently against his chest. His hand stroking the back of her neck, he held her until she brought the tears under control and straightened.

"Forgive me," she began, mortified at her weakness.

He brushed a thumb against her cheek. "It hurts my heart to think of what you've suffered. Can you trust me enough to come to me in future, if you should ever need help? You don't have to be alone any more, Helena."

She looked up into the green eyes gazing down at her, her chest tightening at the strength and goodness and honor she saw there. "Yes, Adam, I will trust you."

As she watched, his eyes changed, their color deepening. She let her lashes drift shut as he tipped up her chin. The gentle brush of his lips against hers was as arousing as she'd imagined, yet so piercingly sweet her chest expanded so she could scarcely breathe. She had desired him before, but this feeling was somehow…different. Larger in scope, more intense. *More.*

At last he drew away, easing her back against the cushions. "Remember, you're not alone." After once again brushing her cheek with his fingertip, he walked out.

You're not alone…. Her mother had been so wise, pushing her to seek out this sense of acceptance and belonging. She now had a family who had come to love her as she loved them. And Darnell—*Adam*—for whom she felt admiration, affection and a desire that made her long for his presence and his touch.

Adam, with whom she feared she had fallen in love.

AFTER DRAGGING A GROOM OUT early the next morning to accompany her on a gallop before it was scarcely light, Helena hurried back so she might visit Charis. Despite Adam's reassuring words, she wanted to see her friend alone, to make sure all was right between them before they met with Lady Darnell at breakfast.

She also wanted to question Charis about Adam's engagement. Despite indulging in a few midnight fantasies of how wonderful it might be to pursue passion and tenderness in his arms, neither admitting her love for Adam nor the fond regard he'd avowed for her altered her opinion on marriage for herself.

In the prosaic light of day, Adam's kindness last night only emphasized the enormous gulf between the character of a true gentleman and the male who had sired her, making her all the more resolved never to risk passing his bad blood to another generation.

Blood would tell, Mad Sally had always said. Should she somehow become an honorable man's wife—Adam's wife—how could she subject them both to the horror of watching a child grow up to become what her father had been?

She would deny herself passion—and love—a thousand times over before she would allow that to happen.

In addition, her experience since arriving in London had demonstrated how unprepared she was to become the wife of any man from Adam's world—unless he wanted to abandon Society for as wild and isolated a place as Lambarth Castle. Both Adam's home here in London and his country estate at Claygate required a mistress capable of directing a large household and a hostess skilled at entertaining.

Adam had promised to protect Helena. Should she not return the favor? If she had to endure seeing him wed another, it seemed only right to try to insure he had at least a chance for happiness. Helena wasn't sure that Miss Standish, despite her other qualifications, possessed the sweetness of character to promise him that.

As soon as she entered her friend's chamber, Charis dismissed her maid and came over to seize Helena in an embrace. After mutual apologies and a few tears from Charis, her friend poured them each some chocolate and invited Helena to sit while she finished her toilette.

"You still look radiant!" Helena said. "The dinner with Lord Blanchard's parents was a success?"

"Yes, they gave us their heartfelt blessing."

"Then they are most perceptive," Helena said with a smile. "I cannot help but notice, though, that Adam does not seem nearly as excited about his upcoming nuptials as you and Lord Blanchard did yesterday. Or perhaps he is not given to demonstrations of affection?"

Charis sighed and set down her hairbrush. "No,

Adam is usually quite affectionate. I must admit, I had hoped his inclination might lead in a different direction—but before that could happen, he offered for Priscilla. I expressed my reservations to him when he first informed me of the match. He replied that he had a high regard for Miss Standish that would deepen over time. Which is what continues to trouble me."

"In what way?" Helena asked.

"I've not warmed to her—how could I, when she takes every opportunity to snipe at you? But more important, after watching them carefully on many occasions, I can detect no evidence of increasing warmth between *them*. I know she must care for Adam, but I worry that so reserved and critical a girl will never make him happy."

Secretly glad Charis shared her opinion of Adam's fiancée, Helena said, "If affection has not developed as he'd hoped, why not admit he made a mistake and break the engagement? It seems idiotish to me to go forward with a marriage that shows so few signs of succeeding."

"You don't understand. The engagement has been publicly feted at any number of balls and routs. Should Adam terminate it, Miss Standish would be humiliated, her chances of contracting another alliance severely damaged. 'Twould also be a stain on Adam's honor to break his word. Were she twice as shrewish and cold, he would not do it."

"Even if she will make his life a misery?" Helena asked, aghast to find Society's rules so inflexible.

Charis sighed again. "Since nothing can be done

now to free him, I can only hope that once he gets her away from the influence of her insufferable mother and that friend of hers, Lady Cordelia, Priscilla will display more of the character that first attracted him."

"You're certain nothing can be done?" Helena asked. Now that Charis had confirmed her suspicions, everything within her rebelled at the idea of abandoning Adam to the emotional desert of a marriage to Priscilla.

"Not unless Miss Standish changes her mind. To jilt a gentleman, though frowned upon, is forgivable. But let us not speak any more of Adam being unhappy, which is far too distressing! I trust a merciful Providence will find some way to make things right. Come, shall we go down?"

Deeply disturbed, after arranging instead to meet the ladies once she'd changed out of her habit, Helena went to her room. It appeared, she mused as Nell helped her into a morning gown, she would have to abandon her vague plan for using the attraction between them to try to induce Adam to break his engagement. Though she couldn't imagine a man like her father expending a moment's thought about humiliating Miss Standish or staining his own honor, the Adam Darnell she loved would do neither.

If, at least at the moment, she could think of no honorable way to prevent the match, she would have to try to tolerate Miss Standish with as good a grace as possible. Despite the girl's continued hostility.

A resolution which, she suddenly realized, she would have to put into practice immediately. Yesterday's tumult had made her forget until this moment that she would encounter Miss Standish on two occasions today.

The first meeting had been scheduled two days ago, when the Darnell ladies called on Princess Esterhazy and found Miss Standish and her mother also present. To Helena's surprise, Miss Standish had made her way through a knot of Helena's admirers to her side.

Entering the conversation during a pause in the entreaties of the gentlemen trying to extract Helena's agreement to race her black against them, Miss Standish said, "I've heard so much about your horse, Miss Lambarth! What a pity he is so unsteady you cannot ride him during the promenade hour, so we might all admire your skill."

"I believe Pegasus could be induced to behave himself even then," Helena replied, keeping her tone cordial with an effort. "But I prefer a gallop to the slow pace one must maintain in the park in the afternoon."

"I agree! Schooling a horse to a walk is much more difficult than giving him his head," Miss Standish replied.

Though Adam's fiancée was entitled to her views, Helena couldn't help but think her remarks were more an attempt to disparage Helena than a statement of opinion.

Before she could reply, one of the gentlemen hooted and said, "Well, Miss Lambarth, that sounded like a challenge! Why not ride Pegasus in the park and show just how well you can manage him?"

"Miss Lambarth, if you think it possible, I would be

delighted if you could ride with my cousin Francis when Darnell next drives me to the park. With you disdaining so many social events, I haven't had much opportunity to get to know you better. Darnell speaks so highly of you."

Seeing no polite way out of it, she'd reluctantly agreed, and the outing had been set for this afternoon, prior to the Darnells' dinner at the Standish mansion—another event Helena did not anticipate with much enthusiasm.

At least Mr. Dixon had promised to lend his presence to the first excursion. Since at the most recent musicale she'd attended, she'd been compelled to rake her nails over the hand Francis Standish had placed on her derrière, she was glad of any company that spared her having to give her full attention to Miss Standish's odious cousin.

So that afternoon, gowned in her favorite scarlet habit, Helena met Mr. Dixon and proceeded to Hyde Park a bit in advance of the fashionable hour, that they might run the horses before she would have to confine Pegasus—and herself—to the boredom of a walk. They'd completed one full circuit of the park before she spied their party.

Sighing, Helena put on a smile and slowed Pegasus to the pace of the Standish landau.

During the general greetings, she could not keep herself from looking at Adam—or feeling the rush of awareness his presence always triggered, deepened now by an intense swell of affection. He smiled back, his eyes warming, until Miss Standish, glancing in the direction of his gaze, tapped his sleeve to reclaim his attention.

Affection changed to an ache as she watched them, trying to stifle again the sadness that his handsome countenance and sterling character were to be bestowed on Priscilla Standish. A sharp, venomous irritation Helena feared must be jealousy deepened her regret.

So distracted was she by this tangle of emotions that when Mr. Dixon excused himself to ride on and speak with a friend and Francis Standish suggested they dismount and walk apace with the carriage, she absently agreed.

"Well, Miss Lambarth, I must admit I'm impressed," Priscilla said, reluctance in her tone. "Your Pegasus appears better behaved than I was led to believe. Or did you have a gallop around the park to tire him first?"

More amused than annoyed now by the girl's continual attempts to belittle her, Helena said evenly, "We cantered one circuit around the park, but he is still vigorous."

"I'm sure he is," Francis said, leaning close to Helena as he stroked Pegasus's neck. "We gentlemen do so appreciate a passionate creature," he murmured, so near she felt the warmth of his breath against her ear.

While Helena stepped away, wishing she might remount and catch up to Mr. Dixon, Adam sent Priscilla's cousin a warning look, to which he smiled blandly.

"Won't you both join us in the carriage?" Priscilla

asked. "You can tie your horses behind. We could converse more easily—don't you agree, Adam?" she said, making a show of tucking her hand under his.

The cozy familiarity of that gesture made Helena want to snatch Adam's arm away. Under no circumstances did she wish to sit opposite the couple while Priscilla demonstrated her ownership of Adam—if such were her intent. Neither did Helena trust her restive mount to behave if tied close to another horse with no rider in control.

"Thank you, but Pegasus is unlikely to trail us like a docile pony," she said at last. "And I do prefer to ride."

"Yet I understand you intend to buy a carriage," Priscilla said. "Surely not a high perch phaeton, as I've heard! Though challenging enough to show off a gentleman's skill, Francis tells me controlling one would take more strength than a *lady* could hope to possess."

Meaning, Helena thought, that if she chose a phaeton, she must be both ill-bred and a show-off. But before she could master her irritation to frame some innocuous response, to her surprise, Adam pulled his hand from under Priscilla's and frowned at his fiancée.

"Though it would not, as a general rule, be advisable for a female to attempt driving one, a lady who possessed sufficient expertise should have no more trouble with a phaeton than she would handling a curricle or a gig—which, Miss Lambarth, I believe you once mentioned you used to tool about in quite competently."

Warmed by Adam's praise—and the flash of disapproval in Priscilla's eyes at Adam's defense of her— Helena said, "Yes, I drove often as a child. However,

Miss Standish, I do intend to take instruction before I attempt a phaeton."

"So intrepid a rider as Miss Lambarth must be fretting herself to flinders, poking along as we are," Francis interjected. "What say you, Miss Lambarth? Shall we take the side trail up ahead and let the horses trot?"

As loath as Helena was to accept the escort of Francis Standish, even on horseback, she was hardly happier to be trapped here while Priscilla tossed little barbs at her—annoying Helena and disturbing Adam.

Before Helena could reply, Miss Standish said, "Miss Lambarth has already admitted Pegasus is not docile enough to be trotted now that the park is crowded, Francis. If she dare not tie him behind, 'tis wiser that you walk the horses and keep pace with us."

Enough, Helena thought, her small store of patience exhausted. Crowd or no, she was confident she and Pegasus would be able to outride Francis Standish and circle back to find Mr. Dixon. To avoid looking at Adam, whose quelling gaze directed at Standish a few moments ago seemed to indicate Adam didn't consider the man a very trustworthy escort, she turned to Priscilla's cousin. "Yes, Mr. Standish, I should like to ride ahead," she replied, confident she would not suffer his company for long.

She ignored the leg up offered her by the smirking Francis, electing instead a groom's assistance. Anxious to get away, she vaulted into the saddle, Pegasus sidestepping and snorting as she shifted her weight against the pommel. She'd scarcely gathered the reins in hand when he reared up, neighing loudly, and exploded into a gallop.

CHAPTER TWENTY-TWO

WITH PEGASUS NEIGHING and bucking as if possessed by demons, for the first few seconds Helena devoted all her attention to maintaining her seat. Once sure of her balance, she leaned low over her mount, talking into his ear to try to soothe him while she used reins and heels to slow his flight.

She'd just managed to get him under control when she heard hoofbeats thundering behind her. Worried the approaching horse might cause Pegasus to panic again, she half-turned to wave the rider off—and saw it was Mr. Dixon.

"We're all right!" she called. "Keep your distance."

He slowed his mount to close the gap between them at a more gradual pace. "Are you injured?" he demanded.

"No, I'm quite unharmed."

"Thank heavens! Did Pegasus graze a branch when he bolted past that last tree? He's bleeding."

"I don't think so," Helena said, concerned. As soon as her horse, blowing and sidling, slowed to a walk, Helena jumped down. "Where?"

"There—" Mr. Dixon gestured, dismounting and

coming to take her reins "—at the corner of the saddle blanket."

Still murmuring to the horse, Helena gently ran a hand up under the blanket, then gasped as she pricked a finger.

"Hold him still!" she commanded. Working the edge of the blanket free, she pulled it up to reveal the wound—and the large, wicked-looking thorn at its center.

After ripping the ruffle from her cuff, carefully she pulled the thorn free, wiped the blood from her horse's flank and wedged the linen strip back under the blanket against the still-oozing wound.

She turned to see Dixon frowning. "No wonder the animal bolted. I don't recall riding through any briar patches on our way here, so someone must have inserted that thorn intentionally. As pranks go, I don't find it very funny."

Helena heard more hoofbeats approaching and looked up. Only then did she notice that on the crowded carriage path a hundred yards away, all traffic had halted. Ladies and gentlemen leaned from their carriages, staring and gesturing, while several riders had set off across the field toward them. To her shock, she realized that the rider now closest to them was Adam, apparently on a borrowed mount.

"I see we've provided quite a spectacle," she said dryly. "Though not as amusing as it might have been had Pegasus managed to unseat me."

"Amusing?" Dixon retorted. "You might have been killed! If I ever get my hands on—"

Just then Adam reached them, reining in his horse and leaping down from the saddle. "Please, say nothing!" Helena said to Dixon in an urgent undertone. "Let me handle this in my own way."

He had only time to give her a reluctant nod before Adam ran over and grabbed her by the shoulders. "Are you all right?" he demanded urgently, fear and anger in his voice as he looked her up and down. "The devil take that horse! If I had a pistol, I'd shoot him where he stands."

"I'm unharmed, so you mustn't malign poor Pegasus. But I don't wish to ride him home." And compound the injury the animal had already suffered, she added silently.

"I should think not! A groom will see to him. Come back in the carriage with us. Miss Standish will be relieved to see that you've sustained no injury."

I'll just bet she will, Helena thought, resolved to walk rather than share a carriage with Adam and Priscilla. "Can I prevail upon you to lead Pegasus home, Mr. Dixon?" she asked. "You will know what to tell Johnson when you get him to the stables."

"I will indeed, Miss Lambarth," Dixon said grimly.

Several other riders reached them then, exclaiming and offering assistance. After declining them all with thanks, Helena felt a guilty pleasure at allowing an insistent Adam to take her arm while Mr. Dixon followed with the horses.

Far too soon, they reached the carriage and Adam let her go. "Miss Lambarth, are you unhurt?" Miss Standish cried. "Adam, help her in! She has had such a fright! I was near to fainting myself, just watching."

Anger flamed in Helena that someone had callously injured her horse in an attempt to embarrass her—perhaps this girl. But though Helena now suspected the invitation to the park had been offered in the hope of putting her riding skills to the blush, unless Miss Standish were a better actress than Helena could imagine, the girl's pale face and trembling lips argued that she had no role in arranging *this* part of the adventure.

Helena had a sudden memory of Francis Standish leaning over to pat Pegasus. He had been close enough to insert the thorn, which would then have rested harmlessly beneath the saddle blanket until she'd remounted, driving it into Pegasus's tender side.

Francis Standish, who was nowhere to be seen. Was this how he'd decided to repay her for rebuffing his insolent advances the other night? Though she couldn't prove he was responsible, neither could she imagine any other way a thorn could have gotten where it had. She would have to think carefully about a suitable retribution.

"I am fine," she assured Priscilla. "Nor would I wish to soil your gown, riding with you in all my dirt. Mr. Dixon, would you summon me a hackney?"

"Yes, and follow you home."

To her surprise—and delight—with his fiancée and the interested crowd still looking on, Adam reclaimed her arm. "I shall escort Miss Lambarth to the hackney and return in a moment, Priscilla."

"Really, Adam, I'm sure Mr. Dixon can—"

"Miss Lambarth is my responsibility," Adam said curtly, cutting her off.

Color rose in Miss Standish's cheeks. "You might see to your cravat before you return, then," she said stiffly. "You're looking most untidy."

As Adam tucked her hand firmly under his arm, Helena savored his solicitude as much as his touch. After she'd said her good-byes, he led her away.

Once they had distanced themselves from the crowd, however, he grasped her hand to stop her. "Are you sure you're all right? There's blood on your cuff."

"It isn't mine."

"You're certain?" When she nodded, he exhaled an explosive breath. "Praise Heaven! But what a fright you gave me! I thought you were going to…" He swallowed hard.

"But I didn't," she said softly, loving the feel of her fingers entwined with his and compelled by the tingling force between them to look up into his eyes.

Gazing back just as intently, Adam lifted his free hand to her face, as if to stroke her cheek. Even as her eyes drifted shut, anticipating his touch, he stopped, clenched his fingers into a fist and thrust his arm back at his side. With a small sigh, he urged her forward.

Disappointed to have the moment cut short, Helena walked silently beside Adam to the hackney stand, where he engaged a driver. After giving the man instructions, Adam cast a glance back over at his shoulder toward the carriage trail, where a doubtless impatient Priscilla awaited him. "I must return to Miss Standish now."

"Of course you must," she agreed, no less regretful for acknowledging that truth.

Adam handed her into the carriage, not letting go of her elbow until the last possible moment—as if as reluctant to release her as she was to send him back to his fiancée.

He gave her a smile that looked forced. "Try not to run off with this carriage before it can convey you home."

She smiled back. "I shall try."

"As for what happened with your horse…we will talk about that later."

Not until I've decided what I mean to do about it, she thought, returning a noncommittal murmur.

Adam shut the door and the vehicle lurched off. Helena caught one last glimpse of him standing by the road, watching her as the coach pulled away.

Shaking her head, she tried to dissipate the lingering effect of his sensual spell and regather the thoughts his nearness had scattered. She needed to consider the circumstances of Pegasus's injury—and Francis Standish's probable role in it. Since she was almost certain to encounter Priscilla's cousin at dinner tonight, she had best decide what she wanted to do about it quickly.

AS THEY ENTERED THE dining room that evening, Helena was satisfied to discover she had been seated beside Francis Standish. Since she knew Priscilla would not have done her the honor, she wondered if this were an attempt by Priscilla's father to allow his heir to try to charm her and her wealth, or whether Francis wished to see up close the effect that had been wrought by his trick in the park.

Whatever the reason, she thought, setting her lips into a determined line, she trusted that by the end of dinner she would have induced in Francis Standish a firm resolve to avoid her permanently.

As she had been avoiding Adam. Expecting he would have checked with his groom upon arriving home and thus be even keener to discuss the incident in the park, she had delayed leaving her chamber until the carriage had been brought around, then sidestepped his attempt to speak with her in the parlor before dinner. Tempted as she was to fling in his face this evidence about the true character of his betrothed and her cousin, if Adam were barred from severing the engagement, she would rather spare him the distress of learning of their behavior from her.

Priscilla had evidently recovered from her momentary concern for Helena, for as soon as the company was seated, she said, "May I commend your fortitude in rebounding so quickly from your ordeal this afternoon, Miss Lambarth. How fortunate Mr. Dixon was able to bring your horse to a halt! I only wish you had allowed Adam to choose your mount." Smiling at her fiancé, she squeezed his hand. "I'm sure he would have found a more suitable one."

"My papa always warned me reckless behavior leads to a fall," Miss Standish's friend, Lady Cordelia, added from her seat opposite Francis Standish. "Though we are all glad, of course, that you did *not* fall, Miss Lambarth!"

To Helena's surprise, Adam removed his fingers from his fiancée's grip. "Far from falling, she controlled the horse magnificently—with no need of assistance from Mr. Dixon. 'Twas a marvelous display of horsemanship."

Priscilla's smile faltered and Lady Cordelia's smug look faded. Before Helena could respond, Lord Blanchard looked up from gazing adoringly at Charis to add, "I only wish I'd been present to see it! Her sangfroid and skill were the talk of White's when I stopped by this evening."

In the short silence following Blanchard's remark, Priscilla's expression soured further. Having received so unsatisfying a return from her efforts, she turned and directed her conversation to her mother. At the other end of the table, while Mr. Standish monopolized his dinner partners, Helena was free to concentrate on Francis.

At first he seemed guarded. But after two courses during which she ventured only deferential replies to his occasional comments, he relaxed and began regaling her with anecdotes in which he played the principal role.

Finally the fruits, nuts and sweets were brought in. Selecting an apple and a sharp knife, Helena waited for a break in his monologue.

When Standish paused to fill his mouth with syllabub, she said, "Have you traveled abroad, Mr. Standish?"

Francis swallowed and gave her a patronizing smile. "I have not. Though some tout the improving nature of a Grand Tour, one has only to recall the rapacity of the French and the inability of other European nations to prevent Napoleon's rampages to know all the benefits of a superior culture are to be found here in England."

"But such an amazing variety of civilizations exist in the world! I've read a number of accounts written by travelers to distant lands and find them fascinating." She picked up the apple and began slowly paring off a long, hair-thin slice of the red peel.

"Too much reading burdens the mind, especially a female's. You would do better to follow Priscilla's example and let your thoughts be guided by gentlemen."

"Ah, but one might miss so many…pointed details, were one to leave observation only to men. And one should always seek to discover the truth of what happens around one, do you not think?"

His air of assurance faltered a little. "I…I suppose so, Miss Lambarth."

"But I was speaking of foreign cultures. Recently I read a mesmerizing account of travel among the *peaux rouges* of America," she continued, paring off another slice. "It seems the savages have a barbarous practice of scalping their enemies, often sneaking up under cover of darkness to overwhelm their victims as they sleep. Is that not incredible?" She peeled another slice, cutting this time deeper into the flesh.

Francis's gaze dropped to the slow work of her fingers and he swallowed hard. "Yes, um, incredible."

She laughed softly as she continued paring the fruit. "I suppose it's the fault of my sadly deficient upbringing, but I find myself rather in sympathy with the savages. If someone were to hurt some object or person dear to me—a horse, for example—I should strongly consider taking just such a bloody revenge."

Finished, she dropped the naked apple onto her plate beside the curl of peelings and gazed up at him. "London nights are so very dark, are they not?"

His eyes wide in a face gone suddenly waxy, Francis stared back at her. Then, dropping his napkin onto his plate, he sprang up, almost knocking over his chair.

"Good heavens!" Mrs. Standish exclaimed. "Francis, whatever is the matter?"

"I am feeling…suddenly indisposed. You will excuse me, please." Hand to his mouth, he hurried from the room.

AT HIS END OF THE TABLE, Adam had to smile at Francis Standish's loss of composure. For once paying little attention to his fiancée, he had been surreptitiously watching Francis and Helena all through dinner.

Though his ire had cooled somewhat, he was still furious after speaking with Johnson when he arrived home from the park. As incredible as it seemed that anyone would be reckless or mean-spirited enough to deliberately cause Pegasus to bolt, there appeared no other explanation for the thorn Dix told the groom Miss Lambarth had removed from the animal's flank. Johnson had adamantly insisted nothing of the sort would have been overlooked when he saddled Pegasus before her ride. Nor were there any bramble patches she would have traversed in the London streets between St. James Square and Hyde Park.

Besides, Pegasus had behaved perfectly until

Helena remounted after walking the animal beside Francis—who was the only one close enough to have tampered with the saddle blanket. Though Miss Lambarth's performance with the apple tonight had been outrageous, he could only applaud the fear she had so cleverly induced in Francis Standish. Which showed the man to be a coward as well as a sneak.

Standish deserved more than a good fright, Adam thought fiercely. His breath hitched as he recalled the horror he'd felt when Helena's horse had bolted. Were it not for her exceptional riding skill, she might at this moment be laid out in a winding sheet instead of sitting at this table. A shudder rippling through him at the thought, he uttered a silent prayer of thanks for her safety.

He didn't know why Standish would have wanted to perpetrate such a prank. But though he refused to believe Priscilla would have initiated such a scheme, given the disparaging comments she had addressed to Helena during the drive and at dinner tonight, he suspected she might have encouraged Francis to do something to show Miss Lambarth at a disadvantage. He intended to interrogate her about the matter as soon as they had an opportunity in private.

Recalling Priscilla's petty remarks in front of the company earlier this evening, Adam frowned. The ladies met frequently when making social calls. Did his fiancée speak as slightingly to Helena when he was not around to object? Though Miss Lambarth had never complained of such treatment, he meant to question Priscilla about that, too.

Belatedly he noticed that Mrs. Standish had risen to lead the ladies out and jumped to his feet. Since all the guests were proceeding to other entertainments, he would be spared making stilted conversation over brandy and cigars.

His mind still racing, Adam watched them file out. Helena, gowned once again in her favorite scarlet, walked out last, her head high and her carriage graceful.

He'd hardly seen her since that night in the library. He hardly knew what to say when he did see her.

He'd hoped that if he stayed on his guard and concentrated on his role as head of the family, he might keep his attraction under control. And he *had* honestly meant only to comfort her when he'd taken her in his arms.

But once she'd calmed, he simply hadn't been able to let her go without finally, finally tasting her lips. True, he'd kept the kiss gentle, hadn't parted her lips and plunged his tongue within to ravage her mouth as he did in the dreams that troubled him far too often.

In fact, he realized suddenly, though desire and pleasure had sung in his veins as he held her, he hadn't *wanted* to ravage her, not with her still so upset. Somehow lust and tenderness and compassion and affection had gotten all mixed up inside him, until he wasn't sure where one left off and another began. He certainly couldn't predict when one irresistible impulse would shift to another.

He both regretted kissing her and was thrilled he'd kissed her. He'd felt as if his whole soul expanded with gladness and humble awe when she granted him her trust—she who had been given so little reason to trust any man.

Lord, it was such a muddle.

All he knew was that he'd felt more terror while he watched Helena cling to that bolting horse, more tenderness and affection as he held her in his arms, more desire as he gently kissed her than he'd ever felt for his fiancée.

It would be dishonorable to break the pledge he'd made to marry Priscilla Standish. But how could it be honorable to wed a girl he was becoming increasingly convinced he did not and never would love?

Especially when he was beginning to believe 'twas Helena Lambarth who had captured his heart.

CHAPTER TWENTY-THREE

HAVING CELEBRATED HER ESCAPE from the company at Grosvenor Square, Helena was dismayed when, halfway through the musicale the Darnell ladies attended after dinner, she looked up to see the Standish party arrive.

The group halted at the entrance to the refreshment room where their hostess had escorted her guests while the second set of musicians tuned their instruments. Though Charis and Lady Darnell at once walked over to greet Adam and his fiancée, Helena hesitated, not sure she could force herself to be polite to Priscilla three times in one day.

To her surprise, Miss Standish and Lady Cordelia waved and began walking toward her.

Satisfied as Helena was to have put a scare into Priscilla's cousin, she doubted Francis would have had time to warn Priscilla not to trifle with her again. Still, how much damage could she do in a drawing room? Helena need only parry the girl's falsely sweet words without losing her temper—difficult as that might prove.

"Dear Miss Lambarth," Priscilla said as they

reached her, "we have yet to manage a comfortable cose today. Shall we rectify that omission? Cordelia told me of the extraordinary adventures you were relating at dinner."

"I recounted some incidents about which I had read."

"And you are so well-read," Priscilla commented. "Charis tells me you are studying philosophy—in Greek!"

"Even if Papa were to permit me to examine such a heathenish tongue, which I'm sure he would not," Lady Cordelia interjected, "I should never presume myself clever enough to study a subject normally reserved for gentlemen."

Tired of hearing what females were or were not supposed to do—and under no obligation to be conciliating to Lady Cordelia—Helena said, "How fortunate that you recognize your limitations."

Lady Cordelia flashed her a look full of animosity. "But I understand you are more enterprising than a gently bred female in many ways, Miss Lambarth."

"Indeed," Priscilla said. "Traveling all the way to London on the common mail coach—without even a maid!"

From the periphery of her vision, Helena noted other guests drawing near, heads inclined to catch the conversation. Miss Standish had aimed enough barbed comments at her during various afternoon calls—when Adam was not present—that his fiancée's hostility to Helena was probably well known.

Why not give all these eager observers the show they were expecting? Helena thought. Having worn out her patience for ignoring Priscilla's baiting during their previous meetings today, she replied, "I rode on the roof, too. You mustn't omit that little detail."

"But that wasn't the boldest of her adventures!" Lady Cordelia said. "Priscilla, did you not tell me Miss Lambarth actually prowled about London at night, disguised as a boy? Oh!" she exclaimed, putting a hand to her lips with a look of mock dismay. "Dear me! I forgot I wasn't supposed to mention that. Pray, excuse me, Miss Lambarth!"

Someone gasped and the matrons nearest them froze. A sudden silence spread across the room, until even Darnell and Lord Blanchard, conversing near the door, looked up.

Miss Standish glanced at Helena, both anxiety and triumph in her eyes. "Oh, I'm sure 'twas all a hum—wasn't it, Miss Lambarth?" she said nervously.

"No, it wasn't!" Lady Cordelia interposed. "Priscilla, you swore to me 'twas absolute truth!"

Stricken to realize that Darnell must have divulged her escapade to his fiancée, Helena studied the girl, who seemed unable to decide whether she was glad or sorry to have her betrayal of Darnell's confidence revealed. But though Miss Standish had offered her a possible avenue of escape, Helena never considered taking refuge in a lie.

Besides, true or not, when added to her previous social missteps, the allegation alone would probably achieve Miss Standish's obvious desire: creating an on-dit scandalous enough to permanently discredit the girl she perceived as her rival.

"Why, no, Miss Standish, 'twas quite true," Helena replied calmly. "I even watched the horse of Lord Blanchard's friend outside White's." Gesturing toward the diplomat, she switched into the tones of one of Dickon's street mates. "'Old yer 'orse fer a copper, me lord?'"

In the now silent room, her words carried clearly to every guest. While Lord Blanchard's jaw dropped, Helena watched shock and disbelief wash over the faces of those nearest her. Despite her paucity of experience, she knew there were limits to the eccentricities Society would excuse because of her wealth. In the outraged or dismayed looks she was now receiving, she read that she had just bypassed those limits.

But when her defiant gaze met Lady Darnell's stricken face, she realized her downfall would not be hers alone.

Not unless she acted quickly to distance herself from the family that had become so dear to her. Already Charis, recovering from Lady Cordelia's pronouncement, had stepped in her direction, while Adam, a furious scowl on his face, was striding toward her.

Before he could reach her, she said softly for Priscilla's ears alone, "If you expended as much passion trying to please Adam as you have in disparaging me, you'd both be much happier."

Meanwhile, like marionettes controlled by the same strings, the rest of the guests drew back. Stepping forward to intercept Adam, Helena said urgently, "Don't bother about me! Tend to Aunt Lillian and Charis."

"You can't think I'll just abandon you—"

"Please, Adam! Don't let my disgrace become theirs."

For a moment he hesitated. Then, recognizing the truth of her words, he nodded. "All right—for now. But don't think this is over yet." After giving her hand a quick squeeze, he proceeded past her to his fiancée.

With a withering glare, Adam clamped a hand on Priscilla's arm and led her toward Charis, Lady Cordelia scurrying after them. Standing alone in the center of the floor, Helena could almost see opinions that had been teetering between amusement and censure turn against her.

How sad Society is, she thought. All these people so trapped by their ridiculous code of rules that matrons and suitors who had flattered her and solicited her company a moment ago no longer dared meet her gaze.

Even Lady Jersey, after giving Helena a tiny, pitying shake of her head, turned away without speaking. Other guests hastened to follow her example. Helena was wondering whether she should wait until they had all exited before departing herself when a voice rang out.

"Pray, Miss Lambarth, lend me your arm."

Helena turned to see Lady Seagrave approaching her. After first encountering the woman in Lady Jersey's parlor, Helena had often noticed Lady Seagrave watching her when they chanced to be at the same gathering, had even exchanged a few words with her at several functions. Toward the mother of the wild young man *Helena's* mother had loved and fled to,

Helena felt some of the same mix of gratitude and resentment she'd always harbored for the son.

Those emotions gave way to puzzlement as Lady Seagrave reached her side. Had the exile of Gavin Seagrave for killing a jealous husband in a duel made his mother sympathetic to other victims of scandal? Helena wondered.

"Madame." Helena curtseyed to the older woman.

Lady Seagrave placed her hand on Helena's arm. "I find the room has grown suddenly...chilly. I wish to return home. Would you drive with me, please?"

Helena, too, had to get home—and it would not be wise to count on claiming a seat in the Darnell carriage. Still curious why Lady Seagrave was suddenly befriending her, Helena said, "Are you sure you dare take me?"

The older woman smiled. "Are you sure you dare leave with me? Yes? Then let us go." Murmuring her thanks to their still speechless hostess, Lady Seagrave clasped Helena's arm and guided her firmly out of the room.

As if by agreement, neither spoke until they were seated in the carriage. "Thank you for your assistance, Lady Seagrave," Helena said. "If you would set me down at Darnell House, I should be most appreciative." She smiled sardonically. "I expect it would be prudent for me to begin packing at once."

"Don't you wish to know why I intervened?"

Helena shrugged and raked the woman with a scornful glance. "Because it amused you?" she suggested.

To her surprise, tears began to glimmer in the older woman's eyes. "Ah, how like him you look—full of scorn and ready to defy the world! So like your father."

Helena stiffened. "I would thank you not to liken me to Lambarth, madame."

Lady Seagrave smiled through her tears. "Never would I do so, my dear! I meant your true father—my son Gavin."

"My true—! Helena gasped. For a moment, shock held her immobile. "Are you claiming that Gavin Seagrave is my father?" she demanded at last.

Lady Seagrave nodded. "Indeed I am. 'Tis a rather long story. Why don't you come home with me and let me tell it to you?"

Numb with astonishment and silenced by an incoherent jumble of disbelief, grief and curiosity, Helena allowed Lady Seagrave to conduct her to her North Audley Street town house and shepherd her up to her parlor.

When they were both settled, Lady Seagrave began, "From his earliest years, Gavin was wild—passionate, impulsive, ready to fight at the first perceived slight, just as quick to forgive. He'd wooed his share of ladies, but when he met your mother, they fell instantly and completely in love. From that moment Diana favored only Gavin, ignoring Vincent Lambarth, who had courted her for months. Though her family—your late grandparents—thought Gavin too unsteady and refused his suit, she would have wed him anyway—if not for the duel."

Lady Seagrave sighed. "A trumped-up affair. To

protect her actual lover, the married lady in question named Gavin as her paramour, expecting he would deny it and that her husband would let the matter drop. But once insulted, Gavin insisted on having satisfaction. They met, the husband died and Gavin had to flee England."

"So what makes you think he's my father?"

"Diana, as you could imagine, was heartbroken at Gavin's sudden departure. Then within the week, her family announced she was to marry Lambarth. Even at the time I thought the unseemly haste more than just an attempt to distance her from Gavin's disgrace, but being persona non grata to the Foresters, I was not permitted to see her. Even if I had, suspecting what I did, how could I urge her to refuse Lambarth and wait for Gavin, when neither of us knew where he was or when we might hear from him again? By the time he did contact me, 'twas too late. Diana had married Lambarth and gone with him to Cornwall."

"All you've told me are your own suspicions," Helena said flatly. "Have you any real proof?"

"Patience, my dear. After a few years, I heard there was a child. I kept hoping Lambarth would bring the family to London, but he never did. Then my son contacted me, saying he'd sent agents into Cornwall to check on your mother and learned she was grievously unhappy. He was determined to rescue her and her child, and take them back to the estate he'd settled in the Caribbean. As you know, that rescue was not entirely successful. It wasn't until after his men brought the hysterical Diana to him that she told him

the child she'd borne—the child they'd failed to free—
was not Lambarth's daughter, but his."

"Mama told him that?" Helena demanded.

"Yes."

"You swear this is the truth?"

"I swear it."

"But…" Helena shook her head. "Mama wrote me
letters—many, many letters over the years. Not even
when she knew she was dying did she inform *me*
Lambarth was not my real father. Why would she not,
if it were true?"

"After their second rescue attempt failed, Diana and
Gavin believed Lambarth when he vowed he would see
you dead before he would relinquish you. Not daring
to attempt another rescue, Gavin engaged the best
lawyers in England to find some legal way for Diana
to wrest you from Lambarth. But as his acknowledged
daughter, legally they could do nothing. So Lambarth
had his revenge, making them live knowing he held
Diana's beloved child in his power."

"That still doesn't explain why Mama didn't tell
me in one of her letters. Or why you are only now
coming forward, when I have met you on several occasions."

"Since Lambarth refused to divorce Diana or release
you, what point would there have been in telling you?
Your parents' only hope was that you would survive
until Lambarth was dead or incapacitated enough that
you could be freed. Then, as either heiress of
Lambarth's estate or in possession of the fortune Diana
had amassed, you could claim a respected place in

Society. A place that would never be granted the illegitimate daughter of a man who'd fled England in disgrace.

"For the same reason," she continued, "I dared not show too much interest in you, for though in voice and profile you favor Diana, in coloring and stature you are all Gavin. The resemblance would be only too obvious had he not been absent from England for so many years. Even now, 'tis striking enough that some might recall the old scandal and remark upon it, were I to spend much time in your company. And so…I watched from a distance, my heart breaking that Gavin was not here to see you. That I could not claim my only grandchild as my own."

Still not sure she believed it, Helena said wryly, "A grandchild who has caused a scandal nearly as great as the one created by the man you say is my father. Are you sure you want to acknowledge me?"

"Oh, my dear, selfish as it is of me, I rejoice in your scandal! Were it not for Miss Standish's knavery, I should never have allowed myself to approach you. And if you wish to attempt a recover, I shall still let our relationship go unacknowledged. But I could not do so without, just this once, seizing the chance to let you know the truth. But here I'm rattling on, when I meant to show you this first."

Taking Helena's hand, she led her out of the parlor, down a hall and into a small, elegant sitting room. Gesturing to the portrait of a young man that hung over the mantel, she said, "Your father, Gavin Seagrave."

Helena felt her breath leave in a rush. But for the

gender of the subject, as she gazed at the man's snapping dark eyes, curly black hair, tall frame and arrogant tilt of chin, she might almost be looking in a mirror.

It all made sense—perfect, awful sense. Lambarth's rage, the beatings, his twisted desire to keep her a prisoner he seemed at once to both want and despise.

She turned to Lady Seagrave. "Did Lambarth know?"

"Though he, too, was dark-haired and dark-eyed, he must at least have suspected. Did…did he treat you badly?"

Badly. The small word did not begin to encompass what the man she'd called father had done to her. Curling her damaged hand into its glove, she said simply, "Yes."

Lady Seagrave closed her eyes, as if receiving a blow. "My dear child, I am so sorry. 'Twas your mother's darkest torment, to think of you all alone at Lambarth's mercy. Forgive me! If I had insisted on seeing Diana before she married him, perhaps I could have somehow prevented it."

Vowing to conceal what she had suffered, Helena took Lady Seagrave's hand. "With only suspicions, you could have done nothing. Nor should you reproach yourself now."

Lady Seagrave smiled tremulously. "Thank you, my dear. Knowing the truth, you still have a choice. For all her flightiness, Lillian Darnell is a clever lady. If you wish it, I'm sure she can figure out a way to salvage your reputation. It might be best to maintain the fiction that I am simply an acquaintance who, having weathered scandal before, felt sympathy for you tonight. It will be enough for me that *you* know you are my grandchild."

"I have no intention of letting Aunt Lillian risk any more of her social standing trying to redeem me. I shall leave Darnell House tomorrow as soon as I can pack my things. And if…if you will have me, I should like to stay with you until I decide what to do next."

"Are you certain?" When Helena nodded, tears brimmed once again in the older woman's eyes. "Nothing would give me greater pleasure. Why not send a note to Darnell House telling them you will stay the night? Oh, I have so much to tell you!"

COMING GROGGILY AWAKE THE NEXT morning in a strange room, it took Helena a few moments to remember where she was. She'd managed only a few hours of sleep after sitting up nearly until dawn listening to Lady Seagrave describe everything she knew of the love between Diana and Gavin, their reunion after Gavin's rescue and their life together.

Her parents had wed under local Caribbean law, but to their grief had no more children. Having amassing wealth as a privateer, Gavin settled down after their marriage to become a successful shipper of rum and sugar. Tapping his network of trading partners and some less respectable contacts from his days on the high seas, he had watched and waited for the day the daughter he dare not acknowledge could be freed.

She was still marveling at these revelations when Lady Seagrave entered bearing a tray of hot chocolate.

"Good morning, my dear! I would have let you sleep longer, but you said you wished to be up early."

"Thank you," Helena replied, accepting a cup. "But you must be tired, too. You shouldn't have waited on me."

"You would have me send a maid? Indeed not! I needed to make sure you were truly here and not just a dream."

"I am quite real…Grandmama," Helena said shyly.

Tentatively Lady Seagrave reached out her arms. Helena let the woman enfold her in a hug, then clung to her in a wave of gladness. She was finally free of Lambarth, of the man whose cruelty had caged her spirit much more successfully than his castle walls had imprisoned her body.

Lady Seagrave's eyes were moist as she released Helena. "So, have you decided yet what you wish to do?"

"Not precisely. I must remove from St. James Square and it would probably be best if I left London."

"You are sure you do not wish to attempt repairing your reputation? Lillian Darnell can work wonders."

"No, I've seen enough of Society to feel certain I shall get along quite well without it. My only regret is my scandal must cause problems for the Darnell family. Otherwise, I am ready to go elsewhere."

She couldn't bear remaining to witness her beloved Adam married to Priscilla Standish, even at the distance of a news item in the *Morning Post*. It hurt too much to imagine him wed to a gloating Priscilla or to envision how living with his bride's pettiness might slowly stifle his warmth and compassion, until the choice honor dictated narrowed into naught but the bitter fulfillment of duty.

"Should you like to travel?" Lady Seagrave interrupted her dark thoughts.

Helena shrugged listlessly. "Perhaps."

"If you are certain you wish to acknowledge our connection, would you consider sailing to St. Kitts? There could be no greater joy for my son than to finally meet the daughter he has loved and longed for all these years."

The Caribbean—far from Adam and the heartache of knowing he could never be hers. Certainly she was curious to know the man her mother had loved, whom she resembled so closely and had just discovered to be her father. Maybe Gavin, who had borne grief and loss himself, could teach her how to endure it. "I believe I should like that."

"Wonderful! And you will stay with me until arrangements can be made?"

"I will return tomorrow after I have…taken leave of the Darnell family," she said, those few words barely hinting at the heartache performing them would cause.

"Excellent!" Lady Seagrave cried. "Enjoy your chocolate then, my dear. I shall visit Gavin's London office immediately to see what can be arranged. Ring if my staff can assist you with anything."

After agreeing to meet for dinner, Lady Seagrave left. The note Helena had sent to Darnell House the previous night had instructed Nell to bring fresh garments this morning. While she waited for the girl, she would write some additional notes.

To Aunt Lillian, apologizing again for the scandal she'd caused and telling her she would return this evening after the ladies went out to collect her things. To Lady Jersey, asking that she not hold Helena's transgressions against the Darnell family. To Mr. Pendenning, saying she would call this afternoon to discuss plans for her future.

But to Adam she would write nothing. Instinctively she knew he would wait for her tonight, that he would not let her depart without seeing her one last time. She both longed for and dreaded that meeting.

Uncertainty might cloud her future, but one fact was blue-sky clear. Now that she knew not a drop of the blood in her veins came from a wretch depraved enough to beat, starve and imprison a child, there was one last thing she meant to do before leaving London.

Though she would not attempt to trick the man whose honor she so admired into breaking his betrothal vows, while Adam Darnell was still unmarried, she was quite prepared to compromise his honor just enough to seduce him. Before she was forced to abandon him to a loveless marriage, she would give him one night of joy in the arms of a woman who loved him completely.

And if time permitted before she returned to Darnell House, she would seek out the courtesan she'd once seen in the park and ask her the best way to pleasure a gentleman.

AFTER COMPLETING HER ERRANDS and returning to share a simple dinner with Lady Seagrave, Helena was about to set out on her last, most important mission when Nell came in, announcing that Mr. Dixon had called for her.

Though she had assured Nell and Dickon that Lady Darnell would find them other positions after she left, with a loyalty that warmed Helena, both affirmed they would rather follow their mistress, regardless of where she settled. Far from reluctant to leave the city of his birth, Dickon had expressed a great enthusiasm for visiting the island realm of planters and privateers.

Her thoughts consumed by her approaching rendezvous with Adam, Helena's first impulse was to tell Nell to send her caller away and proceed immediately to the address in Covent Garden her disapproving maid had charged Dickon to obtain. The courtesan, Dickon had obligingly discovered, would soon be leaving to meet her lover at the opera.

But Mr. Dixon had been her friend from her first Society appearance. His seeking her out after last night's disgrace could only mean he intended to offer his support. She couldn't repay his loyalty by avoiding him.

Resigned to postponing the meeting with the courtesan, Helena cheered herself with the reflection that, under the terms of her bargain with Mr. Dixon, perhaps she might ask him a few of the questions she'd intended to address to the pleasure woman.

When Helena entered the parlor moment later, her caller rose and came over to kiss her hand fervently.

"My dear Miss Lambarth! How I regret that a dull dinner engagement at my great-aunt's prevented me from attending the musicale last night. I should not have left you standing in the middle of the floor, I assure you! I can't imagine why Darnell was so hen-hearted!"

"Thank you, Mr. Dixon, but you mustn't think badly of Adam. Knowing he needed to protect the reputations of the ladies of his own family, 'twas I who demanded he leave me and see to them. Then Lady Seagrave offered her help."

"Did you really hold Blanchard's friend's horse outside White's? 'Od's blood, I wish I had seen it!"

"Yes, but enough said of that."

"Indeed, 'twas the talk of the clubs! I can't imagine another female skilled or intrepid enough to do so."

"Certainly not a lady," Helena observed dryly. "Instead of discussing that, may I presume once again upon your friendship and ask some rather indelicate questions?"

His eyes lit and he grinned. "Absolutely!"

Thinking about the strange excitement that had filled her when Adam's lips touched hers, she said, "What is it about kissing that makes men desire it?"

Though Mr. Dixon reddened, he gamely replied, "Kissing—and other forms of affection that proceed from it—are…profoundly pleasurable. Shall I show you how much?"

Ignoring the offer, she continued, "Were I to kiss you, how could I make the experience…more pleasurable?"

As she waited expectantly, his face turned scarlet. She was about to conclude she had exceeded even his tolerance when at last he said, his voice a throaty rasp, "You could let me draw you close, so that I felt the whole length of your body against mine. Open your lips, so that I might touch your tongue with my own."

"Doing so would make you want…more?"

His exhaled a gusty breath. "Merely looking at you makes me want more. But if you wish a tutorial on kissing, I am much better at showing than describing."

"You…want to kiss me?"

"More than I want my next breath."

Regretting now that her inflammatory questions had obviously ignited his desire, she thought perhaps she owed him a kiss. A goodbye kiss for a faithful friend.

Perhaps a kiss that would show her whether her passion could be aroused by one man only.

"Kiss me, then."

He moved quickly to take her in his arms. Thankfully he did not try to bind her against him and his lips, though insistent, remained gentle. She found his caress…pleasant, but he engendered no urgent need within her to draw him closer or to open her mouth to his probing.

Unlike Adam. In a rush of sensation, she remembered how he had sparked her to flame with the merest brush of his lips. Made her chest ache with wanting to be encircled in his arms and never let go.

She eased away from Mr. Dixon. Before she could apologize for using him so shamelessly, he dropped down to one knee.

"Marry me, Helena! No man could admire more than I your unconventional, questing mind, your strength, your uninhibited passion. You may ride whatever horse you choose, drive as fast a phaeton as you desire. We can even explore the streets of the city in disguise together! Let Society gossip as it pleases. I shall never forsake you!"

"Please, Mr. Dixon, get up!" she said, dismayed by the direction her inquiry had gone. "You mistake me entirely! I should not have gone out in disguise if I could have explored as I wanted. Nor did I choose a spirited horse just to set Society on its ear. I have never *tried* to incite gossip, but only to live according to my lights."

"Then let me live with you, protect you, love you."

Not sure whether it was love, loyalty or a secret desire to tweak Society that had promoted his unexpected declaration, she said, "Mere words cannot express how honored I am. But I cannot accept your offer. I fear, by kissing you, I have already imposed grievously upon your friendship. I never wish to marry."

"Perhaps you need the right gentleman to persuade you."

"I cannot be persuaded—and I have made you uncomfortable in the bargain. Forgive me."

He rose and took an agitated turn about the room. "It's Darnell, isn't it?" he asked, gazing back at her. "He will never break his word to Miss Standish, you know."

A bit alarmed that he had guessed her secret, Helena avoided a direct answer. "I would not have him break it."

"Then why not consider my suit?"

"I am leaving London soon. May we not part as friends?"

"You are resolved upon this?"

"I've long wished to travel." She gave him a deprecating smile. "I believe I've just been given the perfect opportunity to do so. As it happens, Lady Seagrave is about to set out for the Caribbean, and I have agreed accompany her."

"You cannot be dissuaded? I should always be proud to stand by you and support you, even as just a friend."

"And I am honored by your friendship. But I must go."

He studied her for a long moment, then sighed. "I suppose there is nothing left for me to do but to once again express my deepest admiration and devotion. I wish you well on your journey! Remember, if you ever change your mind, England and I would rejoice to welcome you home."

Bowing low, he kissed her hand and walked out. Thoughtfully, Helena watched him go. Her guilt at refusing him was lessened by noting that he did not appear to be a man whose fondest hopes had been crushed. She suspected that, had she been unwise enough to accept his offer, the admiration he felt for her "unconventional" spirit would have swiftly dwindled once he discovered his scandalous bride caused him not just to be barred from the balls and dinners he deemed "dull," but also to be denied admission to his clubs and cut by many of his peers.

As for her plans for Adam, though Mr. Dixon's kiss had been mildly titillating, it had not come close to igniting within her the intensity of desire, the tenderness or the sense of completeness Adam's had.

A shiver of excitement swirled in her belly. Since it appeared only Adam could create the magic she'd felt in his arms, she was more anxious than ever to recreate that experience and allow all those feelings full play.

Grateful as she was to Mr. Dixon for showing her how to begin, she still wanted a bit more instruction in the art of seduction. If she hurried, she should catch the Divine Alice before she left for her rendezvous.

SOME TIME LATER, LADY SEAGRAVE'S carriage deposited her at Darnell House. Helena entered to find Harrison himself stationed by the door.

"Miss Lambarth, welcome back!" he cried. "Lady Darnell wished me to inform you that she and Miss Charis would like to see you at your earliest convenience."

Surprised and warmed by the concern evident in Harrison's normally impassive face, Helena handed him her cloak. Though she'd suspected her aunt would not allow her to slip away without a struggle, her chest tightened at her new family's demonstration of support even as she dreaded what would no doubt be a heart-wrenching meeting.

All the more reason to get it over with quickly, she told herself. "Then I shall go immediately," she replied. Squaring her shoulders, she followed him up the stairs.

As soon as Harrison admitted her, both Lady Darnell and Charis rushed over to embrace her. "That hateful girl!" Aunt Lillian said through a haze of tears. "I shall leave this house the minute Adam brings her here as his bride. But you mustn't despair, my dear. I am still Somebody. If we retire to the country until the next scandal captures the attention of the ton, we can still—"

"Dearest Aunt Lillian!" Helena interrupted her, feeling guiltier than ever that instead of the reproaches she deserved for bringing scandal down upon them, her aunt was thinking only of redeeming Helena's position. "I cannot tell you how grateful I am, but I refuse to allow you to put yourself out any further on my behalf."

"You cannot think us so poor-spirited as to desert you!" Charis said. "I should not have consented to leave you last night, had Adam and Nathan not both said 'twould be better to let you go with Lady Seagrave and end the incident quickly rather than prolong it by arguing."

"Indeed, we shall all stand by you," Lady Darnell affirmed. "As soon as Charis is wed, let us go to Claygate. By the Little Season, much of the talk will have died down. I doubt the highest sticklers will ever be induced to receive you, and naturally Almack's is out of the question, but my friends, who value you for yourself, will send enough invitations to keep us tolerably amused."

"My dear Aunt Lillian, retire to Claygate if you wish, but I cannot accompany you. Perhaps later, when all has passed into memory, I may visit you—or Charis, at whatever embassy she is gracing as hostess. If you still want to acknowledge me then. For you see, there is more to the scandal even than what Lady Cordelia revealed last night. Something quite shocking, of which I have only just learned myself. Will you not sit while I explain?"

Briefly, Helena detailed what Lady Seagrave had told her, finishing by informing them she meant to journey with her grandmother to meet Gavin. Though at first, Aunt Lillian gasped and nearly swooned, after reviving she declared that even if Helena meant to acknowledge Seagrave as her father, the Darnell family would support her.

"Then you are far too good! Not that I mean to post a notice in the *Times*, but as I plan to spend time with Lady Seagrave, sooner or later, the secret will be out. I'm not sure which would be worse for you—to be connected to a hoyden who sneaks about the city in masculine dress, or to have housed the illegitimate daughter of a privateer."

"To us, you are just 'our Helena' and we love you," Charis said fiercely. "Can we not persuade you to stay?"

Were it for their love only, she might be swayed. But she knew she could not remain and conceal for long the strength of her feelings for Adam—and she had already exposed them to scandal enough.

Feeling the burn of tears again, she shook her head. "I'm sorry. I love you both dearly, and I shall be very sorry to miss your wedding, Charis, but I must go."

While Lady Darnell reached for her handkerchief, Charis gave her a long, searching look. "I understand," she said, giving Helena a hug. "Damn Priscilla! Do what you must, my dearest Helena. Remember that wherever you travel, you will always find a welcome with Nathan and I."

After more hugs all around, Helena insisted they not cancel their plans to attend the ball to which Lord Blanchard was to escort them later in the evening. Leaving them to complete their preparations, she returned to her room to set Nell packing. Then, after the ladies departed, she went to the library to wait for Adam.

CHAPTER TWENTY-FOUR

SEVERAL HOURS LATER, Helena seated herself before the blazing hearth, garbed in the white silk night rail she had worn the first evening she'd encountered Darnell in the library. The first time she'd seen on his face what she later came to recognize as desire. A desire she intended tonight to satisfy to the fullest.

Since she was far too nervous for any book to hold her attention, she was relieved when, after a time spent alternately pacing and sitting on the sofa, she heard his footsteps in the hallway, followed by a knock at the door.

She looked up at him as he entered, her heart swelling with gladness at the sight of his dear face, though its expression was solemn. The tingling awareness of his presence that always struck her when he came into a room enveloped her, comforting in its intensity. Soon she hoped to take that awareness to a new level entirely.

He halted in the center of the room when he saw her. A flash of strong emotion crossed his face before he mastered his expression and walked to her. Almost at the sofa, he stopped again, as if not trusting himself to sit beside her. "I talked with Bellemere this afternoon. She told me you intended to leave us. To leave London."

Hearing the strain in his voice, Helena's own reply wobbled. "I think it would be b-best."

He turned abruptly, anguish in his eyes as he faced her. "How can I ever apologize adequately for bringing this misfortune upon you? I never dreamed Priscilla would breach so sensitive a confidence—a confidence I should never have uttered, had I dealt with her more adroitly. I am deeply ashamed at having broken your trust."

Curling her fingers into fists to resist the urge to smooth the lines from his face, Helena said, "As keen an interest as that lady takes in my errors, I expect she pounced upon the opportunity to wheedle it out of you."

Adam grimaced. "So she did. But that does not excuse my fault in giving her the chance to do so. I haven't been able to talk with her yet about last night's incident—her mother denied me both times I called, saying she was 'indisposed'—but I shall speak with her tomorrow if I have to break down her bedchamber door."

"What's done is done," Helena said, rejoicing to have Adam confirm that Priscilla had tricked the information out of him. "Pray, do not be too severe with her. I...I have ever been an impediment between you. I should like to be one no longer. Leaving will accomplish that— and free Aunt Lillian from the threat of my social disasters."

"You mustn't let this unpleasant incident drive you from London! Bellemere can manage Society and you may leave Priscilla to me. I can no more allow you to go into self-imposed exile than I would permit Charis to do so."

"She has scarcely caused the trouble I have," Helena retorted wryly. "But I don't wish to brangle! Let me convey to you the news that makes essential that I leave."

In a few short sentences she summarized again what Lady Seagrave had confided to her. "You perhaps better than anyone know what I suffered at Lambarth's hands. After last night's incident, I should have wished to leave London anyway, but now I have a more compelling reason than merely avoiding disgrace. I want to meet the father I have never known. You could not ask me to forego that."

"No, of course not." He studied her, his lips curving into the smile she so loved. "How happy you must be to learn no part of Lambarth lives in you."

"You do understand," she said gratefully. "Others see only that recognizing Seagrave will brand me a bastard."

"Better a bastard than the offspring of a man who made a travesty of the words 'father' and 'gentleman,'" Adam said fiercely. "So then…you must leave us. When?"

She swallowed hard. "I go to Lady Seagrave tomorrow. We'll leave as soon as she can arrange passage."

"Then tonight…"

"Must be goodbye," she finished, rising and coming over to stand by him. Her heart already raced and despite her resolve, she was so nervous she was trembling.

She made herself take his hand—the first time she had sought out his touch. After recoiling a little at the spark he must have felt even as she did when their fingers met, he raised her hand and brushed his lips across her knuckles. His breath seemed to come as quick and shallow as her own and the heat she felt emanating from him did not, she was sure, originate with the fire.

"Kiss me goodbye—on the lips," she whispered.

At first she thought he meant to refuse. But then, his green eyes deepening with that compelling, enticing evidence of his desire, he lowered his head. "Goodbye, Helena," he breathed a moment before his lips touched hers.

She felt the gentle brush of his mouth down to her toes and heard a moan, not sure whether it was her own or Adam's. Then, before he could break the glancing contact, she stepped closer and put her hands on his shoulders.

"Ah, Helena," he murmured, but whatever else he might have said was lost as she took advantage of the slight opening of his lips to slip her tongue into his mouth.

He stiffened in shock, but before he could pull away, if such were his intention, she darted her tongue deeper, seeking his. The blast of sensation that rocketed through her when the sensitive tip of her tongue caught the plush fullness of his so weakened her knees that she almost fell.

Fortunately his hands closed on her shoulders to pull her nearer. Curving her body to fit against his, she leaned her weight on him and gave herself up to the exquisite game of fencing tongues, advancing to tease and tantalize, withdrawing to await his pursuit, then sending the full blade of hers gliding across his.

She could feel his heartbeat thundering in his chest and lower, a hard ridge pressed its heat against the thin silk covering her abdomen. She murmured and twined her fingertips in the tendrils at the nape of his neck, pulling his head closer still while she stroked and parried and stroked again with her tongue.

Everything within her seemed to turn molten, coursing in heated waves from her belly, the sensitized tips of her nipples down and outward to knees, fingertips, toes. A throbbing began at the junction of her thighs, pulsing in time to the stroking of their tongues.

She had just decided that she needed hotter, closer, when Adam broke the kiss and took a staggering step backward. "Helena, no," he mumbled, his eyes wide and unfocused, his breathing erratic. "This is… madness."

"Yes," she said fiercely, and brought his head back down to capture his mouth and his tongue again. A second later, with a strangled cry, he crushed her against him.

This time he was the aggressor, his tongue pursuing hers, laving it with quick, hard strokes, hers the strangled cry as she scratched his coat, desperate to penetrate the material and find bare skin. With her other hand, she inched down his waistcoat, straining to reach his arousal. She took his cry in her mouth as her fingers found purchase, shaping and caressing the long hard length of him straining against the trouser flap.

She was working the buttons to free him when he caught her hand. "No, Helena," he panted. "We… mustn't."

She curled her hand around his erection, exulting as he shuddered. "Do you not want this? Do you not want me?"

"Yes…no!"

"One night, Adam. Just one stolen from all the rest of our days. One night when nothing else exists, not duty, not obligation—nothing but you and me and this. Only you and I will ever know. Can you send me away without tasting this for just one night?" Massaging his length as she spoke, she pulled his head down for another long kiss.

After a moment he broke away again, though his hips still angled into her stroking fingers. "Are…you sure? I'm trying to resist, but another moment of this—" he rubbed against her "—and I'll be beyond stopping."

"Don't resist." She caught his bottom lip between her teeth and nipped it. As she slid her tongue back into his mouth, his leaped forward to meet hers, mating fiercely as if they were lovers long parted.

But as her fingers managed to undo the first button of his trouser flap, he thrust her back. "Not…here."

"You'll come to my room, then?" she whispered.

"Yes."

"Now? You promise? For I swear if you are not there in ten minutes, I will come to yours."

He kissed her hard, running his hands down her back to cup and squeeze her buttocks. "I'll be there. I promise."

Like stealthy accomplices, they slipped from the library and hurried up the stairs. In her room, Helena lit a brace of candles, then pulled back the bed linens and tossed her satin dressing gown to the floor.

What would Adam prefer? she wondered. To find her waiting between the sheets—or to have her meet him at the door, candles outlining her body beneath the silk?

Then the door swung silently open as Adam entered. The collar of a shirt peeked out from beneath his dressing gown and his hair was tousled, as if he'd disrobed quickly.

"Adam, my love," she whispered, walking over to him.

He framed her face with his hands. "You are so beautiful," he said hoarsely. "I've wanted you for so long, I can't remember not wanting you."

She took his hand, led him to the bed, stripped off his dressing gown. Beneath it he wore only his shirt, hanging below his waist where it tented out over his erection. She nudged him onto the bed and pushed him back against the pillows. When he reached out to tug at her night rail, she pulled it from his grasp. "Not yet. First, let me please you, Adam."

He let the silk go, his gaze never leaving hers as

once more she gently pushed him against the pillows and placed his hands at his sides. Perching beside him, she leaned over and kissed him, found his tongue and twined it with her own.

The heat of his body through the fine linen shirt warmed her more than the blaze from the library's hearth. But she wanted more, wanted the feel of his bare skin against the thin material of her gown. Still kissing him, she worked loose the buttons on his shirt, pushed it aside and ran the pads of her fingers over his chest, tracing his ribs. He gasped, sucking her tongue deeper when she drew his puckered nipples between her fingertips.

Suddenly she wanted to taste him, his chest, his nipples, the hollow beneath his throat. Laving his mouth with a final stroke, she broke away to trace her tongue across the raspy stubble of his chin, nipping lightly, over the ridge of his jaw, up to the tender curve of his ear, around to the soft skin just behind it. Lowering her mouth to nibble at his neck, she leaned her weight against him and skimmed her other hand from his chest down the flatness of his belly, thrilling to the texture of his bare skin.

He tensed as her fingers approached his erection, his breath little gasps at her ear, then uttered a strangled groan as she grasped his naked shaft. A pulse of exquisite sensation rippled to her core as he quivered in her hand. The skin was so taut and smooth, the head, where a drop of moisture beaded, almost silky to her exploring touch.

Tracing it with one fingertip, she whispered, "Does this please you?"

"Y-yes," he gasped.

But she wanted him beyond speech, beyond any response but the thrust of his hips. Still outlining his length with her fingers, she moved her mouth downward, rejoicing as he shuddered against her when she rasped her teeth across one taut nipple, then the other. Cupping her hand around his shaft, she descended his abdomen, laving, nipping, gliding her cheek across the soft skin.

Finally she moved to straddle his legs. Grasping his erection with both hands, she continued to shape and caress him while she examined him in the candlelight, marveling at the beauty of his nakedness as he lay with his eyes closed, head thrown back, his rigid hands clutching the sheets.

"I want to kiss you—here," she said, drawing one finger down his length. "May I?"

His eyes flew open. "Yes," he rasped, fisting his hands more tightly in the sheets.

His cock leaped against her lips and a long, low moan issued from his throat. Something leaped in her, too, a blaze of sensation in that moist, throbbing spot between her thighs. Murmuring, she widened her legs, rubbing against him as she licked from the thick rigid base of his erection to the satiny tip, then took him into her mouth.

Her heart was beating so rapidly she felt dizzy, impairing her hearing, for when he thrashed his head from side to side and cried out, she couldn't tell whether he was imploring her to stop or continue. But the thrusting motion of his hips seemed to indicate he wanted more.

As did she. She loved the feel and taste of him, the

feral pulsing in her veins, the throbbing at her core, winding her tighter and tighter. She loved the sound of Adam's gasping breaths, the sheen of sweat on his chest and abdomen, the clench of his fisted hands and corded arms. Then he cried out, his whole body going rigid as he filled her with his salty essence.

For a few moments he lay gasping, eyes closed. Worried that she had somehow hurt him, she slid up beside him on the pillow. "Adam, are you all right?"

His eyes opening, he laughed weakly. "All…right? No. Astounded. Transformed." He lifted a limp hand to caress her cheek. "I didn't want for it to be like that, only for me. But you are…amazing. I couldn't control myself."

"Then I did please you?" She smiled tenderly at him. "I did so want to. I listened quite closely to the Divine Alice's instructions."

"'Please' is a thousand times too weak a word—" Suddenly he stopped, his eyes going from dreamy to fully alert as he propped himself up on an elbow and stared at her. "The Divine Alice! You can't mean that you…"

"Consulted her?" Helena said. "Oh, but I did! I've wanted to talk with her ever since I first saw her at the park. After my disgrace at the musicale, I decided my visiting her could hardly worsen the scandal. More than anything, I wanted to please you. I thought she would speak honestly of what happens between a man and a woman." Her smile turning wicked, she traced a finger down Adam's bare chest to circle one nipple. "And she did."

With a growl, Adam caught her hand and brought it to his lips. "And what," he asked, nibbling each finger in turn, "did the Divine Alice say about my pleasing you?"

The sensations evoked by his hot tongue and the nip of his teeth were swiftly eroding Helena's powers of speech. "I didn't…think…to ask," she murmured.

Adam laughed deep in his throat. "Let me be your tutor, my temptress, and I shall endeavor to please you just as thoroughly." Wrapping an arm around her, he pulled her against him and cradled her on his chest.

Helena snuggled under his chin, breathing in the scent of him, more deliriously happy than she'd ever been in her life. An overwhelming sense of having come home filled her, as if she had been made to be here, wrapped in Adam's arms. She refused to listen to the tiny voice that warned how short-lived that happiness would be.

The maelstrom of sensations that had been building within her eased as she relaxed into his warmth. She'd almost drifted asleep when she felt his hands slipping under the hem of her night rail.

She reached down to stay them. "Adam—my back. I…I would rather not remove the gown."

"Do you not know every inch of you is beautiful to me?" he whispered. "Every scar, an emblem of your honor and courage? I want to see you, touch you everywhere." Leaning over to nuzzle her lips, he stroked his fingers over her skin as he slowly tugged the gown up.

Helena would have resisted, but the quiescent tension within her had tightened the instant his clever fingers began their work. Before she could begin to worry, he gently pulled the gown over her head.

And then thought scattered altogether as with his other hand, Adam tipped her chin up and captured her lips, sliding his tongue within as she gasped at the pleasure of his mouth on hers. While he kissed her, his hand wandered slowly up her leg, kneading her ankle, smoothing over her knee, rubbing the tender inside of her thigh.

Groaning into his mouth, she widened her legs, offering him access to her hot, pulsing center. His fingers crept upward at a maddening pace, moving so slowly that she began to twist restlessly beneath his hand.

As his fingertips grazed the thatch of curls between her legs, he broke the kiss and moved his mouth to her breast. In the next moment, his finger parted her folds to caress the nub within while his mouth suckled her nipple.

Acute pleasure seared her where his mouth and fingers worked. She cried out as she writhed beneath him.

"Does that please you?" he whispered against her breast, continuing to slide his fingers over the slick nub.

"Oh, yes," she gasped.

He moved to her other breast, suckling the nipple, teasing it with his teeth, then cupping the whole breast in his hand and nipping the tender skin. Meanwhile his finger slid lower, parting the lips to delve into her body.

The piercing pressure spiraled tighter and tighter until she felt she must explode or shake to bits. Just when she felt she could not stand the torment any longer, something within her released, sending a paroxysm of unimaginable pleasure coursing to every nerve.

For a long time afterward, as the waves of sensation faded, she lay motionless, too drained to move or speak.

Smiling down at her, Adam kissed her forehead. "Did I please you, my love?"

She struggled to smile back. "I never dreamed... such feelings existed."

"Only for you, my sweet," he whispered. "For all of this night."

And for the rest of that splendid night they lay entwined, Helena pillowing her head on his thigh, her hand cupping his spent member to coax him back to strength, or gathered boneless and breathless against his chest while his fingers soothed her satiated skin.

But after awakening near dawn to have the little voice she'd been ignoring cry insistently that their time was nearly over, Helena knew with desperate urgency that she could not leave Adam without tasting just once the fullness of union that, to protect her, he had been denying them.

Snuggling closer, she nibbled Adam's ear while her fingers stroked down his abdomen. She felt his chuckle as his shaft rose to meet her teasing fingers.

"More, my insatiable darling?" he murmured.

"Always," she replied, leaning up into his kiss.

Boldly she sought to conquer the fencing blade of his tongue, but he would have none of it. Chuckling again, he rolled her beneath him, clasped her hands and pulled her arms above her head as he settled himself between her legs. Moving his hips, he pressed his hard length against her, stroking her sensitive center with the hot smooth head of his cock in time to the rhythmic sweeps of his tongue.

Knowing that continuing in this fashion, he would soon drive her beyond control, Helena turned her face away, breaking the kiss. "Can't...breathe," she gasped. Though it was truly not a lie, her plea achieved its aim, for Adam rolled her over and lifted her to straddle him.

Eyes glazed, chest sheened with moisture, his breathing rough, he gazed up at her. "This is...better. I can see...how beautiful your breasts are." He weighed them in his hands as he spoke. "Nipples...pink from my mouth. See the curve of your belly. Touch you." He pushed gently at her knees to widen the parting of her thighs.

Before he could return one hand to tease and stroke and send her crashing over the precipice, Helena thrust her hips quickly downward to capture the smooth tip of his rigid cock. Pushing downward again, she felt a slow burn as at last, at last, she eased him within her.

The moment of discomfort passed swiftly, succeeded by an amazing fullness that massaged and caressed from her throbbing nub down the whole of that sensitive passage.

Beyond thought or plan, instinctively she withdrew and thrust down again, crying out at the wonder and intensity of it. Vaguely she noted Adam catching her arms.

"No, my love, we—" he gasped before Helena leaned forward to cover his mouth with hers and press her knees against his sides as she drove downward, sheathing his length fully within her.

"Love me, Adam," she whispered. "Love me completely."

For an instant he remained rigid, resisting. But when she thrust against him again, with a growl he seized her bottom and pulled her closer, arching upward to meet her.

Though she'd had to trick him to it, he quickly took the lead. Slowing the pace of their movements, he let her drive him in deep, then held her still while he pulsed within her before allowing her to pull back for another thrust. Though he'd several times taught her to balance on the acute edge between madness and ecstasy, this time he held her suspended above the abyss until she was shrieking her need for fulfillment. Then, with an equally savage cry, he plunged in one last time and bound her against him as they both shuddered, spun and shattered together.

The intensity of it, similar and yet so different from the pleasure he brought her with his clever tongue and nimble fingers alone, robbed Helena of breath and brought tears to her eyes as she lay afterward on his chest, both of them spent and gasping.

One flesh. One heart, hammering in unison as they lay wrapped in each other's arms.

But though she'd long sought to ignore it, she was forced now to acknowledge the pale light forming a ghostly halo behind the tightly drawn curtains, its increasing illumination beginning to rival the glow of the guttering candles. When Adam stirred, she sat up, every fiber of her being revolting against the thought of losing him.

She couldn't sail away and leave him. Having experienced this ecstasy, she simply couldn't imagine life without him. Her heart, her soul, couldn't bear the loss.

"Adam, I did please you, didn't I?"

He opened his eyes and smiled at her. "Did we not please each other?" he corrected, kissing her hand.

"Marvelously," she acknowledged, returning his smile. "Then…though of course I do not wish to keep you from your…obligations, would it not be possible for us to…to salvage some time to be together? I could take a house outside London. Somewhere close enough for you to visit."

His smile fading, he looked at her searchingly. "Are you proposing what I think you are?" he said at last. "Helena, I don't want you to be my mistress! I want…" Almost at the point of uttering something more, he shook his head. "Let us not speak of it now."

Her chest felt as if a giant talon had ripped it open. She swallowed hard and blinked back the burn of tears. "No, of course not. Excuse me for mentioning anything."

Of course he didn't want her. Hadn't she caused enough havoc in his life? Why would he wish to take a scarred, ill-behaved, troublesome woman who tumbled from one scandal to the next as his mistress when, should he ever wish to indulge in a discreet affair, with his breeding and charm he might have any woman in the ton?

The day was definitely dawning now, the rosy light at the windows brightening with every passing moment. Belowstairs, the servants were probably already stirring.

Feeling a chill that went to the bone and had little to do with the temperature of the room, Helena slid from the bed and fished her satin wrapper off the floor. "I expect you should go now, before the maid comes to make up the fire. I shouldn't wish to distress Aunt Lillian by creating yet another scandal on my last night in her house." She picked up Adam's dressing gown and the long-abandoned shirt and held them out to him.

For a long moment he stared at the garments, as if reluctant to take them from her hands. Hating, as much as she did, that their night together was ending?

Finally, swallowing hard, he said, "I expect you are right." Dropping the shirt on the bed, he stood and pulled the dressing gown around him. For a few more minutes Helena drank in the beauty of his naked body—the broad shoulders, flat belly, strong legs and now-flaccid shaft lying against his thighs. The body she had kissed and caressed, licked and fondled, pleasured in every way she could devise over the long hours of the night as he had caressed and pleasured hers—even, she recalled, her breath catching, the scars at her back.

As he turned to the door, she clamped her lips shut, stifling the aching need to confess her love in these last few minutes they would ever have alone.

Adam would probably soon feel guilty enough over the night she had coerced from him without adding to it the burden of her love. Better that he think her a wanton who'd decided she couldn't leave his life without sampling the passion that had sizzled between them since that first night in the library. Just one more irresponsible, ill-bred act by a girl who had already committed so many.

Numbly she moved to the center of the room, eyes closed, waiting for the soft click of the closing door that would signal the beginning of the impossibly empty days that stretched ahead of her without him.

She sensed him walking past her—then turning back. Framing her face in his hands, he kissed her, so gently she had to bite her lip afterward to keep from weeping.

"You will stay at Lady Seagrave's?" he asked.

She nodded. She couldn't tell him everything she felt, but she could at least say this. "Thank you, Adam—"

He put a finger against her lips and smiled tenderly. "No, *I* thank *you*...my dear Helena," he whispered, his eyes roaming her face as if to memorize every curve and line before he pulled her once more into his arms.

She had vowed to let him leave freely, but despite those noble intentions, she clung to him, her hands biting into his shoulders and her body molding to his as if to sear an imprint of him into her skin.

At length, he set her away from him. "Nothing is settled yet, so don't do anything rash," he said, one finger caressing her cheek. Then he turned and walked out.

Helena stumbled back and slumped onto the bed,

burying her face in the pillow he'd lain upon, which still carried the faint scent of his shaving soap. She had wrested from him her one night of passion. She now realized she would likely pay bitterly for it for years to come.

BARELY AN HOUR LATER, A GRIM, tight-lipped Helena arrived at Lady Seagrave's town house. After brooding on her love-ravaged disarray of a bed for a time after Adam left her, she'd sprung up with a fierce resolve to be gone from the house before any of the family woke. She didn't think she could face Charis or Aunt Lillian without them immediately suspecting what had occurred.

And as for Adam—she couldn't face him at all. She had thought she'd loved him before, but until last night she'd had no concept of the intensity of connection, the sweet purity of emotion one human being could feel for another.

And having felt it, she knew she didn't have enough veneer of polite behavior to keep herself from approaching Adam again to beg that he reconsider taking her as his mistress. Too little maidenly restraint not to want to scratch out the eyes of Miss Priscilla Standish for daring to marry Adam. Adam—*her* Adam, whose body had branded hers, who belonged with her!

Thank heavens for Lady Seagrave's invitation. Only the width of an ocean between them could guarantee that she would keep her distance from Adam, let him lead the life his honor required.

When she tiptoed quietly into the entry, to her surprise, the butler directed her to Lady Seagrave's book room, saying the mistress had been up for several hours and was eager to meet with her. Trying to summon a pleasant expression, she knocked at the door and entered.

"Good morning, Helena," Lady Seagrave said. "Let me finish these instructions and…" Her words trailed off and her welcoming smile dimmed as she examined Helena's face. "Oh, my poor dear. Saying goodbye was difficult?"

"Yes," Helena replied shortly.

"Then I hope my news will cheer you. When I visited Gavin's office yesterday, I found one of his most experienced captains there. He was to rejoin his ship in Falmouth once the rest of his cargo arrived, but when I told him who would be traveling with me, he proposed we sail immediately. He has been with Gavin long enough to know that bringing him his beloved daughter a week sooner would be worth far more to Gavin than a thousand bottles of Spanish wine. We can set out today—if you are ready?"

Even the prospect of meeting her father could not lift her spirits. Still, she knew she ought to leave London without delay. "I am quite ready."

"Excellent! I'll have Stephen put your trunks in the coach." She came over to pat Helena's cheek, concern in her wise eyes. "Do not grieve, my sweet. Everything will turn out all right in the end."

Helena managed a smile. But though she was about to embark on the sort of adventure she'd always dreamed about, she couldn't see how anything would ever be right again.

CHAPTER TWENTY-FIVE

'TWAS WELL AFTER NOON when Adam finally woke. He crossed his arms behind his head, his body satiated and his spirits bursting with excitement and optimism.

He couldn't recall when he'd last stayed abed so late. But Helena had been so inventive, so marvelously eager, that he'd not wished to waste in sleep more than the time necessary to recover his vigor before loving her again.

He still couldn't quite believe she'd had the boldness to seduce him. But she was Helena, that unique creature who marched to no rules but her own. And in truth, he hadn't tried too hard to resist her. Not when she rose to greet him, her curves lushly outlined by that silk night rail, reminding him of their first night in the library. The embodiment of the fantasy he'd dreamed so often, her untutored, instinctive sensuality had touched him far more deeply than any practiced courtesan ever could.

Who was he, for the sake of a few lines scribbled in a parish register, to deny her what her passionate spirit yearned for? Especially not when he'd already decided that regardless of the stain on his honor or the embarrassment to Priscilla, he simply couldn't let Helena go.

The decision to terminate his engagement had been taking shape for a long time. But after witnessing Priscilla's behavior at the musicale two nights ago, he had known that, even if he'd not fallen in love with Helena, he could not marry a lady who seemed ready to do anything—even forfeit his respect by betraying his trust—to discredit the girl she saw as her rival.

Though he would like to hear her explanation, his decision to end things between them was firm. And though their interview this afternoon was likely to be unpleasant, he was almost looking forward to it. For once it concluded, he meant to head directly to Lady Seagrave's house.

He'd almost broken and blurted out his intentions this morning—until Helena had asked to become his mistress, reminding him before he blundered into the proposal he was not yet free to make of her determination never to marry.

He would have to court her carefully, cleverly, for he would be satisfied with nothing less than persuading her to become his bride. Given her unconventional nature, perhaps he could use some seduction of his own, he thought, happily envisioning such a scene. And after he'd rendered her replete with satisfaction, maybe she could be induced to accept his suit without a murmur.

Seduction aside, he knew he'd begun to win her trust. He need only continue showing her he was worthy of her heart and hand…and she would be his, legally and forever.

A huge grin split his face. The London ton be damned. If they chose to shun him for jilting Priscilla and marrying his scandal of a bride, so be it. His immediate family, he knew, would support his choice. With them, Claygate and Helena, he'd have all he could wish to make him happy for the rest of his life.

Suddenly ravenous, he yanked the bellpull. He'd order a beefsteak and some ale, get his man to tog him out in his best, rid himself of Priscilla—and then seek out Helena.

Would she scan his body boldly when he called, smiling as they silently acknowledged what they'd shared in the night? Or, her mouth still swollen from his kisses, would she blush and look away with the maid's shyness that was also part of the complex character he loved so much?

He couldn't wait to see Helena again. He felt as giddy as one of the lovelorn characters in the silly novels he used to chide Charis for reading. Remembering how he'd dismissed her contention that love should be so much more than the mutual respect and admiration he'd been extolling, he had to laugh at what an ignorant ass he'd been.

He could only be grateful that Providence—and Helena—had intervened before he'd condemned himself to a marriage so much less than marriage was meant to be.

But the right marriage was not yet a certainty. Ready to begin making it so, he jumped from the bed.

AS IT TURNED OUT, ADAM WAS not forced to storm his betrothed's bedchamber. Upon arriving at the Standish mansion, he found Priscilla already in the parlor.

For a moment he simply stared at her, wondering how he could have let a few favorable impressions, flattery and public opinion push him to a declaration before he'd truly reacquainted himself with her character. Or would her true character not have been revealed if she'd not found herself confronted with a rival she was determined to crush?

She returned his stare coolly, but as the seconds passed in silence, she at last looked away, her cheeks coloring. "Won't you sit, Darnell?"

Still regarding her gravely, he took a seat.

"Well," she said, evidently unable to bear the silence any longer. "I might suppose you would inquire about my health, as I'd not been feeling well yesterday."

"And I might suppose that you would begin by explaining why you broke my trust. I explicitly remember obtaining your promise that you would not divulge Miss Lambarth's misconduct to anyone. Yet you confided it to Lady Cordelia—and then abetted her in revealing it in such a way as to cause the maximum damage to my stepmother's ward."

"I never dreamed Cordelia would reveal it! I did try to make light of it, but Miss Lambarth herself confirmed its truth. You cannot blame me for that!"

"You can't deny you have taken every opportunity of late to belittle her or to draw attention to her supposed deficiencies. That episode in the park, for instance. My groom tells me a thorn had been inserted into her saddle blanket—and Francis had to be the one who planted it."

"I had nothing to do with that!" she cried, confirming the truth of what he'd suspected. "Though I admit, when Francis encouraged me to invite her to the park, I may have hoped that she would appear to less advantage in the press of vehicles than she apparently is while riding that showy beast for her admirers in the early morning."

"Even setting aside your flaunting of my trust, how could you be so petty to a girl who had none of the advantages of the cultivated upbringing you received?"

"I might have known you would defend *her*—just as you always do. Have you never considered how *I* must feel? I've seen the way men look at her. The way *you* look at her. Everyone notices the partiality you display for her company. Am I to endure people saying you mean to set up a mistress before we are even wed?"

Though she might have grounds for jealousy, that she would impugn his honor, especially given how tenaciously he'd had to fight to cling to it, infuriated him. "I would have expected you to ask *me* about it, not listen to malicious gossip…from your friend Lady Cordelia, perhaps?"

Priscilla tossed her head, her color heightening. "Is it idle gossip? I'm not disposed to offer my hand and fortune to a man who takes my money while he has eyes for no one but that wild, unprincipled creature."

For a moment genuine curiosity tempered his anger. "Why *did* you bestow your hand on me?"

"You were the hero of my childhood! If I had

known then how…how dead to genteel behavior you can be, I would have not been so precipitous in accepting you!"

"Then we are in agreement at last. For I've discovered I have much more regard for that 'wild, unprincipled creature,' who tried her best to fit into a world she was never trained to enter, than I have for a jealous manipulator with a taste for sly cruelty."

Priscilla gasped. "How…how dare you! She has cast her spell over you, the witch, with her outrageous gowns and shameless behavior. Has she lured you to her bed yet? Cordelia said she would! I just hope you'll remember later, when you discover you're sharing her with half the men of the ton, that I warned—"

In one quick move, Adam reached her side and pressed a hand over her mouth. "I think you've said quite enough," he said softly, resisting the urge to grab her shoulders and shake her until her teeth rattled.

While she clawed at his hand, he continued, "We are agreed, then, on ending this mistake of an engagement? You have my leave to abuse my character to whoever will listen, but if I hear another ugly word about Helena Lambarth, I will know who originated it. And remember, I could spread abroad some facts about Francis that would not redound to his credit."

He removed his hand and stepped back. "May I wish you good health and happiness in the future, Miss Standish?"

Fingers touching her lips, as if she could not believe what he'd just done, she simply gaped at him.

"A good day to you, then." With a bow, feeling as if a tremendous weight had been lifted, Adam strode out.

SO EXCITED HE WAS TEMPTED to race all the way to North Audley Street, Adam could hardly contain his impatience as he tooled his curricle the short distance from Grosvenor Square. He tried to focus his euphoric mind on thinking of something clever to say when he saw her again. Something other than "I adore you! Marry me this minute," which was all that filled his head at present.

Scarcely waiting until the vehicle halted at Lady Seagrave's town house before jumping down, he took the stairs two at a time and pounded the knocker. Cutting off the footman who opened the door before the servant could speak, he said, "I must see Miss Lambarth at once! I'm Darnell," he continued impatiently, offering the man his card. "I must see Miss Lambarth immediately on a family matter of utmost urgency."

The footman glanced at his card and bowed. "If you will follow me to the parlor, my lord."

After five minutes of pacing Lady Seagrave's elegant salon, Adam was about to storm the stairs and initiate a room-to-room search when the door opened. His spirits soared, then plummeted as instead of her lithe form and lovely face, he saw another livried minion.

The man bowed. "I'm Chambers, Lady Seagrave's butler. Thomas tells me you are seeking Miss Lambarth?"

"Yes," Adam replied, ready to grind his teeth in frustration. "Are the ladies at home? As I told the footman, I must speak with Miss Lambarth at once."

"I am sorry, my lord. The ladies have already gone."

"Gone? Gone where?"

"I am not sure that I am at liberty to divulge—however," he added quickly, his eyes widening in alarm as Adam stepped toward him with a growl, "since you are a family member, I suppose I can tell you that the ladies left this morning to sail to St. Kitts on a visit to Lady Seagrave's son. My mistress told me not to expect her return for at least six months."

"Six months!" Adam echoed, aghast. "They left…this morning, you say? From what port is the ship sailing?"

The butler shook his head. "I'm sorry, my lord, I don't know. However, someone at Mr. Seagrave's shipping office in the city might."

"Where in the city?" Adam was out the door and heading for the stairs practically before the last syllables of the address had left the man's lips.

A stop at Gavin's office revealed that the packet taking the ladies to meet their ship in Falmouth set sail from Portsmouth. Scribbling a note to inform Lady Darnell and Charis of his plans, Adam hired a vehicle and left without even a change of clothes.

But though he pressed the hired teams to their limits and paused only as long as it took the ostlers to get a fresh team harnessed, quaffing a mug of ale as they worked, when he arrived at the dock in Portsmouth the following day, mud-spattered and weary, he found the ship's berth empty. Captain Blackman's packet, one of the sailors from a nearby ship confirmed, had sailed on the morning tide.

SIX WEEKS LATER, HELENA SAT fanning herself on a bench in her mother's garden at Gavin Seagrave's estate. The manor and its grounds, carved from the hills overlooking the harbor at St. Kitt's, offered panoramic views of the sea below and the peak of Mt. Liamuiga in the distance. Her father and grandmother were in the house, planning tonight's dinner to introduce her to more of the island residents.

The month-long crossing had been stormy. But except for the time she spent tending poor Lady Seagrave, who along with Nell and Dickon had been extremely unwell, Helena remained on deck, huddled on a cargo chest out of the way of the sailors, the howling wind and crashing seas well matching her mood. Her indifference to the pitching deck and torrents of rain led Captain Blackman to remark to Lady Seagrave later that Helena had taken to the sea so well, 'twas proof enough she was Gavin's daughter.

During the journey, Captain Blackman had regaled her with tales of Gavin Seagrave's exploits as a privateer. Recalling some of her own excursions at Lambarth in the dark of night, Helena realized she had quite a bit in common with her rogue of a father. The one warm spot in the mostly desolate landscape of her heart was the immediate connection that had formed between her and Gavin Seagrave the moment he'd greeted them in St. Kitts.

Despite having seen his portrait, it had been a shock to finally meet him, to see gazing back at her the same eyes she saw when she looked in the mirror. Lady Seagrave's gasp when she saw the two of them side by side reinforced how striking was the resemblance.

In the two weeks since she'd arrived, she'd quickly grown fond of the man who had won her mother's heart. But it was her own heartache that finally melted the last of the resentment she'd harbored for the lover she had always half blamed for luring her mother away from her.

She could understand better now why, in defiance of the law, Gavin had invested such effort and treasure in freeing the woman he loved. Why her mother had risked everything to return to the man she'd never stopped loving. And though Helena took care to keep her damaged hand hidden, having sworn never to grieve her father further by having him discover just how much she had suffered from Lambarth's cruelty, she supposed she could not fully comprehend their devastation at being parted from their daughter until she had a child of her own.

A possibility that did not now look very likely. Perhaps, braced by the love of her family, she would eventually recover some enjoyment in life. But she couldn't imagine ever wishing to marry—ever allowing another man to touch her as Adam had. Ever wanting to caress another as she had pleasured him.

By now Charis should be married and returned to Vienna with Lord Blanchard. Perhaps Adam and Priscilla had set their own wedding date. "Oh, my love," she whispered, the tears welling up, "may you be happy in spite of her!"

It seemed, she thought impatiently, dashing away the tears, that she did little now but weep. Perhaps it was the heat, she mused, fanning herself harder.

Her grandmother, knowing there was little she could do, offered companionship. But often Helena preferred to be alone, walking in the garden of exotic flowers her mother had created or riding the mare that had been her mother's favorite at the small breeding farm she'd established here.

Her father urged her to remain and run the farm with him. She hadn't yet decided whether to do so.

Thinking of that possibility, her spirits lifted slightly. Gavin Seagrave had offered his daughter's companions the same warm hospitality he had extended to Helena. Noticing how frequently Dickon turned up at the stables—and probably knowing better than anyone that an active boy needed occupation to keep him out of mischief—her father instructed the head groom to teach Dickon to ride. Observing the lad's first lesson, Gavin pronounced him a natural horseman, assigned him to be the head groom's assistant, and promised if he worked hard, Dickon might one day become the farm's manager. The boy now accorded Gavin the worshipful respect he had previously offered Harrison.

Nell, too, had told Helena several times how much she loved the beautiful island, its sunny warmth and hospitable people. Though Helena suspected that her father's handsome young secretary, whose attention Nell had attracted the day of their arrival, was the main reason behind her companion's delight in her new circumstances.

Since her grandmother was, of course, thrilled to be reunited with her son, Helena often felt she was the sole island of misery in the sea of gladness surrounding her.

Restless, she rose to pace the garden path. Her mother's touch was evident in the design of the beds with their fragrant displays of Diana's favorite white and yellow flowers. There was even a tiny maze, reminding Helena of the trip Adam had proposed to Hampton Court.

Her breathing stuttered and pain twisted in the hollow of her chest. *Please, Mama,* she silently implored the presence she felt so strongly in this place. *You lived for years without Papa before you were reunited. Teach me how to survive without the man I love.*

As if her thoughts had conjured her father, she looked up to see him approaching. She went to meet him, laying her head against his chest as he drew her close for a hug.

"I'm sorry to be such a poor-spirited guest, Papa."

Tucking her hand under his arm, he strolled with her. "You're not a guest, sweeting—you're the joy of my heart. I only wish I could help you recapture some joy in yours."

Looking up at his face, one brow arched in an expression she recognized as so like her own, she read compassion and understanding. Grandmama must have told him what had transpired in London. Unable to restrain herself, she asked, "How did you endure the years you and Mama were separated? Though I suppose, being a man, you had tasks and adventures to distract you."

He laughed softly. "Oh, I had adventures aplenty—but the ache of missing your mother was always here—" he tapped his chest "—deep within. I can tell you one thing not to do. Don't spend your days repining or regretting any mistakes you may have committed. 'Tis the love you cherish that makes life worth living. Hold fast to it."

"What if that love is no longer possible…like for you now, with Mama gone?"

"Losing her was a blow from which I suffer every day. But all that we shared lives on in my heart. One day we will be together again. And though it is natural when one has suffered terrible pain to try to wall oneself off, let me assure you that the joy you gain from loving someone is always worth the cost. Trust that joy, sweeting."

Tears stung Helena's eyes. But before she could thank her father for giving her a measure of solace, the garden gate clanged open and Dickon came toward them at a run. "Mr. Seagrave!" he called. "Mr. Wittington done sent me to fetch you. Gray Star's foal be a'coming!"

"Then we'd better go help it be born, eh, my lad? Go tell Wittington I'm on my way." While Dickon sped off, Gavin turned to Helena. "Will you come, too?"

Helena shook her head. "I'll remain here a while longer. Perhaps I shall ride later."

"Don't stay out too long. The sun in the tropics is very strong. You're not used to it yet."

"I'll remember. Thank you for talking with me, Papa. I hope someday I may be as wise."

Gavin grinned as he kissed her forehead. "It took a great deal of bad living to accumulate what wisdom I possess—an experience I would spare you! Until later, my dear."

Helena watched as, whistling, her father strode out the gate and headed down the lane that led to the stables. She took a seat on one of the garden benches, but after a time her restlessness returned.

Despite the steadily increasing heat, perhaps she'd ride. A good hard gallop always helped clear her mind.

She was walking toward the gate when a man approached down the lane from the east, a black silhouette against the blaze of morning sun. Not wishing for company, she was about to retreat out of sight when something about his stride, the way he carried himself, seized her attention.

Her breath caught in her throat. But no, the hot Caribbean sun must be making her hallucinate. 'Twas only her grief and her disordered spirits that had turned that featureless silhouette into the image of Adam Darnell. Who was halfway around the globe in London, perhaps already married to Priscilla Standish.

Despite that certainty, she turned her back to the gate, cursing herself for her idiocy in being unable to watch the man walk by and prove the impression false. So preoccupied was she in berating herself that she jumped when a hand was laid on her shoulder.

"I had thought after traveling so many miles, I would at least get a hello."

She whirled to face him. "A-Adam?" She shook her head, but the face that materialized before her still appeared to be his, so impossibly dear her heart lurched.

"Adam," she repeated, reaching out to touch his cheek. Papa had just warned her about staying outdoors too long. But with a delusion this wonderful, she didn't mind becoming delirious.

"Yes, Adam, my sweet," he said, laughing. "Ah, Helena, Helena, how I've longed for you!"

Her hallucination kept getting better, for now he was embracing her. She could even smell, over the aroma of frangipani, the spicy scent of his shaving soap.

"Kiss me!" she murmured, determined, before they incarcerated her in a dark room with a cold cloth on her forehead, that she would eke every last drop of pleasure from this fantasy. Wrapping her arms around his neck, she pulled his mouth to hers.

Ah, it was just as she remembered—the taste of him, the delight spiraling outward from the teasing dance of tongues. She molded herself to him, surprised to discover that a fantasy could have an erection.

After a moment, he broke the kiss. "My dear, unless you wish to cause another scandal in this garden, you must cease kissing me like that. A long-deprived man can only resist so much."

She stared up into those familiar green eyes, lit with amusement and a deeper heat. "Adam?" she whispered. "It…really is you? But how?"

Taking her arm, he walked her to a bench. "I ought

to wring your neck, hellion! I told you to do nothing rash, and less than a day later I find you've run off to the colonies without even a by-your-leave! Before I could tell you Priscilla and I had terminated our engagement. Before I could declare that the only woman I want is the utterly captivating lady I love—you, my darling."

"You...love me?" she repeated, not sure she could have heard him correctly.

"Completely. I was hoping you had become rather fond of me, as well—if your behavior the last night we spent together was any indication."

"You want me for your mistress after all?"

His teasing expression sobered. "For my mistress—and so much more! Though I know you haven't much liking for wedlock, what I truly want is for you to marry me."

Twining his fingers in her hair, he pulled her to him and brushed his lips against hers again, this time gently, reverently, as if she were a priceless treasure that must be treated with infinite care. "My dearest Helena, can you trust me that much? Will you grant me a lifetime to demonstrate how precious you are to me?"

He loved her...she was precious to him. His wonderful, unbelievable words filled up the empty, aching spot in her heart until she felt it must overflow with happiness.

Trust in joy, Papa had told her.

"Yes, Adam, I will marry you."

His eyes widened in surprise. "You will?"

"Yes. Oh, Adam, I love you so much!"

With a crow of triumph, he picked her up and swung her around and around. "Marvelous! Bellemere and Charis will be thrilled! Before I left, Charis told me it had become her fondest hope that we would fall in love." Setting her down again, he continued, "I'm humbled by your faith in me, despite all you've experienced."

Twining her fingers with his, she said earnestly, "After being with Papa—my real Papa—I've come to realize it is not marriage itself, but the character and commitment of the two people who enter into it that make the difference between happiness and misery. I trust you never to misuse the power the law grants a husband. And I can imagine nothing more wonderful than spending my life with you. But…are you sure you want to marry me? You know how lacking I am in the many skills needed in a wife."

"You possess all the qualities that matter most to me. Courage. Integrity. Compassion. And," Adam added as he kissed their joined fingers, "the power to drive me mad with just a touch."

Though she felt a giddy pleasure at his tribute, still she said anxiously, "But what of the scandal, Adam? I wouldn't want you to be ostracized by your peers."

"By the time we return, there will have been a dozen new scandals to overshadow it. The people I care about will always value us. Like Dix, who sent his blessing when I told him I was coming after you. In any event, if it suits you, we shall live mainly at Claygate…when we are not crossing the ocean to show off our children to their grandfather."

He kissed the tip of her nose. "Rapscallion little boys like Gavin Seagrave and adventuresome, unconventional little girls like..." His enthusiasm abruptly cooling, he added, "That is, you do want children, don't you, my darling? I know that your own childhood was hardly—"

She raised a finger to still his lips. "I do want children, very much. I had a mother whose love sustained me through ten years of exile and torment. And *my* children will be nurtured by a father whose love and compassion will never fail them. Which reminds me, the single greatest blessing of this last fortnight has been getting to know Papa. I can't wait for you to meet him, Adam! He's a wonderful man."

"He must be—to have produced so remarkable a daughter. Please, take me to him at once so I may ask for your hand. You will marry me immediately, won't you, my only love? Along with the good wishes of Charis and your aunt, I brought a special license with me, just in case."

"Then we can marry here, in my mother's garden?" Where her parents, after separation and heartache, had finally found happiness together. As she and Adam would.

"As soon as I can find a priest. Today, I hope. I can hardly wait to begin our life together—and for another demonstration of your wifely skills," he said with a wink.

The joy and passion in his eyes sparked an answering fire in her that, after the desolation of the past month, was simply too exhilarating to be denied. "At the moment, Papa is preoccupied with a mare in foal. And it's been so long—" she drew him toward the secluded shade of a great flamboyant tree "—I fear my 'wifely skills' may need refreshing. Before you go looking for Papa, perhaps we should...practice."

Wrapping his arms around her, he murmured, "I shall never get enough of practicing—even outdoors in a flower garden, my dearest, darling, untamed bride."

REQUEST YOUR
FREE BOOKS!

2 FREE NOVELS
FROM THE ROMANCE/SUSPENSE
COLLECTION PLUS 2 FREE GIFTS!

YES! Please send me 2 FREE novels from the Romance/Suspense Collection and my 2 FREE gifts. After receiving them, if I don't wish to receive any more books, I can return the shipping statement marked "cancel." If I don't cancel, I will receive 4 brand-new novels every month and be billed just $5.24 per book in the U.S., or $5.74 per book in Canada, plus 25¢ shipping and handling per book plus applicable taxes, if any*. That's a savings of at least 10% off the cover price! I understand that accepting the 2 free books and gifts places me under no obligation to buy anything. I can always return a shipment and cancel at any time. Even if I never buy another book from the Reader Service, the two free books and gifts are mine to keep forever.

185 MDN EF3H 385 MDN EF3J

Name	(PLEASE PRINT)	
Address		Apt. #
City	State/Prov.	Zip/Postal Code

Signature (if under 18, a parent or guardian must sign)

Mail to The Reader Service:

IN U.S.A.	IN CANADA
P.O. Box 1867	P.O. Box 609
Buffalo, NY	Fort Erie, Ontario
14240-1867	L2A 5X3

Not valid to current subscribers to the Romance Collection,
the Suspense Collection or the Romance/Suspense Collection.

Want to try two free books from another line?
Call 1-800-873-8635 or visit www.morefreebooks.com.

* Terms and prices subject to change without notice. NY residents add applicable sales tax. Canadian residents will be charged applicable provincial taxes and GST. This offer is limited to one order per household. All orders subject to approval. Credit or debit balances in a customer's account(s) may be offset by any other outstanding balance owed by or to the customer. Please allow 4 to 6 weeks for delivery.

BOB206

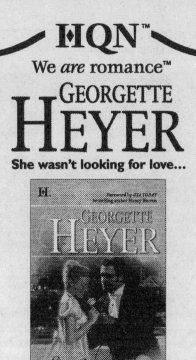